Place
of the
Heart

STEINUNN
SIGURÐARDÓTTIR

TRANSLATED BY PHILIP ROUGHTON

Published by

amazon crossing

Text copyright © 1995 by Steinunn Sigurðardóttir
English translation copyright © 2014 by Philip Roughton

Place of the Heart was first published in 1995 as *Hjartastaður* by Mál og menning. Translated from Icelandic by Philip Roughton. First published in English by AmazonCrossing in 2014.

Published by AmazonCrossing, Seattle
www.apub.com

Amazon, the Amazon logo, and AmazonCrossing are trademarks of Amazon.com, Inc., or its affiliates.

ISBN-13: 9781477818220
ISBN-10: 1477818227
Library of Congress Control Number: 2013917696

The translation of this book was supported financially by:

Icelandic
LITERATURE
CENTER
MIÐSTÖÐ ÍSLENSKRA BÓKMENNTA

Cover design by Anna Curtis
Cover photograph by RAX (www.rax.is)
Maps by Mapping Specialists, Limited

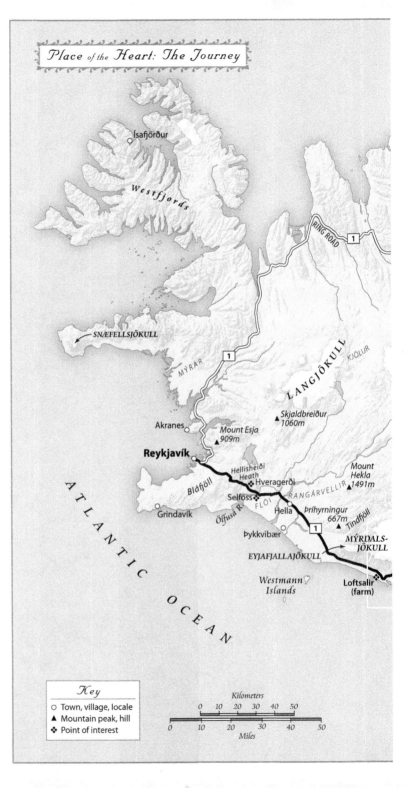

Place of the Heart: The Journey

Ísafjörður

Westfjords

RING ROAD
1

SNÆFELLSJÖKULL

MÝRAR

1

LANGJÖKULL

KJÖLUR

Skjaldbreiður
1060m

Akranes
Mount Esja
909m

Reykjavík

Hellisheiði
Heath

Hveragerði

Mount
Hekla
1491m

Bláfjöll

RANGÁRVELLIR

Selfoss

Grindavík
Ölfusá R.
FLÓI
Hella
Þríhyrningur
667m
Tindfjöll

1

Þykkvibær
MÝRDALS-
JÖKULL

EYJAFJALLAJÖKULL

Westmann
Islands
Loftsalir
(farm)

ATLANTIC

OCEAN

Key
○ Town, village, locale
▲ Mountain peak, hill
❖ Point of interest

Kilometers
0 10 20 30 40 50

0 10 20 30 40 50
Miles

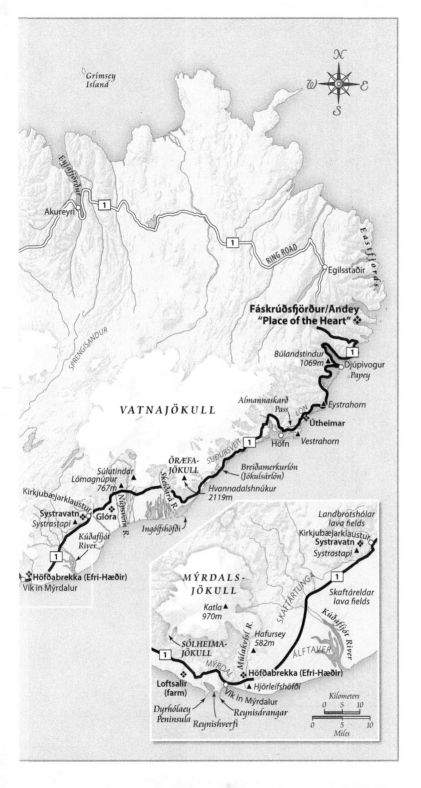

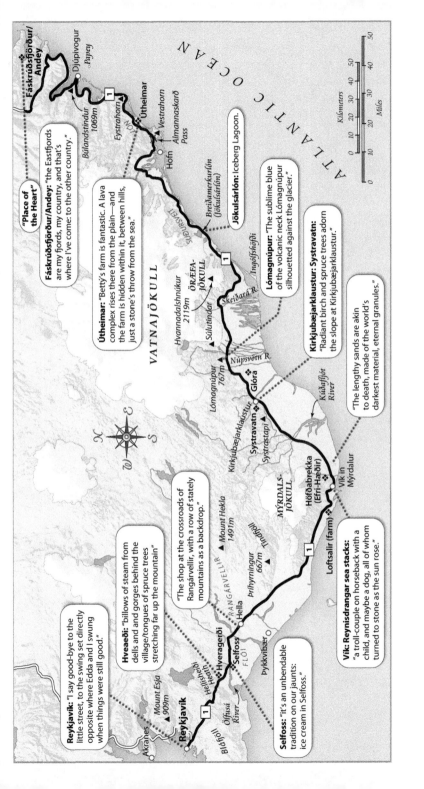

ATLANTIC OCEAN

"Place of the Heart"

Fáskrúðsfjörður/Andey: "the Eastfjords are my fjords, my country, and that's where I've come: to the other country."

Útheimar: "Betty's farm is fantastic. A lava complex rises there from the plain—and the farm is hidden within it, between hills, just a stone's throw from the sea."

Jökulsárlón: Iceberg Lagoon.

Lómagnúpur: "The sublime blue of the volcanic neck Lómagnúpur silhouetted against the glacier."

Kirkjubæjarklaustur: Systravatn: "Radiant birch and spruce trees adorn the slope at Kirkjubæjarklaustur."

"The lengthy sands are akin to death, made of the world's darkest material, eternal granules."

Reykjavik: "I say good-bye to the little street, to the swing set directly opposite where Edda and I swung when things were still good."

Hveaeði: "billows of steam from dells and and gorges behind the village/tongues of spruce trees stretching far up the mountain"

"The shop at the crossroads of Rangárvellir, with a row of stately mountains as a backdrop."

Selfoss: "it's an unbendable tradition on our jaunts: ice cream in Selfoss."

Vík: Reynisdrangar sea stacks: "a troll-couple on horseback with a child, and maybe a dog, all of whom turned to stone as the sun rose."

Djúpivogur
Papey
Búlandstindur 1069m
Eystrahorn
Útheimar
Vestrahorn
Hornafjörður
Höfn
Almannaskarð Pass
Breiðamerkurlón (Jökulsárlón)
Ingólfshöfði

VATNAJÖKULL

ÖRÆFA-JÖKULL
Hvannadalshnúkur 2119m
Súlutindar
Skeiðará R.
Lómagnúpur 767m
Núpsvötn R.
Kirkjubæjarklaustur
Systravatn
Glóra
Systrastapi
Kúðafljót River

MÝRDALS-JÖKULL
Höfðabrekka (Efri-Hæðir)
Vík í Mýrdal
Loftsalir (farm)
Mount Hekla 1491m
Þríhyrningur 667m
Tindfjöll
RANGÁRVELLIR
Hella
Selfoss
Hveragerði
FLÓI
Þykkvibær
Hellisheiði Heath
Mount Esja 909m
Bláfjöll
Ölfusá River
Akranes
Reykjavik

Kilometers
Miles

Bollagata

You wait here, Heiður. This is for my legs alone, I say, trying to come up with a reasonable method of exiting the pickup truck.

Short people like me have a harder time obeying the laws of gravity when getting down out of high vehicles than resisting them getting in. My friend watches from behind the wheel to see whether I accomplish my two-footed hop.

With the solid ground of the Norðurmýri neighborhood beneath my feet, I grab the black bucket that had been rubbing gently against my calf since leaving Laugarás and, for the last time, hurry to the gate of my yard on Bollagata Street.

What do you know—Hreinn Elías slinks out from the basement door, and my heart skips a beat. It's been hammering ever since I woke at the thought that we were leaving today. *Now,* and who could know whether Edda Sólveig would be there, or what condition she might be in. Would I have to start this trip by going to look for her in some sort of dive that until last year I didn't even know existed in Reykjavík?

Hreinn Elías is living proof that my daughter's at home, which is why I bless him in my mind as he slithers up the steps like an amoeba, dangling his head so that his bright angel hair billows over his nose.

Good morning, I say, looking into his small glassy eyes.

He returns my greeting in his flaccid way and keeps his eyes fixed on the sidewalk as he steps into the flower bed to avoid me, crushing a marigold beneath his loosely laced sneakers.

I straighten up and brace myself for dealing with the rest of the gang. I peek in through the door, which Hreinn Elli hasn't bothered to shut. There's no one but Edda in the empty apartment. No need to work myself up.

I should thank my stars that the girl is home, but I've grown so hard-hearted that I'm no longer grateful for anything. As she lies there fully dressed on the living room floor, wearing thick-soled shoes and snoring so loudly that the walls rumble slightly, I view her as an object that has nothing to do with me. Her black leather vest leans upright in one corner, like the seared torso of a bull.

I do the rounds, and my experienced eyes immediately notice the layer of ash covering the room, the residue of beer and soda sticking to the floor and windowsills. The bathroom stinks of urine, and there are yellow splotches on and around the toilet. Edda's friends are incapable of lifting the seat, and it's not for me to say if they've ever heard of doing so. I wipe it off with toilet paper, and as I flush, the noise resounds throughout the basement. Someone threw up in the sink, and I hope that it isn't Edda who's sick. That is the last thing I need on this trip, which has infested my dreams for the past few weeks, and there is no postponing it now.

My eyes smart with smoke and the reek of moonshine. I open the window quietly, terrified of waking Edda, though she should be getting up anyway. Dented beer cans are arranged around her in an orderly circle, and in one corner are vinegar bottles used for moonshine.

Edda's rasping snores grow louder as I scrub sticky splotches off the soil-brown linoleum floor. She's lying on her back with her slightly ratty red hair hanging over her face, including a little matted lock wafting in front of her mouth. Her right hand's clenched on her chest, and her left one is stretched out on the floor. These hands are forlorn, both of them, bony and freckled. The skull ring from her dead friend Rúna underscores their desolation.

I've started cleaning the apartment with unnecessary precision because I'm not keen on waking the creature, but this won't do. I'm just about to say *Edda Sólveig* in a very low voice when a huge blow-fly darts in through the open window, buzzing and popping like a tiny helicopter. In my mind I direct it toward the girl's ear, and what do you know? She wakes with a start.

Are you ready, dear? We're leaving.

Huh? Puh.

I rush to the bathroom with my cleaning supplies, wring out the rag, and empty the bucket into the toilet. I carefully spread the rag over the bucket as if I were laying a tablecloth, letting it hang down equally on all sides, perfectly smooth, my practical gift to the next tenants. Then I wash my hands thoroughly, dry them with toilet paper, flush again, and return to the living room with a shivery feeling, as if I'm coming down with something.

Edda Sólveig's back is turned to me as she stands on a dry island in the damp floor. I look past her, out my arched window, the jewel of this basement apartment, the window that I always keep so clean that you can't even see the pane. Two white poppies swaying in the breeze could just as well be inside. Sunbeams stream through individual couch-grass blades with joints that bend in various directions, blades so long that they would tickle the armpits of small women. The bay willow in the hedge is midsummer green, and there's a hint of russet in the leaves of the rowan tree; its berry clusters are no longer red, but rather orange, although it's still August. Until tomorrow.

Then it'll be September and I'll have gone halfway east, to what was once my *dreamland of spring. Will now be my winter den.*

Which hand do you want?, asks Edda, turning around sharply, like a ninja. In just a few months she's become an expert in taking her opponent by surprise, and her opponent's become an expert in keeping a poker face while expecting anything. Indeed, anything could be in the clenched fist that she holds out. Even a hand grenade.

This one.

She opens her right hand to reveal an Egyptian beetle, my lost scarab.

Where did you find it?

I hug Edda as if by reflex, though well knowing she won't like it. She pushes me away with her famous left-arm tactic, cupping her palm around the scarab.

It was behind the radiator.

And how did you find it?

I caught a glimpse of something when I stood up.

It's been missing for a whole year. I wonder how it got behind the radiator.

Isn't it from the French perv?

His name's Gabriel Axel, and you shouldn't call him that, considering how many beautiful things he's sent you.

The girl hands me the beetle as if she were holding something disgusting between her thumb and index finger and walks out, her shoulders hanging and her steps wavering. She drags the unshapely vest behind her.

I fiddle with threading the scarab onto my old necklace, a gilded beetle with a body of lapis lazuli. There's something otherworldly about this sky-blue stone flecked with gold. I've found myself staring at it and pondering the possibility of its being.

. . .

She's making a run for it, the wee one?

My smirking mother is in a yoga position in front of the radiator, on the damp floor.

When I moved here, Mom, you were already dead, remember? You never came to Bollagata. What are you up to *now*?

Just to practice my yoga.

Your behind will get all wet sitting there. Move it. Far from there.

No.

Did you steal the scarab?

You should ask whether I was the one who found it. Those who don't ask the right questions don't get the right answers.

Good of you to mention questions, Mom. There's actually an old one that I could never cough up. I'm going to fix that as soon as I get to your sister Dýrfinna's out east. She'll tell me, unless you want to answer me now. Who is my father? You have to admit it's a good question. And from what I know, the answer should be a doozy.

That you can count on, little Eisa.

I reach over her, shut the window, and hurry out of this hole in the wall for the final time, towing a garbage bag stuffed with the remains of nighttime excesses left by Edda and company. I bang shut the door, hoping to startle the noisy upstairs neighbors who've irritated me to no end with their masterful thuds, sly bodily noises, and slamming doors.

I throw the bag in the garbage bin behind the building and run back through the yard in the gleaming Sunday sun. My hands are empty. Unbelievable for a person who always has something in her hands: shopping bags, bedpans, knitting needles.

The shiny white pickup waits at the gate, ready for departure. There's something strange about this vehicle, something that's difficult to pinpoint. Somehow it seems to me like an ambulance, but for sick sheep maybe.

Edda sits wedged against the door in the backseat. She's packed in among bags and bundles made of plastic, leather, and cloth, her cat eyes open just a slit in a cloud of red hair. I focus all my energy on getting up into the car, first by standing on tiptoe and grabbing the door handle, then gaining a purchase on the step with my right foot and swinging myself into the seat.

. . .

As Heiður sets off, I say good-bye to the little street, to the swing set directly opposite where Edda and I swung when things were still good, hypnotized by the old spruce trees and newborn clouds rushing past, swinging to our hearts' content at breakneck speed after we both ought to have grown out of such a thing.

I say good-bye to the un-Icelandic view over my Three Towers, as I call them—the two spires of Háteig Church and the Maritime College's one. Behind them is Mount Esja, a bulwark for the capital.

Heiður slips a CD into the player, and an airy Telemann flute composition played by her wafts through the car. With supernatural power it balances out the reek of alcohol coming off my daughter. It's a relief to hear, because early Sunday morning in the city is always such a chasm of silence that it's as if Armageddon has come to pass. Although if that's the case this Sunday, it somehow, incredibly enough, missed three women in an overloaded car.

If you're going to play that crap, I'm getting out, comes a threat from the backseat.

Heiður gives me a flabbergasted look, as if *I* were the one who said it.

I try putting on an apologetic expression, as if Edda Sólveig had said it through me.

Although the car is moving, Edda tears open the door and says she'll jump out if this fluterwauling isn't shut off immediately.

Heiður turns off the music and says brusquely: I didn't know the situation was that bad.

She shifts gears with a harsh scrape that resembles some of the sounds she unleashed from her violin as a child, and might well have caused her to switch to the flute.

. . .

Heiður pulls up to the intersection in front of Hotel Esja, where no one is crossing, and shakes her head in frustration at having to stop. I shake my head in unison, amazed by the first living thing that we see on our way. It's a tall man with a camera, taking pains to frame the historical site of the former Dock Wood. He has long dark hair and is wearing a light-colored suit, exactly like my photographer of old. The man I imagined was a gypsy, with a sad smile and an *angel hand* that he laid on my head. The man I've never told anyone about because of a finger that he placed on his lips, saying something in a foreign language that translated as *hush*. I understood that I couldn't talk about the gold chain he gave me, and I felt safer not saying a word about meeting him, not even to Heiður.

It occurs to me that this could be the same man, that I should go to him as I did then. I feel as if he has something to tell me, and am on the verge of opening the car door when Heiður drives off. He is, of course, a different man.

. . .

Those many years ago, after I arrived at Dock Wood and the tall man had gone his way, there took place the most famous story of my childhood, which exists in many different versions and started somewhere along these lines when I used to tell it to new kids and birthday guests:

Once there were two girls at Laugarnes School. One was terribly small and dark. It just so happens that it was, in fact, me.

From Heiður's perspective, this was how the story started:

When I came to Hrísateigur and asked for Harpa Eir, her mother said: She's gone to Dock Wood with an orange. She's poorly dressed, just in a swimsuit and shorts. Be a dear and go find her.

Between Heiður and me, the Dock Wood account is a horror story, but I cooked it up for Edda in such a way that it became a harmless thriller in which a broken arm is just added spice. The child retold it to her pack of teddy bears and girlfriends missing their front teeth.

Once when poor Mama was a girl she went to Dock Wood in search of wild children who lived in a ditch. It was where Blómaval Garden Center is now, and that's the honest truth.

The site where the story took place has been leveled, the ditches all filled in. Big houses and scattered trees bordered by asphalt islands now rise from the former sward of northern dock plants. But the sculptor's domed studio still stands, bearing witness to the story, along with the hulking cement folk who some said raised us kids in that neighborhood.

When I was out and about with little Edda in those parts, she pointed with her sharp finger and said: That's where you were, Mommy, in your wild-child game, when the Indian and the cowboy came.

I look back over my shoulder, halfway hoping that the teenager in the backseat will ask for the story of stories, but her hostile look reminds me that she's grown out of it.

Tell it, Mama!, demanded my ex-child every time we drove down Sigtún Street or Suðurlandsbraut Road.

I'll tell you:

When Mama Harpa was at Laugarnes School, we kids liked to run around in the huge Dock Wood, next to the domed building where a hundred tons of concrete were playing a game of sculptures. The scrub in Dock Wood was as high as the shoulders of most kids my age, but came up to my nose because I've always been so small. Everyone knew that mysterious beings known as the WILD ONES lived there. They were very small and dark, with curly hair. They were actually wild children but hardly human. It was difficult to explain their existence, although everyone knew that they were orphans, among various other things. They lived mostly on dock, but if they grew hungry in winter they might kill rats for food. They were distinguished from other children by the fact that they had no belly button. That's because they hadn't been born in the usual way. These savage Wild Ones were rarely seen, since few dared to venture deep into the woods. Sometimes, we kids tried to stay hidden for hours, without a sound, in order to lure them out into the light of day.

During the summer following third grade, we had one of those precious warm days in Reykjavík that throw everything out of whack. I wanted to go play in a swimsuit and shorts. Mom didn't want me going out like that, because I was always supposed to be so ridiculously well dressed, but I pestered her hard and she unexpectedly gave in. She slipped me an orange when I went out the door declaring that I was going to Dock Wood.

I was determined to find a Wild Child, even if it meant searching for the entire day. As soon as I'd crossed the plank over the shallow ditch, I crawled on my hands and knees, head bent down, so the Wild Children wouldn't notice me right away. They were, in fact, incredibly timid, which was one reason why so few had seen them. A big boy at Laugarnes School was supposed to have come across a girl and boy as they cuddled in a large cardboard box, dressed in skins like Stone Age people, with hay for a blanket and mattress. But the boy, who was called Friðrik or possibly Ingvar, had quit school and moved, to Grenivík or Grindavík, and that's why it was impossible to get hold of him and ask him more about it.

When I came to the Deep Ditch, over which there was no plank, I stood for a while on the bank, gathering my courage to muck through it. When I finally did, my feet got all wet and muddy, and I scraped my knees as I groped my way up the opposite bank.

Now I was on unfamiliar ground. I didn't recognize a single pipe, stone, or stick. I'd gone past the last landmark, the hut that the sixth-grade kids had cobbled together and named the WILD HUT. Rumor had it that the Wild Ones took shelter there on stormy nights.

In this new territory I transformed myself into Kamala, the foster daughter of wolves. Mom was always talking about her. Wild Kamala from India, who'd sucked the teats of she-wolves rather than her mother's breasts and preferred to play with young goats instead of children after she was captured and kept in the orphanage of Reverend Singh. I scurried around on all fours between pipes, sniffing the dock and snapping at it with a howl.

I wasn't a whit afraid of the Wild Ones anymore. I felt a strange sympathy for them, and could hardly wait to meet them.

As soon as I caught a glimpse of them I'd say: *I'm not Harpa. I'm the foster daughter of wolves. May I join you?* You poor Wild Children, who have no beds to sleep in, no dad to read to you, no walls to shelter you from the wind, no roof to protect you from the rain.

If they allowed me to join them, I could teach them to sew so they wouldn't always need to wear skins. Under the cover of night, I could make off with my mom's hand-crank sewing machine and bring it to the Wild Children. Mom wouldn't miss it, because she had a brand-new Pfaff machine that did embroidery and all the other tricks.

If it were true that they just shrieked and couldn't produce any words, I would also teach them to speak. I would point at myself and say: *Girl*. Point at some dock and say: *Dock*. Point at the sky and say: *Cloud*.

I sat down in half a concrete drainage pipe not far from the ditch, a genuine rocking pipe in which I rocked myself, pretending it was a fishing boat in Grandmafjord. I looked forward to going to the countryside and getting to travel alone on the coastal ship *Esja* or *Hekla*, all grown up, with a malt drink and a banana for a snack. To going east to my fjord, Fáskrúðsfjörður, and feeding milk from a bottle to the orphaned lamb, greeting new calves, and visiting with dear Grandma, who was always warbling *fee fie fiddle-ee-i-o* as she worked in the kitchen and slipping me hard candies and blood pudding with raisins.

I tore off a strip of orange peel and bit into the fruit so that the juice ran down my neck. I tried to wipe it off, but my hands were muddy and just left a dirty smear. Besides that, I was all caked with dried blood from the scrape on my knee. My appearance suited me well, because the Wild Children would probably be bolder about approaching me looking like this than if I were clean and tidy. They might also be less shy if they saw that I ate everything like them, so I gobbled down a dock leaf and some orange peel.

Just then, I heard a shout, and three boys leapt up out of the Deep Ditch. One had a crew cut and was wearing a feather headdress and brandishing an ax; another was wearing a cowboy outfit and carrying a gun; the third had on shorts but no shirt.

Wild One!, shouted the Indian with the ax. *Surround it!*

Two of the boys took positions at either end of the pipe and one next to it, staring at me in terrible surprise. I imagined that they must be from Langholt School, since I'd never seen them before.

I told you it was true. The Wild Ones do exist.

No one ever said they ate dock.

Yes, they do.

She's all smeared with rat blood.

Damn, she's disgusting, and black.

My name is Harpa, and I live on Hrísateigur Street. The blood is mine. I fell and hurt myself.

This one speaks. I was told they didn't know any words.

Of course I speak. My dad teaches shop class at Laugarnes School. His name is Axel, and he lets the kids make leather folders.

There's a shop teacher there named Axel, supposed to be a really good guy. How does she know that?

Maybe she's telling the truth.

No, no, this is a genuine Wild One, said the Indian. Let's attack.

I cried out as he swung his ax to strike, aiming at my head. I just barely managed to twist away, and the ax thwacked my upper arm. In my nightmares I still hear the scream that came from me following the blow in Dock Wood.

Girls never eat dock. *Let's kill the Wild One!* He swung his ax again, but the blow missed and hit the edge of the pipe.

Help me!, I cried to the cowboy and the boy in shorts, who both stood there paralyzed, frightened. At the same time, I jolted myself into action and jumped up out of the pipe, screaming loudly. But I only managed a few steps before the Indian caught hold of my hair and shoved me to the ground. They all stood over me, the Indian still brandishing his ax.

Let's finish off the Wild One!, he howled, kicking my thigh. *Otherwise, it'll kill us!*

What if it's a girl?, said the cowboy. She spoke. I've also heard of a little black girl at Laugarnes School—I just didn't know if it was true.

She has a gold chain around her neck. That's not like a Wild One.

Let's check if she has a belly button. Wild Ones don't have belly buttons.

The Indian bent over me and yanked off my shorts.

Help!, I screamed as loudly as I could.

The Indian said: Hold it, and cover its mouth.

Are you crazy?, exclaimed the boy in shorts. A Wild One can't be wearing a swimsuit. They're always in skins.

In a frenzy now, the Indian shrieked: *Hold the Wild One! It's dangerous!*

The cowboy covered my mouth, and the other boy crossed my arms and held them. I struggled and prayed *Now I lay me down to sleep* for what I thought was the last time. As long as I live I'll never forget the frenzied hatred in the eyes of the crew-cut Indian, and the terrified hatred in the eyes of the other boys.

Then from not far off, Heiður shouted: *Harpa, Harpa, where are you, Harpa?* Hearing her, my strength doubled and I kicked the boy covering my mouth, making him lose his grip. I squeezed out a gruesome wail that stunned the boy.

She said her name is Harpa!, shrieked the boy in shorts. Someone's calling for her! This is just a girl, who speaks and everything. You're crazy, Bragi.

I heard Heiður approach, hurriedly pushing her way through the thick dock, swish-swash. The hatred in Bragi's eyes transformed into sheer terror.

I'll kill you all!, screamed Heiður, swinging a long piece of nail-studded wood.

As the boys ran away, she screeched: I'm calling the police! *You're going to jail!*

I came to my senses on the stretcher as it was slid into the ambulance. A sharp pain shot through my twisted arm. I said, "Arm," and thought at the same time how shameful is was to be wearing nothing but half a swimsuit. It had been pulled down to my waist. Even today, I still have nightmares about being half-naked, wearing torn shorts in public.

. . .

I'm certain they would have finished me off, those fucking pricks, if you hadn't come with that nail-board, Heiður.

You've never told the story that way before, Mom, says Edda, thrusting her face, and her bad breath, toward the front seat.

I suppose it was only to be expected that something would happen. I looked like the first immigrant.

How did you actually get to be like that, Mom?, asks Edda, in a genuine tone of surprise. She who's lived with my looks all her life.

If only I knew.

I giggle, just to be on the safe side, but Heiður doesn't join in. She stares at the road, insecure behind the wheel of her father's pickup. She knows the truth. The question of my appearance has bothered me so much that it trips me up both day and night.

God, I'm glad I don't look like you, Mom.

I understand completely, I say.

But your mother's so beautiful, interjects Heiður.

Heiður will likely end up as a hunchback or at the very least get a slipped disk from taking up the gauntlet for me year after year, from car floors, lawns, kitchen floors.

And this faithful soul is still saving my life, even though I turned thirty-one the day before yesterday, August 29.

I celebrated my thirty-first birthday at the old folks' home at Grund. Harpa Eir, the youngest birthday girl at Grund, ever.

Took the bus to my dad's with a cake that kitchenless I, having packed up everything, got to bake and decorate in the realm of Saga Kaaber, Heiður's mom. The cake didn't endure the trip intact, but luckily Dad's sight is very poor now. His roommate, however, gave the poor wretch of a battered cake a highly puzzled look.

My steps were heavy from the Line Six bus to Hringbraut Road, with the sharp August wind in my face—steps I was taking to say good-bye to Dad. I stumbled with my crappy little cake and nearly fell on my head, which would have landed on a fire hydrant if I hadn't managed to put my hand out. It would have been fitting for the treacherous daughter to be knocked unconscious as she went to abandon her dear old dad for an entire winter, maybe forever.

· · ·

Why is it necessary to have red lights so early on a Sunday morning?, whines Heiður as she stops at the last traffic light in town. There's no one around.

Are we no one?, I say.

I wouldn't say that, says my mom, out of the blue.

I was talking to Heiður, not you. *You're not coming along on the trip.*

You won't even notice I'm here.

It's such a long way. You'd smother me.

. . .

How do you feel, Harpa?, Heiður asks, jerking us into motion, freeing us from the traffic lights.

The bridge over the Elliðaá River is behind us. Rauðavatn Lake and the spruce trees of Heiðmörk are ahead. Soon we leave the outskirts of the city, and the countryside takes over. At our journey's end are a fjord and its valley, around which turned my dreams. Once upon a time.

I don't know, I answer Heiður. It's hard to leave Dad.

Didn't he take it well?

Of course. You know Dad. Since when has he ever thought about himself?

How I wish that snow could have covered my wretched tracks to the old folks' home at Grund when I went to tell him the news at the start of summer. How I wish that I could erase the scene when I pretended I'd come to ask for my dad's advice when I'd already decided to move east for the winter.

THE FALSE DAUGHTER: A narrow two-person room in a rest home. Dad on his bed with the gaudy blanket that Mom crocheted. Me on an uncomfortable chair opposite him. A twenty-year-old radio on the nightstand, a Blaupunkt from my youth, a prop from my former life on Hrísateigur Street resurrected for this absurd drama at Grund. This degradation was never even imaginable when it was a newly purchased state-of-the-art device and center of attention on the homemade teakwood kitchen table. The extra in the play, the deaf roommate, can neither listen to the radio nor our conversation. He's completely out of touch with the world. He has such a trivial role that he says not a word while other paupers in other plays are at least allowed to croak *Good master!*

Dad sees immediately that I'm feeling low. He probably also realizes, before I utter a word, that I've come to betray him. I'm a female Judas, a false daughter who's come here just to leave, to leave him, my bleary-eyed sad old dad. The dad who gave me good memories, the dad who read "Hansel and Gretel" and *Oh How Strange It Was* with incredible dramatic emphasis, modifying his voice and singing in falsetto to amuse his little girl. Dad, the shop teacher himself, who created things day and night, artful little rotary grindstones and puzzles. Dad, who substituted for Jón Pálsson, the master hobbyist and host of National Radio's *Leisure Time Program* when Jón's voice became too hoarse.

Here he sits, red-eyed, in the blue-gray sweater vest with bright-yellow elbow patches that Mom designed. I remember him in the new sweater holding Edda when she was just a few months old. I also remember Mom stitching on the patches after she became sick. I said: Mom, these don't go together at all. And Mom said: Can't you see how crazy fun this is? Being one who wants everything to match, I just shook my head. Those indestructible patches are still on his sleeves. They'll survive me, said Mom. Now it also looks as if they're going to survive the sweater's owner, and the sweater itself, for that matter.

I get up from the chair, sit down on the bed, and with extreme sentimentality lay my palm over Dad's cold hand. I, an archlurker, have come to betray. I should be ashamed of myself; it's the least I can do. I'm ashamed of myself, Dad. Of course I am.

Clouds shadow the Heiðmörk conservation area. Evergreen trees nourish hungry eyes in the yellow-gray moss-covered lava, summer winter spring and fall. Sun dapples the flower-filled hollows where we sit, drinking cocoa from plastic cups and eating malted bread with cheese.

Dad with his flat cap off, imitating birds. Dad, patient Dad, teaching us to make grass whistles. If someone falls and scrapes himself, and there's always someone falling, Dad pulls a Band-Aid from his pocket, blows on the cut, and bandages it. As gentle with Heiður as if she were his own daughter, as gentle with me as if I were his own daughter.

She who comes to betray at the start of summer:

Dad, Dýrfinna came.

She visited me, too. She gave me some of her homemade ointment to treat the sore on my foot.

I know. I can't believe she's still making it.

I stroke the back of Dad's hand.

She wants, she wants—

Yes, she spoke to me about it. She thinks it would do Edda Sólveig good to be out east, with Ingólfur and Margrét in Andey.

Exactly . . .

That's right, and she said that you could stay in her attic, if you wanted to be close to Edda.

That's what I was going to talk to you about.

You should hurry and go. It can do nothing but good.

I hate to leave you behind, Dad.

Your brother will look in on me. You have more than enough on your plate, without having to worry about me. All that matters is for little Edda to get back on track. A change of environment could be the way to go.

I don't even know if there is a way.

It'll at least be a try, my dear. Even if it fails, you can always say you tried. The worst is to do nothing.

I'm so downcast that I can't think of anything else to say, and now it's Dad who pats my hand. His hand is cold, a veiny, gaunt claw, with brown spots and cracked yellow old-man's nails. The same hand that's so warm in my childhood memory, the grip firm and trusty.

You won't be anxious if I go?

To be anxious is the privilege of the young. I don't know how to be so anymore. Just wait, dear girl, you'll be surprised when the time comes. How nice it is to be old and expect nothing, to take delight in all the trivial things—little sunbeams that come slanting in through the window to warm you, a gentle voice on the radio, a cup of coffee in the morning. We'll talk on the phone, my dear Harpa. I'll be fine here.

I pat his shriveled paw and say that I don't know what would have become of me if I hadn't had such a good dad.

You can tell me that as often as you like, says Dad, laughing with his young voice, the same that laughed at Pippi Longstocking's shenanigans after I'd crawled into bed on Sunday mornings and said, *Read, Daddy*, driving my ice-cold toes into the backs of his knees. Dad's grown old now, prematurely, old in every respect except for his voice. Sometimes I shut my eyes and listen to it and imagine that time stopped before everything came pouring over.

DAMNED SLOW-ASS!, shouts Heiður.

To be on our way is all that matters, and the indigenous Icelandic art of holding up traffic doesn't bother me at all today. But my friend at the wheel can't restrain the impatience that's in her blood. How this impatient person can stand practicing the flute hour after hour, year after year, the same notes, the same lifeless scales, is a mystery to me. I've questioned her—asked her straight-out—and even read up on the lives and working methods of musicians, but I still don't get it.

Heiður leans on the horn. I glance over my shoulder, startled, to see whether the passenger in the backseat's going to rain curse words down on us from her hungover trap, but she doesn't stir.

Just ahead of us is a rusty Land Rover, and in front of it an ultralong American car.

Please don't honk the horn like that.

Heiður hammers the dashboard with a clenched fist, bellowing: *These people don't know how to drive! They're like damned cows out on the moors!*

It's not car number one, but car number two that's the slow-ass, I say. It should pass. The trouble always starts when car number two hangs on the tail of car number one.

Huh.

It's a beautiful day, Heiður. Let's go slowly and enjoy the scenery.

Near and far.

Neat rows of midsummer-yellow dandelions line the edge of the road, defying the blowballs, the future that they don't know awaits them.

Spread over the banks of the small Sandskeið pools is the sedge that all children think is cotton but isn't.

Nothing is as it seems. Neither before nor since, neither near nor far.

In the complex massif of Hengill are secret green valleys and white clouds of steam.

Soon the white patches on the Bláfjöll Range will expand, transforming into glistening snowfields accented with skiers in out-fits of all colors. Last winter, it was in fact one of my escapes. On cross-country ski trails I would forget my overwhelming concerns while chatting with apple-cheeked, oxygen-deprived people, some with sleds and warmly dressed children in tow. It made me recall little Edda tearing down the toboggan slopes with me.

Heiður, far from happy with the slow progress of traffic, keeps honking into the wind, while the slow-ass drives his Land Rover at a steady pace down the middle of the road. Maybe he's hard of hearing and unaware of us, or maybe he's just being obstinate. It's all the same to me, but my driver, her long chin topped with a vigorous frown, says nothing as I explain my sudden realization, after all my trips east, that the broad mountain Skjaldbreiður can be seen for just a brief moment from this road, even though it seems as if it ought to be invisible from here at the Svínahraun lava field. I feel like an explorer of an unknown territory, and I shiver with joy at seeing one of my favorite mountains make an unexpected cameo on this frequently traveled route.

I add that she can even see the summit of Snæfellsjökull if she looks in the rearview mirror.

As if I didn't know that, she says, irritated, before changing the subject. How did you manage to conjure up a necklace during a brief stop at an empty apartment?

Heiður is extremely dangerous in the way that she notices everything. Even before I did, she saw what was happening with Edda Sólveig. It's antisocial behavior, she said, and she was right. One sign, in retrospect, was how the girl stopped greeting visitors. She would just go straight to her room and shut the door. When Edda started hanging out downtown or who knows where until dawn and came home either smashed or stoned, it was Heiður who realized right away that it was something more than normal teen drinking and attitude.

Edda's nickname for Heiður is *The Scanner*. "I can't stand that damned Scanner" has been a common refrain from my daughter the last few months. Heiður had rented a movie with this name, about a man with X-ray vision who used his amazing psychic powers to explode people's heads.

Wouldn't you know—Edda found the creature behind the radiator. It had been lost for more than a year.

What is it?

Don't you remember? I always wore it after I came back from my summer in Perpignan.

Yes, of course. What is it again?

It's a kind of beetle that was sacred in Egypt, called a scarab. It symbolizes rebirth. Gabriel Axel gave it to me.

Is that the guy who's always sending you and Edda things?

Only for Christmas and birthdays.

Weird. You just sort of randomly met him that summer in Perpignan and he can't forget you?

The man is close to seventy. We're pen pals. Maybe he took to me because he doesn't have kids.

And gives you a good-luck charm in parting?

Seems logical to me. A lucky charm for an unlucky creature. The funniest thing he's sent me so far is a large compass, from his shop, which is called The Art of Sailing. He sells everything you can imagine for people who own boats, big or small. Ship's bells, sea charts, pilot wheels, books about sailing and repairs, stories and novels of sea voyages: *Moby-Dick, The Old Man and the Sea.*

How did you meet him?

I've told you that seven times.

Tell me eight times.

Every morning, as a favor for my landlady, Widow Dumont, I went to the bakery to buy croissants for breakfast and, on Sunday mornings, *petits pains au chocolat.* One Sunday I had to find somewhere new, because the bakery on the corner was closed for the summer. As I walked past the sailing shop, I happened to drop the glass bottle of mineral water I was holding. It shattered on the street, and as I gathered up the pieces, I cut my finger. Gabriel Axel saw this from his apartment, which is above the shop, and he invited me in and bandaged me up. I was in a rush, because I knew Widow Dumont wouldn't be happy if she had to wait too long for her *petits pains au chocolat,* which would no longer be warm, not to mention the Sunday edition of *Le Figaro.* But Gabriel Axel asked where I came from. You should have seen his face when I said Iceland.

He threw up his hands and said: *Yes, but you don't look like it!*

I know, I said, but it's not my fault.

Then this noble man laughed and invited me for coffee or a drink next time I was off work. I didn't hesitate to accept, though Dad had warned me about the white slave trade. I figured no one in the white slave trade would want dark little me, anyway.

When I paid Gabriel Axel a formal visit, it turned out he'd been to Iceland—isn't the world small and strange? Naturally, I was surprised that he hadn't told me that right away. You didn't mention that the other day, I said. He gave me a peculiar look before replying: I suppose I'd just forgotten it.

Were you bored by Iceland?, I asked.

I wouldn't say that, he answered.

I was curious to know why he'd gone, and he said he'd gotten lost.

Oh, where were you planning to go?, I asked.

That's just a way of putting it, he said.

He'd sailed over on the *Gullfoss* at Christmas, and I said that visiting at that time of year was absurd; it's so dark that you can't see anything. But he said he'd wanted to see the dark days, those renowned northern days of darkness that are more like night.

Too bad they can hardly be seen, I said, and suggested that he come back in the summer. He said that he very much wanted to, especially to see the summer in my fjord to the east. But he never mentions visiting in his letters. I don't know why. I think he has enough money.

He's so wonderful, just like a ghost—

How can ghosts be wonderful?, interrupts Heiður.

You'll understand when I introduce you to him. He's long and thin, with a matador's physique, and he walks with a Seville swing, because he grew up in Seville. His father was French and his mother a Portuguese Jew, so, strictly speaking, he's Jewish—it's based on maternity. He's fluent in French, Spanish, and Portuguese.

I need to practice and then show you how they walk in Seville, with a deep swing, leaning back. Gabriel Axel has such an air of grandeur, the kind of melancholy grandeur that doesn't exist in the north. He isn't married, but keeps company with a famous Catalan flamenco dancer named Elvira. She's such an incredible character, with the widest smile I've ever seen. It reaches completely up to her nose and all the way out to her ears, and she has a gap in her front teeth. But her dark-brown eyes are sad, like the eyes of her boyfriend, full of sorrow but never dull. I saw her dancing once, but being well over sixty years old now, she mainly teaches. I've never understood the logic in flamenco. It's one of the most difficult things that the body can undertake, yet it's still possible to dance it until the day you die. Elvira was a total star, dancing throughout Europe and America. I saw clippings from *Die Zeit, Corriere della Sera,* the *Times, Politiken, Frankfurter Allgemeine, Neue Zürcher Zeitung,* the *Washington Post.*

How do you remember all this?

I've told you all this before, and you obviously don't deserve to hear it again since you're so horribly senile.

Heiður grins, and apparently not caring to listen anymore, she turns on the radio. We listen to rhythmic Bach, who gives us faith in glorious order and rule, faith in our existence. Faith in Sunday light, a fresh day over Hellisheiði Heath.

Which inches its way up along the beveled edge to its yellow sunstead.

Lends intense luminosity to the dense green moss-covered lava after the damp of night.

The white-flecked blueness of Mount Hekla and the enchanting ice cap of Eyjafjallajökull, promise of another land farther east, of what the travelers get to see up close:

Radiant mountain stars, from other angles.

The view from the crest of Kambar isn't dependent on the season, or on any time for that matter; it's unreal. The coldly gentle light overenhances naked contours, and a traveler thinks: This isn't real, I'm not here.

If you venture beyond the shelter of a window—car, house, airplane—the land doesn't become unreal, but rather, superreal. A cold gust of wind gets caught in your throat, enters the naked individual, chafes the ears, and you think: It shouldn't exist, I shouldn't be here.

Heiður, weren't you scared of Kambar when you were little?

Me, scared? No, for me it was fun when the view opened up after the tedium of the heath.

I didn't notice that you could see anything, because I was so terrified of the steepness and the narrow road. Plus my ears hurt or they got stopped up, which sometimes lasted for several hours.

But now I see

Hveragerði

billows of steam from dells and gorges behind the village

tongues of spruce trees stretching far up the mountain

the green plain cut by the Ölfusá River

silver sea

mountain glory and glacier

which pulls us in

Nothing at this moment tells us that the summer is retreating. Even the lone snowdrift on Mount Skálafell pretends to be something it's not. It's the only one that didn't melt in the summer, and could actually be an April drift, with style. Nor do any birds reveal the season—they're nowhere to be seen, gathering for departure over the seas. There's no hint of autumn in the air, and it's impossible to tell from the color of the sky and the light following dawn that summer is fading fast.

Behold the glory. Let's breathe.

Breathe. We've forgotten to breathe in this car, which smells like a small pub, and no one's had the sense to roll down a window.

On the Crest of Kambar

Heiður pulls the parking brake after coming to an abrupt stop at the turnout. I thought we were going to go over the edge, but I kept my mouth shut. Maybe I hoped deep down that she'd let us fall. Then she dashes out and takes several spasmodic steps around the panoramic dial. Heiður certainly does lurch her way through life. She walks and talks in fits and starts. But everything changes when she plays her flute. When she walks onstage, she transforms. All of her hastiness and testiness vanish. She becomes peculiarly supple, as if harnessing her innate jerkiness in order to travel out to the very edge of fluidity and seesaw over the abyss just beyond the brink, balanced against an invisible weight.

And in the third row, her assistant-nurse best friend, who can neither play flute nor anything else, feels a little twinge of admiration and envy.

My daughter in the backseat has opened her eyes, and I dare to address her:

Would you like to get out and stretch a bit, Edda?

She arches her back aggressively and sticks out her tongue at me.

I cautiously hop out of the pickup as a nearsighted person would do. We small-statured folk carry ourselves like those who are nearsighted. It's not surprising; the world's so far from us. We've got to get right up close to it in order to function.

My daughter's attitude hasn't escaped Heiður's notice, of course, and she asks whether Edda's making any progress.

Not that I've noticed.

You've been far too kind to her. You let her walk all over you.

Remind me again that it's all my fault.

Since when did you become so sensitive?

Don't be so cross. Have you forgotten how miserable I am?

I never forget it, says Heiður, laughing. Look, not a single cloud over Eyjafjallajökull. And the Westmann Islands are so vividly blue, as if they've just stepped out of a deep-sea bath.

She stares at the sea, narrowing her eyes as if she intends to heave the Westmann Islands archipelago from it with mental energy. As her eyes grow smaller, her nose elevates and her chin grows longer.

I lean against the gleaming-white car, and the curtains of my mind draw shut as the sun itself bursts forth from its cloud-cage and long pale sunbeams point at the shimmering bends of the Ölfusá River all the way south to the coast, where they spread out before the sea takes over.

You're so pale, says Heiður. Are you carsick?

No.

My nausea is none of her business. It's a reminder of my stupid life's work, child rearing that went down the drain, a single seriously ill infant of fifteen years. Is it true that she's mine? How did I do this?

Maybe I'm making the next-biggest mistake of my life with this trip, though there have certainly been enough to choose from. I have to resign myself to the fact that I won't discover anytime soon whether it was right to leave or stay, and that I might never discover it.

Look, they're turning, I say.

Thank God, says Heiður.

The two cars that had kept us at thirty miles per hour across the length of Hellisheiði Heath had both turned into the town of Hveragerði. This Sunday morning the traffic eastward from Reykjavík consisted of three cars precisely, forming a little caravan. How incredibly skilled some Icelanders can be at holding up other cars on the road, and frugal. One single car is all they need for their caravan.

. . .

To torment myself on the way down, I look at the old road, how it twists in tight bends, precipitous and narrow from the lowland up to the heath. The combined miseries that I've suffered on Kambar are not insignificant. One of my first memories is of Mom's fear of heights manifesting itself here, her calling for Jesus to save us and me screaming in the backseat.

I'm ashamed to say it, but I still sometimes feel dizzy on this broad, winding road with its steel guardrails. My sense of balance is probably a bit out of whack. Heiður's driving doesn't help, as she accelerates and decelerates by turns, for no apparent reason.

How much I wish I weren't in this overstuffed vehicle that reeks of moonshine. This isn't the day to be here. It's a day to be nowhere, except in Grandma's Grove, tending to sweet little trees and listening carefully to every keen word uttered by my very own streams and waterfalls.

I don't want to be thirty-one with my life behind me, all because of an accident when I was small and stupid and didn't know how to say no to a shy but pushy boy. I want to be a fourteen-year-old girl, me as I was *before*.

Fourteen years old on the coastal ship *Hekla* or *Esja*, on my way to the eastern part of the country, running thirsty eyes over waves and crests and skerries, with salty sea-air in my lungs.

The seas cover three-quarters of the earth, land only one-fourth, Dad taught me, turning the illuminated globe on his desk.

Fortunately, the lands are small and shallow compared to the seas.

Fortunately, my land is an island surrounded by a very large sea.

Everything seems gentler from the sea: the island is bluer, the fjords greener, and the glaciers softer. When I was at Laugarnes School I wrote THE SEA IS MY LAND, a story for the school paper about sailing east to my countryside.

For half the year I looked forward to sailing east, just as much as I feared Sunday drives, steep slopes, and narrow bridges with bends in them, and Mom running her mouth nonstop. No matter how hard I tried to shut it out, her hoarse voice crashed into my ears and filled my head.

There was nothing to do but bite the bullet and curse under my breath. Dad remained ridiculously focused behind the wheel, his shoulders stiff and his chin thrust forward. Whenever possible, he peeked over his shoulder and smiled at me and my brother, Sibbi, as we pinched and scratched each other in secret to the sounds of Mom ranting.

The old Škoda is the first car I remember, its color a peculiarly washed-out yellow-gray-brown-green. Mom had just returned from getting her hair permed and colored, her hair white and dull, her red mouth running like a machine in a monologue about sloths, which take eight days to digest their food, and about the foster daughter of wolves, Mom's all-time favorite subject during my childhood. Amala and Kamala in India, raised by wolves, discovered by men, and taken into Reverend Singh's orphanage. Amala and Kamala dashed about on all fours with tangled hair down to their waists, terrifying civilized men at midnight with their howling and devouring carrion, bloody from their mouths to their ears.

Sibbi started teasing me early, saying I was a foster child from the Far East. With my looks, I believed him, and I cried myself to sleep at night. Kids don't know that such things constitute normal sibling torture.

I wanted to raise myself above the wretched status of foster child and instead become a fantastic and very rare foster daughter of wolves. I practiced it like a circus act when I was home alone. Wearing only my underwear, I crawled and howled across the kitchen floor as fast as I could. Once, my mother caught me. I thought she'd gone to town, but she'd actually only stepped out to the nearby fish shop. She'd come all the way into the kitchen and clearly witnessed the whole thing, but acted as if nothing were out of the ordinary. I was terribly ashamed and wanted to cry, but instead said: *Bak pú vó.* It was one of the few things that little Kamala ever learned to say, and means *doll in a box.*

Fish, said Mom, pointing at the haddock.

Yes, of course. This is what I'll name my autobiography, which will never be written: THE FOSTER DAUGHTER OF WOLVES, the name of a book that exists and is about something else.

I roll down the window, and Edda shouts: Do you want to kill me? I promptly roll it up again.

No, it isn't fun to be the goddamn wimp that I am. In fact, it can be dangerous. Edda wouldn't be in such a state if I were tough enough to deal with the world and her.

Edda, should we stop at Selfoss as usual and get ice cream?

My only child doesn't hear. She's in her own world, with her Walkman headphones in her ears and her eyes shut. Her face is pale, and she has light-green circles under her eyes, and she isn't particularly well washed. A red scar from an ugly injury runs from the top of her ear over her cheekbone and almost all the way to her nose. Edda's an emaciated child with more life experience than a seventy-year-old man. She's wearing a leather vest over a torn sweater and greasy black stretch pants, with a spider in her earlobe, and a skull ring from little

Rúna on her index finger. Defenseless Rúna, who didn't survive the world that my daughter entered this past year.

Will you please stop in Selfoss, Heiður? Edda's got to have an ice cream.

Edda?, Heiður asks. Ice cream?

It's an unbendable tradition on our jaunts: ice cream in Selfoss.

You call this a jaunt?

Let's say it's a jaunt. That we're just on an outing to Selfoss, and when we set off from there, we're not going any farther east than to Hella. If you divide up the route and shut the gates in between, it becomes bearable—many short jaunts.

You're quite the expert.

Those who have delinquent children become experts in time and space, I say. They learn to cut time into pieces in order to survive it, change the road into turnouts and splice them together into one main road.

Heiður asks whether it's worthwhile to stop, since the girl would probably just be irritated.

Yes, and that's also how she'll be if she doesn't get ice cream. Sounds familiar, doesn't it?

There's a slight twitch around Heiður's mouth, in the sensitive flute-nerves adjacent to the base of her powerful nose. She's in no mood to discuss the vicious circle of my life right now.

Where is everyone?, she asks.

Nowhere. We're alone in the world.

Queen of the road!, sings Heiður, accelerating in the middle of Ölfusá River Bridge and taking a reckless turn into the sleeping town.

Have you lost your mind?, hisses Edda, after tumbling over.

You should be wearing a seat belt, dear.

I'd need a life belt, the way you drive.

Strange that the creature sometimes seems to have a sense of humor. Delinquent children generally don't have a good eye for the absurd side of human life, as far as I've seen.

Aren't you going to stop, woman?, exclaims Edda.

At the last moment, Heiður swerves into the parking lot in front of the ice-cream shop, and brakes with a piercing screech.

Selfoss

Shall I get you something from the shop, Edda, or are you coming in?

She says nothing, but her crooked old smile reappears and her face brightens momentarily.

Heiður skips perkily into the shop, like a five-year-old girl on a playground, while Edda drags along behind, her shoulders bent in the world's glummest slouch.

The morning sun shines brightly, the day is calm, the view extends far into the highlands—into the heart of my country, which I've never had a chance to explore. To me, Sprengisandur and Kjölur are terrae incognitae; the routes over my own highlands are unknown to me.

I lean against the bed of the little white pickup truck, where selected bits of my household belongings lay piled beneath a canvas tarp. I breathe so deeply that I grow giddy from the heavenly air and the view of the glacier, wishing simultaneously that the truck would change into a helicopter, Heiður into a pilot, and Edda into the good girl she once was, and that we could waltz on polished, airy dance floors over the highlands all day long and sing all the songs that came to mind.

Heiður's standing in the shop door as I enter, and she gives me an anxious look, making her even more long-faced and as off-putting as the figure in *The Scream*, the painting that hangs in every last hotel room in Oslo, troubling the dreams of international travelers.

Edda's chatting with a lanky fellow in sap-green leather pants. They lean against the counter, as if incapable of standing up straight. The back of the boy's head is shaved from his neck up over his ears, and a greasy ponytail hangs down between his shoulder blades. Oh, the Chicken is here. No wonder I didn't recognize him right away; he's changed his haircut.

The posture of the two at the counter reminds me of the scene when the Chicken came to Bollagata with Edda broken-armed, her face bruised and cut, a remarkable spring-night pair oscillating awkwardly at the front door like spastic Siamese twins.

I walk slowly into the restroom as if I were on official business, with Heiður right behind like an assistant, holding on to a child's ice-cream cone dipped in chocolate and sprinkled with puffed rice. Why should it bother me if some teenage boy makes a trip to the countryside?

Who's that?, Heiður hisses.

That damned Gerti Chicken from the gang.

Why in God's name is he called "chicken"?

His parents kept chickens in an old Dodge in their yard, in one of those charming fishing villages down south by the sea. They felt it unnecessary to pay a fortune for eggs, not when they had such fine facilities at their doorstep. They were astounded when the Public Health Authority started asking questions.

Heiður laughs her spasmodic laugh, which inspires more dread than cheer in those who aren't used to it.

That boy cuts an awful figure, says Heiður, after regaining her composure. He's like a seventy-year-old wino who's borrowed a leather outfit from the Hells Angels.

He came very close to shooting himself into the great beyond last year.

Oh my God, are these people into heroin?

Not as fancy as that, as far as I know. No, they grind up aspirin tablets and inject them. The poor Chicken definitely got hold of something stronger.

God, I've never heard anything more funny and pathetic. What sorry excuses for addicts.

It isn't so funny. Even if the stuff isn't that strong, they could still contract AIDS or hepatitis.

Edda shoves open the door with a loud crack and storms in, chin protruding.

Gerti's going to Reykjavík. He offered me a ride.

We're going the other direction, remember?, I say, acting as unaffected as possible. If I show any signs of weakness, all is lost.

Yes, maybe *you're* going the other direction. But I decide where *I'm* going.

Don't be so ridiculous, says Heiður. It's a done deal.

Maybe it's a done deal for Harpa Eir, Edda says.

It doesn't bode well when my child starts calling me by my baptismal name. Now my every little move has to be considered carefully, because one misplaced word would be enough, or simply a look that Edda Sólveig Loftsdóttir doesn't like, and she could be in a car with Gerti Chicken, heading back toward Reykjavík, in order to finish herself off slowly or quickly, depending on circumstance. It occurs to me, and not for the first time, that I should maybe indulge her.

Keep out of it. It's none of your business, I say so brusquely that Heiður sputters and coughs over the sink, the melting ice cream in her hand. Hopefully, she'll understand that I needed to bristle at her, despite it being ludicrous, if I'm going to win this round of the match.

I'll wait out in the car, I say, and hurry out of this stupid restroom, cursing Gerti, Heiður, and Edda in my mind. I treat everyone equally, you can grant me that. As I walk past Gerti, hanging bowlegged from the counter with a can of Coke and a Camel cigarette, I resort to the excellent idea of sticking out my poetic tongue at him. The hand holding the Coke can freezes halfway to his mouth, but his expression doesn't change, not one bit.

Unluckily, a young backpacker, a foreigner in a red down jacket, witnesses my mockery, and his southern face screws up from his forehead to his chin and out to his ears. I smile to show him that I can do that as well.

It's a refreshing relief to come out under the bare sky, and I feel good about my negotiation of human relations. Maybe I'll make it a rule to stick out my tongue at assholes and hoodlums. But, hmm. It would be a lot of work. I'd be like a lizard, constantly shooting out my tongue and having time for nothing else.

Gerti's yellow car is parked outside the gas station next door. It's a smaller version of a delivery van with a high roof and no rear side windows, and goes by the name *The Little Yellow Hen*.

I've got to be careful not to let Edda intimidate me. She's coming with us. I don't look back; that would be fatal. If Edda noticed me looking back to check on her, she'd turn me into a little pillar of salt and rush off to Reykjavík with her brain-damaged friends.

Edda's left her bag in the car. I open it up and find two pill bottles, one half full of acetaminophen, the other full of valium. Her hangover kit. No suspicious tablets, no powder. I confiscate a small portion of both types, assuming she hasn't inventoried her supply. I must remember to reiterate to the Andey couple to hide all their medicines, worm medicine included. Unless that's what Edda needs. An anthelmintic to drive out worms.

I hear footsteps, but it's not Edda. Edda drags her feet like a storybook ghost. It's Heiður's jerky gait. She climbs straight into the car.

What fucking fuss was that?

Sorry, Heiður. You don't deserve this. I was trying to save the situation by scolding you. I had to do it to prevent the girl from actually going back to town with that idiot.

Oh, of course, I should have realized that. What do you think she'll do?

Who the hell knows? What do you think of Gerti's car?

It's funny. Is he a delivery boy?

Yes, he's a delivery boy for the father of Hreinn Elías, who's one of Edda's so-called friends. We saw Hreinn Elli outside the house on Bollagata this morning. The poor boy is sometimes called Hreinn Brain for some reason, and his father, who's called Pituitary, brews moonshine on a large scale. Theodór the Ringleader—by far the biggest shithead of Edda's friends—manages the sales, and Gerti makes the deliveries.

Theodór's in charge? Isn't he the same age as Edda?

He just turned sixteen. Celebrated his birthday in Hotel Saga's Homestead Room, with coffee and sandwich cakes, traditional refreshments for wakes. He's a soft-spoken businessman to whom picking up the phone and dealing with hotel managers comes as naturally as ordering pizzas does to most kids his age.

Edda rushes back and squeezes into the backseat among all the luggage. My daughter's grown out of buying ice cream in Selfoss. She's holding a can of Pripps low-alcohol beer and a pack of peanuts.

You stuck out your tongue at him, you rude bitch.

Hold on a minute, says Heiður, with a laugh.

You stuck out your tongue at Gerti.

Did the Chicken complain to you?, I ask, cool as day, while fiddling with my twisted seat belt.

. . .

Why did you stick out your tongue at my friend? I'm fucking ashamed of you.

Your mo-hom has never stuck out her to-hongue at anyone, says Heiður in between bursts of laughter, distracted from steering the car out onto the highway. That friend of yours has had a little too much of something.

It isn't funny, you snobby cunt, says Edda, in a choked-up voice.

Hey, what kind of language is that?, exclaims Heiður.

I can call you *flute pussy* if you like it better.

My rude daughter sounds as if she's on the verge of tears over my behavior toward Gerti. Interesting that it should bother her so much. Inwardly, I'm dying of laughter, but I mustn't laugh when my child is so foul-mouthed toward her benefactor.

I prepare for a long silence in the car, maybe even all the way to Vík in Mýrdalur. I don't feel like talking, anyway.

What a Sunday jaunt. I don't understand what Gerti Chicken is doing out here. Gerti's so stupid that the idea of following us couldn't occur to his shaved, ponytailed head. No, he must be on more important business, picking up moonshine from some distillery, for example.

I look over my shoulder, just as Edda's head is turning back after having looked over her own, and she grimaces as we catch each other in the act. We're both looking for the yellow van, which isn't in sight.

I glance askance at Heiður. Her expression is formidable, as might be expected after the last exchange with her hopeless passengers. HOPELESS PASSENGERS wouldn't be a bad title for one chapter in little Harpa's biography, or as a subtitle for the book.

The road cuts across a moor, and cars travel it in wavelike motions, making passengers' stomachs gurgle as the tall grass stands nearly unmoving at the roadside. For now, think deeply, focusing on the silo silhouetted against Mount Hekla. Then surge along the undulating moor road, listen to the inner gurgling, become one with it and the rising feeling of nausea as the sun warms the light-yellow blades and reddish ears of the autumn grass between the wire fence and the road.

THE DAYS HAVE COME.

The days have come when you say, I find no pleasure in them.

The day has come when I travel east out of necessity. The day is today. The paradise of childhood is transformed into a prison yard. I who could always flee east when all other doors were shut. Now it's the place that's shutting me in.

Where shall I flee when my blessed Andey has become a lair for a viper that I've suckled at my breast? For what shall I be homesick?

Almost every spring until Edda was born I came east to the glittering springs that foreign businessmen see as potential, to Grandma in her garden where the trees grow tall and straight: birch, rowan, aspen, silver fir, red spruce, pitch pine, hackberry. Where the flowers spread: meadowsweet, harebell, Icelandic burnet rose, pyramidal saxifrage.

The dreamland where everything grows, where even my soul took root. Apparently my mother's soul was there as well. This came to light when she told me of the fairy-tale fjord that in the spring transformed into a floating tent city. She spoke at normal speed as she recalled the fishing boats in the shape of majestic migratory birds, and her voice warmed as she told of Martin the Frenchman, the doctor on the hospital ship *Lodestar* who saved her life by removing her appendix, and, when he returned the following summer, gave her the imperishable doll, Cosette.

Edda was also homesick for the dreamland when she was little. When it was too bitterly and grimly cold to play outside, she said she wanted to go to *Addey to dab*, meaning "build little dams." I'll never forget her in Grandma's Grove, her first summer there when she was two years old, calling out *mommappa* to her mommy, Harpa, under the pitch pine that grows just inside the garden wall and leans out over it to reflect in the pool at Andá River when the weather's calm. Her wretched little mother was just eighteen then.

I mustn't lose sight of Edda as she was those summers, a plump-faced girl with freckles, wearing firecracker-red shorts, her gleaming copper hair in braids, chasing speedy blowflies and the tails of cats, showing her mom the remains of an old farm, a bleached-out leg bone that she found beneath a rock, or a fragment of a shiny shell. I mustn't forget that the child and I existed a long time in a world in which we could clearly see our hands in front of our eyes, before the sorcerous fog descended.

I mustn't forget that in the darkness I still have people who try to light my way. My relatives to the east who shelter Edda and me. The friend who's driving us east in her dad's pickup, and the good spirits who gave me good advice, above all Jói and Dýrfinna.

But I should have listened to Dýrfinna sooner. Mom jokingly called her Prescient Finna, without realizing that she'd hit the nail on the head. Aunt Dýrfinna is one of those people who can see farther than the tips of their noses, not because she's in contact with another world, but because she thinks clearly.

Before anyone else, Dýrfinna saw signs of where Edda was headed, though she didn't say it outright. The summer that Edda was thirteen, Dýrfinna said that Ingólfur and Margrét wanted to have Edda stay on with them in Andey that winter. The girl was up for it. But I felt that the only acceptable thing was for me to take care of this child of mine. I was no invalid, damn it, though I might be a wimp. Other single mothers had toiled away in poverty and brought their children to adulthood. How could I justify to myself putting her in the hands of others? I who had sacrificed everything in order not to be dependent on others, ahem, to no one but the dwarf I lived with at the time, who was really not the best choice.

If I'd recognized the signs of the imminent tragedy, I would have taken Dýrfinna's advice. Then it all hit that winter. My child, the changeling, was exchanged before I could say so much as "Damn it," and I found myself with a little bag lady instead. Of course she wouldn't hear of going to the Eastfjords the summer after; instead she wanted to stay in the broken glass in the park at Arnarhóll, like others of her kind. But what Aunt Dýrfinna saw, what signs she noticed that indicated Edda would be heading straight off the map, I still don't know today, not even in hindsight. I saw nothing until it was right before my eyes.

Now the child is finally on her way east, where she should have been the entire time, on a late, special trip, with her mother and Heiður and the doll Cosette, which was named after the character in *Les Misérables*.

If I'd had any backbone, I would have taken the opportunity given to me by moving and slaughtered old Cosette or sold it. It's probably a valuable antique. But what did I do? I packed it securely into my best suitcase, the precious treasure from Gabriel Axel. It was even the first thing that I packed.

Cosette could have represented any one of the many unfulfilled dreams in Mom's unsuccessful life. The boat trips that were never taken, discourses on everything and nothing, the infidelity that led to my birth. She kept that foreign doll in a locked glass cabinet where nothing else was allowed to be, a little idol that I wasn't allowed to touch unless Mom was watching. A symbol of her chaotic dreams that weighed so heavily upon us and threatened to suffocate us alive. What a grudge I bore against the totem doll in the cabinet where Mom stood with her hands clasped, poised as if worshipping. Once when she wasn't at home, I stole the key and took out Cosette. I started caressing her extremely hypocritically, acting as if I didn't know what I was up to, then produced a long darning needle and stuck it in the doll's rump.

This dandy of a doll was also a symbol of the treatment Dad received, Mom's practical method for torturing him. She acted as if she and the doll belonged together, so elegant and distinguished, while Dad was just Icelandic scum. Dad was of course far too good for Mom. His was a beautiful soul, which Mom abused.

Do you ever see Alli the dwarf?

The few times that Heiður breaks the wall of silence, she's careful to choose unpleasant topics. It irritates me to no end how nosy she is about the men in my life, maybe because there's not so much to be nosy about, but I forgive her privately by thinking that she just envies my options. She's well set now with the incredible German baritone Dietrich Bacon. He was mine from the start, backstage after the concert at the Old Theater; it couldn't have been more obvious even if it completely escaped Heiður. I let her have him out of sheer obtuseness, or general stupidity.

I go out of my way to avoid little Alli if I see him on the street, I reply. The man is so boring he could put a slug to sleep.

Is he still in contact with Edda?

He calls her now and then and occasionally gives her money. If he happens to run into her, he invites her to go for a hamburger, even if he's terribly busy. Terribly busy. His wording never changes. He always brings her a Christmas gift in person, something nice.

Can't that be called loyalty? Hasn't it been five years since you quit living together? He's not even her father.

Even mental dwarves have their qualities.

Don't be saying bad things about Alli, Edda chimes in. You were awful to him and then left him.

Have it your way, Edda.

What does Alli do now?

Alfredo Bibelinni is a debt collector and a binge drinker, as he was when we were together. Imagine taking a five-year college-degree program to become certified to collect debts. Wouldn't it be more economical for society to shorten such a degree to half a year at a vocational school? But no matter how many televisions Alli collects from pensioners and the crying mothers of reprobates, he never has enough money for alcohol, fashionable jackets in increasing sizes, sports cars, and complicated gadgets. Too bad no female ever sticks around for long in those furnishings of his, nor in those excellent negligees that he collects. They're usually out of their negligees after about a month, then leave fully dressed and never again show themselves in the Seltjarnarnes suburbs.

Well, says Heiður, it's been no more than a month since he cried on my shoulder for half an evening and said that he loved Harpa, the magical creature. Couldn't forget her.

I know. You've told me that. Do you really think we can take such people seriously? He was probably so drunk that he meant it at that moment, but after half an hour had already changed the love of his life. He's a sentimental bastard, and that is, let me tell you, a poisonous combination.

Aren't you saying this just because he made fun of your poems, Harpa?, Heiður asks.

You think it's *just* because of that?

No, of course not.

There were so many other things as well—and each of them in itself would have been enough to make him unbearable.

His response to your poetry was extremely ugly, of course.

He was truly adroit at finding a weak spot. Maybe there's a class called WEAK SPOTS in the debt-collections program at the university. There's no more certain weak spot than the poems of nonpoets.

She kept them in the crotch of her dirty panties in the laundry basket. It's no wonder he found it funny, says Edda, squeezing out a little bleat of laughter.

The laundry basket was the new hiding place after he stumbled on some lines of poetry under the dish towels in a kitchen drawer and read them aloud, to my disgrace, to the drunks he dragged home from Gaukur Bar, smashed on low-alcohol beer mixed with vodka. Unfortunately, I hadn't gone to bed when the troops showed up. I was watching a video in the living room, in one of those precious kimonos he gave me, wouldn't you know it. Alli drawled out the poems in a loud voice, punctuated by a little trail of spittle, and laughed loudest at the poem about the heart and death.

I remember it, says Heiður. I found it a very interesting poem, although it wasn't long.

Fucking bullshit, that poetry crap, says Edda.

She doesn't mince words, your daughter.

Something's sifted in from all the books that were read to her.

Close to my heart, death,
bright death of the heart,
beating life.

No wonder Alli found it funny. But he could have skipped reading it to the drunks from Gaukur, bursting with so much laughter that he could hardly get out the words and sputtering over his drinking buddies. Then he asked who wrote this through me, and I said it was the sister of the man who drank through him.

I slunk away from this sophisticated party and went to bed. Edda came into my room, because she'd woken to the entertainment and asked whether I wanted to come and sleep in her bed. It didn't strike me as the stupidest thing I could do in this situation. At least her room was far from the drinking ruckus.

When Alli decided to hit the sack early the next morning, he grabbed at empty air in the king-sized bed with its built-in stereo system. He went to Edda's room to look for me, and to his credit didn't try to wake the child; instead he poked at my shoulder and asked in a low voice what I was doing there. I dragged myself out of the room so as not to disturb the girl any more than she'd already been disturbed, and crawled without a fuss into the broad upholstered bed, where the lunk threw himself on me in a beer-vodka haze and drove his short, broad dick into me—a tireless creature, and quite nimble.

It was the last straw. Not officially, but in my little artificial heart. I stepped up my devious operations to rid myself of the mental dwarf and strengthened myself by coming up with many different starts to stories, such as: ONCE THERE WERE TWO LITTLE DWARVES in a heterosexual relationship sharing a magnificent home at Undragrandi in Reykjavík, along with the woman's daughter. The man was a mental dwarf but the woman a physical one, so to speak.

Alli never got to know what it was that I could least forgive him for. It was part of my revenge. He, who has wandered into my private sphere in filthy shoes, will never be given any explanation, though I have a very detailed one, with a long register of sins; he'll get nothing but a "just because," and I hope it's true that he loves me to distraction, incessantly.

There's a trick to getting rid of a man who thinks he's in love, and maybe even is, to get rid of him without his noticing it, gradually. One day you leave, *just because*. And it was inevitable, just because. And the way that you've behaved makes him feel incredibly relieved, and he can hardly hide his relief that you're gone, just because. And you've behaved in such a way that it's difficult to pinpoint exactly what was so unbearable, just because.

There'll never be any closure—you're just done, though it's never said straight-out. Instead of a pop and a bang, a dead hand is laid over the relationship. I made life miserable for the dwarf, *no problem*. He roamed around devastated and didn't know why, exactly, and counted himself lucky to be rid of us when Edda and I hired the moving van, no problem, and moved to the basement apartment on Bollagata that was ready and waiting for us and that I'd even painted in my favorite colors, no problem.

The peculiar thing was that I continued to hide the poems at the bottom of the laundry basket after I moved from the penthouse to the Bollagata dump, and what was even more peculiar was that as time passed, Edda took over the role of Alli the dwarf, and once when I least expected it, she snatched the shreds from beneath the dirty socks and underwear and read them out loud, to my shame. I felt as if it were clear that I shouldn't exist, neither in Iceland nor on earth in general. I simply couldn't, when I wasn't even allowed to scribble my more or less stupid poems in peace. Poems that I wasn't planning to publish anywhere, or show to anyone but Heiður at most, and then only if she asked or demanded to see them.

It's like her to ask about my poems, my friend who encourages me to shine and wants me to feel that I'm something. But she needs to be careful not to take her praise to the point of flattery, which is something other than what it is. Her enthusiasm also becomes laughable when she says that I ought to gather my poems into a book or publish them in magazines. I don't want to be a demented assistant nurse who publishes poetry.

When I was a kid, I didn't need to be ashamed of my verses, which I composed especially for Dad and sometimes Heiður. She encouraged me immediately and said that it was terrific and that she wished she could do the same. Even today she still remembers my prize poem from the Laugarnes School paper and sometimes recites it when least expected, in order to promote Harpa Eir's boundless talents.

The butterfly jumps off the edge of the day,
swims the butterfly stroke in the pool of the sky.

Then say the kids with the yellow ball: Now day fills the air.

When the ball sinks
to the bottom of the pool,
the kids get out and dry off.

They chase the butterfly through the night
and sing in children's choir: Fun is the darkness.

Even my brother, Sibbi, praised me. He wasn't all bad, the poor boy. But it was impossible to draw Mom's attention, whether with prize-winning poetry or anything else. She was on her original saunter in weightlessness and had no points of contact with reality as she floated out of reach, standing on her head or lying on her side.

She thought that whatever I undertook would never amount to anything. Sibbi was her baby; she pampered him in secret, behind Dad's back, and stood up for him no matter how absurd it was. She even stood up for him when she found out he'd been teasing me and he'd been the one to start it.

Dad was extremely careful not to show favoritism and tried to hide the fact that I was his favorite. Occasionally, however, it happened that poor Dad couldn't control himself. He was so proud of the prize-winning poem that he had me recite it to his bridge-club friends. I'll never forget the embarrassed look on the face of Ingi the barber. He was apparently not a man who understands poetry.

Whether Mom understood poetry, I don't know, but every time Dad mentioned my gift for poetry, Mom interrupted him in midsentence and changed the subject, a conversational technique that she'd developed so thoroughly that it verged on being a new art genre.

Mom, how can I make sense of you?

You can't, my dear Eisa.

Stop twisting up my name. You've done more than enough damage by twisting up my paternity. You're going to get quite the shock tomorrow night when Dýrfinna lets the cat out of the bag and I find out what lout you were carrying on with behind Dad's back.

You and Prescient Finna can scheme together until you're blue. I'm not afraid of that.

Of course you're afraid. The unveiling of the century is at hand. The truth about my paternity will echo over the entire fjord.

Are you planning to get a bullhorn?

Don't try to pretend you don't care.

I suppose it's not going to affect me much, as things stand.

It never has, if I remember you correctly.

A great victory will be won the day that you remember me correctly.

Let me out, I need to pee, Edda says, thrusting her head toward the front seat, as if she thinks that otherwise she won't be listened to.

We'll soon be at a shop, says Heiður.

I'll just pee out here.

You can't wait five minutes?

Damn this long trip. I'll go out of my head.

This isn't that difficult of a trip, says Heiður. Your mother had to travel to the countryside by boat when she was little, before they built bridges over the sands.

I even went alone when I was just six years old, with no one special to take care of me. Some woman at the wharf was asked to look after me. Not as much fuss was made over me as over you. You who have two of your own ladies-in-waiting.

I turn around to check whether the girl sees something funny in this, but she replies with an elaborate grimace.

Didn't you feel insecure about going alone?, asks Heiður.

Not a bit. It was fantastic to get cookies from strangers who asked where I was going. I looked forward to it for months, starting at Christmas, to get to sail east and be a big person on my own. Those who see the land from the sea when they're children gain a different perspective on it from those who only get to travel over horrific bridges spanning ravines and on dusty horse-tracks, after which they blow black dust from their noses for three days. The most fun was going in May, as soon as school was over. The countryside had such different shades of green—greenest under the Eyjafjöll Range and at Dyrhólaey, on the southernmost plain. If the weather was clear, the glacial caps lorded it over the landscape. In many places the ice overflowed, nearly spilling into the sea.

I can't believe I never went with you.

Things were much stricter when we were little.

The Shop on the Plain

W e arrive at the shop at the crossroads of Rangárvellir, with a row of stately mountains as a backdrop on this clear and calm day. There's snow on Mount Hekla's northwestern slope, but not the cloud that some say is a fixture. The Tindfjöll Peaks, Mount Þríhyrningur, and Eyjafjallajökull Glacier make a resolute landscape. All of nature promises a brighter journey ahead, all the way east to my old refuge.

Heiður extends her leg from the high door and immediately has solid ground beneath her feet. Despite her clunkiness, she tries to look sporty, wearing a light-green tracksuit with violet stripes, and aggressive sports shoes. She has on a blue headband that makes her look even sharper and emphasizes her high nose. Over her shoulder, she's draped the strap of a terribly expensive sports bag, where she keeps her hair spray and gold flute. In this guise, the flute player

Heiður Jensdóttir could very well be an undernourished long-distance runner on her way to a race.

Inside the shop, Heiður scurries here and there to examine the goods: prunes, balaclavas, rye flour, screwdrivers, window varnish, cat litter, potatoes from the new harvest in Þykkvibær. Near the back, behind a pitch-black pot holder, protrudes the corner of a picture that I nearly drop when I pull it out. It turns out to be *Weighing of the Heart* in Egyptian style, from *The Book of the Dead*. The same sort of picture hung on the wall of my faithful friend Gabriel Axel in Perpignan. When he explained what the picture was supposed to represent, I thought that Monsieur Axel didn't need to fear his heart ending up on a scale. I didn't know then how well I had understood his heart. If the beautiful letters from Gabriel Axel and his nice gifts hadn't been part of the equation, it isn't certain that I would have made it in one piece through the Year of the Changeling. To know that someone cares about you without having to, someone who doesn't need to pretend to care about you and doesn't require anything in return, is magnificent and can be lifesaving.

I'm paying for the picture when Edda comes from the bathroom, jabbering about how I can't afford it, that I can't afford buying some piece of art junk and always claiming to be dead broke.

You never stop nagging, do you?, I say, even though the salesclerk can hear.

Edda glares at me with her spiteful yellow eyes and stomps out.

Heiður comes to the cash register to pay for a ceramic mug decorated with a picture of a fisherman from Lofoten. He's wearing a yellow slicker with a long sou'wester hat and holds a huge cod, closely resembling Gunnlaugur Scheving's portrait of a true Icelandic fisherman.

We walk light as feathers from this cosmic store, framed by crossroads and the sky, with a Norwegian tankard and an Egyptian picture in our hands. A cream-yellow Bronco pulls quick as a flash into the parking area. An old model resembling a soapbox car, waxed beautifully and not a single dent to be seen. At the wheel is a rosy-cheeked bald man of around sixty, his face so smooth that it's nearly taut. Next to him in the front seat is a finely dressed woman in her eighties. She steps out, nimble and straight-backed, with fresh waves in her blue hair, and goes straight into the shop, the man behind her in crackling new overalls.

A sheep's bleat is heard, as unexpected as from the fog of the sea on my boat trips to the east. I look around and see a sheep sitting up in the backseat of the jeep.

I'd best put a belt around it, Mom, says the son, turning back.

Where do you think they're heading?, asks Heiður.

They're taking the boy to mass.

From the high seat of the pickup truck, I have a good view of the farmer tussling with the sheep in the back. He tries to shove the creature into an older-style seat belt, a so-called lap belt.

I'm hungry, grunts Edda as soon as she's back in the car. I want a Coke.

Can't you wait? We'll have our lunch soon.

Not too stingy to buy useless things, but too stingy to buy a Coke.

Do you want an apple?

She says nothing. I root up an apple from the bottom of a bag and hand it back to her. She frowns, yet takes this forbidden fruit and munches it loudly.

. . .

Farmers have rolled hay into white plastic bales that are spread out across the fields. At a row of leaning trees, leafless on the leeward side, a bay horse grazes peacefully this Sunday morning.

A sheep, her bottom clotted with dung, walks slowly along the wire fence with her two lambs. Her tidy-looking offspring attack her teats and jostle their mother so much that her gait is undulating, while the lambs' stub-tails spin like tops. The sheep is impatient, doesn't want to wait, hurries onward as her lambs get tangled underfoot.

That's how you would have behaved if I'd been a lamb, Mom, I say. You didn't want to have me at your breast. At just two weeks old I was on the bottle. You turned me into a stray from the beginning, and what's more, I'm the scamp daughter of an unknown sluggard. Shame, shame, shame. It's awful.

There was no milk in my breasts. Was I to blame?, says Mom.

You didn't want to breast-feed me. You were a lousy mother—that's why there was no milk.

You definitely need to get yourself out of this blame game, my dear. You're old enough now to understand that it's no use blaming others for your mistakes. It doesn't lead to anything. You can't change a single movable thing in your life if you're always barking up the same tree.

It's new for Mom to resort to social-counseling tactics. It would be best if she got a dose of her own *Change Your Tune, Inc.*

I saw a documentary from Australia the other day, Mom. It showed the shell beach that you talked about sometimes. But you've probably never seen it for real. Wave after wave, nothing but light-colored little shells as far as the eye can see, rough at the edge of the sea in eternal sunshine. And not a soul to be seen anywhere.

That's what's nice about Australia, says Mom drily. There's no one there.

Oh, right—there's a terrible pile of people where you are? It's no wonder, of course. All those pitiful people who've died ever since the dawn of history.

Naturally, we don't live in the same luxury as in Australia, where you can drive around the wide expanses for days on end and meet nothing but marsupials and Aborigines until the most beautiful place on earth appears before your eyes in perfect simplicity.

But it isn't possible to waltz around on Shell Beach without damaging it. You take one step and grind up hundreds of shells.

I'm rather afraid that a shell beach is much more for looking at than walking on.

You could say that about the entire earth, says Mom.

Is that how you experience the earth when you're free from it?

It doesn't change the fact that I longed for such a beach. I saw so little, always bound to Iceland.

You're not a prisoner anymore, Mom.

What do you know about that?

You don't have anything resembling a shell beach where you are?

God forbid, Eisa.

Oh?

Here there's nothing.

Maybe no one, either, I say, hoping to scare Mom away.

Mount Þríhyrningur has changed from a triangle to a wide-open tulip.

To what could Gunnar and Njál compare their mountain when they rode about the plain? They'd never seen tulips.

The sea is a pond and the Westmann Islands blue dream-blocks that a child puts out to float on the pond.

When are you going to Copenhagen?, I ask Heiður.

In a week.

Are you nervous?

Yes.

But you're so used to it.

I never really get used to performing. It always makes me nervous. It's a complicated solo piece, for computer and flute. I don't understand the composer's intention. It's unplayable, but not so bad otherwise.

Is this your sixth or seventh trip abroad this year?

Something like that.

Will you see Dietrich?

Yes, he was singing in Bergen earlier in the week, and he's planning to take it easy at home in Stuttgart before he sings in Berlin and Venice. We can have two days in Venice, during the regatta.

Oh, don't say that. I'll turn green with envy.

I'm quite happy with my Ditti—I'll admit it.

You're so lucky to travel everywhere free as a bird and have people admire you.

It's not just a pleasure; it's also a damned hassle.

Yet you're using the talents that God gave you.

Let's hope so.

I won't ever make much of mine, but maybe there were never enough to make anything out of.

You've been learning languages, Harpa, and reading all kinds of books.

Yes, but it's of no use to me.

Yes, it is of use. You can be sure of it.

Heiður looks in the rearview mirror to check whether the monster is awake, before saying: Ever since Edda was little, and especially now with all of her nonsense, your hands have been full. No one who has a small child or a problem teenager is free to go anywhere.

There were a few years in between, I say. What did I do then?

You studied to become an assistant nurse.

Yes, don't you think I aimed high?

People don't always take a straight path to their goal.

If I'd only had a goal.

Your goal may still come into view. First sort out the girl, then get down to business.

It takes money to get down to business. Everything gets stuck. There's no money.

What isn't there can come. Who knows, maybe you can scrape some together starting this winter.

Of course it's economical staying with relatives. Ingólfur and Margrét don't want to take anything for having Edda, and Dýrfinna refuses to let me pay rent.

Will the health center pay you reasonably?

Better than in Reykjavík. There's a living allowance. I might have a bit left over after the winter, even after I pay my bills. On the other hand, my savings, if there are any, won't be enough to get me much more than some crappy rental.

The basement in Dad's house on Hraunteigur Street will actually be available in the spring or fall, says Heiður. You could probably rent it for next to nothing, and you wouldn't need to pay a deposit.

FROM BASEMENT TO BASEMENT. That's what I'll call my autobiography.

Hey, it's not a basement as such. It isn't belowground. It's more ground-level.

Then I can call it FROM BASEMENT TO GROUND-LEVEL. Oh, sorry. I just feel sometimes as if I'm a mole that will never be able to chew its way out into the light. I'm always dependent on others.

Bullshit. You've had to stand a bit too much on your own two feet.

Don't you think this trip proves it?

I'm starting to think you're sulking.

I'm always sulking.

It's all going to be all right.

You can't be sure of that. But at least I get to be all by myself in an apartment, even if it's nothing but two closets at the eastern end of the world. It'll be a luxury not to have to wait for my only child to come home battered or pale as a ghost, a luxury to be able to walk from one end of the house to another without having fists swung or abuse hurled at me.

Don't forget that you're in the prime of life, in perfect health. You're beautiful and intelligent, and people care about you.

What good does that do? I'm chained to a monster, and the monster doesn't care about me.

Heiður takes her hand off the wheel and strokes my cheek, letting the car veer out of the lane just as a bridge pier looms ahead of us. She immediately gets it back on the right track again, and I smile at her, so utterly shocked that the impending collision with the bridge doesn't particularly shake me. Heiður grimaces apologetically. I smile again to show that it doesn't matter one bit to me how she drives, that I'll ignore all her flaws and take her oversights lightly, whether in driving or anything else, while imagining that it's I who am saving her and I who hold the reins along the way.

Where glacial mush oozes down ravine-cut slopes.

On a trip in distorted time. An infernal autumn expedition.

On the ocean side is a time-warped field, a bright-yellow square that looks like it belongs in another country, in the spring.

I want to be on a spring trip, seeing lambs gamboling on the rims of ditches.

See a little lamb on its mother's back

beneath a gentle sky that opens its bright arms to the newborn earth.

No, here it's horse heads that look up from the grass tufts in the ditches. Nature raises a curse-pole against me on the road. THE CURSE-POLES OF NATURE would be a splendid name for my first book of poetry, which won't be published anytime soon.

Our roles in my friendship with Heiður haven't changed: rescuer/rescuee. The relationship began as a rescue operation and has continued almost uninterrupted as such on Heiður's part. When she managed to protect me from becoming the most famous child in Iceland—MURDERED BY HER PEERS IN THE LAUGARNES NEIGHBORHOOD—she saved my life for real.

Our story began when Heiður was in fourth grade and I was in third grade. She was a star with a velvet-lined violin case, scraping on the instrument at festive occasions, wearing velvet dresses that were purchased abroad and came out of gold-lettered boxes labeled Harrods, Bloomingdale's, El Corte Inglés. Once when I was upset with her, I called her *Heiður the Velvet Bitch*, which is one of many things packed away but not forgotten. The violin suited dear Heiður better than the flute; there's no denying it. It went better with her dramatic and volatile temperament. But maybe it's best for musicians to choose instruments that go directly against their character, because it would create exciting tension. Who am I to say?

She became a soloist during her first year of study and certainly was majestic when she performed in the auditorium. She played "Mary, lofty and mild" the final day before Easter break, just before the morning devotion.

It was sung in the auditorium every single morning, while the red horses of the art teacher, one of the nation's foremost painters, grazed on the school's walls.

I was as noticeable as Heiður, but for other reasons. I was called *Paper-Doll Harpa*, as little as Thumbelina, with curly pitch-black hair, Bambi eyes, long eyelashes, and dark skin. Mom made me dress in strange getups that highlighted my uniqueness. I tried to fight against them, but it was a losing battle. Every day I was outfitted in extremely impractical and easily soiled clothes, like white angora sweaters and vivid pink blouses. One Christmas, Mom ordered me a sailor jacket and matching sailor pants from a German catalogue, with the help of Erika, her sister-in-law. Then she put ringlets in my hair, no doubt outmoded, and stuck a sailor hat on my head, with an inscription in gold letters reading "Gorch Fock." I looked like a confused young transvestite. When I walked into the auditorium for the school Christmas celebration, I received a round of applause. I shrank back out and ran home crying.

Heiður ran after me, though she didn't know me, and caught up with me by Laugarnes Pharmacy. It wasn't cold out, but the ground was covered lightly with snow. Neither of us was wearing appropriate shoes, and we had trouble keeping our footing as we ran. Heiður's dress was thick, with fabric like plush upholstery. She was wearing white lace pantyhose with a fancy pattern, black patent-leather shoes with low heels, and a señorita comb in her hair. She towered over me, and I felt a sting in my heart because she was tall and her clothes were so incredibly nice. But no matter how elegant she was, she couldn't be called pretty, which perked me up a bit. She was slightly sunken-cheeked, with a sharp nose, rather thin lips, a long chin, and light freckles. For a freckled girl with bright-red hair, her dress, the same pink as Bazooka bubble gum, wasn't the right choice.

You're really pretty in your outfit, Harpa. Stop crying. You were by far the prettiest at the party. The kids were jealous of you because you're sooo cute.

Yo-our dress is much pre-ettier, I blubbered.

It's awful. I have to wear it because my mom ordered my dad to buy a dress for me when he went to Madrid. Do you think my dad can pick these sorts of things? It's a child's dress. But you look great. Come on.

Heiður tried to convince me to go back to school, but I wouldn't hear of it, so she walked me home and missed out on the Christmas party as well.

How do you know my name?, I asked when I was able to speak again.

Everyone knows who you are.

You think I don't know I'm called Paper-Doll Harpa?

The girls are jealous of you because you're the cutest in the school and the boys like you.

You must be nu-huts. Who do you think would li-hike someone so little?

It's sooo cute to be so tan all year long. You also have such great curls and long eyelashes.

Oh, you don't know how boring it is to be so little and ugly like me. My brother calls me *The Ugly Duckling* and *Little Black Sambo*.

I'll beat him up for you.

As we approached my so-called house on Hrísateigur Street, I almost lost heart, because I was so ashamed of it. It had been transported from Skerjafjörður and looked like half a house, not a whole one—as if it were cloven at the shoulders.

I saw Heiður look in surprise at the sawed-in-two shell-sand stuccoed box where I lived, but she said nothing. I usually recall this when I'm frustrated with her. I think about her old nobleness until I calm down and the frustration passes.

I started plucking off the sailor suit as soon as we got inside, huffing to Mom that it was a carnival costume I'd never put on again. She delivered a short monologue about the poor black children at the Icelandic mission in Konso, Ethiopia, and how they received used woolen clothing—sweaters, scarves, hats, mittens—from the missionaries. They, my mother insisted, didn't refrain from showing their delight and appreciation at receiving such nice Christmas clothes. My mother told me that I should be utterly ashamed of myself. Heiður was dumbstruck, and I led her to my room as Mom went on chattering in the hallway.

Heiður looked around my room respectfully and said it was awfully nice, making me feel proud that the richest girl in the school should feel that way. She was in awe of the little church on my desk, which Dad had crafted as a Christmas ornament for me. It resembled Laugarnes Church and was lit up electrically. In the sparkling snow surrounding it were Yule Lads out for a stroll under the guidance of their mother, the ogress Grýla. One had a candle made of a match, with wax melted over it, its wick made of superfine crocheted twine. Heiður had never seen anything so cute as that miniature candle. Yet what she liked best were the embossed shelves that Dad had made for me, full of books, even foreign picture books.

She said that there were no pictures on the walls of her room, so I gave her one that I'd cut out of *National Geographic*, of black monkeys with white stripes, which we called zebra-monkeys, and another of parrots in rainbow colors that Dad and I had pasted on cardboard and framed.

Sibbi was hovering outside my room, warbling one of his songs: *There goes Harpa-larpa-lo. She's ugly from head to toe.* Heiður slammed the door in Sibbi's face, already defending her dark little friend.

Damn, she snorted, I'm lucky I don't have brothers or sisters.

I started feeling sorry for Heiður, the rich, spunky girl who had no pictures to put on the walls of her room. Setting up shelves for her was always on the back burner, so her books were kept in wardrobes or drawers. I began to realize that just because you're an only child with a rich dad doesn't mean you get everything you want.

Yet this nouveau-riche dad of Heiður's certainly has been incredibly helpful to her, and to me as well. I almost certainly wouldn't have taken this trip, this salvage expedition to the east, if I didn't have a friend whose dad owned a pickup truck. Or the country's most isolated villa, the summer palace at the foot of the volcanic neck Lómagnúpur where Jens Kaaber and his wife, Saga, are providing us accommodation.

I don't want to remember the real reasons for this trip. Heiður and I are just out for a lazy jaunt through the countryside.

Over the fresh green Eyjafjöll fields

the eastern sky with a little jar of cloud puree

the ruins of sheds on rugged cliffs, stoutly built barns and silos that I call ICELAND'S CASTLES

calves on steep slopes

dog-lazy ewes dragging their lambs behind them in the rust-red brush at the feet of slopes

patches of green

millions of rocks on the road to the south.

The *Moonlight Sonata* soft and dark. In sharp Sunday light.

Now my friend should play something happier.

A sunlight sonata.

Dad played Beethoven's *Moonlight Sonata* over and over, on the piano as much as on the record player. Mom couldn't bear it, calling it the wail of ghost, like that of an infant left out to die. Dad's eyes would then turn red and his chin would twitch vulnerably. Everything was used against Dad. What was dearest to him was used most against him.

Do you remember how you acted toward Dad when he played his favorite song?, I ask Mom. You must regret it.

A new month in your life starts tomorrow. September, after August. Stop talking about the past and focus on what's to come.

Strange that you should say that, as someone who stopped existing ages ago and refuses to leave.

Mom's behind the wheel of the pickup truck now, wearing her traveling outfit from my childhood. Light-brown moleskin pants and a sweater the colors of the Icelandic flag, with a Norwegian pattern and fancy metal buttons. It figures that she and Teddi, the chief evildoer in Edda's gang, dress in a similar vein. Norwegian ski sweaters are something all evildoers share in common.

Why do you want to drive, Mom? You never learned to drive. Have you forgotten that?

Don't think that we sit idly in the beyond. I've earned my driver's license, dear. I really could use the practice. It's good to be able to take the wheel down here on earth.

Are all your roads paved?

Yes, they just put permanent surfaces on all the roads. It was a huge project and they had to take an unfavorable loan, but it's a completely different life on our roads now.

There's one thing that I've always wanted to talk to you about, Mom.

Don't start talking about Dad now. I'm not in the mood.

It has nothing to do with Dad. It's something that I've never mentioned to anyone. Sometimes I think I dreamed it, but I know it was real.

Oh, please don't hassle me with your nonsense.

Once, just after I'd returned from the hospital after the boys attacked me in Dock Wood, I woke in your arms like a baby wrapped in a blanket, and you were crying and upset and you rocked in your seat and wailed and you were saying: *What have I done?*

You must have been feverish.

I was almost nine and you held me like a dead infant in the blanket and you hurt my broken arm.

Once you had a high fever when you were that age. You're talking about that.

You know that's not true. I'd like to understand why you broke down like that.

You'll understand it if you think long enough, and warmly enough. When you've finally understood that, you'll understand everything.

I've never told Dad about it.

You're a good girl in some respects.

It's here, our picnic spot, I say to Heiður. Stop, stop.

Where?

Here on the left, by the corral.

Ugh, look at all the cows, says Edda, like a city girl who's never visited the countryside.

Heiður brakes so abruptly it's like being rear-ended.

The Corral at the Foot of Eyjafjöll

You're going to kill us all, says Edda from the backseat, in a deep doomsday voice. Sometimes, it really does sound as if her voice is changing.

Did you doze off, my little chick?, I ask, thinking immediately that I shouldn't have said something that might make her think of Gerti.

None of your business.

Aren't you hungry, ladies?, I ask, as the keeper of our provisions.

Not me. I'll wait in the car.

Says she who was complaining about being hungry.

Heiður and I step out, two slightly stiff dames, and fetch the picnic basket from beneath the tarp, where it sat at the base of my slim Electrolux refrigerator. It's not just all the sitting in the car that makes it hard to move now, but also the density of the calm air, like a palpable material that we have to break through, preferably with a jungle machete, like explorers. Mom called this type of weather *murderous mildness*. Was that supposed to be funny?

The sky is calm along the Eyjafjöll Range, the gusty region where sheep are blown up onto cliffs and end up starving or having to be shot. I can't help it, but sometimes I remind myself of a sheep that's been blown onto a cliff and doesn't know whether it should let itself fall or wait for someone to be so kind as to come and put a bullet through it.

Barbed-wire fence. An obstacle that I've struggled against since my very first days in the countryside, like Don Quixote in the guise of a girl fighting with fences. THE GIRL WHO DIDN'T GROW UP. I still have to struggle, come up with a strategy, locate a suitable place to clamber over—from a tussock, for example—or move a rock to stand upon.

Now everything's easier because there are two of us. Heiður goes first, swings her legs over, one after the other, without needing me to hold down the barbed wire, but I do so anyway with one hand, holding the picnic basket in the other. It's a sophisticated container of the English variety, wicker on the outside, lined and partitioned on the inside, with straps to hold down the crockery and cutlery with rosewood shafts. It was intended more for trips to the forest in the Lake District of England than in the Icelandic countryside, where everything is endlessly being blown away. One of the few things left from my relationship with Alli. He gave it to me as a birthday present but intended it mainly for himself, because he found it so fun to have me prepare the food for countryside picnics, during which he'd get drunk. He preferred to crown such outings by doing it out in nature under various weather conditions, after bothering to find level ground, of course.

Heiður holds down the wire, and I clamber over with the utmost caution. Still, I barely avoid getting caught on the barbs—these are no legs at all, these stubs of mine—and ripping my newly ironed snow-white trousers, which go so well with my fuchsia-colored cotton

V-neck sweater. My white jacket, the other half of my pantsuit, I've left behind in the car, choosing instead to bring my rain jacket.

You look absolutely stunning, says Heiður, as if she'd read my thoughts about how tremendously chic I am. In freshly brushed moccasins and all the rest, on a stroll through the cow dung. As if you're on a yacht.

Heiður swings the picnic basket, many yards ahead of me, the woman with the long legs. How good she has it—and then there's poor me, short and faint-hearted. It's a grand shame being so petite, and just so hard. Life would have been different for me if I'd been over five foot three. At five two, oh, I hardly can be called a person, damn it, not lengthwise, anyway. At least I'm all woman crosswise. At my worst moments I think of my fellow sufferers, short men like Sammy Davis Jr. and Napoleon, and I remind myself that it's twice as bad for a man to be small.

Heiður's walking slowly up the slope, past the corral. Her gait's steady now, and she's stopped swinging the picnic basket. It's as if she's playing her flute but fluteless. Such is the effect the calm weather can have on a jerky person between a belt of cliffs and the sea.

After the early-morning jump start on the bliss, the landscape now looks worn-out, like it's taking a Sunday nap. The seagulls screech softer than usual, slightly hoarse, and sail lazily over a black cliff, which in the summer is embroidered with herbal-dyed yarn. Now the green yarn has become somewhat frayed and reddish beneath the diligent sun, which was at work all day and all night at its peak. The final day of August has arrived. The feast of the beheading of Saint John the Baptist and the birthday of little Harpa, August 29, has passed, and the angelica has already yellowed here and there. Otherwise, autumn shows few signs that it has already begun. The grass is vibrant green in the morning sun, brighter and more aggressive than it ought to be right now.

A black cow snuffles ahead of its sisters, coughs loudly, looks us over, takes two cautious steps, stops. The one nearest it looks at us and tilts its head shyly. Its belly is black and white and gray, patterned and textured like a glacier tongue. Its female friends stretch their snouts toward us and swing their heavy heads in unison.

The racket deepens. The seagulls branch out on their cliff-carousel, and the echo of their chatter travels far, while the poor flies buzz slowly over the open picnic basket, so languid that it wouldn't surprise me if their wings stopped beating and they plopped straight into the smoked salmon.

Now I put on sunglasses, as is suitable in so much light, and start arranging our provisions on a little tablecloth that I embroidered with care in home economics class, before putting it aside for a time, and finally finishing it just before Edda was born. ONCE THERE WAS A PREGNANT CHILD WHO KEPT STITCHING A FULLY STITCHED TABLECLOTH.

You sure are taking your time with this, Heiður says.

Just making sure everyone's going to be happy, I reply. These are yours, dear; no butter.

A real picnic!, exclaims Heiður.

All we need are the woods. Typical, don't you think?

Is that silly girl just going to mope there in the car?

Heiður, let's pretend the girl doesn't exist for the time being. The only way to survive her is to eliminate her from your mind at regular intervals.

In calmness and sun, we sink our teeth into the salmon-topped bread and stop existing except as consumers of precious open-face sandwiches.

Then after a break of forty-five seconds or so, the car door slams shut, and we become participants in life once more.

Edda Sólveig has thought better of it and is on her way up the picnic slope. She clambers straight over the barbed wire, without bothering to hold it down. Those who do so usually end up tearing holes in their pants, and that's what Edda does. Her demeanor is far from inviting as she strides up to us, stepping in a cow pie along the way, naturally.

I'm bleeding, whines the girl piteously as she approaches, in the same tone of voice she used after scraping herself when she was little.

I have a Band-Aid, I say, reaching into my pocket.

Always prepared for everything, says the flutist. There's no one like you.

No one like me but my dad, to whom I don't belong. He's my model for always having a Band-Aid in my pocket.

The girl has to take off her pants in order for me to put on the Band-Aid. Blood oozes in two thin lines from a cut on her inner thigh. It reminds me of horrible things, and I feel faintness spreading through me, from the small of my back, first down and then up, all the way to the crown of my head, with a slight tingling from my temples to my forehead.

Heiður smiles at me, and I absorb her reassuring currents, gather strength, buck up, put my foot down. There's so much that I mustn't think about on the way east. I mustn't let the bad things that Edda and I have encountered this past year get hold of me now. I would be lost. It's true what they say, that life's struggle is the struggle to gain control over our thoughts. Control them according to our own traffic signals. Green: think. Red: don't think. I'm here to enjoy a picnic, not to recall the worst.

My injured wretch in torn stretch pants is eating a salmon sandwich.

Does it hurt, Edda?

Yes, a bit, she says miserably, like a little girl trying to pull herself together.

Flies still hang over their potential catches, but they seem to be suffering sunstroke, because they make no attempt to get hold of anything.

These are absolutely delectable, dear, says Heiður.

Then try to behave like a civilized person and eat with your little finger raised, I say, and Heiður laughs.

Edda looks at us like we're unbearable old maids making fun of her. She stands up and hurls away a piece of her sandwich. A bird shoots up where the slice comes down. Just as well it wasn't a rock.

I notice Heiður's temper flare. It's clear what she wants to do. Punch the girl. I want to, too.

What a sorry excuse for a mother I am. To want to work over this pathetic figure who's walking as if one leg were shorter than the other. The bad mother's conscience stings me, knowing that somewhere inside the sorry soul before me is the adorable red-haired stripling who gathered dandelions in Grandma's Grove and kissed dogs on the lips to the displeasure of three generations. It's impossible to hate her for real, except briefly. She's so ill, this monster, and so young.

Oh. I can never feel any feelings undivided, not even anger at myself. Everything is mixed and intertwined, half persons, half a life, one quarter from something else, maybe not from life. Not even my pessimism is unpolluted. Even if everything looks hopeless, you can still experience, well, I wouldn't say happy days, but good moments. I'm not pessimistic enough *not* to go east, though I have no hope— or, should I say, little hope. I have to try something; I refuse to see the only thing that's mine fall to ruin.

The cows stand huddled together, alternately mooing softly and staring moist-eyed at their female friends from the capital. I feel as if they're focusing on me, a dark-skinned woman in white pants out in the wilderness, with her rain jacket conscientiously spread on the ground so that she won't soil her clothes. The mottled lead cow sets off, heading toward the little woman, very slowly yet steadfastly, and the others follow at a distance. They walk lazily, giddy in the voluminous warmth, their recently emptied udders swinging. They sniff at me and the last drops of Chanel No. 5 that I splashed on before we left. It's just like me to squander the final fragrant whiffs on beasts of the field.

See how fond my spiritual sisters are of me?

It's not normal. They arrange themselves in an orderly semicircle around me and moo softly. They don't even blink an eye at Heiður, as if she doesn't exist. Maybe they feel a real connection with me, or maybe they're just disoriented by the muggy weather, chewing their cuds sluggishly.

The cream-colored Bronco comes driving by.

I'm relieved to see it, even if it's just that old lady and her son, says Heiður. I was starting to get a bit of a "last person in the world" feeling.

If only we were dreaming, as the last person in the world might wake to discover he was doing.

It's not that bad, Harpa.

As I put everything back in the picnic basket, folding the tablecloth and the napkins, I'm engulfed by the desire to wet them with a flood of tears. To blow my nose in them, my face swollen, and lie down to sleep on this slope without ever, ever having to wake up again.

The jumble of cows retreats when I stand up. I call it a touch of respect, something that hardly anyone else shows me. Heiður takes the basket from me and rushes ahead down the slope. It's typical of her to want to lead the group, whether it consists of one or more. She waits for me on the other side of the fence to help me cross over accident-free, and for a moment the consideration shown by this impatient person makes me feel so small and weak that a little tear slips out into the world.

How fleeting were our good times in the grass just now. After I'd bandaged Edda, after she'd sat down with her snack, before she sprang up violently and flung food at an innocent curlew. They'd lasted only two or three minutes.

Can the secret to life be to prolong the good moments? As they're being experienced, if possible; otherwise in memory.

Moments experienced in the blink of an eye. Two minutes in the grass. If only we could continue to live in those moments as we move on.

The art of turning back on the journey into the murky woods, reining in the darkness, sharpening it into the bright point that it originally was, and focusing our attention on it like a yogi. TO REMEMBER THE GOOD, that will be the title of one chapter of my autobiography, as well as a suggestion to others as to how we should perform that task. If we're able to gaze at the *bright spot*, life will become as wholesome as it possibly can. It's the only way to make a bit of sense of it. In that point is crystallized a fragment of the wholesomeness, the good that was, at least at one time. That could possibly be again. I focus on it and call on the clouds as my witnesses that it was so, as I remember it, all the clouds in the skies of the world that never return in the same form.

. . .

I'll be damned if Edda isn't looking shamefaced in the backseat, still sipping from her Pripps can.

Do you remember the raven at Andey?, I ask her.

Huh?

It laid its eggs on the cliff above Grandma's Grove and did all sorts of damage. It even attacked the lambs as they were being born.

As they were being born? Gross, says Heiður.

Yes, my dear. Ravens are villains. My cousin Ingólfur tried to destroy its nest. The raven made air raids against him, flew over him with rocks in its claws and dropped them on him. Ingólfur returned looking none the better and on the next trip took his shotgun with him. He hates no creature as much as the raven. When he was a kid, he played at being the mother of thrush chicks in their nest, putting butter on blades of grass and giving it to them to eat. But one morning when Ingólfur came out, a raven had killed all the thrush chicks.

I think ravens are awesome, says Edda. I'd like to be a pitch-black raven.

They're cruel, Edda, I say.

I'm cruel, too.

Edda pops on her headphones to indicate that this communication is finished—over and out—and closes her eyes.

I do too, tired after our *déjeuner sur l'herbe*, tired after having removed everything from our Bollagata hole, having scrubbed my hands sore, tired from everything that's occurred, before and since, especially since. TIRED OF LIVING, the subtitle of my autobiography. Tired of living, YET I SHALL STILL STRUGGLE. Struggle on, avoid the pits into which I'm always stumbling.

I must not allow myself to eliminate the bright point, cover it, and expand into outermost darkness, mourning the beautiful and good that once was, wishing that it had never happened because the regret is so deep.

Regret for the man in the January night whose private name for me as a child was *The Foreign Girl*. A man who's nowhere—Ísafjörður wiped off the map.

It was Heiður's fault that we met again, after never even having spoken to each other since the damned swimming lesson twenty years ago. My prima donna friend had spent an entire day practicing an unusually complicated modern flute piece and said that she deserved a Campari with a view. After a considerable amount of persuasion, she dragged me along to the bar at Hotel Esja on a brilliant June evening.

Heiður had ordered her drink in her usual way: *I'd like something strong, for five hundred krónur*, and on the basis of this lively opener ended up in an energetic conversation with a childish fellow with frighteningly light-blue eyes.

Drunk people of both sexes were giving me attitude when the top dog walked in the room with some foreigners, the center of attention as always, without even trying.

I retreated to the window with a Campari and soda and was looking over the snow-white places of my youth in the Laugarnes neighborhood, the concrete domed building and the former Dock Wood. Suddenly, someone laid his hand on my behind and said: *You're the most beautiful woman I've ever seen.*

It was a pencil-thin old man with leathery dark-brown skin, his hair dyed blue-black, curly and glossy with Brilliantine. He was wearing a striped suit, a white shirt with a red-and-black silk tie, a clunky silver tie-clip with a red ruby—the kind that Icelandic boys got as confirmation gifts around 1960—and a red carnation at his breast. This elderly gigolo smelled strongly of aftershave that I didn't recognize, but the smell was good. He moved closer, put his arm around my waist, smiled straight into my face, and made himself ready for a cinematic kiss. He had false teeth and had forgotten to trim his nose hair.

I retreated from his death-kiss, bumping backward into the nearest person and apologizing over my shoulder before I saw that I'd splashed the drink from the top dog's glass and drenched his lapel. I felt awful, so I took out a newly ironed cotton handkerchief and tried to dry off this man. Luckily, he'd only been drinking water.

The man stared with great interest at the handkerchief, since modern women always carry tissues. Then he pointed at the gigolo and asked: Is that your dad?

Yes, we always drink together, I said. At the same time I recognized the water man, although our acquaintanceship had begun and ended almost two decades ago.

Hi, he said.

Hi, I said.

Do you still swim?

Not at the same pool.

We'd both taken swimming lessons from Jón Ingi at Austurbæjar School one spring. I wasn't more than ten years old, and he something similar. It was a particular trial for me to take those detestable lessons, but Mom forced me. I was suffering the misfortune of having my breasts develop far too prematurely. The left one was a sight larger, and the asymmetry caused me added shame. I went around slightly bent to draw attention away from these embarrassing bumps and developed complex strategies to make them less noticeable—for instance, wearing baggy sweaters though they weren't in fashion, and trying to keep my arms crossed over my breasts and hide both of them behind anything available, such as schoolbags, pillars, posts, and even light poles when handy. It wasn't exactly high on my wish list to display myself in a swimsuit or take showers in public. I still find it a shock to see photos of myself from that time. I look like an eight-year-old in overall appearance and height, but my chest is noticeably developed. A big-breasted little girl. What a perverse sight.

How is it you remember me?, I asked, partly to tease him, because naturally I knew. He blushed—yes, blushed—and said: You stood out because you were so dark, and so *precocious*.

He checkmated me with his frankness. Then he added: You were also so polite.

I was inhibited.

It came out as decorum.

It was his turn: And how is it that you remember me?

It isn't hard. The top dog.

In your opinion.

This fellow from the Sogmýri neighborhood, whose name I never knew, was a self-crowned prince. It was always clear at the swimming lessons that he was number one. He was the most handsome, the coolest, the most fun, and, so rumor said, he had the best grades as well. He always appeared to be dressed elegantly, but he was probably just wearing ordinary clothes that looked good on him. All the girls had crushes on him, which could cause big problems. One girl with a massive crush sometimes left chocolate-coconut treats in a brown paper bag on his front steps. He didn't eat them. It was impossible to imagine that he did nothing to be so admired. He put on no airs and didn't try to draw more attention to himself than the others. I didn't know his name, since I never asked and was never interested in knowing, and was one of few who didn't have a crush on him. I was so ashamed of every last inch of myself that I couldn't have had a crush on anyone.

He was exactly as I remembered him from the swimming lesson at the sinister fortress of Austurbæjar School in the old days, open and forthright and free from self-aggrandizement. The methods that he uses to force his way into others' consciousnesses are of such a nature that the others are caught completely unawares. He wrinkles his forehead, especially when he speaks—creating three deep lines crossing lengthwise—and he addresses you with a certain intensity, although he doesn't come too close and doesn't intimidate you with a straight-on stare. His eyes have a greenish luster, and there's a sheen to his darkish hair and skin as well.

After the adventure at the Hagkaup store and the forehead kiss, I christened him THE FOGGY BOY in a poem of the same name, which I tore to pieces as soon as it was finished, sticking the tatters into an empty milk carton and making a special trip to the trash bin with it.

Did you see his russet shoes? Holy crap, the man's got style, said Heiður as we put on lipstick in the bathroom.

They're red as wine. Are you color-blind?

He's awfully cool.

You don't say, I said.

Where do you suppose he got that jacket?

Isn't he wearing a sweater?

Is he married? It looks like he's wearing a ring.

I hope so.

Instead of going back to the bar as I'd planned, I snuck down one flight of stairs, then took the elevator and briskly walked home to Bollagata in the evening sun that painted the mountains purple. Along the way I regretted the fact that I hadn't taken more than two or three sips of my drink. I also felt bad that Heiður might be searching frantically for me all over Hotel Esja.

Edda was hunkered down on a kitchen stool, eating a shortbread cookie. She gave me a fugitive, hateful glance as if I were an executioner who had tortured her for years with highly advanced techniques, and not the mother who'd scratched her back before she fell asleep, warmed her toes beneath the quilt, and knitted stacks of sweaters and yards of scarves with multicolored patterns. Her mother, who read her *Orla Frogsnapper*, told the story of the Wild Children from Dock Wood and stories of Andey from when Grandma Sól was a child and a French ship's doctor cut out her appendix so that she wouldn't die, sang "I'm Forever Blowing Bubbles," and called her my little girl.

I knew beforehand that it was no use to try to talk to her, yet I asked all the same if she'd been out. Keep your nose out of what's none of your business, she said, rolling her eyes. I looked away and down at the shiny kitchen floor and Edda's bare toes, brown like raisins.

Wouldn't you like to take a bath, Edda?, I said, taking care not to be gruff, but she sprang to her feet like a wild animal and abruptly struck my upper arm with the back of her hand.

Think about scraping off your own shit, you fucking mare.

I did nothing, just stared at the child, straight into her wild eyes. She kicked me in the shin. I stood still and we stared hard at each other. After a few moments I went into my bedroom and locked the door, sat down on the bed, and tried to cry, but my eyes were too dry. I started thinking of the swimming-lesson man with the wine-red shoes.

There are three clouds high in the sky where none were before, two round ones over the sea, and a third a vertical stripe hanging negligently over Sólheimajökull Glacier, shining bright, just like the time when Dad said: The new-fallen snow makes it glisten so.

It snows endlessly on glaciers without us knowing, while it's summer in town or late summer, and no one thinks of snow except for folks who dread winter. Now it has snowed behind the glacier, even though it's still summer on our side and August hasn't passed.

Snow falling softly on a glacier
in my heart a hailstorm.
Big mellow snowflakes my foreign heart would have
far more than cruel hail.

We head south, to the southernmost hayfields in the country. In these parts is the farm that Dad said had the most beautiful name in Iceland: LOFTSALIR—SKY HALLS. The fields here are the first to turn green in the spring, and I remember their color as I beheld it from the other side, from my sea voyages to the east. Hayfields lying near the sea are a different green from those farther inland. Here they contrast with the dark volcanic rock of Dyrhólaey and the beach of polished black pebbles that diminish in size the closer they are to the water's edge. Sibbi and I went there once with Dad, on our way to see Erika and my uncle Beggi in Vík. It was absolutely special to walk on the clattering pebbles that the sea had fulled, giving the beach the feel of cloth. We looked down at the pebbles, ignoring sea and sky, and filled our pockets with them. The smallest variety went into one pocket, bigger pebbles into the other. Harpa Eir, ever-sorting, ever-arranging, looking forward to creating something out of this haul, threading pebbles together with silver wire and painting them with a slender paintbrush.

Look at the rainbows.

At first I think my ears are playing tricks on me. It couldn't be Edda speaking, this time in the sweet voice of an innocent girl who's never known anything bad about the world, let alone taken part in anything you might call bad.

It's a double rainbow, at the southernmost spot in Iceland. The bows are of blossoming colors that have their roots in a tepid field and grow on wings of pure air. We blaze south beneath the bows, out toward the sea, where I always wanted to go sailing.

What makes a double rainbow?, asks Edda.

I can't even say what makes a single one. It has something to do with electricity in the clouds, but I think that a double rainbow is a sign of good luck.

Wasn't it also a sign of good luck this morning when I found the creature from the French pervert? You're terribly superstitious, Mom.

Not really.

Yes, you're all wrapped up in superstitions. You'd have probably been burned at the stake in the old days.

Yes, if I'd lived back then.

Don't you think we can live over and over, as some people say?

I'm not sure. At least I don't think it pays to put faith in the idea.

But it could happen, of course.

I don't think we can count on a next life. I think we have to live here and now as best we can and not expect any do-overs in the next life. If there should be one.

Some people remember all kinds of things from their previous lives, Edda says.

Not me. I don't remember anything at all. But if I did exist before, I would probably have been a wimp in all my lives.

You're too sharp-tongued to be called a wimp, says Heiður.

A sharp-tongued wimp, that's what I am. A toxic combination. No one realizes that's what I am—even me—because it's so unbelievable.

If a whole lot of people claim to be the same person in a previous life, it sure must be lively in travel groups, Heiður interjects. I heard about a tour guide in Egypt who ended up in quite a predicament, with seven reborn Cleopatras in the same group.

Heiður laughs at her own humor, gasping as if she has whooping cough. She's welcome to laugh. It's funny.

In Mýrdalur there's a ravine with a red cottage at its mouth. The area has quite a few trees, and I've always wanted to have a look around, to hike up the ravine and examine it up close and see how it is and what grows there. But there's never any time on the road, least of all now, on this trip all the way out east. When we were kids, we didn't get to decide where we stopped. It was one of the things that we thought would change, but it hasn't. Time and place are apportioned to us in advance. On this trip I'm obligated to stop and see Erika at Höfðabrekka, Uncle Arnbjartur at Glóra, and particularly Aunt Betty at Útheimar. It's just like in life itself—no one determines his own stop. It's determined ahead of time, as far as I can see.

The here and now is uncontrollable, the moment is past before it began. Life is one continuous follow-up, processing and then preparing for the future, the next moment.

DAYS ON THE ROAD will be the name of one chapter in my autobiography, which will never be written, and the old road up out of Mýrdalur will get at least a page.

As soon as Kambar was behind us, I could start to feel apprehensive about Mýrdalur, though it was far, far ahead of us. I shuddered at the thought of whether it was worse to travel up a steep slope or down, and realized that both were equally bad.

I used to ask Mom to let me know before we came to the frightful road just before Vík so that I could spread a blanket over my head in time and avoid the torment. It ended with both Mom and me spreading the blanket over our heads and my brother, Sibbi, having a fit over the scandalous behavior of the idiotic women in his family. At the same time Dad talked about how the stretch all the way down to the bottom of the ravine above Vík and then upward could be life-threatening, not least on ice and in darkness. I knew a man who died there, added Dad; his car slid off the road down into the ravine *here*. Dear Dad, he didn't always realize exactly what he was saying, and Mom and I whined in unison like two owls—ooh hoo—beneath the blanket. When Dad said that it would be safe to take off the blanket, I saw a thick white line in the sea beyond the village.

What's that?

It's called surf, replied Dad.

How's the surf born?

The surf isn't born. It always exists on the sea.

Like children. Do children always exist, also before they're born?

Yes and no. Half of them exist in women, the other half in men. Which sperm from which man meets which egg from which woman is a coincidence.

What's a coincidence?

I never got an answer to that question, because Mom broke in and said: It's more a miracle than a coincidence how an individual reproduces.

Can't it be both, dear, coincidence and miracle?, asked Dad.

You can spend a lifetime on this, wondering whether you're a coincidence or a miracle, if not both. I suppose for a person with my appearance, it's certainly something to consider. Mom said a miracle. Why didn't I get down to business and compel her to tell me the whole story while there was still time? What miracle am I, Mom? I'm me, I'm supposed to be here still after you're dead, I'm entitled to know what I am. Hardly a truly Icelandic miracle. And don't start talking about Hans Jonathan. I know that he was an immigrant from the Caribbean, born in Saint Croix in 1790, and he lived in Djúpivogur, in eastern Iceland. He was pitch-black, but none of his descendants could look like that now. Anyway, according to the parish registers I'm not related to him.

The parish registers don't necessarily tell the whole story, little Eisa.

Mom, we're well into the twentieth century, don't forget. I still look like a mulatto.

It doesn't matter who your father is.

I know it doesn't matter to you, because you're dead. Nothing matters to you anymore.

Mom guffaws, her mouth open wide, displaying her long lipstick-colored teeth.

Damn, that was funny, says the mouth. You're making progress.

It may not be that funny.

She raises the volume of this terrible laughter of hers, which always drowned out my own. I'm so wary and so afraid of laughing like her or some other idiot that I almost never laugh out loud except when I'm alone. My friend Jói noticed this. THE WOMAN WHO DOES NOT LAUGH. That was the name of the little poem that he wrote for me two and a half weeks before he died.

. . .

Heiður stops on the slope above the village to take photos. She says that the light's special here. With half the sky blue and half lightly gilded, it resembles a glacier beneath the shining sun.

The sea adjoins the sky. It's good to be where sea and sky meet.

Heiður runs off up the slope. I lean contentedly against the trusty old pickup truck that's transporting Edda and me far to the east, to a foggy valley lush with vegetation.

Seen from above, the village appears fast asleep: not a car on the road, not a soul stirring, not a blade of grass wavering. Only one thing is moving, in its entirety: the sea. Even in calm weather, the industrious sea's incomprehensible powers create currents that quicken like a kind of life, turning to breakers beneath a little village far to the planet's north, on an island where few people live, scattered along shorelines. The surf's a squirming foamy-white streak, ineffaceable from this northern village that is in fact southern, because it's southernmost in its own land, southernmost on this big island, a green village with bright-green cliffs from the lowest ledge to the highest. There the massed seabirds line the rock pedestals with droppings, transforming them into cushions for themselves and their own in immense bird parlors.

I first saw the village of Vík in Mýrdalur and the Reynisdrangar sea stacks from a ship when I was just a tot, but I recall them very clearly and that entire land of plenty, the south coast with islands just beyond the sandy beach, the inland mountains, the huge green fields, and the broad bulging glaciers.

I learned that the Reynisdrangar stacks were originally a troll couple on horseback with a child, and maybe a dog, all of whom turned to stone as the sun rose. Dad and Mom and me in a previous existence, but the dog a stray. I found it a clever arrangement that we stone-folk should be able to be reborn in flesh and blood, and I was downright happy that Sibbi didn't exist at the time.

The village has certainly chosen itself a beautiful location, although it's vulnerable to sea and land as it cuddles beneath crags and peaks and a real glacier containing a malicious volcano.

The volcano is called Katla, said Mom as we stood out on the ship's deck, and no one knows its whereabouts in the glacier for certain. But after it erupts, it floods everything, with ice chunks as big as apartment buildings. People have to abandon their houses and flee for their lives.

No one knows precisely where the crater is, precisely where the lava spews up out of the earth. It's impossible to pinpoint, like the craters in the volcanic zones of our souls.

Raindrops fall from the sky, not large, weather that's useful in the spring, for the grasses and trees, but which now, as autumn approaches, is like a funeral hymn of nature. The plants are gone, as are the leaves on the trees. All as the one blossom, growing up from level ground. They should flee now while they can, the plovers and terns, this final day in August, before the storms hit. I should make my way in the same direction as them, by sea, steal one of the amphibious vehicles parked near the shop, drive it down to the beach with its chimney smoking, and set out across the deep.

When Edda and I were on autumn break once with Erika and Uncle Beggi in Vík, we walked down to the water's edge, threading little paths around lyme-grass-covered sand tussocks, and the roaring of the surf hit our ears as we fled fast-moving waves on the wet sand just before they reached our toes. It's been twelve years since Edda played with the waves, jumping into her mommy's arms—at that time a good mommy and a sweet mommy—and sticking her nose in the crook of her mommy's neck. Mommy kissed her behind her ear, and then the little girl was ready to rejoin the game. She ran out after a wave, fled frantically from it into her mother's arms again, gathered courage, and ran out once more in pursuit of a wave on the gleaming wet sand, as far as she dared.

This is why we exist, I then thought. To take a child in our arms so that it can warm up and gather courage before running out into the world. This is why we exist. To be an open embrace for our own children for as long as life lasts.

Erika pampered us and taught us how to make German Christmas decorations even though it was only September. She spoke straight to the point with me in her broken Icelandic about me being such a young mother. People usually avoided the topic, fortunately, but Erika can talk about everything without any qualms, a trait she shares with Dýrfinna. At the same time, she pointed out to me what I'd heard said and knew examples of myself, that the children of children are often born under lucky stars.

Erika and Þorbergur had both retired but looked after the seismograph for the Institute of Science. Edda Sólveig was so well behaved that Erika had no worries about this unusual home decoration and taught her to say "seismograph" with a German accent, of course.

I sent her the nice photograph that I took of two-year-old Edda in the lyme grass, wearing a white Aran cardigan with little leather buttons that Heiður had brought back from Ireland. It was the same picture that hung on the wall in the kitchen at Bollagata, enlarged and in a gold frame, until Edda threw it to the floor a year ago,

breaking the glass. I still have that sweater, in a
CLOTHES 0–4 years, stored in a stack of bc
garage on Laugarásvegur Road.

In the photo Edda is between tufts of lyme g
the hems rolled up over yellow-and-red boots that l
head's bare, and she's clearly saying something, becau ⌐outh is
open enough to reveal her sharp little teeth. Her hands might have
been a bit cold—she's not wearing mittens—and she has placed her
left hand over her right. Behind her is a piece of driftwood in a tangle
of bright-green grass, and vegetation that's turned orange and brown.
The girl's copper-red curls blaze in the sun, and the summer has
speckled her face with numerous dark freckles. However things turn
out, this photo exists. This is the way the world was for one moment
in autumn more years ago than I feel I've lived.

The mommy, who isn't in the photo, had just turned eighteen.
An unhardened teenager who was supposed to be a shelter to her
child—and there was indeed shelter in her. Her little one was safe
and smiling with her little mommy, who had her daddy, Axel, to
thank, as with everything. He who protected the mommy when she
was little. From shelter is born shelter, as evidenced by the forest.

. . .

Through the open car window comes the sound of bells ringing in chorus, from the bowels of the village: *Soo-oon, he-eralding
the morning.*

Combined with the surf.

The latest craze in all these villages around the country is bell
choirs, says Heiður. They're replacing brass bands.

That's a shame, I say. Do you recall the obituary that stated it was
well known that brass bands are the best places for making friends?

Bright bells ring out like the voices of children who know no
evil: *The su-hun will shine fo-o-orth.*

though I can't read the clouds, it looks to me as if the wind going to pick up; there are wind-clouds in the sky, what most people know as cirrus clouds. I would feel much more secure if there were more movement in the air. I start feeling uneasy if the sky is too still for too long. One of those who always thinks: *Treacherous calm before the storm.*

Heiður and Edda already know the story of Grandpa Óðinn, yet I tell it again: Grandpa Óðinn, Dad's dad, perished in these breakers when he was only thirty-seven, just beyond the beach as they were coming in to land. Folks from the village watched their dear friend drown within earshot and could do nothing. He had five children, the youngest two years old. He lived at Höfðabrekka when it happened, where the rest home is now.

Why isn't your dad at that home rather than at Grund?, asks Heiður.

He can't stand the building. He says they've wrecked the most magnificent farmstead in the country.

After Grandpa died, the family at Höfðabrekka was split up. Dad was eleven, and he was placed with foster parents in Skaftártunga, given little to eat, and made to do far more work than he was capable of, like fetching water in freezing weather and snowstorms, causing him to fall on patches of smooth ice with full buckets. They came very close to killing him—he contracted pneumonia and wasn't expected to live. Grandma Sigríður went to get him after he started to recover and found him a place on a farm in Flói. There he was treated well and received enough to eat. The couple on the farm had lost a son, and Dad reminded them of him. They became his surrogate parents and supported his education.

For the second time in his life, my dad is being abandoned by his closest relatives, this time by a false daughter. Sibbi's betrayed him even more, taking from him the fruits of his life's work: apartment, car, savings. Is this what parents live for, to witness their children's treachery, in spirit and in truth?

What will I live to see Edda Sólveig do?

You should turn here, I tell Heiður.

Edda sits up abruptly as we turn off the main road and asks: Where the hell are we going now?

I promised your grandfather I'd bring dried halibut to Erika. You knew that.

What am I supposed to do in the meantime?

Why don't you just come in too and have a look at the seismograph? And the house—it's so wonderfully original.

To this I receive no reply in words, only a low murmur of disapproval, as if from a deranged choir member who wants to ruin the performance.

How did that actually come about, this thing with the seismograph?, asks Heiður.

Uncle Þorbergur was a self-educated geologist, one of those Icelandic farmer's sons who long to get an education but can't afford it. Actual scientists got wind of how he took the pulse of movements in the ground without any instruments and got him to watch over the seismograph in order to keep track of any signs of an eruption in Katla. He put forward theories that were debated in learned journals, both domestic and foreign. One was called the pseudostub theory or something along those lines, about an eruption that occurs under great pressure, at the seabed, for example, or beneath a glacier. According to his theory, pseudostubs then emerge but aren't always clear, because the forces of nature can carve them so sharply and transform them. The Reynisdrangar sea stacks or Dyrhólaey, I don't remember which, are exactly like that—yes, stubs, according to Þorbergur's theory. And guess what? He actually predicted the Westmann Islands eruption.

The man must have been clairvoyant, says Heiður.

To see Alexis Papas's rest home rise from the hills after a steep and winding journey is unlike any other sight in human history. I squeeze my eyes partway shut and squint toward a monster of an old-fashioned turf farmhouse in the middle of a potato and vegetable field. The field's fenced with sky-blue filigree-like wire mesh, high above the plain. There's a wide view over the sand, as far as the eye can see, across the sea and out to the horizon, where the sky begins, and from the middle of the sea of sand rises the checkered-green island Hjörleifshöfði.

Go-od, who had this awful thing built?, Heiður wonders aloud.

Alexis Papas, the old Greek. Don't you remember? So much was written about it when he bought the farm and had this replica of an old-fashioned gabled farmhouse built.

I must have been overseas.

Alexis Papas was a shipping magnate who lost his family. Not one single gene of it is left. His son was murdered, his wife took her own life, and I don't remember any more except that the old man gave almost all of his possessions to help the needy in India, and a sizeable part went to Mother Teresa. With the little he kept, he built this three-story farmhouse on an Icelandic heath. It can accommodate forty residents, but it's never had more than twenty or so. Alexis Papas set admission requirements. The old folks must have an interest in organic farming, and work at it if they have the strength. Apparently, however, Icelandic senior citizens are just so headstrong that they'd rather hang around helplessly at home than pretend to have an interest in organic farming. Erika, on the other hand, didn't need to pretend. She was bitten by the biodynamics bug long before it became fashionable in Iceland. I recall having seen her in my childhood with a copy of *Biodynamics Journal* that had photos of bright-yellow potatoes and phosphorescent carrots.

Pointing at a picture, she said: Zev has not been poison zo fahr.

Efri-Hæðir

Edda remains behind in the car, and I have the good sense not to utter a peep. Though it's tempting to remind my daughter how well Erika has always treated her.

A lively gust of wind blows us along to the high iron gate. EFRI-HÆÐIR is spelled out in chrome letters swinging beneath the gate's arch. UPPER HEIGHTS.

God, the rest home is called Upper Heights? What a hoot!, says Heiður.

Yes, didn't you know that? Alexis Papas got a nutty Icelandic language scholar to help him, and this was the result.

And what is *that*?

Heiður points to a tiny building way back in a corner of the vegetable garden. It looks like a turf-roofed dollhouse, with a cross on top. It reminds me of something that Dad put together at some point, but I can't remember what.

I think it's a replica of the chapel at Núpsstaður, the smallest house of worship in the country. I heard about Alexis creating this replica, but I thought it was a joke.

Sheesh.

He liked that little cemetery over there so much that he bought it as well.

What's he going to do with a cemetery?

Just own it, I think.

So does he own the people in it, too?

I hope not. My grandma and grandpa are buried there.

A long gravel lane leads to the house. On a sign next to the lane, the image of a car is crossed out.

How do they get the things they need?, asks Heiður.

Everything's brought by horse-drawn wagon up the last bit.

Organic home delivery, says Heiður, gasping with laughter at her own joke.

Didn't the fellow check how damned windy it gets up here before he went and built his rest home? Here it just blows and blows. When Dad was a kid the church blew away. One morning people woke to find nothing but debris strewn around the property. Pieces of the organ were scattered all over the hayfield. It was a gold mine for the children and provided raw material for all sorts of workmanship for a few years afterward, especially the pipes. Some had been blown up into the hills. Half the instrument was stuck in the stream, and the keyboard lay on the bank, split in two yet hanging together. Like half a rib cage from an unknown creature that maybe went to get a drink a hundred years ago but then, like Lati Geir in the poem, lay there lazily until it died. Sheet music with hymns and funeral marches was cast across the slopes, while on the grave of Great-grandpa and Great-grandma lay an open hymnal, as if someone had placed it there neatly.

We've just come to a black-lacquered door when a short man with thick glasses appears from around the corner of the house. He's wearing a tan cobbler's apron over a checkered work shirt and is carrying a spade. A patch hides one of his eyes.

Did you say magnate or pirate?, says Heiður.

He's a war hero, my dear. He's one of the Greek heroes who blew Nazis to bits during the war.

God, he looks like Onassis.

They're related, as well.

That's a damn lie.

They're something like second or third cousins.

You're joking.

Ask Erika if you don't believe me. We're lucky to catch a glimpse of him. You almost never see him except when he's puttering in the garden. He even eats alone and never really speaks to anyone but Erika. They both speak German.

The doorbell at Efri-Hæðir is a golden convex apparatus that you hesitate to touch. It resembles a little breast with an exaggerated nipple.

A gray-haired woman in a white bathrobe, her shoulders bent, opens the door. Right next to her stands a man with angel hair and a baby face. They're both the age of people who live in rest homes, but the woman has a nursing symbol on the lapel of her robe, so she must be on staff. Unless there's a special arrangement here that the residents act as staff members on a rotating basis.

I've come to see Erika, I say.

She's up on the second floor, says the woman, pointing at a golden elevator door. The final piece of the puzzle—an elevator in a traditional gabled farm.

The man with the angel hair tilts his head toward the gray-haired woman's chest, and calls out softly: Mommy, Mommy, hello. He's wearing a light-yellow tracksuit, and together he and Heiður are like an avant-garde advertisement for these overused garments.

Tracksuits are one of the most appalling inventions of recent decades, belonging only on tracks and in gyms. Yet entire rest homes, rehab centers, and all sorts of other asylums are chock-full of people in these uniforms. There's no better way to shear people of their individuality than to put them in rustling, shiny tracksuits. I prefer good old bathrobes: checkered English wool robes with a belt around the middle, colorful velour robes with abstract patterns from Finnish designers, electric-blue nylon bathrobes with tasseled belts, short robes over spindly legs, wide American terry-cloth robes that make people look like little bears, Chinese silk robes with coloring-book flowers. I forbade Sibbi and his wife, Bagga, from giving Dad a tracksuit. He'll be allowed to maintain his dignity, in polyester trousers and a blue-gray vest, with morbid-yellow elbow patches from the psychedelic mind of his dead wife.

Erika's room is remarkably small compared to the size of the building. There's nothing in it but one bed, one chair, and a transparent box in place of a nightstand: the seismograph itself. Adorning the bedroom are the white, pink, and purple flowers of African violets that fill the window, and beyond them shines the green ecosystem of the broad-leaved vegetable garden that sits almost under the clouds, while sand and sea lie far down below on the earth. Erika, small and slim, in her snow-white tracksuit that's too wide at the shoulders, tends to the seismograph. The dear woman's begun to lose her hearing and doesn't notice me until I touch her shoulder.

Oh, hello zere, teer, she says in her accent, which is still very German after forty years in Iceland. She embraces me like the most loving mother.

How are you?, I ask.

Ve feel vell, she says, pointing at the box. I vas jahst vinishing changing zis. New papeer und ink in ze recorter.

Erika motions us to sit on her bed, while she picks up a tin decorated with illustrations from paintings by the angel-master Stefan Lochner, her countryman. Under the lid covered with robust-looking angels are cookies, perfectly shaped, colored appropriately, glossy half-moons and plump meringues.

Did you bake these?

Cehrrtahnly. Ich have aczess to ze kitchen.

In Erika's window, a statue of Christ hides among the flowers. Erika's a strict Catholic. She was even on the verge of entering a convent before she came to visit a girlfriend of hers who'd married a farmer in Reynishverfi. Instead of becoming a nun, she married my uncle Þorbergur. She called him Beggi and always said he was "compleetlee vunderbar." And now she spends her life looking after her and her late husband's seismograph in a newfangled retirement home not far from the roots of a glacier. They had the apparatus in their own home for fifteen years, and understandably didn't want to leave it behind when they moved to the rest home. Beggi tended it even after he became bedridden.

When he died, people came from Reykjavík to disconnect the seismograph, but Erika had already met with the home's directors and it was formally agreed that the apparatus would remain there, that new generations of elderly residents would be allowed to adopt this fine device rather than put it in the hands of strangers who have no feeling for the earth's movements.

I recall that Alexis Papas was so enthusiastic about this plan that he offered to donate money to make it possible to set up a network of seismographs in all the rest homes in the country, but geologists felt such a distribution to be too random, and the billionaire withdrew his offer in a huff.

How tas your vader veel?

Dad has really slowed down, but he's in good shape mentally.

I can feel the tears start pushing their way from my soft brain, trying to break out into the world. I try rubbing my eyes so this can't be seen, the so-called daughter devastated at being reminded that she's abandoned her bereft father.

Are you und Etta plannink bote to be in ze Eastfjords zis vinter?

Yes, I'm having trouble with her. She's going to be in Andey with Ingólfur, and I'll stay with Dýrfinna.

Iz ahbsolutely right to leave ze gank. She maybe vill be goot. Und Tjurfinna und Ingólfur, zey ahre one of a kind.

Yes, I'm hoping it'll work out, my dear Erika. We've got to try something.

Iz hohrrible in Iceland vat young people end up in zo much. Zere ist no reahl upbringing here, ahnless ze kid ist goot himself.

This isn't the first time I think it's a shame that Erika and Þorbergur had no children. Both so gentle, yet so firm. Then there's Erika's exemplary housekeeping; she's punctilious and meticulous, yet without being nitpicky—an atmosphere in which children and flowers thrive. Such is the world. Those who should have babies don't, while the scoundrels multiply like rabbits.

Und ist Etta just out in ze car?, asks Erika.

She's so rebellious, I say, feeling terribly ashamed of my worthless excuse for a daughter, who won't even deign to look in on her old benefactress. She does everything opposite of what I want, I add.

Strange, says Erika. She vas such goot little girl.

Yes, it's strange.

The old man with the white hair who was at the door when we came in pushes into the room and calls, Mommy, Mommy, hello.

Ja, ich bin here, says Erika.

You're not my mommy. She doesn't talk like that.

Heiður takes the man's hand and leads him back into the hallway.

Ich found him in my bet wahnce. Ich var terribly frightent. He ist cahmpletely baby now, und cahn damage ze rrecortehrr.

She takes out a box of chocolates, puts it in a brown paper bag, stretches a rubber band around it, and says that it should be for "Tjurfinna."

Vill you alzo stop at Arnbjart's?

Yes, I promised to look in on him.

Zen ich shall give you here brant-new biodynamische potatoes zat ich gazzered for zahmwahn elze.

She grabs a plastic bag from beneath her bed, and I have no heart to object, though I have no idea where I can fit in this addition to our luggage.

Erika turns every place and everything into a distribution center, even the final institution in life, decrepitude itself.

I give Erika dried strips of wolffish from the Westfjords, from Dad, goods that are sold in secret at his rest home. The staff at Grund have tried hard to disrupt the dried-fish ring, and its consumption is strictly prohibited indoors there. The stuff's stench is unbearable, and it makes an inordinate number of crumbs. Sometimes I've seen old folks standing out by the wall on the Hringbraut side, shivering in their cold slippers as they tear off and eat pieces of the contraband fish. They form a circle and pass around a jam jar filled with butter, for dipping the pieces in. Dad doesn't want it going around that the dealer in the west is on the village board in Flateyri and either personally brings the goods south or sends them by way of go-betweens, even in the suitcases of children who are coming from the countryside.

Erika says that wolffish is the very best thing she could be given and blesses me for bringing it in airtight packaging, before adding: But ich must go to a bench outsite to eat, zis ist so uncleanable. She brushes imaginary crumbs off her white tracksuit.

Now Herr Doktor Papas will also be happy because he lahfes vell-vuhrked hartfisch.

When we come out of the room, we find Edda in the hallway, in an animated conversation with the angel-hair man. He's stopped calling out for his mommy and is listening to Edda, who's telling him that Erika's husband, Þorbergur, was her great-uncle.

We were confirmed together, says the feebleminded man. Beggi was enormously intelligent, which was proven when he foretold the eruption on Heimaey while all the Icelanders were taught in school that Helgafell was an extinct volcano.

I can tell that Edda is ashamed about not having come with us immediately to see Erika, to whom she owes so many thanks: for kindness, homemade toffee, and angora caps with tassels and visors.

Now, like a normal person, she asks how Erika's doing, starting a lively discussion with her and the man.

Here at the old Greek's rest home is where Edda should have been left behind. This is clearly the place for her. But who could have known that in advance? A lack of imagination, of course, is what vexes people most.

Erika suddenly announces that she mustn't hold us up, but first she invites Edda to her room.

As Heiður and I stand on the steps outside, gusts of wind tear at our hair. The swollen potato plants sway in the billowing wind, and far below us the sea is topped with white crests, big and little, which race up onto the sand strip stretching into the distance.

Heiður and I hurry down the gravel path. The damned organic potatoes are quite heavy and do nothing to alleviate the muscle pain of this little assistant nurse.

As soon as we step out through the arched gate of Efri-Hæðir, a cream-yellow Bronco roars up the path at high speed. It's the same one from the shop in Rangárvellir. The farmer and his alleged mother step out. The woman looks exactly the same as before, but she's wearing a different overcoat, light gray, all-weather. There's no sign of any sheep inside the car.

The sheep must be napping, whispers Heiður.

After mother and son have gone through the gate, Heiður and I walk over to their car and peek determinedly through the window. At first it looks to me as if the sheep is in the backseat with the seat belt fastened around it, yet it turns out not to be the sheep, but its fleece, or that of some other sheep, neatly fastened with an old-fashioned lap belt. The backseat also holds a scythe and a sleeping bag, and on the floor next to the seat is a mop bucket covered with a wet rag.

Home-butchering, on the road, says Heiður.

If it's only that.

Edda suddenly appears next to me.

Are you crazy, Mom? Peeking in people's windows, for fuck's sake.

Sorry, darling, but it's just a car, I say, terribly submissive out of old habit, and apologetic, as if I've played a nasty trick on her.

See what she gave me. She said she had another one.

Edda shows me the little statue of Christ from Erika's window.

It looks to me as if my beast likes this gift. Who would have believed it?

And she gave me five thousand krónur.

God Almighty. Hopefully, you thanked her.

Of course, says Edda, highly insulted. You think I don't have manners?

Down down down
all the way down to the field.
It goes quickly. Yet the wind is against me.
Not even the wind is with me.
A dead-tired woman
of a highly uncertain origin.

The odor of alcohol emanating from Edda has intensified. The old man must have given her one for the road.

Heiður grasps the steering wheel tightly as she navigates the curves down the slopes. She bites her thin lips as she works hard to counteract the wind.

MANY FACES are made in such a way that any one part of them can live an independent life that is unconnected to the face or the individual associated with it, like a part that has survived the death of the body and is now a ghost. These parts of the face are little used, more often than not—think of someone with glassy eyes or a frozen upper lip—and, with their lack of use, point either to death or a former life, despite their independence.

I don't know what life Heiður Jensdóttir's regal nose has come from, but it would fit just as perfectly on a falcon as a man, preferably an Arabian sheik. This falcon's beak is little noticeable when Heiður speaks, laughs, or thinks, and she never wrinkles this piece of furniture. Instead, it sits like a stone somewhat in the middle of her face while her mouth moves and she narrows her quick eyes. Although her nose does nothing while awake, it certainly does in sleep. Heiður snores loudly, a fact she does not find humorous at all.

Heiður's masculine nose transforms only under one circumstance as far as I know, and that's when she plays her flute. Then this majestic nose stops ruling over everything as it's put under the control of instrument and notes. It's only when Heiður blows into her flute that her nose melds perfectly with her and acquires a life that's connected to the rest of her.

Do you remember, Edda? *That's* where Grandpa saw the monster, there on the slope where the footpath runs from the sand high up to the brink where he lived when he was a kid. The rest home is built right on top of the farmstead.

Dad was nine years old, and there was another boy of about the same age with him. They went down the slope, where the path turns, in order to fetch the cows. It's called Kaplagarðar; you can see the track. It was midsummer, in calm, sunny weather, with unusually high temperatures. After coming halfway down, they saw a gray-white behemoth the length of two full-grown cows trying to climb up the bottom part of the slope, slow and cumbersome, murmuring as it inched its way up, legless, or so it seemed. It tumbled down several times and took a very long time regaining that ground. Dad says they weren't afraid, because the creature wasn't making any great speed. The boys ran up to the farm, and farmhands were sent to the scene, but they saw nothing. They went all the way down and fetched the cows, but it turned out to be impossible to drive them up the slope where the beast had been seen. The locals guessed that its odor or even slime frightened away the cows, though human noses could smell nothing.

The river's right near there, says Edda. The monster must have gone into it.

Yes, the Múlakvísl River. That was one of the theories.

What can it have been?, asks Heiður.

Nobody knows. Dad thought it resembled an elephant seal, but the creature didn't have a balloon on its snout, as elephant seals do.

It was a walrus, says Edda.

They didn't see any tusks.

It was a huge seal, says the girl.

A manatee, says Heiður.

A legless manatee?

You two sure can bullshit, says Edda Sólveig, in a voice that reminds me of both an old bitch and a bad actor playing a flamboyant gay man. She's getting a very good grasp of this variant, which is newish and incredibly grating on the nerves. If she continues using this tone during our trip, I'll throw myself out the window.

Hey, what's this?, Heiður asks, before answering her own question. We've come to sand.

She's distracted once again, and the car veers toward the edge of the road. Yet crashing there wouldn't be so swift a death, because the drop is no higher than a foot and a half, followed by level black sand.

Someone has a fake driver's license, says Edda.

The sand's starting to blow. Look at that bank there.

It's some sort of dust cloud. I hardly think it could be a real sandstorm. But it's quite windy.

I asked up at Efri-Hæðir, just to be sure, but was told there's no sand.

Funny wording, that there's no sand. This is an absolute desert.

Should we turn back?

No, damn it, says Heiður. But it wouldn't be good to ruin the paint on Dad's car. It costs more than a hundred thousand krónur to spray-paint a car.

The sand's bad for the windows, too, says Edda. It dulls them.

It's something, no question about it, says Heiður.

Maybe we should turn back, I say.

There's plenty of time to turn back, replies the driver.

We continue halfheartedly. At least it's halfheartedly that I continue. I'm careful not to say it out loud. I mustn't make excuses for my own escape. Halfheartedly, like everything else I decide to do. HALFHEARTED—that would be the perfect title for my autobiography. Got pregnant as a teen, halfheartedly. Lived with a man, halfheartedly. Fled to the peace of the countryside, halfheartedly. Will die halfheartedly, and come back as a ghost, halfheartedly. Ugh.

All out of luck, little loner.

An only daughter, not even loved by her dead mother. You'd think Mom could at least have given me that.

Following us are sinister birds, a skua and great skua, sent from Mom with a message that I'm making this trip for nothing, to remind me that I'm doomed to lose. That Edda, the only thing I have, will end up destroying herself in a hell of her own making, which is my doing even though I don't even know how I managed it.

The birds aren't from me, little Eisa. It's absolutely no use pinning them on me.

I'd certainly believe you to be capable of sending flying monsters my way.

Those noxious birds have nothing to do with me. I stand by that, you little nervous Nellie.

Mom, I know it's difficult to cut the cord, almost impossible. Yet I beg you, let's stop, instead of talking like this to each other.

I'll think it over.

We've got to learn to reconcile if we're going to survive.

I *didn't* survive, my dear. That's the whole point.

The route over the sand has shortened since I was a kid. Back then it seemed endless. On a bumpy road, in a big cloud of dust, and Harpa frightened as could be, worrying about the possibility of a devastating glacial flood from Katla. I tried to spy escape routes for us. Where the closest refuge might be *now*. On the other side of Hjörleifshöfði? On top of Mount Hafursey? On this trip over the sands there are serious difficulties—a mad sandstorm is a relief. To know what one should fear is so much easier than to fear everything and nothing, vaguely.

Blowing sand. A cause for fear that this little coward somehow missed back in the day.

Shouldn't we turn back for real, Heiður? Look at the sand cloud. We're about to drive into it.

The sand can't possibly be blowing much. I'm sure it needs time to get going for real. The wind's only just begun to stir itself up.

It certainly was windy up at Efri-Hæðir just before.

The world ahead is a deep-brown cloud. Its limbs reach out to us and scratch the car.

Both blizzards and sandstorms have a brown hue. Every hampered view is like the next, akin to death. Death itself, master at self-consistency.

I've never encountered such a thing before, says Heiður.

Me neither. I'm terribly worried about the car.

It'll all be fine.

Gusts of wind-driven sand slam against the car.

The wind picks up, accelerating the pounding.

Damn, I should have turned back, says Heiður.

This is nothing. It was much worse when I went with Sibbi, says Edda.

The sand's a punishing rod that flogs the car with immense force, as if trying to tear off pieces of it and turn it into a sand sculpture. We can still become famous: modern-day Reynisdrangar sea stacks on the sands—three fossilized wenches in a pickup truck.

The devious pitch-black grains penetrate the car and settle on the dashboard, where they multiply. Nothing in the world apart from these particular particles could reach us through the battened-down seam of shut windows and locked doors.

There's a bridge ahead, says Edda. You should stop on it and wait.

What do you mean? Hunker down on the bridge?, says Heiður, foul-tempered.

It's the right procedure if you run into sand, says Edda. I landed in a sandstorm here when I went east with Sibbi. He had the sense to wait and there wasn't a scratch on our car. But when we got to Kirkjubæjarklaustur, we saw another car that'd been stripped of almost all its paint.

I can stop, no problem.

. . .

The world is goddamned blowing sand and nothing else. Sea and shore and our mountains gone. The sand itself is gone. It dissolves into blowing black snow, a substance that seems not to be made of sand.

PRECIPITANCE.

That the earth should take it upon itself to pound on us and block our sight. Even the soil is hostile to this precipitance.

My entrance into this world was due to the precipitant rush of a neurotic mother into the arms of a foreigner. Who is he? Where is he?

MY PATERNITY

is a poem that I haven't bothered to jot down
not even on a little scrap of paper kept with the dirty laundry.
I've compared my looks to the pictures of the nationalities
of the world
in a beautifully produced book belonging to my dad.
I could be anything on my father's side, though hardly Asian.
My face is mainly reminiscent of sculptures of Mayan Indians,
but where could Mom have gotten hold of one of their descendants?
It's more likely that, by chance,
a Frenchman, Italian, Spaniard came here,
some sort of American, yes, it's most probable that Mom got together with a soldier,
an aged soldier's gal.

Why? Because that's what they did then.

I could also describe myself as gypsy-ish, or Indian-ish.

My dad could therefore be called Lofty Lion, Young Toe.

He could also be called Hernandez, Colombo, Hugenbüttel, Rambo, Root-Renfrew, Nandor, Disney-Smith. *There's no lack of names.*

Harpa Disney-Smith. Harpa Hernandezdóttir.

Those who don't know their own fathers don't know their own names.

They call themselves whatever they like until the truth is revealed.

If I were in your shoes, says Edda, I'd keep going. It's better for the time being.

Heiður shakes her head. I don't know why, maybe in disbelief that the beast had addressed her tactfully, or from frustration at having ended up in such a predicament in her father's pickup.

What do I mean by this? What do I mean by dragging my busy friend out onto the roads of Iceland, and even into financial loss that I wouldn't be able to help redress?

. . .

Heiður sets off, driving straight. The pitch-black sand hammers the car as if it comes from the jaws of a sand-spewing dragon that can't be seen through its own dust cloud.

Excuse me, says Edda from the backseat. You can't drive fast in a sandstorm. The sand hits the car with more speed and is even likelier to damage it.

Heiður rolls her eyes and decelerates, until we crawl along at thirty.

I suppose that's logical, I say.

A small Jeep with a Z plate number, from the local district, inches toward us.

It must be true, since the locals drive so slowly, I say.

Of course what *I* say doesn't matter, complains Edda, insulted.

My unpredictable delinquent child. One moment a boor, using language like the worst street kid in a big-city slum, and the next thing you know, a responsible guide who takes two older ladies to task on the Mýrdalur Sands. You couldn't even call her a changeling, but rather, a constant-turnaboutling or something—I don't know. But I get qualms when she behaves herself decently, because she usually regrets it right away and changes back.

A yellow car rushes past us at lightning speed.

That guy knows nothing about driving in sandstorms, since he's going so fast, I say, flashing Edda a smile. She's wearing a strange expression as she peers out the windshield. I'm struck with the horrible feeling that the car looks surprisingly similar to Gerti Chicken's fucking delivery van. If this is the Chicken, then I implore all the forces of evil to scratch each and every particle of paint off his car and sandblast his windshield until not a speck can be seen through it.

Gerti the brainless chicken, who was always present when the worst things happened.

Edda and Gerti's dance on the basement steps was world-class choreography, a pair lurching apart and together and out and down, the female dancer badly battered. Gerti pretended to be supporting Edda when she was supporting him no less. Gerti Chicken, with dirt-colored greasy hair hanging down to his shoulders, his face russet except for the stone-gray bags under the hollows of his eyes and flourishing clusters of pimples with yellow nibs crowding their way out of the dungheap of his cheeks. His head's short and square-shaped, lacking a chin, and his deep-set eyes are really like a chicken's, so vacant that you're afraid to look into them. It's no exaggeration to say that in appearance, Gerti Chicken is the greatest wretch of all the damned wretches that Edda Sólveig's been keeping company with. Emanating from him is a stench that at times perfectly resembles the smell of shit, so strong that you can hardly breathe. When I told Heiður that I used hospital disinfectant on the furniture he'd touched, she burst out laughing and said that it wasn't hard to understand why the daughter of a woman who was a neat freak had chosen this very friend.

I hadn't replaced the porch-light bulb and didn't notice immediately what bad shape Edda was in. All I saw was the masterfully executed, distorted dance of these two young bums at the front door.

Did you know there's gold in the sand from Katla?

Sand from Katla is in fact what's hammering us now. A flogging with gold.

A new type of perversion.

The sandstorm picks up again, lashing the car with a frighteningly crunching grumble. Nothing's visible but a thick cloud. Now apprehension flies at me like the grains of sand, in through invisible chinks in my soul, even though it's supposed to be armored, like a little tank.

Skua, great skua, and raven. What will happen to these flying creatures of darkness when the sand ascends to their paths? Won't the black mass pile up on their wings and crush them into the dust? Will they be buried in sand holes, with only their beaks poking out?

How silly I am. These winged creatures can fly out of this disaster. Winged creatures, as I am in spirit. It's been a game of mine through everything that's come my way to imagine myself with wings, to imagine that I can ascend above all of this after a prolonged takeoff, like a swan taking off from water, dragging its black feet along the surface a long way, coming to full steam like an airplane along a runway, and driving itself into the blue in order to view the earth from the sky on wide wings, from a lofty distance.

More often than a swan, though, I'm a martyr, an angel with one wing.

You inherited it from me, little Eisa.

Is that you, ghost Mom?

You can't fly far on your one wing, my dear.

Well, I just sort of flutter and flap it a bit.

You've always looked slightly lopsided.

I use my wing rather infrequently. It's mostly ornamental.

Maybe being caught in a sandstorm isn't such a bad thing, Mom says. It's exciting to find oneself in a bad place in life, feeling claustrophobic and suffocated.

To move along the road, a reprobate hussy in a movable cage of roaring sand?

To be defenseless against a sandstorm, she says. There's worse defenselessness than that.

I'd rather be defenseless against the sand than against people. With all that they entail.

. . .

Although the storm has let up a bit, Heiður stops on a bridge, and I'm not about to interfere.

To think that all these greening measures still can't prevent the sand from blowing, I say.

Conservationists are always protesting the planting of foliage in the black sands. They say the sands are a natural wonder, existing nowhere else.

Lucky they exist nowhere else. They're a horror.

I check the backseat to make sure Edda has her headphones on.

Hey, guess what?, I say to Heiður quietly. I could swear I thought I saw the Little Yellow Hen dash past us earlier.

You think they've chased us all the way here?

If it's the Hen, then they're chasing us.

Do you think the sand has you seeing things?

I don't think so.

Those assholes.

Gerti's always in the middle of it. He's the one who brought Edda home, with her arm broken and her face all beat up.

But he still had the sense to take her to the emergency room?

A man of his intellect couldn't have come up with that himself. Someone must have sent him.

And no one knows what happened to the child?

Maybe the person who attacked her.

Could she have fallen?

It looked more like she'd been beaten.

And in the middle of all of it, Dýrfinna arrived.

She arrived the day that I was going to kill myself. For three days straight Edda had been playing Guns N' Roses at full blast. Then she attacked me when I offered to give her headphones. My leg still isn't quite right.

Heiður is silent. It's not a good sign if she says nothing after my repartee. She's so impatient that she usually doesn't even let me finish what I'm saying—she's very bad about interrupting. With her there's no pausing for effect, except when absolutely necessary. In other words, when she's onstage.

She's crazy, of course, says Heiður softly, breaking this unusual silence.

That's not what my doctor says.

Your doctor? What does *her* doctor say?

You don't remember? She stopped seeing her psychiatrist, that guy named Dúddi. In her mind, he's so stupid and idiotic and dresses so lame and uses such ridiculous words that she absolutely can't see him.

Too bad I was abroad. Tell me again exactly what happened.

The third evening that Edda was at home recuperating, a soft knock came on the inner door just before midnight. It was the noise-maker from upstairs, my landlord, who loomed over me like a natural disaster what with his constant commotion. I stared expectantly at his limpid, flabby cheeks, his blubbery neck, and the sloughy red eczema that flourished at the boundary between his baldness and his tufty hair. He said in a ministerial voice that things couldn't go on like this any longer. The loud music had prevented him and his wife from catching a wink of sleep the last few nights. I said: Me too, and took one step back from this physically repulsive yet courteous man. I apologized to him and confessed that I had no control over it. The girl kept herself in her room with her broken arm and beat-up face, and she was so stressed or something that she couldn't sleep. I sighed this out, on the verge of tears. My landlord saw how I felt and laid his scaly hand on my shoulder. That sorted me out for the moment, since his physical disgustingness was stronger than my tears. I think I more or less shook the man's hand off me as I came up with the clever statement that I ought to have thought of long before:

I really should buy her headphones, because I'll never get her to stop playing her music at full blast.

Would it have more impact if I spoke to her?, asked the poor man.

She doesn't want anyone to see her in such a condition. But of course I'll let her know that you came.

I went into Edda's room. She was sitting in the lotus position on the crappy bed that her mother, the assistant nurse, hadn't been allowed to make, despite considerable pressure. Along with the blanket and pillow, the bed was cluttered with a sweater, an orange-juice carton, a plastic bag from the Hagkaup supermarket, a hairbrush, cassette tapes, and slippers. Edda was staring at the heap, looking terribly pitiable, her face damaged, her arm in a cast, wearing too-small pajamas and holding a brightly smiling teddy bear.

I'd thought about how to speak to her without upsetting her. My dear Edda, I began. I'll buy you headphones first thing tomorrow, but will you please turn down the music? The landlord stopped by and said they haven't been able to sleep the past couple of nights.

Where are you going to get the money for headphones, you famished whore?

I'll borrow it.

My daughter replied by reaching over to the stereo and turning it up.

Edda, I'm begging you, this can't go on. The people upstairs will end up calling the police.

No, you'll do it yourself, if I know you right, you loose bitch.

However she managed it, she lifted herself quick as a flash from the lotus position and kicked my kneecap with all her might, causing me to drop to the floor with a wail. She hit me on the shoulder with her cast as I cowered on the floor, making me cry out again. I completely lost it—from pain, anger, despair, I don't know what to call it—and screamed with all the powers of my life and soul, drowning out that infernal music.

Then the man from upstairs appeared. I tried to stop wailing but couldn't, and I also found that wailing helped me withstand the pain. But I shed not one single tear, no more than the foster daughter of wolves would have done. The poor man looked like a fish out of water, but he offered me his hand to help me to my feet. I waved him off, but suddenly I realized that it felt really good to scream, and I made a game of continuing to do so. I tried to change the scream into a genuine howl that I would have been completely content with during the heyday of Kamala the wolf-girl.

In the midst of all this, I was deadly calm inside and I thought of a comment a certain doctor made: I would rather that the patient let me know I'm hurting him than for him to start crying after everything's done.

The man from upstairs changed his focus to Edda and looked thunderstruck at her scarred cheeks and swollen lips, and one eye sunken behind a frame of dark blue and red. She stared back hard. After several minutes of taking in Edda's face and my cries, the man turned down the music and said: For the love of God, what's going on?

Edda: Eat shit and start with your toes.

The man with eczema: Should I call an ambulance or the police?

Edda: The fire department.

The man: Where does it hurt?

I pointed at my knee and shoulder but couldn't speak through my screams. I would have preferred to stop screaming now, but it was impossible. The more I fought against my wailing, the more acute it became.

The man: Did she hit you?

I nodded, and the wailing turned into a sobbing that pumped out tears with each exhalation.

The man (to Edda): That, you simply may not do.

Edda: It's none of your business, you sack of eczema.

Unfortunately, the man's wife had come to the door, an obese woman who moves slowly and definitely doesn't look like an unbearable noisemaker.

The wife: How dare you say such things, child!

Edda (shouting loudly): How dare you come barging in here! It's an invasion of privacy.

The wife (to me): Who should I call?

Edda: Call the Salvation Army.

I realized I would have to stop crying and try to say something in order to put an end to this abominable situation. Between sobs I squeezed out: Ih-hit's oh-h-k-hay.

The couple from upstairs looked at each other. Tears were welling in the poor fat woman's eyes.

I tried to stand up and thank them for their help, but my knee gave out and I sank to the floor.

The man (to his wife, and pointing at me): She's broken something.

Me (on the floor): N-no-o (pointing at my knee). Th-hank you.

The man: I'll drive you to the emergency room. No question.

I shook my head and said, Th-hanks. No.

The wife said: Come get us or call if you need anything. It doesn't matter if it's in the middle of the night.

Again I moaned out th-hanks and the blubbery couple drifted out the door like sailboats on a superslow wind.

I didn't try to get up again. I crawled out of the room on all fours, without looking at Edda, but saw out of the corner of my eye that she was hesitant, for a moment. She quickly put the music back on, a tiny bit lower than before, I thought, though I could have misheard, numb as I was. After taking two potent painkillers, I fell asleep. The following morning I limped to the phone and called in sick to work. I was burning with pain, both in my leg and my shoulder, and knew I should go to the emergency room but couldn't fathom making the trip, so I took a sleeping pill instead. I had a supply from my nervous breakdown on New Year's Eve. You know, I have to carry around a miniature version of my medicine cabinet in my handbag, and I sleep with the pill bottles under my pillow. I can't let the girl get hold of anything. That's what these people do to you, drag you all the way down to their level. And you end up with drugs beneath your pillow, exactly like them.

There was little to stop me from swallowing enough pills to ensure I wouldn't wake up again, and I knew pretty much how many it would take to do the job. I felt as if I had no choice but to do away with living, and do away with looking in my child's face, in such bad shape as it was. I felt I never should have been born, much less have given birth. I'd never be strong enough to save myself. What an absurd stretch to imagine trying to save the child. I'd realized all of this earlier, admittedly, but just then I saw it with uncanny clarity.

As I was swallowing sleeping pill number two, the doorbell rang. I was so out of it that I automatically marched to the door like a robot, when it would have been best to ignore it. It was Aunt Dýrfinna. I had no idea she was in town, since she's never in town. She'd taken a taxi to my place, and this was what she found.

There was no way that I wanted visitors, and in the doorway I said, in a slightly hostile tone, that this was really not the right time. Dýrfinna said that it didn't matter one bit and invited herself in. She must have known that there was something afoot other than my lover waiting for me in bed, naked and impatient. Otherwise, she wouldn't have barged in like that.

It's curious what people notice, even when under immense physical and mental strain, including seriously contemplating suicide. I thought of the gray wool coat that's about the same age as me, because Dýrfinna was wearing it when she came to fetch me for the first time down at the dock out east. I also thought of her handbag— where and when she found that, I have no idea. It's a big, clunky container made of brown leather, with a sturdy iron latch; it would be well suited for holding rusty old medical instruments in a museum.

I took my aunt's gray coat and forbade her from removing her orthopedic shoes. Under her coat, she was wearing a drably colored classic wool blazer with a pleated skirt. The buttons on the blazer were covered with the same fabric and edged in gold. Underneath the blazer she was wearing a brownish-pink silk shirt. After taking off her coat and putting down the Reformation-era midwife's bag, she looked like a future member of Parliament for the Women's Party.

She sat down ponderously on my old couch, which I'd just recently covered with beautiful upholstery fabric from your parents' house. It was decorated with blazing tulips—red, yellow, and blue—which somehow looked perfect in my Bollagata living room. Dýrfinna remarked more than once that everything at my place was so lovely and tidy. That there was no question of my exemplary housekeeping skills, which I'd possessed ever since I was a little girl. And one could see quickly in children what sort of adults they'll become. I couldn't help thinking, however, that my experience as a parent seemed to refute such a theory.

I put coffee on, went into the living room, and abruptly grew wings. I was free from my sad earth, floating in neutral tranquility over my vale of tears, and I wanted to hear about anyone other than me and my delinquent child. Yes, as I recalled, Dýrfinna had retired relatively recently from her midwife job after almost half a century.

You never lost a child.

Never lost a child.

You also lost no woman in childbirth.

No one died.

You're a bearer of health and happiness, Aunt.

I've been lucky.

It isn't luck. You're just so smart.

That's not enough, Harpa. There are energies around me that I don't recognize. It could be dead people joining with me—it's said that the dead accompany some spiritual healers—although I don't feel this relationship directly. I've sensed the presence of my dead mother, but it's in a completely different manner from how some spiritualists describe it.

I certainly don't have to worry about getting help from that direction, from my mother. It isn't a nice thing to say, but that's how it is.

Harpa, we should be careful of what we say, and of judging others. We don't know what's under other people's skin. Your mother was so neurotic. She probably would have ended up in an asylum if she hadn't had such a good husband.

Poor Dad.

He was tremendously fond of her. And presumably still is.

I don't understand a life like Dad's. The hardships he suffered as a helpless child nearly killed him, and then he continued to be a martyr in his marriage.

Love isn't martyrdom, Harpa dear. We know so little of others' rewards. Plus, your father has you and Sibbi.

Yes, he *has me*, Aunt, but *am I his*? She's the only person I can ask, but I'll probably never get the words out. What on earth should I say? How is it, Aunt? Is it possible that I really belong to my dad? I mean to that side of the family. I'm so dark-skinned, like a black sheep.

The only person I can ask. But how do I go about it? No one's prepared me for asking strange questions about my family and origin, calling into question the fundamental details of my own existence, which have always been taken as true.

How's it going with Edda?

The question catches me completely by surprise, and because I'm so unprepared for it, I can think of nothing better than to start crying. She seems to find it natural for me to shed a few tears and lays her hand on mine. After a brief moment I point at Edda's door, which I'd shut, but I try not to say anything, because I know that nothing will emerge but a whimper.

Aunt Dýrfinna stands up, supports herself on the edge of the table, then on the doorjamb, and hobbles into Edda's room. I continue sobbing in the living room like the most miserable crybaby. I can't deal with anything, yet try to keep it quiet so that I don't wake the monster.

In the middle of an onslaught of sobs, my curiosity kindles and I change chairs in order to see into Edda's room. My aunt is kneeling by the bed, which her swollen knee-joints certainly can't make easy. I'm worried about her trying to stand up unaided, so I drag myself in and stand next to the bed, fully prepared to help my aunt to her feet after she's finished praying at the bedside of the battered girl. I'm careful to keep my eyes lowered, looking down at the blue-speckled vinyl tiles from IKEA that I laid myself, and not at the injured soul beneath the covers.

Aunt Dýrfinna heads back into the kitchen and sits down at the little round kitchen table.

It's awful, she says. People are such beasts.

I don't even know if someone beat her up or if she banged her head on something.

But they're not just beasts. Some are angels at times. We must never forget that. Nor must we ever forget that light may kindle when all seems most hopeless, the darkness deepest. You and your daughter must come east and spend the winter there, you with me, and Edda in Andey. After that we'll play it by ear.

No, Aunt, I can't let you—

You're both like my own daughters, though I never had any.

You mustn't start—

It's really nothing, my dear. You'll stay in my attic. We might need to paint and lay new linoleum in one of the rooms. You know how to do that, I'm sure. And the girl will be perfect for helping out with the farmwork. She's so well acquainted with Andey. You'll see. The ridiculousness will drip off her like melted butter as soon as she gets up on a horse.

What about school?

She'll just get a ride there, like the other kids in the area. It's easy. Ingólfur drives the school bus.

I can't imagine she'll go for it. And anyway, how am I supposed to occupy myself?

They need people at the health center, my dear.

You're pretty smooth.

There's nothing else to do, my dear, but what's obvious.

. . .

I'll just keep going, says Heiður, driving on.

The sandstorm is no longer a storm. It's transformed itself into little spurts that sweep stutteringly over the road at ground level, scratching powerlessly at the tires, not even reaching the hood to give it a poke. It's the harmless remains of a natural disaster, nothing left but a little dabble in the sand, a little fiddling by the wind, which has grown tired of its own fury.

Behind us, the sandy cloud blocks our sight. No Hjörleifshöfði, no ocean. All that exists is what's ahead. Maybe we've avoided the worst? Maybe time and wind direction have been favorable to us, the wind's decided to side with us after all these years? Finally, after all these years.

And then what?, asks Heiður.

Haven't I told you all this before?

Not precisely.

Unless you've simply forgotten.

I got her with that one, because Heiður forgets everything I tell her. I've often been dreadfully hurt when things I've told her, things that are important to me, completely slip her mind. At those times I feel like an even smaller bug than usual, and I'm forced to remember how everything that Heiður does is much more important than what I do, that everything having to do with me is so damned insignificant that it doesn't stay more than a moment in the head of my best friend. It just goes in one ear and out the other.

Okay, be upset if you want, Heiður says. I was just asking what happened next.

When Edda, with her deformed face, finally left her room and came into the kitchen dressed in pink paper-doll pajamas to find Dýrfinna sitting there mild and mighty on the kitchen stool, dressed in her Sunday best, the girl's face was a true achievement in composition: both hostile and happy at once. You should have seen how my aunt handled the conversation at the kitchen table. She looked straight and firmly into Edda's injured face and asked how she felt. And the girl said, *Fine, thanks*, and my aunt said that she would be herself again in ten days. Edda said triumphantly that she would have a *scar* on her cheek. The doctor had said so. Aunt Dýrfinna said that it would never even amount to a blemish. Edda growled: Like I could care.

Just before my aunt ordered a taxi, she handed Edda knitted socks and two thousand krónur and said: We need a winter farmhand in Andey. You should come out east, dear, with your mother. Ingólfur's horses are in top form. You and Dreki didn't make such a bad team there two years ago.

Had it actually been only two years since she was in the countryside? Those two years had taken as long to pass as an entire century.

Edda Sólveig Loftsdóttir's expression of disapproval was so deep that it was clearly visible through her triple-sized lip, damaged cheek, and sunken eye.

It could be nice to get out of school, she said.

She has the tendency to be disgustingly crafty in her replies if there are others besides me within earshot. In place of giving a direct no, as she wanted to do, she came up with a cunning countermove. One might even be led to think she'd attended a training camp for slyness and duplicity.

Well, you'd still have to go to school, like everyone else your age. You've no choice but to finish the one year that you have left. Especially as intelligent as you are.

School's a waste of time.

Don't say such a thing. Everyone needs an education. You're not going to spend your life scrubbing floors, Edda.

I can work in a fish factory.

What sort of a future is that?, asked my aunt, looking directly at Edda. Plus, the cod are disappearing. Yes, I think a change will do you both good.

You're fucking plotting something behind my back, said Edda after I'd helped Dýrfinna out to the taxi. It had become so difficult for Dýrfinna to walk that I could hardly believe she'd undertaken such a trip.

You know very well I would never have suggested such a plan. Aunt Dýrfinna simply sees that something's really wrong.

Ings eally ong, mocked Edda. Yes, there's something really wrong—you're nuts with that silly poetry shit that you keep in the hamper. What do you do with it—use it for toilet paper? I've told Dúddi that you're insane, that you keep poems in the bathroom. And that you hate me. Dúddi says so too, because you got pregnant so young—

No, it's *you* who hates you, I interjected. That's why you're so awful to me.

You're a damned whore. When I turn sixteen, I'm going to kill you.

Why put it off?

So that I can get into a real prison with genuine criminals and not some fucking juvie-nursery.

You wouldn't get anywhere farther than Kleppur Psychiatric Hospital, where you'd sit and stew with all the genuine psychos.

She slapped my face hard enough for my ear to ring.

I stood still as stone, not moving, not blinking an eye.

You're welcome to do away with me, little Edda. It'll save me the trouble.

Kill yourself, you slut.

I stuck to my old method of retreating to my room, locking the door, and sitting in the rocking chair. I tried reading a book but I couldn't concentrate. Instead, I thought about how much I didn't want to live—the most useless thoughts in the world, because for the moment I was forced to continue living, sad to say. I realized that I was only just pretending to be about to swallow the pills before Dýrfinna came, and even if I had forced them down, I wouldn't have managed to give up the ghost completely, because Edda would have found me before they did their job, or the couple upstairs would have come to check on me.

No, suicide for a person like me is not something that can be rushed. It demands preparation—careful, systematic planning. Everything must be arranged so that nothing can go wrong, that no one can come before the mission is accomplished to ensure eternal sleep. Yet you shouldn't contemplate ending it at isolated areas near the sea or in open countryside, because then a search for your body would have to be conducted. To make those who remain uncertain of what happened is not the point.

The lengthy sands are akin to death, made of the world's darkest material, eternal granules. I imagine them as deceased souls in the deserts beyond. Rock-hard, cunning, compacted, pushing their way into a perfectly secure vehicle. Not like the vanished souls in Australia, an expanse of shiny shells that vie with each other in gleaming at the sun and sky in multiple waves by the sea, on the shell beach that Mom spoke endlessly about.

Poor you, Mom, to be a little black grain on the ugly Icelandic sands and not a shiny shell on the beach in eternal summer on the other side of the globe. You didn't deserve your fate.

You ought to remember that more often, Harpa baby.

I don't even know what happened to you, Mom.

If you look in the mirror, you'll come a bit closer to knowing.

I've often looked in the mirror, but I'm not there.

Whether the sand's blowing or not, it's pretty frightening, says Heiður.

This is one big field of destruction.

Field of destruction.

Yet volcanic eruptions and floods haven't managed to rip up everything and tear it all down. They've always left an inhabitable strip of land at one corner of the sands framed by the Kúðafljót River to the east: a tiny oasis, called Álftaver, where swans and sheep sing in chorus and take strolls in the gloaming by little ponds. It even has a few farms, which have been there a long time, and at one time it had a monastery, where some say *Njál's Saga* was written, on the plain in among jagged knobs of lava filed by water and wind and frost. From the plain there's an extensive view of the glacier and the sky. The people who live there are as little of this world as the oasis that they were allotted. Their faces are as scored as trolls', and they're better natured than the best elves. Descendants of monks? Who knows.

Shouldn't we pile some rocks as a waymarker?, asks Heiður.

No, those who cross the sands for the first time are supposed to add to the cairn at Laufskálar.

Laufskálar—Arbors—changes into desert.

That's the way many lives end.

The farm Laufskálar was located here, in this waste of sand. Funny, isn't it?

There was never anything funny about this desert, I say. It used to take people at least one day to cross it by foot, with everyone scared shitless that a flood caused by Katla might come and take them. Dad crossed the sands first when he was twelve and still recovering from pneumonia. He got caught in bad weather and made it to the other side haunted and bedraggled.

Poor folks have endured and struggled in this country, and with it. All those wet footprints of children and adults in tattered shoes over moors and heaths, scree and stone. All those journeys over trackless mountains and rivers. All those who drowned, died of exposure.

Some made it to their destinations wet, exhausted, and cold, and then died. Made it back only to die.

Like my Edda, maybe.

Somewhere around here, so it's said, was the settlement with the beautiful name Dynskógar, Clattering Woods, which was destroyed in volcanic fire many hundreds of years ago.

When you say it, Dynskógar, Dynskógar, you can hear hooves clattering long, long ago in bright late-June midday sunlight when the glacier glows its whitest, between brand-new birch leaves, and a bird throws itself down from the clouds and lands sure-winged on a branch.

Those who lived long enough hundreds of years ago witnessed the transformation of the fertile plain into wasteland following eruptions and glacial floods. Those who live long enough, at all times, see their friends fall, their faithful friends, their children. None of my relatives have died apart from Mom, and Jói, though I can hardly count him. The sad thing was that I never got to miss my mom wholeheartedly because I was more or less relieved when she stopped getting in the way of all of our lives: Dad's, Sibbi's, even her grandchild's. She could have been a better sort, this one parent from whom I'm certain to have come. She who only allows me to miss her halfheartedly.

I'm allowed to miss my friend Jói with all my heart, he who helped me exist, though deathly ill himself. He suggested that I flee to the east. But even missing him is a polluted feeling, because I'm ashamed of myself for mourning him but not Mom. I'm ashamed of myself for feeling as if he died and left me, he who was so young and died and left others so much more than he left me. I was neither family nor an old friend, nor a lover. I was merely a simple assistant nurse.

Jói was already very ill by the time I first met him. Every time I walked past his bed when he was sleeping it was a reminder of how ill he was and how he couldn't live. But as soon as I talked to him and saw his face light up, especially his soft brown eyes, I forgot that there was anything wrong with him, and it didn't occur to me at the moment that very soon I would have to be without him entirely.

It was selfish. It was about my loss of a friend, not his loss of life. The egocentric side of love reveals a part of our inner being that is hardly beautiful. Even young people who are going to die are entwined in the selfish love of those who fear most being left behind. The heart of the matter is overshadowed. A young person is taking leave of the world: life and colors and smells and sounds and touch.

In my experience, death is generally overshadowed by something that has nothing to do with it. Maybe because no one can bear to face pure death, the ultimate finale.

Except for Mom, the greatest daydreamer I've ever known.

Jói was my very special friend, and I will never have such a friend again.

I found it nice to be able to tell this friend how I was doing every time he asked, though I had a hard time understanding how a twenty-three-year-old man could be so wise and such a good conversationalist.

As I sat by Jói's bedside, this young man wasting away from disease seemed almost relieved to listen to my troubles. I felt as if I were doing him a favor by describing my troubles to him. I never really understood how it helped him.

The next time I was on duty after Edda attacked me, Jói noticed that I was limping and had a bruised cheek, though I'd tried to cover it with makeup. Jói asked what was wrong, and I said that it was such a long story that it would take me an extra shift to tell it. He laughed and asked whether it would be possible to make that happen. When my shift ended, I sat down beside him and told him everything, concluding with Dýrfinna's visit. At first he had to drag it out of me, and then the words came out in one big messy gush. By the time I left, Jói had grown so tired listening to my confessional flood that I was terribly concerned I'd exhausted a patient who was supposed to be in my care.

Go east, he said. I believe in it. Your aunt Dýrfinna knows the score. Why do you think she came in your greatest hour of need?

It just seems so hasty, like running away.

Many a man has saved himself by running away.

This is running away from myself, and Edda, and it can't work. Both of us would be making the trip.

Don't give up, Harpa. It's not a mathematical equation. You'll go east because your gut tells you to go.

My gut tells me nothing, Jói. I have no feeling about it.

I do. Go east.

It occurred to me sitting there next to Jói that the counsel of doomed men hasn't always been considered lucky. At least it wasn't in *Njál's Saga*.

Jói, Dýrfinna, Heiður, and Dad led me to this road, which lies over deathly sands from the netherworld. Jói showed me even more roads, and he taught me. He reconciled me with the fact that there are more un-poets than me, and what's more, I came to understand that the worst lot is to want to compose poetry but not be able to because you've ceased to exist. Then I felt lucky, having the chance to continue to exist and breathe and capture experiences in order to create a poem or not a poem, a little mood that I scribbled down so that I wouldn't forget it.

After Jói died I sometimes felt that I loved him, although he was dead. Or because he was dead. I recited my poems in order to feel his presence, and sometimes I felt that he was closer to me than the living, breathing beings around me, beings I spoke to with words and saw with my own eyes and smelled and touched. Sometimes I felt he'd become part of me, and I still feel it. It's hard to explain.

You dream me only as darkness
in a narrow corridor.

You do not hear my words.

Speak, then, and make your words mine.

Whence I come no light shines
no word is heard.

Because I am in the light, and in the word itself,
as in the beginning, before it became.

I was on duty when Jói died. His family had been with him for his last few days and nights, but his mother happened to leave for a few moments. He was sleeping when I came to take his food tray. I put the tray on the cart, and when I turned back to his bed I saw that he was going. I rang his bell, pulled the curtain shut, and said to Herbert, a patient in the bed by the door: Go to the duty station and tell a doctor to come immediately. I looked into the brown eyes of my friend, for the last time, hugged him firmly, and whispered in his ear, *My darling Jói*, because I know that hearing is the last thing to go. He whispered something back, which I thought sounded like, *Harpa and Jói*. I thought I heard him laugh, but it must have been something else. He would be the first person I knew to have died laughing. When the doctor arrived, Jói was gone. I stopped hugging him, but continued to hold his hand, just in case. This was around the end of my shift. When I got home, I went to my room without saying anything to Edda, locked the door, and cried myself to sleep before dinner. It might be shameful to admit it, but my behavior was more out of self-pity for my own loss than Jói's lost life, combined with jealous sorrow for not being dead like him.

Jói imposed an obligation on me. He implicitly demanded that I remember him, keep him in mind in a way that only I could do. It was his way to stick around and keep his presence alive, even if only in one soul—in the mind of the assistant nurse who some comedian of a doctor called Black Florence. I thought of him with all my heart when he was gone—I felt it served me right to love a dead boy—and I still raise him to life, my life, in his own words. I don't understand how to reconcile longing for both that damned man who moved to Ísafjörður—his body, anyway—and the soul of this dear boy who dwells beyond the darkness.

I would do right to remind myself more often that some people have better reasons than I not to write poems. Some people are simply dead.

That's at least less than what I am.

A raggedy-winged raven dives toward our car, as if planning to perch on the hood. It's not a sinister bird, but rather a black envoy of those who are going to determine my fate, some of them palpably at my heels. Gerti Chicken and company in a yellow van. Naturally, my fate was determined long ago—the raven over the margin of the sands is just one little link in a long chain of defeats, a chain of dreams. Harpa Eir, a descendant of dreams that are never fulfilled— it's passed down in the maternal line—who had a grandma who was going to travel and never traveled, who had a mom who longed to travel and to be more than she was, different than she was, yet who never became anything but notorious, though not any more widely than among her closest relatives. A mom who gave birth to a little runt of suspicious appearance, and who indifferently attributed it to the wrong father. Let me tell you, it's no joke not to know who your father is. It must be incomprehensible to anyone but those who've experienced it. It's the recipe for half a man. That's it, I'll call my autobiography HALF A MAN. It would be appropriate for a little woman, as well.

Another raven flies in an arc before the car. It seems almost as if it's pulling a strip of sand behind it, the final grains that the wind can haul up at the end of the desert.

The sand-lion on the road that stretched out on its front paws and was going to growl us back, back to square one, has changed into a cuddly house cat.

Making it out of a sandstorm feels similar to pain subsiding.

When you're in pain, it's difficult to imagine it ever stopping.

When you end up in the darkness of a sand eclipse, you can't see that the darkness will eventually sink, flatten, and lie down where it belongs.

You can't imagine a stripe of light being born along the edge of darkness.

Dust receives us where the sandstorm leaves off. One car coming toward us is all it takes to create an extended plume. I envision myself blowing black stuff from my nose for the next three days. The vehicle rattles terribly on this bad dirt road, the sort that Heiður's not used to driving on. Granted, she is driving slower than usual, afraid of losing control of the car on the loose gravel.

Damn, I'm hungry, says Heiður. Can't we stop near that thicket and eat?

It's too windy. We'll have coffee at Arnbjartur's.

Recluses never bother with coffee.

Sure they do, I say. Arnbjartur bakes sand cakes.

Maybe mud pies as well.

With this joke, Heiður gets her revenge. But before she can say anything more, she veers sharply toward the side of the road, where the car skids on the gravel. I hadn't noticed the speeding car barreling up the road behind us. It passes us with such violence that Heiður has only a perilous instant to get out of the way. The cream-yellow Bronco—none other. Gravel shoots out from under its tires and pops loudly against our windshield.

We barely missed being smashed, says Heiður, braking abruptly in shock.

Then the dames would have been in trouble.

Look, there's a nick on the windshield.

Fucking rude of them not to slow down on the loose gravel. It's dangerous. What's wrong with those people?

The Bronco reverses at high speed, heading straight toward us.

He's really trying to hit us, says Heiður, furious.

Looking like a child's drawing of a remarkably square soapbox car, the Bronco stops just in front of us. The driver steps out and examines our windshield, his face ruddy and taut, with bulging eyes and rosy lips. From a distance he seems a handsome man, but he awakens a slight apprehension upon closer inspection.

Heiður rolls down her window.

I felt gravel go flying, says the driver, and was a bit scared when you stopped. I thought maybe your windshield had shattered.

We're lucky it didn't, says Heiður, pissed off. You couldn't slow down?

We're late for a baptism in Kirkjubæjarklaustur. We were delayed by the sand.

I see, says Heiður.

Bye, dear, and sorry about this.

Bye.

The farmer jumps into his Bronco, energetic as a foal, and tears off, once again spraying gravel against our car.

The silver-haired woman in the front seat, the one I still believe to be the driver's mother, looks over her shoulder to see where the pebbles and stones land. I'd swear she smiles. Heiður slams her hands on the wheel and lets loose with a mighty string of profanity, mixing in words such as *goddamn hillbilly*, *namby-pamby*, and *motherfucking psycho fit for the grave*, as she drives off into the brown cloud left in the Bronco's wake. Her language brings joy to the backseat. The monster has woken from its dreams—less than beautiful, I should think. But the bizarre noise it makes isn't laughter, isn't human; it's a surly growl that stops when it's high but not low, abruptly, as if its engine has broken down.

He should have spared us the polite chatter and been chivalrous in his actions, I comment.

How many windshields do you think he's shattered, this guy? Doesn't his mama give him hell?, growls Heiður.

Did you get his license number?

It's L 666. Baptism in Kirkjubæjarklaustur, my ass!

Glóra

My uncle Arnbjartur's single-story farmhouse snuggles between the ridges where elves dwell and kindle lights at twilight. Tall rowan trees stand erect, like guards, at the house gable.

Rusty wire mesh, barbed-wire fences on the verge of falling, and artistic driftwood posts surround the property, looking like installations by famous modern artists. The posts are infinitely varied in composition: wide, low, high, narrow, knotted, planed, and everything in between.

The finely crafted ironwork farm gate is made up of two wheels with spokes, some bent, others poking out into the air. The gate's divided into two parts, hanging slanted on hinges, half on the way up, half down.

Rusted tractors and other farm machines, the oldest one of which could be from before World War II, stand in a discontinuous row reaching from the farmhouse all the way down to the private cemetery. On the other side of the house are the remains of three cars, in various states of decay. One of them is so far gone that it's on the verge of changing into something other than a car. Yet it's missing nothing in particular except for the hood and one door. It's as if it ended up in a scrap press where the workers changed their minds and stopped after starting to crush it.

I get out to open the gate but can't undo the knots that hold it shut. Heiður comes to help me, after putting on a pair of work gloves. She's constantly looking after her flutist fingers.

We regard Arnbjartur's mailbox reverentially. This piece is a true achievement of the imagination. He's taken a tire, poured concrete into it, and stuck a pole in the middle. An iron box is tied to the pole with a frayed string.

On my little stroll to the house, I take a deep breath and rest my eyes on the gigantic angelica plants on the ridge by the stream, watching how they struggle against the wind before yielding to it. The farm's generator is in a crooked, rickety shed with a collapsed roof, a refuge for birds and mice.

A stone wall at the bottom of a steep hayfield surrounds the notorious farmstead cemetery. From there it isn't far to the trollish lava and deeply reddish-brown river. The river's loud, heavy rush frightened me as a child, but now it gives me a sense of serenity. The sound itself hasn't changed in all of these years.

Heiður has driven up to the house and parked next to a pickup that's an exact replica of the one we're in, including its color. She comes galloping over to me, swinging the bag of organic potatoes from Efri-Hæðir. Sometimes she's much more mindful than I am.

How old's Arnbjartur?

Eighty-two, as I recall.

A curtain of pink frosted plastic, looking better suited for a bathroom window, is pulled over the pane on the front door.

Arnbjartur opens the door before we manage to knock. He's followed closely by a little sheep. Arnbjartur's a nimble-footed grayhaired man with bright eyes like a child's, and he's still sharp as a tack.

Hello, dear, says Arnbjartur, taking my hand like I'm a first-class member of Parliament, then Heiður's hand. He introduces himself like a soldier, bowing his head. Arnbjartur Óðinsson. I'm just waiting for him to click his heels.

Welcome. Out with you, Lambsy.

Lambsy understands human speech and steps outside immediately.

It's a little cosset from last year, explains Arnbjartur. It only feels comfortable when it's right behind you. Did you run into some sand?

A bit, I say. Edda instructed us to wait at the bridge.

Is the car okay?

Yes, fortunately.

As I say this, my uncle glances quickly at the car, sees Edda, and says nothing.

The house stinks of iodine. A veterinarian smell.

How many animals' lives have you saved recently, Addi? No one but Mom would have asked him such a thing, or called him Addi. It was one of her methods for demeaning people, to come up with demeaning nicknames. She called Dad "Seli" and me "Eisa." Occasionally, she called me "Harpa baby," though that name was well meant.

My uncle's wearing brown moleskin pants and a brown checkered shirt under a large blue sweater. He really resembles a Scandinavian intellectual from around 1970 and even wears an intellectual's clogs. He has thick, unruly hair reaching below his ears. He shows little outward signs of aging, except for some missing teeth.

I pass on the greetings from Erika and Dad, and explain the organically grown potatoes. Arnbjartur reaches for a potato and takes it into the kitchen to get a better look at it under the light.

Gosh, it's pretty. Maybe I ought to switch to biodynamite.

He places it at the center of the kitchen table, a perfect fruit of the earth from the vegetable garden at Efri-Hæðir.

This potato is a daughter of the sun and has the same color as its mother. I could write a little poem about it, if only I would.

In the kitchen everything's spic-and-span. The sink and faucet gleam, and there's not a crumb on the floor. On the other hand, the walls haven't been painted for several decades. In some places the bare stone is visible, cracked through and through. The linoleum has peeled off in the corner by the Rafha stove, perched on slender legs. Seeing the disrepair and tidiness collide in this way is so mind-blowing that Heiður and I sit there silently.

In the hayfield beyond the barn, human movement can be seen. A man in grass-green overalls presses sluggishly against the wind, his hands in his pockets, Lambsy following closely.

Have you hired a farmhand?

No, that's just Liggjas. He's been here a week now.

What's that you say?

He's Faroese. His full name is Liggjas-under-the-Waterfall, but don't bother teasing him about it. He'd just retort with a comment about Icelandic children being given names like Ljótur and Ormur. Why would anyone name their children Ugly and Worm?

What's he doing here?

He first came here last year with a friend of his from Klaksvík who spent his childhood summers in the countryside at Bjarnarstaður. This spring they were traveling, completely broke. I put them in Steinka's room, and they found it so comfy that they stayed half a month. They were on their way to work in a fish-processing plant in the Westfjords, and I gave them money for gas to get there.

A one-man charitable organization, you are, I say.

I wouldn't go so far as to say that. But there are quite a few disadvantaged Faroese in the countryside here. I think we should welcome them, because sooner or later we'll end up like them.

How so?

As far as I'm concerned, we won't be celebrating the hundredth anniversary of the Republic of Iceland in 2044. We'll have thrown away all our chances, I'm sad to say. There hasn't been any control over anything here, and the economy's in ruins. A lot of people have utterly disgraceful wages. There'll be a mass exodus from this country. I don't even know what people are waiting for.

I've often thought along those lines, too, says Heiður.

Luckily, I'll be dead, which is fine with me, Arnbjartur says. I wouldn't want to have experienced this country gaining its independence and then losing its independence again. It'll be good to be allowed to die in the meantime.

He starts making coffee, and Heiður's expression amuses me. She's pathologically afraid of germs and isn't happy about being served refreshments from the hands of a recluse.

Arnbjartur places a pair of coffee cups decorated with golden flowers on the kitchen table, which is covered with a worn oilcloth bedecked with the Icelandic Yule Lads. It's a match for the red Christmas lights shining in the kitchen window. Then he reaches for a parcel wrapped in brown paper, with two types of rubber bands around it. He takes his sweet time unwrapping a blue velvet box, folding the paper neatly afterward, stretching a rubber band back around it. He takes three polished silver teaspoons from the box and lays them on the table, sitting down unexpectedly at the same time, though the kettle's in fact boiling. He looks straight at me with wide child's eyes and asks: What's this trip you're taking?

It's quite a story. I look at Heiður and ask: Where to begin?

That's for *you* to know.

Well, it's best not to beat around the bush, I say. There are problems with Edda, and I saw no better option than to head east. Edda will be staying in Andey with Ingólfur and Margrét for the winter, and I'll be staying with Dýrfinna.

So you're going all the way east. Maybe it'd be best if I came along. I've always had a crush on Dýrfinna, and she's a widow now, by God.

You're not going to tie yourself down now, are you?

Better late than never.

Do you think Dýrfinna would have you?

Maybe if I get myself a new pair of teeth.

Sorry, but there's just no room in the car with us.

I could of course take the bus, after I've seen to the teeth.

Wouldn't it be a housekeeper that you need, Arnbjartur?

Not now. It's been fifteen years since Steingerður died. I didn't feel like getting another one.

Is she buried out here in the cemetery?

Who told you that? Who told you that? Arnbjartur jumps to his feet with a smack of his clogs and pours the coffee into the pot in such a state that I'm afraid the boiling liquid will splash over him.

I thought Mom mentioned it. Never mind.

You couldn't always trust what your mother had to say, dear. Sad to say, sad to say. There's hardly anyone in the cemetery. That's the truth.

Heiður and I sit timidly as mice. My uncle continues pouring coffee into the pot with a vengeance.

There's nothing at all buried in the cemetery but a leg, he goes on. Which should never have happened.

My uncle normally speaks with a drawl, and when he's upset the drawl tightens. Then it shoots up to high C, and down again in a steep curve.

He quickly opens the lower cabinet, takes from it a tub that could have been a paint can in a past life, pulls out a sand cake and a package of Frón shortbread cookies and arranges them neatly on an old cake platter, white with a gold pattern that originally depicted a Christmas tree. The silence is growing uncomfortably long.

A leg?

Yes, a leg. Strange that your mother didn't tell you about it, while she was blabbing about Steingerður.

Well?

There was this man who lost his leg, which can happen to anyone, of course, except that he demanded that the leg be buried. He apparently found it an unpleasant idea to toss his leg in the trash, so when Steingerður died, he asked my permission to put it into the coffin with her, though I didn't exactly own her body.

But Steingerður's daughter Lóa attended the burial, and the damned cow threw a fit when she saw that they were going to put a hairy male leg in her mother's coffin, though it was wearing an intricately knitted sock. I asked whether it would have changed anything if it had been a female leg, and she gave a shout, cursed me in front of the priest, and said that she was taking her mother away, that she didn't belong in that utterly empty cemetery. It was difficult to lay Steinka to rest, bless her soul. Her daughter ran off with the coffin, and I was stuck with the leg. I wasn't about to buy another coffin for it, so I felt it my best option to bury it out here in the cemetery, in consecrated ground. I constructed a rather good-quality box and even warbled "What a Friend We Have in Jesus." But apparently that wasn't elegant enough, because the cursed leg's returned to haunt us. It kicks open doors.

What?

I'm serious, he says. Though I've never heard of an individual leg returning from beyond the grave. No such thing in the book.

Does the man the leg belonged to know it's haunting you?

I didn't ask him.

Is the leg causing trouble elsewhere, or just here at your place?

Doors are constantly being kicked open throughout the area, and I'm being blamed for it. The old hags on the farms around here are sending spirits back at me. They believe I'm empowering the leg against them. It's nonsense. I'm not sending that thing anywhere. Wouldn't you think I'd drive it away from myself and others if I had the chance? I'd be damned relieved to go out east with you to Dýrfinna's. It's impossible having this leg hanging over my head. Especially during the black of winter.

Wouldn't it hunt you down even if you left? Isn't it good at getting around?

It shoots all over the place like a bat out of hell. It's a damned disgrace for this entire district. But I doubt the rascal can follow me out east. I highly doubt it'd like it there anyway, to be honest.

Arnbjartur vehemently pours coffee into our cups, and at that moment Edda storms in, her brows knitted.

Hello, darling.

Hello.

Won't you have a seat and join the fun?

Edda looks around, and when she sees the Christmas pattern on the tablecloth and the lights in the window, she frowns like a respectable but displeased lady. Evidently the darling child's had a bourgeois upbringing.

What may I offer the lady?, Uncle Arnbjartur says.

Nothing.

That's really not much.

A short-legged creature with a long furry tail and brownish fur darts into the kitchen from the hallway and hops straight into Arnbjartur's arms.

What's that?, asks Edda.

It's a tomcat, my dear.

My God! Just look at that.

I see what Edda means, because I wasn't able to figure out what on earth it was, with its tiny eyes peeking out through its tufty hair, and sharp-pointed ears standing straight up on its head, as on an Icelandic dog. Even more bizarre, the cat and its owner have similar hair, right down to the style.

Heiður, how about taking a photo of the kitty? It's so funny, I say, with the subtle scheme of capturing Arnbjartur and the cat in the same photo because they look like cousins.

Heiður gets up and goes out to the car for the camera.

What kind of cat is it?, asks Edda.

It's a Gothic Viking cat.

Can I hold it?, says Edda in a high-pitched pampering tone that's in glaring contrast to her hard-boiled shell.

Arnbjartur hands Edda the lousy cat. It curls up contentedly in the arms of this obdurate girl and purrs with a grinding sound that's grating to the ears. Edda's thoroughly motherly with this furry monster, which she now props on her shoulder, like an infant needing to be burped. Somehow, seeing Edda hold this wretch of a cat like a baby makes me queasy.

What's its name?, asks Edda.

It was baptized Drengur, but is called Deng in honor of the Chinese leader.

Edda laughs and strokes the creature gently, with both hands.

I feel almost dangerously nauseous, so I stand up and announce that I'm going to check on Heiður.

She's standing in the yard, trying to keep control of her hair in the strong wind as she points the camera that she bought in Hong Kong. It's a Nikon, the sort of thing whose price you don't ask about.

It's absurdly beautiful here, says Heiður, if you turn from your uncle's trash dump toward the river and the lava. Then she lets out one of her famous cries: Oh my God! You're not looking very well, dear.

I sit down on a horse block in the yard and take deep, slow breaths.

Are you ill?

I shake my head and try to swallow the rising vomit.

The coffee was far too strong, Heiður suggests.

I shake my head again.

Are you going to barf?

I nod and feel that I have to yield to this force from my abdomen, stand up, grab the door handle on the pickup with one hand, to give me a grip on something in existence, and vomit with the wind over the horse block.

God Almighty, do you think the smoked salmon was bad?

I shake my head, retch again, and notice as I do so that I'm standing with my left foot in sheep shit. Damned sheep, tearing up the land and shitting at people's doorsteps.

I grope in my pocket for a tissue and wipe my mouth, wipe my shoes on the grass, and start to whimper, chilled to my bones.

Heiður puts her arm around me and declares that everything will be all right, that there's nothing to worry about. She opens the car door and gets me inside. Suddenly I'm sitting behind the wheel of this minitruck. I lean my head on the wheel, feeble, wiped out, and I hope to God that the three wretches—man, cat, and daughter—don't come out of the house while I'm recovering.

HARPA EIR AND THE THREE WRETCHES.

Heiður gets in the passenger side, puts her arm around my shoulders, and asks whether something unusual happened.

Edda was holding the ca-hat, I say with a sob.

That couldn't have been so awful, says Heiður.

She held it like an infa-hant.

I don't understand, Harpa dear. Tell me more when you're feeling better. You're just nervous and out of sorts because of the trip. Such a situation makes your mind go all sorts of places. It's natural. This is such a big change, and you want so much for it to go well. You know, Harpa, I have a feeling that this is going to work out. You're doing absolutely the right thing.

Heiður wipes a splotch of vomit from my shoulder, strokes my hair, and says that I should take it easy now while she goes in to chat with the others. Before leaving, she tells me to remember that she's always there for me, no matter how things go. But that they're certainly heading in the right direction.

A door bangs shut. Edda comes out from the farmhouse with that cretin of a cat on her shoulder. I quickly lean my forehead on the steering wheel so that I don't have to witness this.

When I crack one eye open, I see the cat jump from the girl's arms in the direction of the cemetery and disappear into a bunch of yellowing angelica. Edda comes over and asks what I'm doing.

I didn't feel well.

Are you ill?

No, I think it's passing.

We're leaving. Heiður's on her way out.

Yes, I say, realizing that I won't look very good dangling on the wheel like this. My uncle steps out of the house, and I sit up quickly and prepare to hop to the ground with my new technique, but I'm somehow so clumsy that I land on my knees in slow motion, straight onto some fresh lamb droppings at Edda's feet. She pulls me up with a rock-hard hand and asks in a dismayed tone: What's wrong with you, Mom?

I'm dying. Isn't that what you want?

I barely manage to refrain from launching a dreadful stream of curses at Edda, in which the terms "soul murderer" and "walking abomination" would be among the more harmless ones.

Mo . . . wha . . .? She looks at me in disbelief. I've never hated her more than right now, as I lean completely exhausted against the pickup. I want to strangle her with my bare hands, this viper who's poisoned my life so thoroughly that at this moment, nothing's left but the poison. At the same time I feel a pang in my chest and can't move, not even to commit my crime.

Edda helps me to the other side of the car and pushes me in. She's strong as a lion, and I'm moved to tears of self-pity thinking of all those times that I've supported her when she was helpless, even though I'm the smaller and weaker one of us. As I recall, she's never supported me before.

I try to sit as upright as possible, in order to preserve my dignity upon departing, and spread a scarf over the shit blotch on my knee. Blazing bright fish are swimming on the scarf, one of Gabriel Axel's beautiful gifts.

How I long to be with you in your abode, Monsieur Axel, where the windows have pale-yellow silk curtains and special guests such as Harpa Eir are served champagne and pâté de foie gras. How I long to go to a gentler world where laughing people sit in rows beneath striped umbrellas on the patios of cafés.

My attempt to appear normal is useless. Arnbjartur takes a hard look at me as he shakes my hand in farewell and says: Don't worry. This will all work out.

Edda swings herself up into the backseat and gives her regards to Deng.

Arnbjartur asks whether he should send the cat out east by parcel post, and then immediately answers his own question: No, I'll just bring it myself.

How do you think Dýrfinna would react?, asks Heiður.

Not nearly as badly as she might let on.

And this you say in advance, says Heiður.

Too bad there's no room in your car, Arnbjartur says. Well, I can always just leave tomorrow.

Who's going to take care of the farm?

No problem there. I'll just keep Liggjas here. He's got no future anyway.

Good-bye, Uncle. Take it easy.

Good-bye, you three. May fortune be with you.

The little sheep has followed us and is standing next to Arnbjartur.

Be-e-a, says Lambsy.

Watch out for the car now, dearie, says Arnbjartur. Don't get run over.

Bu-u, says Lambsy.

Aw, the poor thing's so terribly limited, Arnbjartur remarks.

Good-bye, Uncle, and thanks.

. . .

I wish myself away, away, away. Shut my eyes tight, wish myself back to my summer as an au pair in Perpignan, buying cherries at the marketplace and strolling lightly dressed between old houses in warm, fresh air. I wish myself away. To a place where I can speak French all day. Be a foreigner. Which I am.

You run out of your uncle's house and vomit? What in the world's become of you, child?

Oh, Mom, I'm so tired. Will you give it a rest?

I can't.

You've always lacked self-discipline.

You know that I don't feel too well on this side.

You mean the other side.

Don't twist my meaning.

You never felt well, Mom. What did you think would change?

I thought I'd be allowed to rest in peace. But it didn't turn out like that.

Fucking misery. Will we meet again, then?

If you should die.

Oh, Mom, you're so spacey. As you've always been.

I turn on the radio in the hope of disrupting the broadcast from the evil woman. The radio's playing Mozart's 40th Symphony, performed on original instruments. I envision lovers who are forced to part for the final time after having spent the day riding an old carousel.

I listened to this for days after Jói died.

Transparent butterflies with frosted wings are granted permission to fly over misleading spiky knobs sticking up from the ash-gray expanse of lava. The lava becomes gray like this when it hasn't rained for weeks.

You'll never again conjure up butterflies in your mind, you who are gone.

How differently dead you and Mom are, Jói my friend.

How do you feel?, asks Heiður.

Just fine.

It's handy that we're on a new road now. I wouldn't have liked taking the old puke-road through all the lava. It even made people who couldn't imagine being carsick feel like they needed to throw up. But the old road's good for walks, and for getting to know the lava field. I read that in a book.

It's a genuine achievement in road construction. Can you imagine dozens of men with chisels carving a path through all that lava over the course of many years?

Many years. *Most things take many years. Changes come slowly. If anything seems to change overnight, it's actually taken many years to change. The mind has been chipping away with a chisel for years. Without a blow being heard.*

The precursor of most things is invisible.

In these parts, the precursor of winter is invisible.

There's no sign of the true season—time has vanished—and I imagine, I conjure up the idea, that autumn is far, far off, this autumn and those to follow. I've taped almost two thousand torn-off pages back on to the calendar. It's an early July day, and I'm on vacation.

The roses in the flower bed by my arched window in the Bollagata basement have started to bloom, early and with exceptional vigor. When I sit on the couch, I have a clear and direct view of these violet briar roses with beautiful leaves and thick stems. Sometimes they've lasted until November, because I nurture them well, calling myself THE STEPMOTHER OF ROSES, but they actually belong to the fat woman upstairs. She's their true mother. I can't imagine many such noble views of roses from the windows of the city, and arched basement windows are rare pearls. Yet Edda and I have these, at least, though we're wanting other things. She comes and sits close to me on the couch, cuddles her bony ten-year-old body up to me and says that she's looking forward to going east. I am too, my darling, I say, as I stroke her fiery-red hair.

That was the trip when my brother, Sibbi, drove us in the big jeep. He'd taken out a loan for it, like everything else, and ended up bankrupting both himself and our father, sweeping away my modest future dreams of returning to France and visiting my friend in Perpignan. A true Icelander, my brother. Heiður had planned on going east with us, taking a little break. She felt she deserved it, having just won second prize in a flute competition in Montreal. I was jealous, though happy for her in a distant corner of my heart. At the last minute, however, she decided not to go, because she'd been offered a project that she wanted to take on. Same old story. Everything had to give way to eternal projects that couldn't wait. An annoying word, *project*, for those who don't have any major ones, and instead are bound to plod on with their lousy menial tasks. In my selfishness, I felt she'd betrayed me.

I wasn't going to bother about this too much, though. I had other things on my mind, having just left Alli the mental midget and feeling relieved to have done so. The burden gone, along with its fat dick. Things were different then, entirely different, though only a few years have passed since. Then, I had a normal child who cuddled with me in the evenings. I still felt as if I could restart my life, and though it might not happen right away, I could wait. Edda and I, daughter and mother, got along well, and we enjoyed many a good day together in our poverty. We lived as it must be pleasing to God. I toiled away, and Edda did her homework at the kitchen table in the evenings as I washed the dishes and tidied. Two evenings a week I baked bread, having calculated that by doing so I would save around 10,400 krónur per year. I helped Edda with her homework as best I could, and brought her a glass of milk and a home-baked slice of sand cake or a crepe before she brushed her teeth and went to bed, no later than ten thirty. We had no television but always listened to the evening news on the radio at seven o'clock as we ate, as long as I wasn't on duty. If I was at work, I left something in the fridge for Edda to eat and when the clock struck seven at work, I knew that she'd taken out her dinner, heated what was necessary, and was sitting at the table, listening to the news like a big girl. Sometimes Dad looked in on his granddaughter. Occasionally, we made a deal that he would buy some food and cook dinner himself. Normally, however, I would have already prepared something and then there would be two servings in the fridge, in sealed jars, or bowls with plastic wrap covering them tightly.

Now I feel, no matter what I thought then, that during those years after we moved into the Bollagata basement, out of the fat embrace of the debt collector, Edda and I lived a decent regular-old life, though we had little space and not much variety, aside from an unnamed man who came to visit, albeit rarely. He took up a considerable amount of the time available to me in my private thoughts and was a thorn in Edda's side. But there was no imprudence except in my affairs of the heart, if you could call them that. Sufficiency and efficiency were practiced in all respects. Handsome old garments from the market benefiting the Cat Friends Society were stitched up anew, modified, and improved; fish chowder was made from leftovers; sweaters were knitted at home, from remainders when possible. Ironed and neatly folded linen was placed carefully in the closet. The odor of Ajax hung in the air, dust from scouring agents. You could see your reflection in the toilet bowl, and the floors were scrubbed thoroughly. I was also careful to polish the windows regularly, not least the "rose window," as I called it. I was lucky that the windowpanes at Bollagata had been replaced just before Edda and I rented the apartment. It makes all the difference to have a clear view. This winter I can expect to have hazy windowpanes.

Edda helped with the housework. She had specific tasks and was conscientious about performing them. When I came home from my evening shifts, my child would be sleeping beneath clean sheets, an edifying book beside her, most often from the City Library on Þingholtsstræti. If her cold toes peeked out from under the blanket, Mommy came and covered them and stroked her child's cheek.

As if a hand were waved, everything changed. No child in bed when Mother came home from work in the evening, food untouched in the fridge, the living room smelling of cigarette smoke, butts in ashtrays all over the house, the odor of moonshine hanging over everything, glasses on windowsills, in the bathroom, on top of the fridge. Then the night shift began for the worn-out assistant nurse, after her evening shift at work. The wait, perhaps until five or seven in the morning, or later, for that matter. And when the changeling finally stumbled in, the home nursing began. Sometimes it was necessary to help her to the bathroom, to hold the forehead of my vomiting child, or bandage wounds from the downtown battleground, at times from broken bottles or cigarettes. The poor mother never got a sound night's sleep. She'd wake with a start after a short slumber and go into the child's room to check whether she was breathing, to turn her over if she were lying on her back. Many a dissolute person has died from choking on their own vomit.

The acrid taste of vomit is still in my mouth. I have an Ópal breath refresher. It's a cure-all.

As are images in the lava, endlessly new—moss to sink in, deep down and sideways. The moss is a cradle of the soul. Now a green cradle, because it has rained.

Transparent butterflies and angels in colorful raiment soar above the lava to the Carousel Symphony.

New lava fields are hostile territory and razor-sharp to traverse. They're too hot to walk on in some places, and may emit lethal fumes. *Old lava fields*, like the two-hundred-year-old Skaftáreldar lava field surrounding us, are blissful places with piles of moss, hollows and overhangs where pale-green bracken grows, and all sorts of grasses, butterwort, and broad-leaved willows. The willow leads by example, growing from nothing, the very picture of tenacity, this gnarly gray-brown plant. Before I die—if I live—the trees standing here and there by the road will have formed a corridor, a low Icelandic willow allée.

We'll never drive through it in your four-by-four, you who used to call me *the foreign girl*. That's just the way it is.

You ran off from Esja, he'd said the next time we met, between the cloves and the apricots in the supermarket, past the cured lamb rolls and flare fat. Easter was approaching.

Did we make some sort of deal?, I said, tossing two packets of dried apples into my cart, though I never ate that at home, then or at any other time. I hate dried fruit. It's probably the result of all the prune compote I was forced to eat as a child, which caused me major digestive problems.

It isn't easy to decipher this man's expression, but it seems to me to be both derisive and hurt, which isn't such an easy combination.

Are you still working at the National Hospital?, he asks me respectfully, if not a bit awkwardly.

Yes, I say, wanting to get out of this pointless conversation with this unostentatious, elegant man who's filled his cart with gravlax, avocados, beef tenderloin, tonic water, lobster, Quality Street tins, fresh pineapple, cream, and ginger ale. I hope he's too distracted to notice the oatmeal, margarine, dry yeast, onion, and chickpeas in my cart, besides the skim milk and those detestable dried apples.

Preparing a feast, are you?, I say.

No, I—we're going to our summer cottage.

Yes, and where's that?

Out west in Mýrar.

I've never been there. I always go out east by the sea.

He asks me about the sea to the east.

I tell him all about Grandma's and Mom's French fishing boats, and Grandma's Grove where everything grows, concluding with the family homestead of Andey, which has the dubious distinction of being the setting of the shortest Icelandic saga ever preserved, the *Tale of Dittur of Andey*, by no means a masterpiece.

I realize that I've been jabbering away, and say that hopefully he doesn't have too many frozen items in his cart.

He says he hasn't noticed any leaks.

We set off on our journey between the shelves, side by side, pushing two shopping carts that have merged into one double cart. We never slip up in our driving, gliding gracefully past islands of goods, and the wandering shadows of other customers shoot around the corners when the double cart comes sailing. It turns out that we're on the same course, because he has forgotten several items and is taking a reverse route through the store, starting in the produce section. And we're both in need of some of the same hygiene products, like toothpaste and cotton swabs. It's a comical shopping trip with a gentleman whose name I don't even know and who asks whether he might drive me home.

What type of car do you drive?, I ask, and when he says a Range Rover, that's good enough for me.

After a smooth drive, the supermarket man slips sideways through the front door of Bollagata, carrying my groceries. What a joke it would be if the bags got mixed up and he went home with my oatmeal and chickpeas, the provisions of a low-wage woman, instead of beef tenderloin and gravlax. I wonder if such a man has ever eaten oatmeal and dishes made with chickpeas.

My guest is polite and doesn't rush straight in. He stops in the small hallway, pressed in by walls and doors and the radiator and shoes, and waits to be invited into the living room. The door to my bedroom was open, and he wasn't ashamed to look that direction and take stock of the situation, as much as it was possible from the hallway. This he did unabashedly, with the same attentive regard he gave the side-view mirrors on our way to my place. Yes, the bed was made—nothing to complain about there. The black crocheted blanket is laid smooth and folded over the bed, and the shiny green rubber tree leaning over the headboard.

He gives me a straight look, having decided to set course into this bedroom, though not necessarily on this day. My expression is neutral as I glance back, pretending not to have any clue what he's thinking.

He sits down in the main chair in the living room, the tapestry chair that Mom wanted me to have after she was gone. This nameless driver looks around the room, proudly, as if he's personally accomplished something, and says: How pretty you've made everything. I wait for him to add: If I may say so myself.

Funny to hear the man praise my abode, because he surely must have something far more impressive than my excavated pit with tiny holes for windows. Except for the arched window, of course. But it was true that I'd tried to endow the place with life and color. Everything tidily arranged, nothing lying about, except for one of Edda's dirty shirts on the back of a chair and my own raggedy slippers beneath the glass coffee table. These I hurriedly remove, before going to the kitchen to make coffee and put the milk and margarine in the fridge.

When I return, I see my dugout home in a new light: the blue walls, the white ceiling, the white lace curtains, and two diligent impatiens flowering white in the windows between all sorts of cacti. And in the corner, the masterpiece: an Easter cactus with a hundred light-violet flowers, on the old oval table from Mom, covered with the tablecloth that Aunt Dýrfinna eye-stitched, embroidered, and hemstitched in the Home Economics School at Eiðir half a century ago. I look at myself in the mirror in the golden frame, my face between the palm branch that is and the other that's reflected, and am pleased to have put on the rosy sweater that I designed and knitted. No other garment of mine fits me as well, though it's undeniably kitschy.

I secretly admire the man's pale-green wool sweater, which goes perfectly with his eyes, not to mention his light-brown khakis and ochre boots. Visible above his shoes are the cuffs of his high-quality socks, in the same color as his pants. This isn't one of those slick scented fellows. He's simply attractive—and all the more attractive the closer you look. But I don't know exactly what this is all about. We say nothing, two utterly relaxed perfect strangers.

The sand is far behind, buried, and forgotten, whether it's rising or still, ahead of us "the manifold mountains of Síðufjöll," as Jói called them. Modest willow stubs along the road are a comforting sight. They weren't there just a few years ago. Some things do grow here entirely of their own accord. The vegetation recovers as the numbers of sheep are reduced. I want to live here after half a century, not earlier.

Then Mom and I could walk freely through the abundant trees. We could lie down when we felt like it and steal sheep to keep ourselves alive. Sheep thieves, eating ill-gotten shanks in radiant sunshine and viewing the glaciers from the opposite side, from poison-green hidden valleys. Then perhaps she'd finally tell me my story. It would be interesting to know, though I might hardly care by the time we got to that point.

The truth is that I want to cuddle up to Mom and listen to her heart as I did before I can remember. Her heartbeat must have been heavy and strange when she found out she was pregnant, with the risk that when the child was born it would look like I do.

Much of the good that happened is *beyond your memory*. You're absolutely right, Eisa.

Don't call me Eisa. You ruin everything when you do.

I want to ruin everything.

How did you become like that?

Like what? Dead?

Malicious.

But I'm not so bad that you wouldn't want to join me as a ghost.

You really think that would work?

Who would we find to haunt?

Bimbirimbirimmbamm!

Ha ha.

Would we need to find someone?

Oh yes. Someone always needs to be found. I wouldn't be wandering around if it weren't for you, Eisa.

Say Harpa Eir.

Harpa Eir.

It's so beautiful the closer we come to Kirkjubæjarklaustur that a wayfarer with any sense of shame might feel like covering his eyes or looking away, instead of taking in everything the eye desires. A great number of mossy pumice hills, for example, which make excellent elf-homes, stunning crags that the sea has licked full-length, blue rivers and white rapids in the lava. Systrastapi, the mossy rock formation, like a giant bone standing on end. The sublime blue of the volcanic neck Lómagnúpur silhouetted against the glacier.

For many hours the glacier lords it over the entire view from the Ring Road, dominating everything else. But it's also of such a nature that it draws out the particular characteristics of whatever surrounds it, whether big or small. In its vicinity the sands deepen, the waters rise. It amplifies the impact of the fiery-yellow buttercups and violet-pink dwarf fireweed. It vivifies the colors and forms of the thickets. The majestic bastion of Lómagnúpur would be diminished on every side if it didn't appear against the white giant. It's as if the mountain would simply wither away if it weren't in such close proximity to the glacier.

Kirkjubæjarklaustur

I'm going to walk up to Systravatn, says Heiður. I've always wanted to see it, and we have time now. We'll be at the cottage early enough.

Early enough. Her wording is less than auspicious.

Radiant birch and spruce trees adorn the slope at Kirkjubæjarklaustur. Everything's gleaming after the autumn cleaning, the landscape and the buildings. Could Icelanders, those kings of clutter, reside on this tidy set? No garbage anywhere, just picture-perfect houses and well-tended gardens. Everything one needs is here: an Agricultural Bank, a National Bank. For a hundred residents.

General appearance: un-Icelandic, unreal. It's like a model in full size.

But not a single local is in sight. Where is everyone?

Stunned by the infusion of oxygen, the magnetism of Vatnajökull Glacier, and the unexpected delight of unseasonably warm weather for the last day of August, the three of us stand there, mesmerized travelers next to a white pickup truck. Even the wind is warm, the same wind that whipped the sand straight at the car but didn't manage to scratch it. Not a single bit.

A young outdoorsman, the last backpacker of the year, appears without warning, from where, God knows, the sun reflecting off his fiery-red down jacket. He smiles, exposing first-rate teeth that have grown harder and whiter in more southerly cleansing fires than cod liver oil and hardfish. His smile lasts a surprisingly long time. It must be because of the incomparable trio that has tumbled out of the pickup: dwarf mother, scrawny daughter, stick woman.

In fact, this is the foreigner in the red coat who saw me stick out my tongue at Gerti Chicken back in Selfoss. Hence the prolonged smile. I smile back and nod as if he's an old acquaintance.

At the start of the trail to Systravatn there are signs that I can't decipher. One shows a man and woman holding hands, and the man is carrying a walking stick. Does this mean: BEWARE OF MEN WITH WALKING STICKS?

On another sign a person in some sort of skirt falls backward off a precipitous cliff, rocks tumbling behind. How is this to be interpreted: PRIME SPOT FOR PUSHING?

Heiður puts on the little backpack holding our lunches and heads up the slope to Systravatn, the lake on the heath at the top. Lakes like these have a strange magnetism. There's a fundamental difference between mountain lakes and lowland lakes. In my experience, a hike to a mountain lake is always rewarding. You're sure to find swans on them, under enchanting moving clouds, or an even more spectacular panorama than the book says.

A foaming stream runs down the long light-red bedrock alongside our path and branches out around a large lush islet where the birch grows out horizontally between moss-covered stones. A remarkably loud gushing comes from this forked waterfall, which I inform Heiður is named Systrafoss—Sisters' Falls—and she looks at me and says: *You know everything.*

Heiður leads the way in her tracksuit and hiking boots. I've curbed my pretensions and put on sneakers in place of my moccasins, since this would be a real hike. The sneakers are brown, which means dirt on them blends in, and just as well, because it's a dirt path in places. We're the only ones hiking up along the stream's steep route, between gnarled old birch trees with peeling bark.

There's endless life on the verdant slope. Clusters of shiny red brambleberries grow by the trail, on heather that's gradually turning red and blue. Honeybees buzz vigorously and alight on the blue blossoms of the wild vetch that stretches out in wide tangles at our feet, along with meadowsweet and fading woodland geraniums. Two black snails lie side by side on a rock, ink-black slime splotches with two tiny snouts sticking out of their pinheads.

Heiður stops just as we reach the rim of the slope and waves to Edda, who's been following at a distance.

The lake up on the heath comes into view, puckishly twinkling waves dashing between its banks on a considerable breeze. Systravatn— Sisters' Lake—was named after the nuns in Kirkjubæjarklaustur. They came here on fair-weathered days many hundreds of years ago, in full-length skirts and flapping headgear, always in groups of two or more. It's said that they bathed in the lake. Maybe they thought about the same thing as me, at least some of them, about the one and only lover who is and always will be away. From good times— who knows.

The lover who lives in a secret place.

Yes, who lives in the secret dwelling place of the mind. One of the things that's never spoken of, except to myself. The secret of the little un-poet.

The view from up here is a panorama of ocean and the estuaries of numerous lakes in a sand-haze and dust cloud, and the glacier, the colossus that somehow looks smaller. The heath before us, grassy, in numerous shades of green, is framed by the bluish line of mountains and a bunch of white sheep on the other side of the lake. Of course, it's by an Icelandic heath lake that everyone should die. Yet who has a chance for such luxury these days?

Not a cloud is visible, though they could well be hidden behind the haze of the August sky. The last sky of the year by that name. I'm going to call it THE MISTY SKY OF UNCERTAINTY.

The sisters' path to the lake would have been through a birch thicket and willow scrub, which once covered the entire area. At that time it was called Skógahverfi—Woodland District. Grazing sheep, poor people, and falling ash ensured the trees' disappearance. These days not a single self-sown shoot is to be seen anywhere but in little niches by the glacier, besides the thick brake out east by Lómagnúpur, so tenacious that diligent sheep haven't managed to finish it off. Jens Kaaber, Heiður's dad, has a fancy cottage there, where we drifters can spend the night.

DRIFTERS I

Once upon a time there were two Icelandic women, one short and the other tall, plus one delinquent teenager, who were heading east. The trip was intended as an escape from a barbarous gang of coarse youths, as well as a search for the father of one of the women, the grandfather of the little drug addict. The mother was certain, due to her highly unusual appearance, that she couldn't be a purebred Icelander, even though that's what her birth certificate and upbringing indicated. There was no suggestion that her genetic father was none other than Axel Óðinsson, a former handicrafts teacher at Laugarnes School, now residing at the Grund rest home.

The three women's vehicle was a white pickup truck, owned by the father of the driver, Heiður, a flutist and friend of the protagonist. Beneath a tarp in the pickup's little bed were the most essential household appliances that belonged to the poor mother and her daughter, who had little financial means but were well disposed for the most part, at least the mother, who had the unique and intriguing name Harpa Eir. Her mother, who also had a unique and intriguing name, Eva Sólgerður, chose her daughter's name because she had wanted to learn to play the harp among other things. Eva Sólgerður, who little Edda called Grandma Sól, had even more aspirations, but appears to have pursued few of them and been terrifically suppressed. She had a job serving coffee at the Marine Research Institute until her strength failed her, quite prematurely.

Are you seeing what I'm seeing?

Edda is sitting on a rock at the edge of the slope. Her back is turned to us and she's damming up a little streamlet. Ten summers ago I spent half a day sitting with her in Grandma's Grove as she, in her sunny yellow rain pants, worked on changing the course of the stream that runs into the Andá River. Mommy sat by to make sure the child didn't put herself in danger. This was during the *Book of Verses* years:

Evil brook, from here on out I shan't forget, not once, you see.

It was possible to leave her to herself on a tiny islet in one place, where the water was shallow on both sides. Mommy could wander a bit and plant one thing or other, pluck grass that was choking new saplings, gather moss and leaves for vulnerable plants at the onset of autumn. But she never let Edda out of her sight. Small children can drown in almost no water at all, before you even notice it. Their faces end up in puddles, and they don't think to lift them out. Doesn't this remind you of something? The lives of some people as they live them?

Grandma Sól was with us in the garden sometimes. Four generations in Grandma's Grove. I've never understood the purpose of life, except on nice days there, a bit in Perpignan, and then maybe right during a kiss. The forehead kiss, for example, which led to other kisses. Nearly an entire gestation period beforehand.

Are you seeing what I'm seeing?

She's making a dam.

I must be getting old and soft, because I can't stop the tears that push their way into the corners of my eyes, as mucus sticks to my palate and throat. The changeling is exchanged once more, and the tough delinquent child turns into a little girl who arranges stones in a streamlet.

It doesn't add up.

Any more than the day itself. The mist is not Icelandic, and the same can be said of the temperature. Even way up here, the wind is warm and the grassy heath deceives us with the green colors of summer: *September is* not *tomorrow,* lie the grasses, or the next day or the next.

On the way down we find ourselves a picnic spot resembling a proper glade. Heiður sits and plays the dutiful housewife, spreading out the little embroidered cloth on the lush slope and laying out smörrebröd, apples, a thermos of coffee, and cups.

My friend notices a little tear. Don't be sad, dear, she says.

I can't get over how quickly the wild beast can become a child.

It's good that she wants to be out under the open sky. She really can use the fresh air, as burned-out as she is.

No one knows better than I how burned-out she is. But I can't bear to hear *Heiður* say it. I want to punch her for blabbing about what's none of her business. This monster's mine, and it's best to leave her to me to deal with, as best that I can.

I lie down, being careful not to crumple the geraniums, which are still in bloom, as if they've been waiting for me in particular. I mustn't pay them back by crushing them. A robust branch of an old birch hangs down over my face, and through the leaves I catch a glimpse of the hazy sky. The branch transforms itself into a fluttering fan. The stream babbles in my jaded ears, the same stream that delighted the nuns of old. If they were troubled, the same sound would have soothed their anxiety, like the anxiety that gnaws at me constantly, even though I might not always notice it. Now my troubles yield sweetly to the murmur of the stream. It will be all right, it says. Everything will be all right.

A kindly blossom, Lord, make me.

I recited this to Edda in the evenings.

With smiles for all in store
in frost and heat my heart carefree
and tranquil to the core.

That's how I would want to be. In frost and heat my heart care-free. I've been so anxious about so many particular things in my time, and about all possible things in general, that I'm sure my anxiety will soon be used up. Blessed be the day when it happens. The day of my death, or thereabouts.

There's a rustling of aluminum foil. The insatiable Heiður gobbles down sandwiches. She must burn enormous amounts of calories, this spindly woman. She can eat if she wants. To sleep is what I want.

Footsteps approach. I imagine that it's Edda, but it's not; it's the red-jacketed man with the backpack. The outdoors freak from somewhere south, the fellow who saw the most petite woman in Iceland stick out her tongue in public. I sit up on my elbow and bid the man *bonjour*. He replies and smiles widely once more, lengthily. From my standpoint, he's sparkling, his skin, his smooth black hair, his teeth. He lingers longer than a total stranger should in this women's stead.

I lie back down, contrary to decorum, and say nothing more. Heiður takes matters into her own hands and asks the man in English to sit with us and have a bite to eat. A pity she doesn't speak French, the poor girl.

The foreigner puts down his backpack and confidently sits between us. Heiður offers him bread and coffee, and in strongly accented English he thanks us profusely. Boor that I am, I turn on my side, not bothering to sit upright in the presence of a guest, yet toward him, at least. The sound of the chatter between Heiður and the foreigner makes me drowsy. I think I hear him say he's studying geology, and last summer went to the South Seas to have a look at volcanic islands, some of which resemble Iceland. But the climate there is better. He laughs, and there's great brightness in his voice. I think I'm not dreaming that his name is Yves. Heiður has also introduced herself and he says "Ei-dur." This is my friend Harpa Eir, Heiður says. He tries to repeat it, "Arba Ire."

As I awake from my slumber, Yves is pronouncing Edda's name flawlessly. She snarfs down one of my sumptuous open-faced salmon sandwiches, her knees muddy after her dam work. I contemplate whether I should still pretend to be asleep, but I decide to be alert, since I'm awake anyway. I sit up like a fully functioning person, and Yves acts nervous, as if he's afraid of upsetting me, which is perhaps no wonder, considering what he caught me doing this morning. He hurriedly says that these are remarkable sandwiches, the best smoked salmon he's ever tasted. I realize that I haven't heard everything. I'd dozed off for real. Heiður's gone and offered the boy lodging for the night at her father's summerhouse. There's enough space, she says, after marking the location on a map. She explains how we can't drive him because the car is packed full, but the house is only a half-hour walk from the highway.

I ask about his travel plans. He'd been planning to go to Skaftafell National Park that evening, but maybe he'd come to our place instead. It could be fun to sleep under a roof for a change. He's going to continue eastward, take the ferry from Seyðisfjörður.

Edda sits at a distance and nibbles a sandwich like a little lady. Yves smiles at her, and she does so in return. She's done throwing sandwiches, for the moment, anyway.

So you're mother and daughter, says the foreigner, pointing at Edda and Heiður.

No, says Edda, alarmed at the thought, pointing between me and her.

Luckily, I don't have any kids, says Heiður.

The man swings his head up in awkward surprise but tries to nullify his embarrassment by reiterating: You look more than a trifle alike.

No one knows what to say. Heiður and I smile politely. Edda shakes her head, with the look of an insulted gentlewoman.

What was Heiður thinking by offering this stranger accommodation at her parents' wilderness palace? How will it be if he comes? Could it be that Heiður has her eye on him? That her interest in Dietrich Bacon is starting to flag and she's planning a little action? Or did she do it just for the heck of it? Could she have thought that Edda would behave herself better with a foreign guest added to the mix? It isn't a clever thing on Heiður's part, because I'm dead tired and I can't imagine having to carry on a conversation with him as the day wears on, not to mention having to pamper him with dinner, and work myself into a huff to boot because my French has grown so terribly rusty.

Buzzing in my head on the way down is the notion that what the man said is true, that the redheads Heiður and Edda do resemble each other. They're both long, slim beanstalks, jerky in deportment and movement. And what's more, this obvious truth has escaped my notice. On the other hand, my daughter and I resemble each other as little as me and my alleged father. *All things are born under the sun.* Why can't I remember that and stop these lame speculations about my paternity? Forget about pestering Dýrfinna with the question of whom I belong to on my father's side. She'd send me to a shrink.

. . .

Let's hurry down to the shop. I've really got to pee, says Edda.

Buy yourself a Coke or something, as well, Edda dear. I hand her a five-hundred krónur bill. You can keep the change.

The girl isn't accustomed to acts of kindness, and emits an awkward *Thank you.*

It's so strange to see the remnants of manners that stir within Edda. She's still able to say thanks. Occasionally, she still has it in her to say thanks for her meal, even if she turns up her nose at it when she sits down to eat. At times she's even the first one to say good night and good morning.

Remarkable, really. All that hanging about with the rabble and all those harmful goings-on haven't managed to eradicate her manners.

. . .

I'll just be a minute, says Edda, as she steps out of the car.

How exhausted I am, much more exhausted now than I was before my nap on the slope. I want a soft bed, a down quilt that I can wrap around me twice and pull up over my head.

How much there is that needs to be done each day before sleep can come and take me: tend patients, cook food, keep Edda in line, sew buttons, wax the floor. Before night can come today I have to hang around in a car with two complicated women, carry luggage into a house, cook dinner, wash the dishes, and keep up a conversation with a foreigner who has nothing to do with me. Dear me.

I open my eyes and the Little Yellow Hen drives up.

I should have learned long ago not to open my eyes.

Damn it.

Good Lord.

The number of occupants in the yellow van has grown since Selfoss. Ringleader Theodór—Teddi—steps out. You can be sure that he's directing this pursuit, the dapper, pretty-boy crime boss with forget-me-not eyes and a delicate, girlish mouth. Teddi dresses sportily in a stock of expensive ski outfits, but he never goes skiing as far as anyone knows. He always does his own thing, and has no scruples about putting on a Norwegian knitted cap, tassel and all. His comrades would rather be dead than let themselves be seen with such a contraption on their heads, underlings in the gang to which they have to conform. Teddi comes from a so-called regular household with a father, mother, siblings, and cars. Things are going well for everyone in that household but him. He operates an amphetamine-and-moonshine wholesale ring and has two thugs working for him, Vernharður and Nonni, whose job it is to beat up people in the evenings and on weekends if they're late with their payments. One of Teddi's innovations is having a female also dole out thrashings: Erla María, a fifteen-year-old girl from Grímsey. She has a job in a soap factory and works out at the Niflheimur Bodybuilding Clinic. Teddi's favorite beverage is whole milk. He doesn't drink or do drugs. He's known for having a stash of mini milk-cartons and when the others are doing drugs, he takes one out, pokes a hole in the top with the accompanying straw, and starts sucking. This ringleader with the baby face so completely contradicts the stereotype that I've caught myself thinking about him in particular, even when I've been tending to the acutely ill and the dying. It's remarkable that he who is the rottenest bastard inside is the most spic-and-span on the outside. He's so fanatically ill-willed and such a control freak that he chases after his friend Edda to spoil her chances of being saved. I would have been more inclined to think that deep down he was bound to be concerned enough for Edda to have wanted her to get away. How silly of me.

What could be the reason that I saw only Gerti Chicken in the shop in Selfoss? It wouldn't be Teddi's thing to try to conceal his presence. Did Gerti pick him up somewhere on the highway? Perhaps the biggest mystery of all: How did the two of them manage to wake up on a Sunday morning? For about the first time in their lives. Something big must be brewing.

Hreinn Elías has appeared out of nowhere, as well.

Allow me to introduce Hreinn Elías, I say. Also known as Hreinn Brain.

That's hilarious, says Heiður, cracking up.

The trio walks around their vehicle, the bastards, devastated at how badly the sand's damaged the finish on the infernal van. I enjoy watching them running their sad hands over the scratched paint and the sandblasted windshield.

Dear friends, this scene should have been photographed, captured on video: Hreinn Elías, a shabby youth with angel hair, parted in the middle over his low brow and hanging down to his slumping shoulders, and glossy violet bags dividing his face beneath his dirt-gray eyes. The boy is like a cherub that devils have taken and pickled in brine. Gerti Chicken in his slimy-green leather pants with his shaved head and clumpy ponytail, looking like a seventy-year-old bum who's gotten his getup from a biker. Ringleader Teddi: a plainclothes Scoutmaster.

Edda walks out of the shop. An instant hangover-type feeling washes over me, an iron cinch tightens around my head, my eyes can't tolerate the sunlight, there's a buzzing in my ears, my limbs are paralyzed, a film coats my tongue.

To behold this crooked picture of misery that I've nourished at my breast and that appears to limp because one leg is shorter than the other.

What happens now can determine the course of Edda's life, the course of our trip to the east—whether we'll make it all the way or whether it might end here, after we've made it nearly halfway.

Edda runs toward her friends. Goodness gracious, to see her run. It's as if she's never done it before, doesn't know how, is on the verge of stopping at every step. She waves. Teddi walks toward her and greets her with a kiss on the cheek like a caring brother. It figures, that the greatest skunk gives the warmest greeting.

This skunk wants to turn my desperate efforts into nothing, kick us back to the point where we were when the outlook was bleakest. My inner fear is blended with anger, the lame-duck variety that's long been my mistress. Can't they be happy about their friend pulling herself together? Do they have to chase after her, persecute her, knock her down when she's trying to pull herself up?

In my opinion, nothing less will do now than to make an assault on the wall where it's highest, so I whip myself out of the car and take a few authoritative steps.

Hello, I say boldly. Where's Teddi heading today?

Where are you heading?, he asks in return, cheekily.

You must have some idea of that, dear, seeing as how you've come all this way.

They all fall silent.

Oh, look, Gerti's got himself a chicken, I say, pointing at a glossy picture of a chicken that he's stuck on the windshield.

Keep your damned nose in your own business, you fucking cow. Just stick with your fluty pervert there and eat shit, growls Edda.

The lady wouldn't have learned this sort of language from tough Teddi now, would she?, I think.

I can tell Edda's afraid I'll do something stupid again, like when I stuck out my tongue at Gerti. To tell the truth, this pleases me to no end.

Heiður's come up next to me. She stares silently at the youngsters. I know there's little that can shake them, but her piercing gaze is better than nothing.

I'm going to kill you when I'm sixteen, says Edda.

I notice Hreinn Elías and Gerti Chicken react slightly to this, whereas Teddi doesn't flap an eyelash, doesn't move a muscle in his noble face.

Why put it off?, I say.

At that moment Edda spits from where she's standing next to Teddi, aiming at my forehead. She's such a good shot that it lands right between my eyebrows.

MY THIRD EYE. MADE FROM THE SPIT OF MY DELINQUENT CHILD.

Gerti Chicken's sitting behind the wheel, and Teddi, Hreinn Elías, and Edda promptly disappear into the windowless backseat, Edda in the middle. The scene is reminiscent of a movie kidnapping. They even peel out.

What should we do?, asks Heiður.

I'll be damned if this isn't the first time I've heard her speak these words.

We can't do anything, not for now.

What on earth are they planning?

They wouldn't know that themselves. Incredible disposition. Not to let her leave in peace, knowing what bad shape she's in.

What should we do?, asks Heiður again.

Wait. See if she comes back.

Call the good cop.

My cousin Rikki?, I say. What good do you think that'll do?

Call anyway. Maybe the police can put a stop to this.

How? It isn't certain that she's going anywhere with those idiots. They could just as well return right away.

Did Rikki know that you were heading east?

Yes, I always let him know what I'm up to.

No one could have imagined that they would chase after her.

Never. It's completely baffling, what they're up to.

A power play.

We get into the car, look each other in the eye.

Don't give up, Harpa. Maybe you should go back inside and call Rikki. You never know, he might have something up his sleeve.

I've come all this way on just a trace of hope. I quit my job, ended my lease, emptied my apartment, scoured it from top to bottom, loaded all the appliances into the truck, left dear old Dad. After doing all that, the least I can do is make one little phone call now that my rescue operation is threatened. But I want to wait and see first. *Wait and see.* I should know how to do that. I haven't done anything for an entire year but wait and see, in despair.

Just call, says Heiður.

Naw. I'm going to hang on. She might just get herself back here.

Well, we can wait for a little while, says Heiður, tapping the wheel with her fingers.

You who are better at most everything besides waiting.

I know who I am.

Should we go after them?

. . .

We could, of course, just as well do that as hang around here. Damn, those boys are freaky.

Don't assume their character is any better than their appearance. Only one of them, that poor Hreinn Elli, has any excuse. Teddi and Gerti come from so-called normal families, though the fact that Gerti's parents raise chickens in their Dodge could suggest they have some rather exotic ideas . . . Hreinn Elli, however, is the third generation of petty criminals. There's nothing but riffraff around him, everywhere you look. His paternal grandfather, Lilli Ódó, is a famous creature. He's doing time in Litla-Hraun Prison for beating the brains out of his best friend with a crowbar. Hreinn Elli's father, who's called Guðmundur Pituitary or Mummi Pituitary, is a petty criminal and moonshiner, and rumor has it that he uses petty crime as a front for major criminal operations. It's whispered that he was involved in the disappearance of two people. I think it's probably true.

Hreinn Elli's maternal line is no better. They're all drunks, and his grandmother is the worst. His maternal aunt once left a one-year-old child alone in a crib with twenty milk bottles while she went off for a weekend drug binge in Amsterdam. The residents of her apartment building heard the baby wailing, and the police had to break down the door.

Hreinn Elli's been systematically wrecked since he was born. Sometimes when I look in those empty eyes of his, I feel as if there's nothing inside him. I suppose children don't survive such circumstances without becoming quite torpid.

How is it possible in a civilized society to allow children to be raised in such a way that they never have a chance?

What would you do? Take them away from their parents?

Wouldn't that be the only way?

Where would we be heading then?

Oh, there—see, what did I tell you?

The yellow delivery van slips toward us between the breast-shaped hills of Landbrotshólar.

They've changed their minds, the little oafs, says Heiður.

What do you know.

. . .

We wait at the turnout for what comes next, and lo and behold, the yellow vehicle stops.

Teddi gets out and opens the door for Edda. He offers his hand to her like a courteous fiancé, and she steps out with care.

He hands Edda a book, which she sticks in the pocket of her leather vest.

What do you think that's all about?, asks Heiður.

Don't ask me. Maybe they're playing bookmobile.

Edda walks slowly in our direction, followed by Teddi. Just like hostages are handed over in the movies.

I roll down the window, and Teddi declares in a gloating tone: I'll leave her with you for now.

Thanks.

He adds: The sands are still impassable.

Thank you, jackass.

Edda's face pales, and she gives me a look that's more frightened than angry. Teddi opens the back door for her and she steps up into the white pickup truck as docile as a lamb.

Poor you to have such a mother, says Teddi.

I know, says Edda. I really think she's about to start crying.

Heiður laughs sarcastically. It's the first time I notice any reaction in Teddi. Now he's angry. He's not used to being ridiculed, and fear of derision is his Achilles' heel, just like any other tyrant.

. . .

Heiður drives off so abruptly that Teddi's nearly shoved off the road. After regaining his balance, he stands there motionless, as if waiting around for something.

Edda grabs at the door handle, but Heiður has presciently put on the child lock. She floors it, sending gravel flying from the wheels, and barely lets up on the gas despite the road curving toward a bridge.

I wonder what passed between Edda and the boys in the van. Most likely, they never intended to take her back to town, and were just teasing me. *I'll leave her with you for now.* They knew how to word things, those control freaks. They used the sandstorm as a pretext for dropping all their plans. Ridiculous.

Good job giving it to that idiot, whispers Heiður, leaning over to my ear.

I know.

Look at you, whispering like you're at a kid's birthday party. Fucking lesbians. Gross.

Heiður gives another sarcastic laugh. What kind of kids' birthday parties have you been to, Edda?

Fuck yourself with a stick.

Sorry, Heiður, she can't control herself.

That's fairly obvious.

I look toward the backseat, fully expecting the girl to launch a new, fiercer attack with her fists. But at that moment she's spreading a blanket over herself, all the way up over her head, her Walkman headphones in her ears.

I don't even know how to apologize to you, I say tearfully to Heiður, like the loser and fool that I am.

You shouldn't apologize to me. What does it look like inside the head of a child who talks like that?

I have no idea what she's thinking. She's in an entirely different world, like a schizophrenic.

You know, from what I've seen of your daughter today, I find it a miracle that you managed to get her to come along at all.

It was a tragedy, mainly, that led to her agreeing to it. I don't think she would have come if little Rúna hadn't died. It was Edda who found her. To see death with your own eyes isn't the same as hearing about it.

What happened to Rúna?

She choked on her own vomit in her sleep.

Just after little Rúna died, a crack in the icy mass enclosing Edda started melting, and we had long chats. I tried to do everything I could to please her—I pampered her anxiously, made waffles and brought her into the living room where she sat and watched splatter films that Gerti Chicken had given her. The first night she ate the waffles and drank the hot chocolate and we talked into the night, in between bouts of her sobbing and snuggling up to me. I couldn't help but cry too. We met Rúna when she was seven or eight years old. She was in the same grade as Edda, an awfully cheerful and clever girl. Then she changed schools, and she and Edda didn't meet again until after they were both deep in the shit. I've also known her mother since the girls were little, but I'm such a wimp that I haven't been able to bring myself to speak to her since it happened.

The first night, I held Edda's hand until she slept, and then I dozed off with the hope in my heart that things would work out for us, even though I was in absolute shock that little Rúna should have come to such an end.

The second night, Edda ate a quarter of a waffle and said less. She shed no more tears, and the sulkiness and brattiness slowly took over.

The third night, she didn't touch anything and was testy with me. In dismay, I took the tray back to the kitchen, my appetite gone, and threw away the waffles, knowing in my heart that the game was over, at least this round, and probably forever.

Everything went back to the way it had been, and that's when I thought that she really was unsalvageable. You couldn't know it until you've tried it, but pulling back a kid who's being sucked down this road is unbelievably difficult. It's even more difficult to put girls back on the right track. Their identity is much more fragile than boys'. The kids who do manage to get themselves out—when they look back, they say that they would much rather die than go through such a horror again.

I didn't notice any change at all in the boys in the gang after Rúna died. They were as determined as ever to drag Edda into the shit.

Well, says Heiður, it's apparently easier to help kids who've had a good emotional relationship with someone. Which gives me hope about Edda. You and your daughter were such a good pair before this misfortune struck.

Yes, we were, kind of.

I always found her to be such a decent kid, a bit precocious. Well behaved, though not too much. I was impressed with how successful you'd been with her, because you were so terribly young and it was all so difficult, you with your mother on your back and that stupid father of hers.

He played such a small part, just barely enough. My dad was our shelter and support. We would simply never have made it if it hadn't been for him.

I know, Harpa dear. But he would have made no difference if you hadn't done such a good job.

Oh, shut up. I want to look at the landscape.

Passengers can afford to.

The manifold mountain range, rounded and pointed and everything in between, the terraced green slopes beneath the pitch-black filigree of the cliffs.

The dusky blue of the majestic Lómagnúpur.

The spring-blue-and-white Vatnajökull Glacier sprouting cloud cushions that add to its height.

A bellowing dishwater-gray river between sandbanks in lava tracts without end.

Have we lost those damned pricks?, I ask.

Pff, they're not going to bother us again. I'm sure they've turned back.

They can't turn back, because they can't cross the sands for now. We'll have to make sure they're not still following before we take the turnoff to the cottage.

If they show up at the cottage, I'm taking out the rifle.

Skip the nonsense, Heiður.

I'd just shoot into the air. A little warning shot. They're complete wusses. They'd take off instantly.

That kind of thinking can lead to accidents. We've got a total wacko in the car. She shouldn't come anywhere close to weapons. You've seen how she behaves when she gets riled.

Edda couldn't do any harm. She doesn't even know how to work the safety. But I'll take care not to wave it around unnecessarily.

I'm not dignifying this nonsense with a reply. I'm going to take a nap.

Good night.

My destiny tonight is to cuddle in a soft bed in the house beneath Lómagnúpur and wrap myself in downy quilts, dreaming about what once was, chattering with my lover from the supermarket who went west.

I remember nothing about the house itself, though I visited when it was new. I've given it so little thought that it might as well have not existed. Might it be due to jealousy of those who own homes in the glorious tract on the eastern side of the ever-blue mountain? How did Jens Kaaber manage to get hold of a piece of land there anyway? I thought the area was protected.

We approach the glacier slowly but surely, and I can hardly believe that we're privileged to spend the night alongside it, with a perspective that few have had through the years. APPROACHING A GLACIER, whether by air, sea, or car, or on foot, is a special feeling that's impossible to describe. Most people in this world have died without having this experience, no matter when they lived.

If only you were here by my side instead of having to tough it out in the Westfjords, where the sun doesn't show its face for a quarter of the year.

If you were here with me, we could talk about the glacier, and I could tell you how it is at the top, though I haven't been there. From the glacier you can see other mountains, trifling cone-shaped piles. When a person's on a glacier, he's king of the world, especially on Vatnajökull, the biggest glacier in Europe. You don't want to come down, you want to remain in that icy universe and gaze down at the land. I should point out that an expedition up onto a glacier is one of the most remarkable things you can possibly do in this life. A GLACIAL SUN doesn't resemble the sun anywhere else on earth.

I would tell you everything about when I was a little child out east, because I know that you long to hear more. I would tell you how it felt to have a child while still a child. I wouldn't be embarrassed. I would tell you how it is to be an un-poet, a poet in secret, without being ashamed of myself. I would be fun, and I would tell you how it was in Perpignan, and where to find the nicest places in all sorts of foreign countries, because I know where they are though I've hardly been anywhere. I've read about places and heard about them from Heiður. I would tell you where I'm going next, with you, and I would tell you how it was to have you by me day and night. It's not love in secret but *love in memory*, because it was a memory, just a memory. I wouldn't take the advice of the English verse:

Never seek to tell thy love
Love that never told can be.

I would let it all out. Everything about love, in detail. I would tell you everything about our first time, which was also the last time. Tell you how it was, in as much detail as possible without being rude, or maybe I could be that as well, just for fun—surprise you, catch the opponent off guard.

Reddening clouds are sailing in multiple evening-sun ponds.

If only he could see this with me, he who occupies my mind— the glory of the landscape to the southwest on the final day in August. The man I recall and can't forget.

He couldn't stop for long, because then the frozen groceries waiting in his four-by-four would thaw.

He looks at me with his greenish eyes, blue-green, green-blue, which call to mind neither people nor the earth, but rather, cats and oceans.

His green eyes
are not of human kin
but of the kin of cats.

Eyes of the sea, not land.

Cat's eyes,
sea eyes.

Would they see me in the dark?

Would it be sweet to drown in them?

He says nothing. There's no need for words now. Yet I'm a little curious about some things. Why bother to hold back?

Have you worked at sea?

I was a deckhand in the summers, because my dad was a helmsman.

One explanation for why he always looked so stylish was that his clothes suited him so well. But it was more than that. He wore clothes that couldn't be bought in Iceland. Everything fit together to make him the top dog—at swimming lessons, at school, wherever he went.

So you were raised at sea.

During the summers, and in my mind too, he said.

Did you get to travel at an early age?

Yes. I was five years old when I first went overseas. What about you?

Not until later.

I always thought you were foreign. My own name for you was "The Foreign Girl." I remember how surprised I was to hear you speak Icelandic. I thought you'd simply learned it well, but I had imagined that you spoke with an accent, which of course you didn't. So you're not foreign at all?

Not that I know of.

He smiles, and I say, I'm just an ordinary changeling.

He looks at me with a gleam in his eye, a sweet, playful gleam.

He adds a smile so wide that his green-blue eyes became narrow slits. It's how a cat's eyes can become when it purrs, if anyone should deign to stroke it. I'd seen him laugh, though it had never lasted long, and I'd seen his half smile. But I felt as if the smiles I'd seen had merely been practice for this special smile. Like a singer performing in concert, giving his all to the high C after having only hummed and warbled and half-sung it in practice. Not only is it an absolute smile, but it's unusually long-lasting, unless my sense of time has become a bit messed up. The high C so drawn out that the audience holds its breath, a note that doesn't stop all at once but dies out gradually.

The teeth in his bottom gum are slightly crooked, and he has warlike canines that he no doubt hates, without realizing that they're charming. Maybe it's because of his canines that these complete smiles of his are so rare. Or maybe they're rare because he saves them for only the absolutely perfect occasions.

The smile leaves behind long streaks of shimmering silence. At first he looks a bit at my face, just a bit, next at my feet, which are in moccasins of nubuck lined with rabbit fur, embroidered with strips of colorful beads. A gift from Heiður after a Canadian tour. Warm and fuzzy shoes on the cold floor of the Norðurmýri basement. It's unclear whether they increase my sex appeal or erase it altogether. Size four and a half. Plainly problematic to find a pair of fashionable women's shoes. Poor woman. Always at risk of being caught in the children's shoe department. Can you believe it?

I set the coffee down on the living room table.

Where's the cottage, then?, asks a voice from the backseat politely.

Yet another U-turn. It would actually be better if Edda were always sassy. It's her bouts of politeness that really throw things out of whack. Because then you get the stupid idea that maybe the clouds are breaking, a hope that's suffocated almost immediately. Which is never painless.

You can't see the cottage until just before you come to it, Edda dear.

Dark spires and towers rise from the rock walls at Núpsstaður, like an illustration for a book of mysteries and fairy tales.

Numerous boulders cast long shadows at the green feet of Lómagnúpur, and sheep graze in the shelter of the shadows.

Where do we turn off the road?

It's a little bit farther.

Eastward, over the vast expanse of sand, to the dullish glacier tongue with a black tire-tread pattern. The giant helmet of the glacier takes over from its creeping offspring and gleams yellowish and steely in the fading sunlight flickering behind the three female travelers in their little truck.

Sharp peaks rise here and there closer to the glacier.

A MONUMENT FOR SOMETHING THAT NEVER WAS. THE FOGGY LAD in the Range Rover. The secret of Harpa Hernandezdóttir.

Roll down the window a crack, and the noise of the tangled courses of the Núpsvötn, Súla, and Skeiðará Rivers hits the ears in a rushing wave, like a repressed memory rising from the deep on the spout of a whale. The act of opening a car window on the Skeiðará sands could be called BREAKING THE SOUND BARRIER: A MEMORY RESURRECTED.

On the earth the sun shines on the piers of very long bridges, and in the sky is an elastic cloud pretending to be northern lights in the making.

Now we travel in the TIME OF HALF-SHADOW.

The last thing the eyes of many a seafarer beheld was the extensive sands of death on Iceland's southeast coast. The eyes of drowning men. The eyes of those who reached land yet froze to death before anyone came to their rescue.

THE SANDS OF DROWNED SOULS. The sands that pummeled us today. *It was today.* Oh, that's funny. The sands from a past life were today.

Added to the sky is the contrail of a jet that I wish I were in, no matter where it's going—the only passenger, free from my daughter, my mother, free from the earth upon which I'm stuck.

That's the road we turn onto, says Heiður.

You call that a road?

Maybe not.

I check the side mirrors and look over my shoulder, but no car is to be seen, not a single one. And definitely not a bright-yellow delivery van on a peculiar mission to pursue my child.

The nonroad running northward along the volcanic neck is an embankment of stone, and the car is no willing vehicle. The bumps could cause a miscarriage if something were kicking in the belly.

Rumbling along a road that's not a road, but rather an embankment. Precipitance under confounded cliffs on the bastion's murky side.

The cliff formations mutate in a blink of the passenger's eye.

Where are we now?

And where are we now?

Uncertainty's found in permanent variability.

The cliffs gleam black in a horrid wet that comes from within.

Cliffs of the very end.

It wouldn't surprise me if one or all of us were to lose our lives in this faraway, fancy abode that I don't recall having visited, though I have in fact been there before. Heiður's threatening to use a rifle. Guns are for killing. I'm traveling with two people who are capable of anything.

I don't understand how they think, don't know what's in their heads.

And Mom.

Mom, who doesn't think. Just *exists*, unapologetically. Things would be a trifle more bearable if I could be free of her. If only I could break loose.

The circles around the little ponds in the light-gray gravel are very green.

The rivers of the wasteland are trimmed with robust rims of moss.

Aren't you tired, Heiður dear?

When have I ever been tired?

Never. I remember now. This landscape is fantastic. Unfathomable, really.

You mean that?, asks the driver, pointing.

Pointing at what wasn't just a few minutes ago: a grassy slope that comes to the fore. It holds elf dwellings, berry hollows, light-green willows, birch shoots, dwarf rocks, little jets that dash down the mountainside, impatient to join a real stream.

Who could have imagined finding this secret place here, out of the blue?

Ruminating sheep with blubbery cushions for sides spring up in alarm. They bleat in unison with their thin-voiced offspring, panicked, as the white danger approaches, a hoarse and rumbling machine over rocks, more rocks, and even more rocks. If I look left, I see the opulence of the slope. To the right are bellowing streams, wasteland. Not a single blade of grass in the scree on our side, not a blade on the sands farther away, where the icy, rugged tongue takes over, rolling up out of the sand like a giant, fantastic beast, at the foot of the proud glacier.

You can't say of the WASTES that they don't BREATHE DEEPLY
I'll join you in breathing
though imminent death might call.

The paper-thin moon, full to the brim, is impaled by one of the Súlutindar peaks.

It doesn't bother the moon.

Nor should it bother anyone.

A long-nosed bird is perched on a mountain peak, like a small torpedo with wings, fully prepared to launch itself at the sound barrier and blast it to pieces.

What's that?, I ask.

The tower.

What tower?

Of the cottage.

A transparent cylindrical tower with a convex top breaks up and out between the gently pointed spruces, an unidentified object hardly flying, and yet, a free-floating tower.

It's like an observatory, remarks Edda.

Yes, it was built especially for stargazing, says Heiður. There's even a telescope in it, to bring you as close as possible to them.

Wow, exclaims the girl.

In a shrub-grown hollow by a stream cascading down a groove in the cliffs is *the house*, hidden from the world by spruce trees. Barbed wire protects it against people, vehicles, and creatures. On the iron gate is a sign reading PRIVATE DRIVE. But the birds of the air don't know how to read, and two generations of wagtails sit by the dozens on the barbed wire and fence posts. The reception committee continues chirping without losing the thread, amplifying its song when the autumn visitors come rattling along in their vulgar vehicle.

In the Shelter of Lómagnúpur

Heiður plunges straight into unloading the luggage from the backseat before reaching beneath the tarp for the cooler. One of the peculiarities of the master flutist is that she never takes breaks until absolutely necessary.

You're so energetic, my dear. I almost feel like I need to tie you down.

She continues working like mad while I take it slower. I'm lazy as a dog after all those years of toil.

I don't get this house, I say.

You've been here before.

Who designed it?

It was Dad's idea.

That explains a lot.

The house is a cross between a castle and a large bungalow in the functionalist style. It's square, with big windows, and is bordered on all sides by a wide deck. It wouldn't look comical in a neighborhood of single-family homes in Reykjavík, but as a summer cottage in the wilderness it tickles the funny bone. A smaller house would have fit in better with the landscape here. A transparent tower juts out from the middle of the roof, where a chimney should be. The actual chimney, on the other hand, is unassuming, standing low and stout at one corner of the roof. It's as if a child lacking manual dexterity stuck on a Lego block.

It may be spectacular, I say, but pretty it's not.

Heiður looks insulted. It's not good enough for you?

It'll do, if I can have the tower to myself. How did your dad get permission to build here? I thought this was a national park.

Stop being so negative, Harpa. Damn, how boring you can get.

Oh, sorry, I say, without meaning it.

Heiður's sulky. She knows that the house is an abomination, and she's ashamed for her father, its tasteless creator. She's stacked the luggage on the deck by the front door, which she opens with a large key. Here *everything*, from the key to the house, has to be *large*.

Edda hurries in ahead of us, draws the pale-yellow silk drapes from the window, and says: Wow.

Wow. Yellow silk drapes, just like in the apartment belonging to my faithful foreign friend, Gabriel Axel in Perpignan, above his shop.

This side of the house has a perfect view of the surrounding glacial rivers, gravel deserts, and sandy tracts, with the Öræfa Glacier and Hvannadalshnúkur Peak providing a backdrop.

On the other side, the windows are in close proximity to narrow waterfalls that rush headlong down masterfully sculpted cliffs. Dropwort grows by the deck, and the bluebell's still in delicate bloom.

It's almost as bright inside as it is outside. The light comes from above, too, from the tower, through the large opening in the ceiling where the spiral staircase ends. Through the convex tower, one of the last clouds of August can be seen floating southward, a milky, thick pillow. A traveling cloud for birds to sail on.

Once you're inside, the brick building transforms into a wooden house. Paneling on the walls and ceiling, and a reddish parquet floor. In the middle is a picture-perfect kitchen, with a giant copper range hood and rods from which hang all sizes of copper pots and pans. On the other side of this accomplished area stands an oval pinewood table with lathed legs and matching chairs, and across from these, there are two deep seven-seat couches along the wall. Porcelain figurines, CDs, and a portable CD player line the shelves. Near the door is the gun collection, small and large rifles—one old, six in total. If the enemy comes, each of us can shoot with two rifles. That should impress Tough Teddi.

Heiður's making the rounds through the house, opening the windows to air out the place, inviting in the remarkably warm evening breeze.

It's nice in here, I say. You can't tell that from the outside.

Heiður says nothing. The last time she decided to quit talking to me, it lasted a month.

Back then I swallowed my pride and called. After all, I'd insulted her; there's no denying it. Now I've got to find a smart way to get her back in a good mood.

I like the way it's been decorated, I add. It's very tasteful.

Edda's on a quick-fire tour of the house. She opens a door, comes back and announces, "Two lovely bedrooms!" She then opens the door to a tiled bathroom furnished with dark-blue toilet fixtures from Villeroy & Boch, gold faucets and mixer taps—in rococo style, no less—and fluffy red towels with the fancy gold monogram *S. K.* hung neatly from towel bars. Saga Kaaber, Heiður's mother, is one of those people who wants her presence known, even when she's nowhere near. But where were she and her decent taste when this box, with its obscene tower jutting from the middle of the roof and crappy little chimney in a corner, was being designed?

Edda's gone up the spiral staircase, and she tramps across the tower floor, making it creak. Come here, Mom! she shouts. You should see this.

I rush up the stairs. This tower may look hilarious from the outside, but once you're up in it, it's like a fairy tale. The view opens up over the spruce trees and the entire stretch of sand, densely meshed by an irregular net of streams leading to the sea.

On this floor, I'm on a par with the glacier.

A red glow at the country's highest peak. SUNSET ERUPTION. Remember to write a poem about it, I tell myself.

This transparent tower must be an architectural achievement, even though it doesn't fit with the rest of the house. Wind doesn't gust into it, and all its joints are made by the hands of a master. To stand here is like having traveled a considerable distance up into the firmament in a glass elevator. All the clouds, except for two, have stopped airing themselves today. They're oval puffs, straight up over the tower, one of black smoke, on its way south, and the other of white wool, heading north. Their goal is union, the conclusion of an important process in the sky, and the start of a new one. Soon nothing will remain in the sky but one unified cloud, black and white—the thin veil of the moon. Then it will slowly grow darker than usual, because we're far from human habitation, before a buxom moon and various seldom-seen stars come to light.

I'm going to sleep here tonight!, I shout.

All the same to me!, shouts Heiður in reply.

You're seriously going to sleep on this crappy mattress?, says Edda. And it's true—the thin mattress with its blazing-bright-rainforest-and-exotic-wildlife sheet could hardly be intended as bedding for an entire night.

Did you want to sleep here?, I ask Edda, constantly afraid of upsetting her.

No, I want to sleep in a proper bed. Hey—see that guy, Mom?, Edda asks as she points outside.

Yes, darling. Iceland's full of backpackers.

Yeah, but isn't that Yves?

Oh, I think you're right. I'd forgotten about him.

Darn! Why did he have to show up?

It certainly surprised me that Heiður invited him. Better to think twice.

It would have been much funner if it were just us three.

He won't exactly be taking up much space.

Where will he sleep?

He can just sleep on the couch in the living room.

Aw, Mom, I don't want him here.

Maybe I can make good use of him and practice my French. I shout from the tower: Guess what, Heiður? The French hiker is on his way here!

What?

Yves.

That's okay. We've certainly got enough food for him.

I carefully inch my way down the spiral staircase, my sense of balance playing games with me.

Heiður's finished bringing in the suitcases and bags and stowing away the food. She declares that she doesn't feel like dealing with the gas refrigerator, not for just one night. It'll be fine to keep the refrigerated goods outside. I see that my friend's still in quite a sulk. Blame her if you like, but she drives me all the way east, and what does she get in return? Scorn and ridicule because of a superb house in an amazing place—free luxury accommodations for a destitute assistant nurse.

I open the door to the deck, and the invigorating mountain air embraces me. The plump-faced moon wants to exist untorn and has moved off the sharp peak of Súlur. When I was taking in the scenery from the tower, I didn't even notice the moon. THE MOON ITSELF ESCAPED MY NOTICE. I want to make coffee, put on my jacket, sit out on the deck with a steaming mug, and watch the sunset on the gleaming glacier.

THE MOON MUSTN'T ESCAPE MY NOTICE AGAIN.

Two wagtails come flying by in jerky fits, reminding me of Heiður. They settle on the deck's handrail, wagging their tails and twittering, a tiny welcoming committee with a carefully rehearsed performance.

Are you hungry, Heiður?

I will be when dinner's ready.

A simple wish like coffee and the sunset on the deck is too complicated to be fulfilled in this life. Something else always has to be done. Something other than what you wish for.

I'll get going with dinner, I say. Go sit out on the deck, Heiður, and have a look at the glacier before it gets dark.

I can see it out the window.

It's not the same as being outside. Take a break now, and I'll start cooking. That was a long day of driving.

Okay, if you insist. I'll make coffee and sit outside a bit with a cup.

As if spoken from my heart, I offer to start the coffee for her.

Isn't that Frenchman almost here?, Heiður asks.

Oh, that's right. Yes, he's almost here. Do you think it was a mistake to invite him? Edda isn't too thrilled about it.

She wants to spend time alone with you. She's jealous, the poor thing. But it's not like she's ever thrilled about anything that you do, whether you're cooking dinner for a French tourist in a mountain hut or coming to find her in a drug den.

Don't talk about drug dens. That was in a past life.

Suddenly I'm beset with weakness in my lower back, leaden feet, dizziness.

Where can I run? Impossible to run anywhere except to a kitchen stool.

I sit down on one next to the counter, with its Gaggenau gas burners, and pretend to examine the contents of a cabinet. Elaborate cast-iron cookware and more copper pots of all sizes. Ceramic plates.

THE RUNAWAY FROM LIFE. That's what my biography should be called.

Can I scream?, I ask.

You can do whatever you like.

I get up and go out onto the deck and try to scream in the most beastly way possible. As soon as I stop, I hear a thud from inside. Edda's lying at the foot of the spiral staircase, holding her ankle.

Oh my God, Mom. Are you insane? I rushed down the stairs so fast that I tripped and fell.

Are you hurt?

Yes. Why would you scream like that?

Are you worried that we'll bother the neighbors?

It's not funny. I might be seriously injured.

I have to take pains not to laugh out loud. I don't get it. I couldn't care a whit if Edda's leg were broken. It wouldn't be such a bad thing. Then at least I'd know where she is.

The French traveler, the one I've forgotten exists once again, comes running as if the Devil's at his heels, his red down jacket flapping wildly. He waves his hands, rushes up onto the deck, and shouts: What's wrong?

Edda fell, I say.

Is she badly hurt?, he asks.

I don't know. It just happened.

Yves has a Swiss Army knife in his hand, blade open. He notices what I'm looking at, folds the blade back inside, and sticks the knife in his pocket, a tiny bit of embarrassment showing at the corners of his intellectual mouth. He'd clearly expected conflict, maybe even murder.

Was it she who screamed so horribly?, asks Yves.

Yes, I say innocently. It's so fun to lie in a foreign language when those who aren't meant to understand don't understand. Heiður, however, gives me a suspicious look.

I'd have probably refrained from screaming if I'd remembered there was a guest on the way.

Where's your backpack?, I ask.

I tossed it off when I heard the scream. I thought it was an emergency.

He must have learned about EMERGENCY SITUATIONS in his Scouting handbook. If a loud scream is heard in the field, not least in the wilderness of Iceland, you must cast off your pack, grab your Swiss Army knife from your pocket, and run as fast as possible toward the noise. If a confused assistant nurse has wailed on a deck for no apparent reason, you should do nothing, but if her problem daughter is beating her up, you must jump into the fray, though not with your knife, unless it's a matter of life and death.

What happened to her?, asks Yves.

Fell down the stairs.

Is she in a lot of pain?

We hadn't gotten that far.

Yves bends over Edda, turns her leg every which way, and asks in his singular English whether this or that hurts. He determines that Edda's ankle is sprained, lifts her from the floor, and helps her over to the couch.

Heiður finds an elastic bandage in her perfect first-aid kit, which appears to be designed for a large-scale accident at sea rather than a minor sprain on dry land.

Yves starts giving effective first aid, the start of Chapter Five, wrapping Edda's ankle with southern élan, hands nearly flying, as Heiður and I shuffle our feet, redundant individuals. Edda sits there with an enigmatic look on her face, acting as if she has no part in this accident.

Do you need a painkiller?, Yves asks his patient.

Yes.

The poor man has no idea that he's speaking to a little junkie.

It crosses my mind that it would be most appropriate to go and get her dope bag and offer her one of her own pills. But this is certainly not the time to be cocky, and the poor girl might well be in real pain, so I give her a tablet from the first-aid kit.

Do you think it'll take her a long time to recover?, I ask.

Just a few days.

The French visitor is a master at wrapping ankles. We really should take a photo of the job he did it's so perfect. But no, now I'm going to cook dinner, no monkeying around.

How about some red wine from our guest's home country?, says Heiður, after taking out a bottle with a lovely label.

Thank you so much, says Yves. Allow me to help. Once again, he pulls out his Swiss Army knife. He examines the bottle and says that the vintage is well chosen, 1987, but of course it would improve greatly with age.

Unfortunately, we don't have time to wait for further improvements, says Heiður.

Yves goes on to tell us that this Cos d'Estournel that we're about to start drinking comes from his neighbor's farm in Bordeaux.

Edda looks at the foreign visitor as if he's stepped out of a Grimm Brothers fairy tale.

It certainly traveled today, didn't it?, asks Yves, with worry wrinkles between his dark arched eyebrows.

What traveled?, asks Heiður.

The wine.

Yes, it traveled with us, she says. By land.

It's preferable not to drink wine the same day it travels. It gets so terrifically shaken, which is bad for the taste.

We'll be gone tomorrow, I say. It'll be too late to guzzle it after tonight.

Yves looks at me and says nothing. I'm not quite certain what this southern gaze of his means, and I look back with so-called inscrutable eyes.

What a magnificent house, says the visitor.

When you look out, yes, I say. You must have missed the exterior you were in such a rush.

Heiður takes three steps to the right and disappears into one of the bedrooms. Yet another faux pas on my part. THE BITCHY ASSISTANT NURSE AT THE FOOT OF LÓMAGNÚPUR.

I take out imposing wineglasses with fat stems. Stately glasses, for use in an Icelandic villa with a see-through silo. I notice Yves giving the glasses a puzzled look. Yes, my friend, this is the way nouveau-riche folk in Iceland like to have things.

Let's let the wine breathe a bit, says Yves.

I can hardly wait, I say.

Lie down and elevate your foot, says Yves to Edda.

She smiles, and I could swear she's trying to be provocative. The tip of her tongue is pushed forward onto her lips, and her head's tilted—pretty darned coquettish. Which is no wonder. Descended from whores on her mother's side, who started early. Turn away and focus on the cooking; that's the thing to do.

Does it hurt now?, asks Yves.

Thank you, it's much better with the bandage. It gives such good support, says Edda from the couch, throwing her arm under her head with a flirty flair. Turn away, ahem, and focus on the cooking, I tell myself again.

I guess I'll go get my backpack now, says Yves, probably a bit embarrassed at having tossed it aside in his perfectly correct execution of the response to an emergency situation in the Icelandic wilderness.

You do that, I say, and sail swiftly out into the immeasurable ocean of culinary arts in which I've been immersed half my life and longer. But I don't really need to put much effort into it now. The potato gratin is ready to stick in the oven, carefully prepared in advance for the trip. The leg of lamb was seasoned yesterday, according to all the rules of the art. But I still have to prepare a salad. It has to be fresh.

Yves gives me a glance and heads down the path.

I light the gas oven and put in the food before selecting cutting boards and knives to cut vegetables for the salad. I rinse off the lettuce, and my eager eyes wander to the bottle of wine standing open on a small table by the couch where Edda's lying. It's Heiður's wine, not mine, and the French rascal said to wait. They're doing their own thing—he out in the wild, she in a huff in her room—while I work on making dinner for them and my indescribable daughter, who now has a sprained ankle on top of everything else, wrapped up by a French male nurse who could, for that matter, be a disguised member of Doctors Without Borders in search of Icelandic patients out on the road. I'm not heeding orders any longer. I'll have red wine when I feel like it.

Edda gapes at me as I fill my glass and asks: Didn't he say it should wait?

I don't take orders from foreigners.

Don't you find it inappropriate to drink alone like that?

It makes sense that you of all people should be concerned about other people's drinking habits.

Edda's surprised. She didn't expect an attack, because she's behaved herself so well for the past ten minutes, or longer. The usual pattern is that when the clouds break in Edda's behavior, I respond like a little wimp, slobbering and muttering meekly, *Good master*, in the most submissive spirit of an Icelandic pauper since stories began. Then I go to great lengths not to make any mistakes and comply with the wishes of this master, a scrawny red-haired teenager with filthy fingernails. The little foot-dryer slinks as quietly as possible through the apartment, but the master leaps on her when least expected, and stomps hard. *Stomp stomp.* Then the little floor-rag cries, heavy torrents of dishwater tears. Wherever they come from, after all the wringing done to her.

What got into you, Mom? Your howling like a fool made me hurt myself.

Hmm . . . Remember the time I hurt my knee very badly? I don't recall any particular sympathy then, least of all from the person who kicked me.

Edda looks at me like a priest looking at a sinner who's committed gross sacrilege, made obscene mockeries of the *Passion Hymns*, made mud pies in the baptismal font.

Well done. It takes initiative to remind her that she's hurt me. I raise my glass to her and take a drink.

I then decamp to the kitchen, where I take another sip. It's an excellent wine, and I can't for the life of me notice anything bad about it, even though it's traveled today. *Traveled.* This poor man is a dreadful sissy. What's he doing out on the road, in Iceland? He fits in much better with those mollycoddled vines of his and pretentious wine connoisseurs.

Damn, you can be a bitch, grouses Edda. Not a bit of sympathy even though I just hurt myself. I totally regret coming with you and that nutcase friend of yours. Ugh.

Settle down now, little Edda, and know your place. You couldn't have thought I'd continue to coddle you, considering how you've been behaving.

Eat shit, whore.

Heiður comes rushing out of the bedroom, a Fury in a short-sleeved T-shirt. Apparently she was trying to nap.

Would you mind shutting your damned mouths?, Heiður exclaims. What the hell is this ruckus supposed to mean? It's like being with a bunch of lunatics.

You're no better yourself, says Edda.

Do you know what you are? *You're a stupid, rude little girl who should be in an asylum.*

Don't talk to the child that way, Heiður. Are you losing it completely?
I say what I want. This is my house, and I'm the one who was silly enough to drive you. It would serve you right if I drove away and left you here.

The pleasure would be mine, says Edda.

You have no shame. You've ruined everything for your mom, and then you just lie on the couch and talk shit.

Don't go judging me and Edda. You understand nothing but violins and crystal glasses. You don't understand the lives of ordinary people.

Look at yourself. You're all torn up with jealousy and envy. You're seething with hatred for people who have a better life than you. No matter what I do for you, it's never good enough. You hate me because I managed to accomplish a small piece of what I wanted to accomplish, while you haven't managed a tiny sliver.

You're the snobbiest cunt I've ever met in my life, is heard from the couch. *Snobby cunt.* I'll bet you've never even let anyone in it. It's probably made of crystal and would shatter at a touch.

Heiður walks straight through the deck door, out to the car, and drives off. I keep cutting vegetables and take a sip of wine, listening to the sound of the engine fade away.

Then I feel like going out for a bit, so I put on my jacket, grab a chair, refill my wineglass, and sit out on the deck, glaring at the white giant before me. Peaks and ridges cast shadows on the vastness of the glacier from which they grow.

THE CLOUDLESS GLACIER CASTS SHADOWS ON ITSELF.

BATHED IN CREAMY YELLOW LIGHT.

The sun is singing on the glacier
the final August song
and tomorrow true autumn begins. September.

The evening cloud veils make mischief around the moon and obscure it.

The glacier and its time mean something to me. The glacier and time, and swans that honk, and the wide expanse, green patches in the shelter of the frozen expanse, beyond the irregularly braided net of the streams.

I belong to myself. This crowd is none of my business. I'll bring Edda east somehow, even if Heiður's gone south in a huff. I'll wait to see what happens next at Dýrfinna's for half a month, three weeks. I'll slip away, I'll write poetry, I'll go to school in Perpignan under the protective wing of Gabriel Axel. He's invited me often enough. Edda will have to stay in Andey or else perish. I'm my own person, I'll educate myself, I'll start another kind of life. It's much better to be dead than to live life as I've done in recent years. I always have an escape route to put an end to that hell. But it would be much better to abandon Edda, live for myself, and let her die if that's what she wants. People like that probably wish for nothing. They get caught in the evil net that the preacher speaks of, in an evil time, and can't move.

But then, apparently, miracles can happen. They break free, and feel afterward that it would be better to be dead than be back in the net.

I need to remember that there are children who have broken free of the net.

Although he's fearfully unreliable, God is still good to let me sit here and see the vault of the glacier draped in golden silk, paling beneath the violet-colored haze of the sky. He's good to allow me to see the light-red-and-blue string of clouds cut across the moon. I get to listen to the streams by myself, sit in an oasis in an evening breeze in steeply declining summer, not a house, not a person, not a car in sight. Instead, only a thrush, a spider, some geese preparing to leave, a blowfly, as I look out over wasteland that isn't empty. That's more than many get their entire lives. I must not take it for granted.

My plan is born. I'll go east and stop only briefly, but I don't say it out loud. It's called GIVING THE SLIP.

Are you going to keep running away, little Eisa?

You're one to talk, Mother dear. You were certainly a great one for escaping, too, in your time.

You don't know the first thing about it, says Mom, laughing vulgarly.

Put on something to keep warm now, Mom, you'll be chilled to the bone in your robe.

There's no such thing as a cold in the beyond.

Mom's voice becomes cloying, and she jabbers on in a sanctimonious tone that doesn't suit her at all: Luckily, the general state of health in the next life is extremely good. Modern diseases are unknown. No cancer or osteoporosis. Colds are unheard of, as is the flu. No one needs to blow his nose in the next life, which is a huge relief and amounts to considerable savings. What's strange is that sometimes there are incidences of obsolete diseases that the modern world has eliminated, such as black death, tuberculosis, and leprosy. Yet God has arranged things so that there will never be an epidemic on the astral plane. The poor souls who are struck so awfully receive extremely good care and a great deal of attention from the highest levels. And by that I mean the *highest* levels.

Mom, you're not playing with a full deck. But come on. I really want to know. Who is my father?

You know the answer.

The time really has come for you to lift this veil of lies under which I've been raised. Of course it's plain to everyone that I'm not Axelsdóttir.

Mom laughs singularly waggish, smoky laughter: You couldn't be Axelsdóttir?

Not unless I'm a mutant.

No one can predict when a mutation will occur. It's a scientific fact. All sorts of things are born under the sun.

Mom starts coughing and tries to suppress it by trying to light a Pall Mall that she fishes out of her bathrobe pocket. But it won't light out on the deck.

We'll have to go inside to light my cigarette, she says.

Damn, you're crafty, Mom, trying to weasel your way into the house.

Well then, girl, stand here and block the wind for me.

I do as she says, so she's able to light her cigarette and suppress her cough.

Mom, your lungs are no good. You should have them checked.

It doesn't really matter, things being as they are, she says, in a martyr-like tone.

Do people really go on feeling sorry for themselves in the next life?

Self-pity is the most persistent emotion. It's not so strange. It's no good to be born and baptized without having any choice in the matter, the way things are in this world. There's so much cruelty, and it really doesn't seem to be getting any better. When the official cruelty slackened for the most part, at least on the surface, when they stopped burning people at the stake, drowning them, and flogging them, private enterprise took over, and now people see to depriving each other of life, all by themselves, often in a horrendous manner. No, Harpa dear, we have no business being in the world.

Should we go and hang ourselves, then?

Wait until Axel's dead, as well.

All right, then.

I want some wine, too.

I won't get drunk with my mother.

Mom puffs, and the cigarette smoke swirls into rings. When I was a kid, I requested that Mama blow smoke rings. Those rings are one of the first things that I remember, how they vanished and were replaced by new ones. But somehow I managed to get the wrong idea in my head that smoke rings were called YEAR RINGS.

What about Edda, Mom? What should I do?

Mom wraps her bathrobe tighter around herself and creates more white rings with her fiery-red pouting lips. I don't know, Harpa dear.

How do you think it will turn out?

How am I supposed to know? Don't ask me. I'm no Prescient Finna.

Sit and watch with me, Mom. For once.

Now the moon hangs unfragmented over the violet edge of the glacier, a moon of white opal, with a pattern similar to the imprint of a coin rubbing.

I go in and shut the door behind me. An aroma wafts from the oven. Dinner will be ready soon. I look forward to eating. There'll be no more chopping vegetables for the time being. What I've already chopped is plenty for me. To eat alone after this damned day is a great mercy. I'm not going to bother about the monster with the elastic bandage. It can look after itself, this time.

I pour myself more wine. What do you know? Almost halfway through the bottle.

I take a seat on the couch and watch two ravens glide in unison down the slope above the cottage, down to the stream as if in search of something at the bottom. Maybe they use the stream as a refrigerator and keep eggs there, like Dad's raven at Höfðabrekka. Suddenly the two black creatures part company. One flies toward the sea, the other toward the glacier, croaking loudly in turn. I nod off. I dream that I'm wearing pointy-toed ankle boots with sugar skin; I bite into the toes and munch.

When I wake, dinner is ready. I've neglected to baste one side of the leg of lamb in the oven, but what does that matter when the chef will be the only one to taste it?

DELIGHTS FOR HER ALONE SHE'LL LAY
THE TRUE GOURMET
UPON HER TRAY

As if it's on fire, Hvannadalshnúkur, 6,952 feet high, flaming fuchsia.

Strange that one of the country's highest peaks, up in the middle of a glacier, should be named after a plant: Hvannadalur. Valley of Angelica. It's nice to imagine the glacier as fertile, bright, with a hint of green in its blue cracks. But there is fertility in the shelter of the glacier—lush vegetation and genuine glacial warmth—here in the wonderland of Skaftafell.

THE GLACIAL WARMTH.

The moon in the fuchsia haze has drawn in the color of the glacier. The mighty moon, jealous, with great attractive force, full, on the final August evening of the year.

I lay the table handsomely, cover it with a white tablecloth, place the leg of lamb in a porcelain dish decorated with embossed oranges. Five wagtails see to the dinner music on the deck railing.

The table is missing flowers, so I go out and pick dropwort, couch-grass blades, and forget-me-not, and arrange them in a square vase upon which fly royal-blue English butterflies.

I've done an excellent job with the food. I'm a gourmet chef. There's no denying it.

Redwings, the best singers of all the birds, have taken over from the wagtails, and reel off Renaissance trills to accompany the one-person wilderness banquet.

Doesn't the birthday girl get anything to eat?

Oh, poor soul, it's your birthday today. Have a seat, then.

Submissively, Mom sits down opposite me, and I get a plate, knife, fork, and glass for her. I slice meat, dish out potatoes, pour wine.

It would even have been a decade birthday. How dreary.

Don't you find it immensely tiresome in the next life, Mom?

No more than in life itself.

You poor thing. Why was everything always like that with you?

I think it's congenital. Just look at my sister Dýrfinna. She was born under a lucky star.

But she's the one who lost her child, even though you were always going on about it, acting as if it were you.

Unnar was one of a kind. That's for sure.

You haven't changed, Mom.

Why should I have done that?

Couldn't you try a bit of watching over me as I sleep?

I'm hardly in any position to do that, my dear. I fall asleep so early in the evenings.

Okay, Mom. I'm certainly no better myself.

Have you completely lost it?, Edda asks. Talking to yourself like who knows what.

I was waiting for you to come eat. Come on, I've sliced you some lamb.

You forgot to call me.

I called you. You just didn't hear.

You were talking to yourself. You said *Mom*.

You were hearing things. Now sit down and eat before it gets cold.

Can I have the wine in this glass?

Go ahead. How's your foot?

It hurts a bit, but I fell asleep.

That's good.

They're not coming back?

I don't know. If they do, they'd better come soon. It's getting dark.

Would you be scared to be out here tonight, just the two of us, Mom?

No, I'm not scared now. I'm preoccupied.

Should I maybe apologize to her if she comes back?

That's the least you could do.

You were ugly to her, too.

I know, Edda. We both have a problem on our hands.

I can't stand that snob, Mom. She thinks she's so great because she can blow that fucking flute of hers. Let me tell you, I was this close not to making this trip with you when you told me she was going to drive. She's a pest. But I guess I can still apologize.

We really owe her that, I say. You know, she's actually a really nice person. Maybe a bit sharp sometimes, which I'll admit can be a bit much.

She's always gotten on my nerves.

That's not entirely true. Remember when you were little and she never failed to bring you back something beautiful every time she went overseas? Heiður was always good to you, and patient if you were naughty. Remember how she babysat you sometimes when I had to go somewhere?

I don't want to think about how I was as a kid.

Maybe you should do it more often. Good memories can be very constructive. You had lots of good times, and we had lots of them together. Out east, for example.

I know that, Mom, but sometimes I feel like it never happened. When I think of something fun from my childhood, I have doubts about it. Like it never really happened. Why is that?

Maybe because the bad things that have happened in the meantime are overshadowing the good things. Think of it this way—every person is made up of memories, good and bad. It's better for us, and wiser, to put emphasis on remembering what was good. Of course, we shouldn't be unrealistic and ignore the bad that's happened. We should deal with it, but then we should pack it away and leave it there. Bad memories can do serious damage if we use them against ourselves, if we let them tear us down. We've got to avoid that, above all.

God, you're so pompous.

I think you understand me completely.

Edda stands up and roots in a drawer, finds two violet block candles, places them on a glass plate, and lights them.

This food is good.

Thanks.

Do you think they'll come back?

If they're not back before it's completely dark, they probably won't come. Here, have some more.

Edda helps herself to more meat and gratin. I pour more wine into my glass, see that Edda's watching, pretend not to notice, take a sip—a laid-back gal in her thirties, chilling out.

I'm never going to panic again. I'm going to stand firm as a rock and never stir, ready for the worst. The worst that can happen is for Edda to perish, but I'm prepared for it. If it happens, I'm going to be able to say I did everything in my power to prevent it. I'm also going to live my own life. I still don't know how I'm going to do it, but I'll do it. I *will*.

I won't let myself be weighed down by a load of dreams, like Mom. Yet I mustn't be DREAMLESS.

I'll keep things separate. Distance them sufficiently. DIFFERENTIATE. Intelligence lies in differentiation.

No one lives his own life, Eisa dear. Desire exists independently, and it blocks everything called life.

How do you know what I desire, Mom?

I have my connections.

Have you started talking to yourself again, Mom?, Edda asks.

Oh, do you think? I didn't notice.

Edda laughs the innocent laughter of a little girl.

The silence of the wilderness replaces Edda's laughter, the silence that's not silence but an intrusive thrum. Right now I'd prefer the babbling streams and gurgling springs of the east.

TO THE EAST OF THE SUN. My dream valley, at the end of a long fjord. It's scarcely imaginable.

Mom, what was up with that man who drove you home from the supermarket that time?

Nothing.

Oh, yes there was. You've seen him since.

Hardly.

Is it that you can't forget him?

I don't need to forget him.

Is he married with children?

Yes.

You shouldn't have anything to do with a married man.

Hmm. There's so much that one should have nothing to do with.

And I glare at the girl, who's still grinning.

Wasn't he also married, that doctor who was sneaking around Bollagata?

Let's not get into that.

I don't think that man was good for you, Mom.

He didn't finish me off.

Oh, listen.

Yes, it must be them.

Man, I just wish we could have been left alone.

We will be, Edda dear. The night's almost over. You can retire whenever you want.

Retire. You talk to me like I'm a senile princess. But I might very well go to my room, just so I don't have to apologize to that pushy snob until tomorrow.

Have it your way, dear.

The girl gets up, thanks me politely for dinner, and disappears into her room, locking the door behind her.

Locks her door. What's that supposed to mean?

I'm not going to speculate.

I want to disappear too—into my tower, up into the twilight that slowly comes down over the earth, the tightly woven net with invisible mesh that captures waking souls and glides with them back and forth until they lose consciousness. *The Sleep Dance of the Soul.* The dance of all souls.

I wish I were invited to that dance now. It irks me to have to stay up to chat with someone I'll never see again. I need peace and quiet to think about one thing and another, peace and quiet to digest Edda's latest about-face. She transformed into a real person for five minutes, a reverse changeling who gives her mother advice about private matters. When the world united against us, she was able to ask about my affairs. *For or against*, that is the question. When the world is against Edda and me, Edda stands with me. When Edda stands with me, Heiður turns against me.

I drag myself out onto the deck for the sake of appearances and wave cheerfully, damned hypocrite that I am. Heiður and Yves come running like a new couple in the twilight, he with his recovered backpack, and she with a bouquet of willow branches, buttercups, and long blades of grass. She hops long-shanked up the steps to the deck, hands me the bouquet, and asks if we can be friends again.

I should apologize, and Edda too.

I'm worried about the child's foul language, says Heiður.

Leave the worrying to me.

Yves putters about with his backpack in a corner of the living room pretending not to hear. How much does he know by now? A thing or two, to be sure. Discretion has never been one of Heiður's gifts. How nice to have your entire life broadcast by your best friend. It's fortunate that she spends so much time abroad. I wouldn't be surprised if during their brief outing Yves gained a huge amount of knowledge about me and my zany little life.

Yves and I picked berries, says Heiður, waving a plastic bag. We can have blueberry crumble topped with whipped cream, an incredibly appropriate dessert for a summer cottage.

Dinner got cold while you were picking berries.

Sorry. I see you two have eaten.

No need to apologize. I'll just warm it up.

I have no idea how I can be so disgustingly yielding. Where did I learn it? Have I always been like that? Of course these people should warm up their own dinners, but naturally, I feel guilty, because I dishonored my savior with help from my rude daughter, driving my savior away. The least I could do was try to make up for it by warming the dinner I cooked, for her and this foreigner.

Heiður lights the candles in the multiarmed chandelier of forged iron over the dinner table and then lights two oil lamps hanging on the walls, resembling a ship's lanterns.

One bright star has appeared over the tower, and it's twinkling as if it's playing a prank, though I don't really get the joke. I know—maybe it wants to shine back at the lights we've lit inside. The cottage is changing into an illuminated elf-city. If only I were in a good mood and could appreciate it, instead of fumbling with lighting the oven and reheating dinner for a complete outsider.

How can I help?, asks Yves softly, uncontrollably French and obliging as I crouch by the oven, my behind sticking out.

You could clear the dirty dishes from the table, and when that's done you can wash the berries. How about that?

Very good.

The tourist puts his all into clearing and resetting the table neatly, all the while gazing with his foreign eyes at the bottle of red wine, but of course he says nothing. My friend, on the other hand, has noticed it in a flash, the old scanner, because she grabs a new bottle, this time from her parents' wine cabinet, and uncorks it. She utters not a word about the wine consumption of her little friend. This sophisticated daughter of the stately benefactress, Saga Kaaber, knows better than to make comments.

Yves is now at the sink, cleaning the berries. Has this nasty catfight been resolved thanks to berry picking? Heiður had driven off alone, badly offended. Where'd she been headed? To Reykjavík, of course. But she returned before dark and started picking berries, just like that.

Berrying berrying
the ogress is away from home.

Her huff is finished. No, never finished—it's there somewhere, waiting to be utilized at the right opportunity. The words that were uttered aren't like snow, which melts. For the rest of my life the ugly thing I said will be remembered. But what Heiður said about my hatred won't melt away either. It'll be stored in my memory like hard stone. It might become a bit weathered, but it'll never disappear.

Now Heiður's sitting on the couch with her legs up, sipping red wine. After all that driving, she certainly deserves to take a break.

Then I bring dinner to the table like a little waitress, fetch napkins, tell the two of them to take a seat, and serve them an expanded and improved salad.

Man, this looks unbelievably delicious, says Heiður.

Oh, you think so?

Please join us, says the Frenchman.

I need to whip cream for the berries.

Allow me to do that afterward, says Yves.

I give him a wondrously feminine smile and make no objection, but I go out onto the deck and take cream from the cooler, find the necessary utensils, and turn my back on the pair as the mixer spins by the substantial strength of my assistant nurse's hands. They chat like a little couple.

How I wish I weren't doing this. But for the single mother of a delinquent child, life doesn't even offer the luxury of going to bed early—not even after a difficult day of fits of tears and vomiting and conflict and fleeing from petty criminals on the highway. If I go to bed now, it would be taken in the worst way. Maybe I'll do it anyway. I'll simply wait for the jolly giggles of the little berry-picking duo to subside.

I put the whipped cream in an elegant bowl that looks as if it's made of stained glass, like a church window from the Middle Ages, sprinkle nutmeg over it, and lay a silver spoon next to it. Then I go to the bathroom to kill time, so that I don't have to carry on a conversation. A ferocious teenager, a French tourist, and a terribly pushy flutist: what company for an ordinary person who toils the year round, on duty caring for the sick and the dying.

Not even the bathroom is a refuge from the jollity of my dinner guests, with whom I don't deign to sit down at the table. Nor are they free of me and my ramblings, because I keep running into one thing and another in the darkness. The dim light from the candle on the sink creates a peculiar ambience here among the deep-blue bathroom furnishings and rococo faucets, in a fluffy forest of thick red towels and frotté bathrobes with big hoods. In this light, even in honest-to-goodness daylight, this could be the dressing room of a new type of pervert.

Only now do I glimpse a flashlight, placed at the end of a marble shelf by the mirror above the sink. I take great pains putting on lipstick by the gleam of the flashlight, ghostly shadows under my eyes. Finally, I'm in the mirror, I who haven't been there, despite my looking.

Would you mind lending me your lipstick?

This one's metallic, brownish pink. It's not your color, Mom. You always wear bright red.

Let me try it, dear. Maybe it'll suit me.

I give in to Mom's nagging, and she applies lipstick like a happy institutionalized woman, and I remark that she should have discovered this color earlier because it suits her very nicely.

I can see that.

It's good to have a color analysis done, Mom.

I don't know what that is, dear.

No, I'm not surprised. It had hardly come into fashion.

It wouldn't be worthwhile doing such a thing here. We're all so clear, sort of.

No way I'm going back out there yet. I'll take a shower. Why didn't I think of that before? Take my time, shower by flashlight and candlelight. That's original. Kill two birds with one stone: wash off the journey's grime and avoid the oppressive company.

Hot water warms me deep inside, to the roots of my heart. Rich scents reach me through the steam—sandalwood soaps and high-end shampoo from Guerlain, fragrances from another world.

In the shower, the middle part of my bare body is illuminated by the atmospheric light: an elf woman's abdomen, a mermaid's breasts, a changeling's thighs. I feel sorry for this utilitarian body, for how so few hands have run over it lately, and for how seldom it's been in the spotlight of other eyes besides mine in recent years. No hands to stroke it but my own when I wash myself, and life is short. If it continues like this, I'll return to the state of a pristine maiden very, very soon, swiftly and surely, and no one will even notice.

He isn't likely to prevent it, my lover who moved to the west.

This entire night I'll dream of him, of the night we made love in so many ways.

There's certainly an abundance of fragrant ointments here— Heavenly Violet's a corny name, completely unsuitable in the shadowy luxury of a bathroom off the beaten path, but the smell of the ointment isn't in harmony with its name. It's terribly seductive, and I take no fewer than five minutes to smear it on, before putting on the biggest and reddest frotté bathrobe that I've ever seen, without a clue as to what sort of chieftain it's intended for, because everyone in Heiður's family is medium-sized. Around my head I wrap a matching towel, creating an enormous red turban, and go out. These people will just have to deal with it.

Come and have dessert, Harpa Eir, invites Heiður, as soon as she hears me.

I walk barefoot into the room and watch how Yves from Bordeaux moves in the flickering candlelight as his cook appears, wearing nothing underneath her robe. The bathrobe wraps one and a half times around little Harpa, and it's not easy to say how a man will take such a getup.

I sit and wiggle my piggy-pink toes and keep my trap tightly shut.

Heiður stands up to get a bowl and spoon for me. That can be classified as an unexpected occurrence. Yves is nervous and doesn't know what to say. I enjoy staring emptily at him, without a smile, enhancing my silence, then eating blueberries as if I've made an art form out of chewing every little berry a hundred times. In between, I put a dollop of cream on the spoon and lick it slowly.

I hope he sees me in the same light as he would have this morning—the woman who stuck out her long tongue in Selfoss.

Yves clears his throat awkwardly, and Heiður starts asking about his trip, in order to say something. These are topics that we've already been through, and I play the ugly trick of letting loose a big yawn.

After answering one of the questions, Yves gets up and goes to the bathroom. I hope my underwear will amaze him, hanging there on a hook, mysteriously illuminated. PANTIES IN MOONLIGHT. That's a fitting sight for interlopers.

I munch loudly on stupid blueberries, decide to get out of here, stand up and bid Heiður good night, and ask her to say good night to Yves. She replies as if all is normal. I pick up one of the violet candles that Edda lit. Heiður offers me a flashlight, which I decline, saying that the stars and moon will provide more than enough light in the tower.

Yves bumps into me at the foot of the spiral staircase. I allow myself the luxury of smiling, though I'm skeptical of how it comes out in the ghostly gleam of the flashlight that he points at my face.

In the tower I breathe light as a feather, all alone with the heavenly bodies, the east wind, the constant murmur of the streams. There are no bedclothes here, but I'd hate to go down to fetch woolen blankets. I lie down on the mattress and wrap the robe tighter around me. I take the towel turban off my head and use it for a pillow. I don't remember having gone to sleep with wet hair since I was a kid. It'll be quite the sight tomorrow. Fuck it. From here on, I'm done with all vanity. It takes too much time. Who the hell would I be dressing up for, anyway?

I blow out the candle that Edda lit for me earlier this evening and I think of her lighting two candles as a hope for hope. One candle for me and the other for her.

There are no doors to my sleep tower. If someone wants to come to me, he can do it directly, without opening a door or closing one after him when he leaves.

Like sleeping outside beneath a warm sky.

I no longer look up into the firmament but pull the red frotté canopy over my head, a nomad of the steppe, and start to glide into the dance of sleep. Slowly, among the stars.

Inviting the man who occupies my mind.

A burst of laughter from the depths of the living room. The cheerful berry pickers are washing the dishes and arranging the pots and pans.

My sleep-intoxicated soul is dancing back into the fine-meshed net of oblivion when I hear a tramping on the stairs, and I sense that he who moved west has found his way all the way to me.

Heiður shines her flashlight into the room. She's hooked the fingers of her other hand around two glasses and a bag, whose contents I'm sure of immediately.

More alcohol— yippee, I say, propping myself on my elbow.

This wretch of a Frenchman is completely useless when it comes to drinking, she says.

I wonder if he's useful for something else.

It wouldn't surprise me. You should take this opportunity.

Are you afraid I have a long, lonely winter ahead of me?

It's hard to say. Better a bird in hand than two in the bush.

I've never understood before how indecent that saying is.

Heiður laughs and pours us wine.

Harpa, I really need to apologize for what I said to you and Edda.

Not unless you forgive me in return. Actually, I've never really understood forgiveness. I don't think it exists. Someone does something to you, and you either remember it or forget it. I understand how people can let sleeping dogs lie, avoid rummaging around in old offenses, ignore things. Anything beyond that, I don't understand. Do you really feel I'm torn up with jealousy and hatred?

Oh, I don't know, I just said that. Of course it upsets you to think that you haven't done enough of what you wanted to do.

It *is* true that I envy you. It's unfair of me. You haven't done anything to deserve it. But I do anyway. I can't help it.

Jealousy is such a common feeling that it doesn't pay to worry about it.

Funny thing for you to say. You don't have it in you.

Of course I do. You just don't notice it.

Not as much as most.

I was always lucky, so I had no reason to be jealous. I can become awfully jealous if someone plays the flute better than me. But my admiration is stronger, as well as the sly certainty that I could beat them next time just by changing one small thing or another. Even when a master plays, I know that I can play at least one or two lines better than they can.

That's because *you're* a master. But when I see you play the flute like an angel, it makes me feel horrible that I don't know anything except how to make a fucking bed.

Stop torturing yourself, says Heiður. You have lots of talent. You can write—you have a gift for languages—but it was your choice to let your kid take priority.

I never chose anything. I just did what I had to do. We both know, Heiður dear, that all this talk about freedom of choice is more or less nonsense. If you wind up in a bad enough situation, there's no freedom. After I had Edda, there was no way out for me.

Wait a minute.

Mom wasn't about to quit her job at the Marine Research Institute. Looking back, I think she did the right thing. I didn't really want her helping me take care of the girl anyway.

You still haven't stopped blaming others for your failures? You're in your thirties.

I'm not blaming Mom for my pregnancy. Then again, maybe it was her fault, in fact.

Well, that's certainly an original way of looking at things.

Real mothers protect their daughters from becoming pregnant at fifteen years old.

Come on, Harpa. Everyone who does it runs the risk of becoming pregnant, until they reach menopause. No protection is one hundred percent.

Mothers who are whores deep-down make their daughters vulnerable.

Whores deep-down? Seriously? How deep is it to our inner whores, do you think?

Mom was a different sort of whore. She ruined things for people, and still does.

Man, I can't believe how much you pity yourself.

No one else will pity me. You know, Heiður, a girl who has a child when she's sixteen never recovers. Something in her dies when the child is born.

You mean she stops aging.

Thanks for the compliment.

That wasn't what I meant.

Something died in me when Edda was born. Not like leaves in autumn, but forever, amen.

Not a single damn thing died. You just say that because you like the way it sounds.

No, I mean it. When a child has a child, the child in the mother dies.

It's supposed to die. People are supposed to grow up.

Those who don't preserve something of the child in them are damaged.

You've never said anything like this before. You were so happy with your little girl.

I've never said anything like this before because I didn't want to admit it. And I'll admit that I was also happy on some level. Your hormones ensure that you raise the child, that you fall in love with your little one, that you'd rather die than let anything happen to your child. But that doesn't change the fact that the soul slowly perishes while a little vampire sucks the milk from a mother who's only a suckling infant herself. It's actually disgusting.

Stop it now, really. Your little family was beautiful.

Maybe it looked beautiful from the outside. But beyond all else, it was barbarous.

When did you start thinking like that?

I think I always have. I only just realized it. Once I decided to spend the winter out east, I started reconsidering my position thoroughly, and that's when it came to me. I'm not saying that I have no good memories of Edda and me when she was a child. I have many wonderful ones and I try to keep them clean and polished, but that doesn't change the fact that bearing a child at such a young age amounts to murder.

I think you're just testing out this theory on me. Because it's so dreadful.

Think what you want.

If it was as murderous as you say, it must have also seeped into the girl.

How so? The terrible shape she's in is due to her mother thinking such ugly things? I suppose it would be best to accept the blame for that as well. Clearly, I contaminated her so much with my thoughts that she went straight to the dogs. It'd be extremely practical to take the entire package of sin upon myself. Then there'd be no need to worry about it anymore.

You already play that game, by blaming your mother. So you shouldn't be surprised if Edda were to blame you for a few things.

Poor Mom was no ordinary case. Remember how she tormented me when it turned out that I was pregnant?

I know she wanted you to have an abortion, but isn't it exaggerating a bit to say that she tormented you?

It wasn't a polite exchange of opinion. She was like one of the Furies making her demands. She wouldn't hear of any other arrangement. She just droned on and on. Get an abortion.

Of course it wasn't pretty.

Definitely not.

Maybe you should have done what she said.

Don't you remember? I was queasy at the very thought. I didn't dare. Those were different times. And poor you, as much a child as I was—you kept trying to convince me that having an abortion done wasn't so horrible. Women had undergone such things throughout the ages. I probably would have done it if my fool of a mother wasn't being so hard on me. She put me into total defiance mode by reacting so vehemently. As if the fetus belonged to her. It's *Mom's* fault that I did nothing. If I had, I might be a famous scientist or famous poet by now, or on my way to becoming one. But now it's absolutely guaranteed that I'll never amount to anything. And just look at the child—she would have been better unborn.

But this trip could change that!

You know what I really think I would do if I could start over? Be alone—from the very beginning, all of my life. That's best by far. *That's* what's worth striving for. Flirt with boys to start with, but then remain a virgin until death. Never let anyone see you naked, except for health care workers, if necessary. Have yourself to yourself, body and soul. No goddamn intimacy, which can never last. Live for yourself and remember that that's how you benefit others best. Have crushes on many, but fall in love with no one, at least not with a feeling close to madness. To be blinded with adoration for someone: what a horror. You should be able to see the light and the other person at the same time. Celibacy is infinitely beautiful. You're free from other people's grumbling, bodily noises, diseases, and defects. You can cultivate your own character flaws undisturbed or try to scrape them off, as you please, and it's no one's business but your own. People who live alone with no descendants can be good to everyone, because their dealings with others are relatively few. Those who have families, even if it's just one child, will inevitably behave badly at times. Shadows will fall on their relationships. Those who live alone can say with conviction when they die that shadows never fell on their relationships with others. Except of course on their relationships with their father, mother, and siblings, but that was so long ago that it doesn't matter anymore.

I wish I'd been a beautiful bachelorette, who charmed loads of people, but was a problem to none. I would have liked to have had a well-rounded education, worked in a fun place, written poetry in the evenings and on weekends, taken long trips out into the wilderness, hiked in the highlands, had a living room with Chinese lacquered screens and two big palm trees and an antique porcelain vase from the Ming dynasty, a view of Snæfellsjökull, a beautiful garden with a variety of species that aren't supposed to be able to grow in Iceland. I would have liked to have been mentally and physically fit, tranquil, to have possessed inner calm, alert and reflective, to have published my first book on my sixtieth birthday, a very long poem that was so amazing that nothing like it had ever been seen, then retired, lived off a decent pension, written when I was in the mood and done some gardening in between, gotten to know lots of other interesting people, died peacefully at around eighty in my own bed, been a smiling, brainy old female corpse, harmless as a lamb, with five pages of obituaries in *Morgunblaðið*, two of which were from wizened admirers who had to use magnifying glasses to write and recalled me as a slightly shy twenty-year-old with long legs and ash-blonde hair.

Won't you even allow yourself to look like you do?

A dark-brown Icelandic dwarf. Would you be pleased to be that? Come on. As beautiful as you are. You just make me angry.

I have a look that people find okay on others, but they'd rather die than have themselves. My fate would have been completely different if I'd been tall and blonde. It's so ridiculous that people's success in life depends simply on how they look. What do you think becomes of a little coffee-brown round-faced woman with wild curls who supposedly comes from thoroughly Icelandic parents? It isn't pretty, Heiður. You've got to admit that.

Are you still obsessed with your misattributed paternity?

Do you seriously think that Axel is my dad?

The way you look doesn't prove anything. All sorts of things are born under the sun.

If anyone knows the truth, it's Aunt Dýrfinna. I'm going to ask her when I'm out east.

You're not in your right mind. I know what's wrong with you. This situation with Edda has twisted up everything in your head.

I've always looked like a freak. It has nothing to do with Edda.

You may as well ask Dýrfinna, I suppose. But I think it's highly unlikely that she'll tell you anything.

If anyone knows what happened, it's her.

It's completely obvious what happened. Your father and mother slept together, creating you.

No kidding. But what father, my dear? That's the question. What father?

Poor Axel. If he only knew what you're thinking.

He doesn't need to know.

Have you ever talked about it with him?

Are you nuts?

Uff, it's all just your imagination.

My father and I bear absolutely no resemblance. Not a bump, not a stump of a finger, not a fragment of a tooth. I've always suspected that something wasn't quite right.

Always suspected? You were at least fourteen years old before you mentioned it to me.

The suspicion was always lurking, but I don't think that children spell out such things to themselves. What's strange is that when I had Edda, I knew that Dad couldn't be my father. I have no idea why I saw it so clearly then. But that's how it was. As the girl grew up, it also became clear that there was no resemblance whatsoever between her and her grandfather, either.

Is this supposed to be a joke? You and Edda look so different that strangers thinks *I'm* her mother. Yves thought so, just today.

There are still one or two resemblances between Edda and myself, if you look closely. The lips, for example. The bone structure of our faces.

You forget how similar you and your dad are, in your mannerisms and ways of speaking.

Anything else would be a pure miracle. I was raised by the man, and we've always been very close.

Harpa dear, does it matter at all? Even if you weren't his daughter, would that change anything? He's the best dad in the world, as you yourself say. What more do you want?

You can't understand something like this unless you've experienced it. Everyone wants to know where they come from. It's a law of nature. It's a psychological necessity.

There must be plenty of children whose paternity is wrongly attributed who never suspect anything.

The suspicion is the key, Heiður. That's what it's all about. As soon as you start having suspicions, you can never go back. Still, if Dýrfinna tells me I'm totally on the wrong track, then I might be able to drop it. She wouldn't lie to me. It's good to be sure of that.

Just ask her then, Harpa. Although I think it's a waste of time. Absolutely nothing will come of it. So be prepared.

No need for us to quarrel. In twenty-four hours I'll get some answers.

And what if you don't like the answers you get? Wouldn't you be worse off?

I'd just have to accept it.

Do you want to go to sleep, Harpa?

I was almost asleep when you came up, dear.

Sorry.

No. I'm glad you came. I had a secret desire for more wine, anyway. Cheers.

Thanks for coming. Sleep tight.

You too.

I listen to Heiður's footsteps sounding in the silence as I lie down again on the mattress beneath the moon wading in clouds.

It's gloomy in my sleep-tower now. Both solace and terror lurk in the gloom.

The soft net of sleep is closing around me, hovering just above the tower floor.

But the merciless earth draws me in once more. This time I'm forced to drag myself downstairs to go to the bathroom, giddy and half-blind in the darkness. I'm fortunate not to stumble and fall like Edda.

Yves is still up, reading by flashlight.

I act as if I don't see him. As if he doesn't exist.

I bump into one thing and another before I find the flashlight in the bathroom. My panties are still on the hook. Best to leave them there.

On the way back, I head straight for the spiral staircase, but I change my mind, walk over to the man from Bordeaux, and ask if he can't sleep.

I can hardly bring myself to sleep, he says, it's so incredible here. And you?

I was talking to Heiður.

Did you solve the mystery of life?, he asks, smiling his beaming-wide boyish smile.

No, we made the mystery of life more complicated than ever, and now my greatest wish is that I'd never been born, I say with a laugh, as a precaution.

I know it's difficult for you, says Yves.

He closes his book and moves closer to the wall to make room. I feel it's going a bit too far to sit down on the bed next to him, and instead pull a folding chair over to the couch. Yves is wearing a white T-shirt. His skin is dark brown, and he has enormously developed arm muscles.

Do you still live in Bordeaux?

I'm at the university in Lyon, but I go home when I can.

What was it like growing up in Bordeaux?

How so?

I want to know how it was to be a kid there, because it seems so different from everything I've experienced.

My father is a manager at a vineyard. I got to be with him out in the fields when he was working and supervising, and in autumn I always took part in the grape harvests when I could—mostly on weekends, because I was in school.

And the weather was always good?

Almost always. I'm not surprised you ask, living in this atrocious climate. I don't think I'd have come hitchhiking here if I'd known just how abominably windy it is.

Yves laughs an infectious laugh, which seems oddly crude in contrast to the rest of his demeanor.

You came a bit late. It's much better in July than at the end of August.

You mean the beginning of September, says Yves, looking at his watch.

Were you allowed to eat as many grapes as you liked off the vines?

Yes, of course. Yves laughs again.

Grapes were a luxury when I was growing up.

Without grapes there's no life, says Yves, earnestly.

Is that a saying?

No, it's just the way it is, he says, almost sternly.

What did you do on your summer vacations?

We went to the beach quite often—there are long sandy beaches close-by—and we made frequent trips to the forest. Sometimes we drove down to Spain or Portugal and stayed for several weeks. Once we went down to Morocco. Two summers we were in Corsica, and we spent one in northern Italy, in Tuscany. It's my favorite place in the world.

You never went north, to England?

We only went there once. We thought it was hopeless. The food was bad, the weather awful, and we could hardly make ourselves intelligible to the natives.

Really? I found it wonderful the one and only time I went there.

It's better than here, of course, he blurts out, before hurriedly asking, in order to cover up his mistake: What did *you* do for summer vacation when you were a kid?

I spent most of my time in the Eastfjords. My mother comes from there. It's like a foreign country in Iceland, with different weather, different people. In fact that's where I'm going now, with my girl.

But this trip is completely different than usual. This is the first time I've ever gone to the Eastfjords in autumn. Before, I always went in the spring, and I always looked forward to it so much. Now I'm running away, because my daughter's been keeping such bad company. It's as if everything has turned inside out. My dream place has become a place for nightmares.

Please don't think like that. Don't forget how curious life is—a simple step like moving can change everything. It doesn't mean that I believe absolutely in a new life, either in this lifetime or another. But I do believe in finding yourself. I know that it's possible to lose yourself, and also that it's possible to find yourself.

How old are you?

Twenty-five.

Do you really think you're old enough to talk about this?

I wouldn't say such things if I didn't think them.

Why don't you ask how old I am?

Yves smiles, sits up straight, swings his legs over the edge of the bed, and looks straight at me.

I don't need to ask. I can see you're not old.

He's wearing silk boxer shorts, incredibly gaudy, with wild orchids and all sorts of tropical birds and endangered fish that flit between jungle flowers with flicks of their tails. It's logical for his large and imposing thighs to be wrapped in such material, and his supple legs appear as if they're about to swing themselves up into a tree in the rain forest or dive in a gorgeous arc off a coral reef in the Pacific. It's a shame that this total beach-hunk, as Heiður and I might have called him in our youthful exuberance, shouldn't have been sauntering in the right environment instead of being bundled up in the wind on an Icelandic highway.

Upon closer examination, I notice that Yves looks Asian, probably Japanese. It's subtle, but there's something not entirely French about his eyes and cheekbones, his straight dark hair, even his olive skin. Nor is his manner entirely French, come to think of it. Yet another one with a false paternity?

Yves gets up and bends down to me on my folding chair. I'm given an innocent but on-target kiss on the mouth. Yves sits back down on his bed.

I want to tease him and tell him that I didn't manage to sleep with a Frenchman when I was in Perpignan, and now would be the ideal opportunity to make up for it. Chances are, though, that he wouldn't be able to take it, so I say instead: Have you seen the stars from my sky chamber?

No. I didn't know they were out.

If you stay awake long enough, the stars come out.

I lead Yves to the spiral staircase and up into the transparent tower that was going to be my private bedchamber this clear night between late summer and autumn.

I turn off the flashlight of my well-equipped traveler, yet we can still see each other in the gleam of the stars.

Icelandic stars certainly are bright.

No need for us to be ashamed of them.

Where are the northern lights?

They're usually later in the autumn.

What color are they?

Sea green or rosy red. If I had some rocks from the east, sawed in half, I could show you. On the inside, some of them are the same color as northern lights, and the veins in them twist and turn like the northern lights in the sky.

Yves puts his hand on mine and says: You should have been a poet.

That's just the way those rocks are. There's nothing poetic about it.

Yves lies down on the floor, on his back, and gazes at the firmament, where the stars sparkle, plump and perky, endowed with new life, far from the noise of the world and the city lights. I lie down on my side, close against him, and lay my hand on his chest. He tells me I'm wonderful, that he's never seen anyone more beautiful, never spoken to anyone so strange and amusing. I'm a heroine from the Icelandic sagas, a fairy-tale princess, with a Nefertiti mouth and nose. Never in his life had he expected to meet such a woman, in this northern hinterland, breasts as if taken from the Song of Songs, a body of glazed porcelain, movements like a gazelle.

He caresses my scarab and says that it lies on its front legs like a little sphinx. For a moment I think of telling him that one of his compatriots gave me the piece, but then I decide that it's none of his business. There's a great deal that's none of this outsider's business.

May I take it off?

If you remember to put it back on again. It's my good-luck charm, and I'd never want to lose it.

I want you completely naked, says my French lover, and he finds new things to say about my body once the scarab has crawled off.

It's a new experience to be loved with words, and I listen motionlessly, saying nothing in return. Odd to think how much of my life I've let go by without sleeping with anyone but Icelanders. I listen for a long time. When I start feeling bored with this delay, I inch my way toward his verbose mouth and dam the stream.

Yves is well on his way to unwrapping me from the frotté robe when I tell it like it is, how I shouldn't be offering myself for such a nighttime task because I'm out of practice. He laughs awkwardly. My admission makes him nervous, throws him a bit off balance. I try to make amends for my offense with tiny kisses zigzagging from his right thigh to his left nipple, my destination being his right ear, with a long stop at his neck. The kisses fall on good soil, and soon it feels as if time in the transparent tower is going at such a ripping pace that it's standing completely still. Years and centuries pass, and here in the tower the two of us sail on the most brilliant wind in the rushing waters of a second, the flood of a minute, the currents of an hour. No, we don't sail. It's the elements of time that creak and hammer around us, while our vessel lies anchored at the island of time, which is made of cloud veils, auroral coils, and sunbeams.

I'll be gone when you wake in the morning, says Yves.

Constellations are born high above our harmonious faces, a satellite sails lazily along, and a rising moon travels trodden paths toward the distant verge of day. This is a well-built house, a summer cottage to the max, and the floorboards don't creak. We play on the tower floor, both zestfully and placidly, and I whisper in his ear, incredibly softly.

You should have been a poet, says Yves once more.

I am one, I say, and he laughs, as expected.

Nothing disturbs us. The few sounds we hear are welcome to our ears. The whistling of streams flowing both forlorn and dangerous down along the sea of sand until the flooding ocean receives them, the tattletale tones of pink-footed geese in autumn moods, the farewell songs of birds I don't recognize, the protracted journeys of planes, and the twitter of the plover saying it has just come to land though it knows very well that's impossible.

Eventually, our bodies have played so much that drowsiness overcomes them and the *Sleep Dance of the Soul* takes over. I lean into his foreign heart, knowing that I must take good advantage of the short time I've been given to sleep tonight.

I float on a fiery-red wind blanket out beyond a little island in the middle of the Caribbean that I christen THE TRANSPARENT ISLAND, though it's made of the same material as islands in general and nothing can actually be seen through it. I'm naked, but next to me on the wind blanket is a big towel that I can grab should a merman come. I shut my eyes.

The man from Ísafjörður, my lover from the supermarket, didn't want to come with me into the sea. He waits for me in a hut on the broad white-sand beach. Columbus is known to have come ashore here. The seafarer's prostitutes resided in a tower that's now in ruins, Maggie's Tower, on a hill that conveniently divides the beach. A group of finely shaped native boys is playing football, and I realize that the supermarket man is bored, that, having grown hungry, he awaits me inside the hut with a giant coral-red lobster and melons that are red on the inside. I swim to land, leaving the wind blanket to sail its own seas. It shouldn't really be possible to glide in water, yet I do, having grown modest in my swimsuit and finding it better not to be naked any longer when I come to the beach, since there are strange boys there. The wind blanket is on its way out to the horizon, and I catch just a glimpse of a red spot. The man who went west welcomes me with a towel fit for a queen-sized bed. Strange to see this white Icelandic male so tanned. How well built he is. The soccer boys' bursts of laughter are silenced. They're sitting in the warm sand.

The cutlery drawer slams. There's a clinking of spoons and knives. In other words: *Wake up!*

I stretch out my hand, and he's gone. I pull a blanket over my head, the blanket that Yves must have brought from downstairs, after I'd fallen asleep, and spread carefully over me in farewell, because I was wrapped in it from head to toe. BLANKET MUMMY IN SKY CHAMBER 1B.

As I lie there in my down-blanket hut, I sense that the weather isn't normal. There's something about the light that doesn't fit. When I opened my eyes earlier, there was a strange half-light resembling twilight, though it was morning already. One star was just barely visible. A fog star.

Plates are tossed onto the table.

Get up!, shouts Heiður.

I'm coming.

In other words: the day has begun. Wake up, all the way.

But I didn't sleep enough. Took on too big of a task.

Dreaming of someone other than the one who's just left.

My dreams revolve around another besides the newly departed.

My dreams revolve around another who went all the way west.

That's how it should be.

The supermarket man who privately called me *the foreign girl* when we were kids was standing by the bookcase when I came back to the living room carrying a boiling hot coffeepot. He was holding a French-language cookbook, about dishes from Provence.

I prepared to answer the question of whether I knew French, but I didn't know the man well enough to realize that he usually takes his opponents by surprise, a trait he has in common with mischievous girls like Edda Sólveig. He's had an astronomical premonition and he asks whether I write.

I'm terribly lazy about writing letters.

I meant fiction.

You rascal, how dare you. I say: I recite ballads to patients at work.

Then it happens. A mighty crash. I had put down the hot espresso pot on a little triangular glass table beside the couch. At the first sound, I don't know what's happening. Then the noise intensifies and the glass plate splits along its entire length with a resounding crack. It now looks like an icy puddle after being hit with a stone, fissures branching everywhere.

This is a godsend. The man's thrown off balance and can't continue with his interrogation. I hope he'll just go home.

Can you get tables like this someplace?

How sympathetic he is about this silly, idiotic, ridiculous accident that nobody except Harpa Eir could have caused.

I hope not.

Oh?

It was an ugly little table.

He stares at the broken monstrosity, which is actually more beautiful all cracked. I could put it on display as an art object, giving it various titles. How about: LOOK HOMEWARD, ANGEL.

Too bad I'd just brought the coffee. Now it'll be impossible to get the supermarket guy off my hands, swiftly and surely. I'm almost inclined to turn off the Jacques Brel as a sign that the conversation's over, as a sign that I shouldn't have accepted a ride in his noble SUV.

A new godsend. The doorbell. It's Edda Sólveig. No one but Edda rings the doorbell like that. I see that the Range Rover man is taken aback, yet again, just as if he'd been caught in the act. Maybe it is being caught in the act, on his sensitive bookkeeping scale.

The man tries to conceal his astonishment when a teenager walks into the room, a lanky girl, bad tempered, and slightly shabby-looking. Yet you've got to give it to her. She takes the visitor's hand and introduces herself. And he actually stands up to greet her but neglects to say his name. It's a wonderful joke. Who knows, maybe he's wanted. THE KIDNAPPER OF WOMEN IN THE SUPERMARKET. How rude not to introduce himself in return. Edda wasn't interested in company, and I sympathize completely. She goes to the fridge. What an incredible eater. It certainly doesn't help decrease the destitution in Bollagata.

You have such a grown-up daughter?

Why didn't he just ask straight-out how old I was when I started doing it? Maybe he's going to wait to ask until he's well into his planned journey, into my bed with the black crocheted blanket.

I reply with a simple *yes*, and Edda saves me again by sticking in her head and asking what bowl she can use for milk for Björn. The neighborhood cat has slipped in with her and now struts cockily to the living room as if he's been invited to give a speech.

The visitor is just over halfway done with his cup, when he suddenly stands up and says good-bye. He tosses another good-bye into the kitchen, and in his modesty doesn't step in over that sacred threshold. He receives a response, though a lackluster one, from all the way inside the fridge, perhaps.

For fun, I help my coffee guest into his light-colored jacket of thick suede. Casual and elegant. I need to stand on tiptoe to slip the jacket onto his shoulders. He's standing directly in front of me in the sea-green foyer that's so short and narrow that the two of us fill it. He's no longer in a rush. Not at all. When was he ever in a rush? He puts his hand on my shoulder, leans toward me, a long way down, and kisses me on the forehead. Maybe that's all the farther he can bend. The kiss is slow, incisive, made with wonderful lips, loose at first and then with a little more pressure the longer it goes on.

This long and thorough forehead kiss shows me that my guest has strong nerves. Which means everything when it comes down to it. Nervous lovers who have ants in their pants do little for building up lust. But why does the man kiss me on the forehead? Is such a thing ever done except to small children and corpses in coffins? It was a mistake for me to put on those childish Indian moccasins with fur trim and plastic beads.

Maxwell House as strong as train oil, bacon and eggs, yogurt for your digestion, chocolate muesli, bananas, orange juice.

Chocolate muesli, my very favorite, shouts Edda, marching across the summerhouse's parquet floor.

I apologize for what I said yesterday, she says so loud and clear that I hear it all the way up in the Sky Chamber.

I'm sorry, too, says Heiður. Are we settled, then?

Yes, *for now*, says Edda, and Heiður breaks into explosive laughter that ends in a deep wheeze.

Rain is falling on the glass tower. I look up at it, listen to it. Such a cozy drip-drop.

From the sky drip big drops, wetting hill and field.

Each drop follows its own course, creating a great many courses, which overlap, spread, disperse. New ones are born, others die out; some are in adjacent lanes that turn into one. Now it would be good to continue napping. Nap for most of the day, nap many days, for long stretches at a time. The odor of bacon wafts up to the freaky structure where I spent a night with a stranger. Let it go and forget it. There's no more space in my head to remember. Have a piece of crispy bacon.

You've got nerve, little Eisa. You want to have a foreign bastard, like I did?

So you admit it, finally. I am a foreign bastard, just as I suspected.

I admit nothing of the sort. I was talking about you and your risky sex life.

I don't have what you could call a sex life, and the risk is none, because I've taken the utmost care ever since I accidentally had Edda. It's you who have no excuse. I know that there were fully reliable contraceptives on the market thirty years ago. You were a full-fledged adult, and you cheated on a true Icelander with some southern oaf.

Don't make me laugh. People need change, Harpa, a little fluctuation. Life shouldn't be so dull, so tightwaddish. People should be left alone to do what they want.

And doing what they want while left alone leaves behind nothing less than a child.

Oh, Harpa, I want some bacon. We never have any bacon. It's only human to want a little slice on a new day.

I put on some clothes and plunk down the stairs to a three-woman breakfast beneath the glacier. My muscles are sore after the night's activity. What does that matter, since I get to sit in a car the livelong day and pretend to be asleep. But maybe I'll just stay awake. As with a lot of other things, I'll see.

The two of them look at me suspiciously.

Edda asks, cheekily: How did you sleep?

I answer, cheekily: Well, but not long.

Edda: And the foreigner has fled.

Heiður comes to my aid: He left a note.

Edda: Suicide?

Heiður: It's a thank-you note.

Edda: For the nighttime service.

I keep myself out of this duet, eat my eggs and bacon, declare it a real feast.

A FEAST AT DAWN.

Damn, you're looking rough, Mom.

Yes, now she actually can poke fun at me, my dear Edda, because she looks as if she's been plunged in a sheep dip. She'd snuck off to clean herself, the darling, when no one was looking. Brushed her hair as well. A new life, in the shelter of Lómagnúpur, on the first day of September. She looks at me and smiles like a real person. That's my dream, for my child to be *like a real person*. I have none other. And yet. To dreams, dreams may be endlessly added.

Overcast weather is my favorite, and that's how it is now, the sky cozy and dim, drooping clouds shrouding the glacier, revealing nothing but the foundation of a superstructure that I quickly build. I enlarge the glacier, though it's big as it is, and make an egg out of it, an upright one. A speckled egg almost all the way up, snow white on top. There's endless space to shape the land at my will as it leans behind a blanket of clouds, and it's a very pleasant feeling to have betrayed a lover to whom you have no access anyway and can perhaps stop thinking about if you continue betraying. To stop thinking about something is the greatest relief. The feeling of giving up a secret love is comparable to that of pain ceasing. The best feeling in the world, someone said.

I longed to witness the sunrise on the mudflats here in the south. When the entirety of the streams, the sand, the glacier, the sky, and the sea form a whole, it isn't possible to distinguish between air or water, because everything becomes a mirror in reflection.

Today, no sun rises where we are. Fog curtains of various lengths hang down Lómagnúpur.

Well-fed terns screech, preparing themselves for the world's longest flight. They raise their young, and then they're gone. A bird doesn't recognize interim states. It's where it is, takes care of its business where it is, and then goes where it goes. It doesn't wait for years as people do, people like me, for permission to travel nowhere.

Edda eats eagerly, but I just nibble, not exactly all there after my spiritual and physical confrontations with women and men. The wagtails are listless in the low pressure of the autumn weather, fearful of flight. One of them sits on the deck railing, a dejected bird at eight thirty on a Monday morning. The first day of September. Does anyone know whether migratory birds sing as they cross the sea? If so, how have those songs been heard?

Though she's limping, Edda helps carry our things to the car. She holds open the door, shuts the door. All of a sudden, she's started making her own journey.

I don't ask her how her leg is. The well-being of others is not my concern today. My own is more than enough for me to think about.

The lusty spruce trees shielding the unusual building are preparing themselves for winter. The damp evergreen branches glow with inner energy in the sunlessness. The smell of pine and birch reminds me of summers as a kid when everything went my way. When the world was me, one dog, and the sun. When the world was my mother pointing out at the fjord where the fishing smacks lay. And later, when the world was me, a little girl that I gave birth to, and the limpid bobbing of the spring-fed streams that we drank from in very gentle breezes.

The grass is moist and the three of us make streaks in it as we walk out to the car. Six long streaks. Today I'm wearing fierce sneakers rubberized all the way up to the ankle, not my moccasins.

THE DAY OF THE VAIN GOOSE is one of the titles I've come up with, I don't know for what.

My days as a vain goose are numbered, however.

Last check, says Heiður, turning around. Whereas I was already out on the sands, my mind carrying me away. Nothing else carries me.

I must make a point of not running into the French traveler after what's happened. Lucky there's no room in the car. If we should catch a glimpse of the backpacker, I'll give Heiður a sign to gun it. I have nothing to fear, though. He's an aesthetic man who's well aware of the boundaries between night and day. He takes one night at a time and won't be seen chatting over cups of coffee in the morning, instead letting himself disappear like a tactful brownie after his impeccably performed job, before the residents rise and shine.

You just can't get rid of the creature.

Which one?

This one. Heiður swings the scarab on its gold chain, making it oscillate before my face like a pendulum.

It was under the mattress in the attic.

So you call the tower an attic? How clever. But thank you for finding this—it's my good-luck charm.

So you said. Such high housekeeping, by the way, taking off your necklace when you spend one night in a summer cottage.

Too true.

Perhaps it was high housekeeping for a Japanese Frenchman to have plucked off me this gilded blue stone animal. Which he forgot to put back on my neck, as he promised.

. . .

It'll be a good feeling to bury my foreign lover when we drive into the wall of fog. I'll then be a sleeping person with stiff muscles after a hard night, and a scraped chin from rubbing against his stubble.

Scarab lost, scarab found, scarab lost, scarab found. The days on this journey start in the same manner. What does this mean? Nothing. It's just the way things go.

Good thing you found the scarab, Heiður. I wouldn't have wanted to wake up in the east and realize that I'd lost it again.

What did I tell you, Mom? You're one big bundle of superstitions.

I admit that I put faith in the creature. It'll do good things for me someday.

That's completely absurd, Edda says.

It was so special how the beast came to me. It was in a golden heart-shaped box inside a big brown leather bag that Gabriel Axel gave me as a going-away present. When I saw the box, I thought: Good Lord, he has a crush on me. But I corrected myself immediately, because he absolutely does not and never has.

No, says Heiður, wrinkling her forehead unusually sharply. It was something else.

You just can't believe how delightful it was to visit him. His apartment above The Art of Sailing is one big fantasy world. It's packed full of antiques, and there's a lamp in every corner; some are art nouveau with chrome leaves that stretch up along the lampstand, and he has an old Japanese silk print, and Indian miniatures. The curtains are made of pale-yellow silk with hand-embroidered flowers, and all over the place are Chinese pots containing strange plants. One is called *Passiflora caerula*, which means something like "passionflower of the heart." It's an odd blue color, like it's made of plastic, and squirming over half of his wall. He has a Louis the Fifteenth bureau with pictures painted on the wood. He has an antique chaise lounge where we sometimes sat like little cousins, including on the day I left. It was on my birthday, in fact, on the Feast of the Beheading of Saint John the Baptist, and he remembered it; he had asked me once when it was. We drank champagne from old Swiss crystal glasses, extremely fine, with grapevines coiling up their stems, and I got pâté de foie gras with it, served on square Japanese dishes.

You should have been a secondhand dealer, Harpa.

Yes, a poet and secondhand dealer. Gabriel Axel and I got to know each other so well that I told him everything there was to tell about myself. He was really shocked when he heard that I had a five-year-old girl, as young as I was. He started talking about how difficult it must be, and I told him at once that such things weren't uncommon in Iceland, but he still got a tear in his eye. It was always his left eye that got teary. He asked where Edda was. I said that she was in good hands with relatives she knew well in East Iceland, and that this would be the one summer in a long, long time that I could count myself free, because I would always have to provide for us. I told him that my father had helped me go to France, he who never travels except in *National Geographic*, because he knew that I had this dream to spend time there and learn more French. Then he asked whether I had a good dad, and I said he was the best dad in the world and that my dad was called Axel, just like him. And then he became so seriously teary-eyed that a little brooklet ran down his left cheek, and my eyes moistened in polite sympathy, though I actually didn't find it sad to have the best dad in the world.

Sheesh, is he so sentimental?

He's really one for atmosphere. His place is just full of atmosphere. And it's always so fun as soon as you go there—you just can't believe it. It's kind of magical.

Why don't we visit him if it's so fun?, says Edda.

What's that?

Are you deaf?

No, I heard you. We'd certainly be given a warm welcome. But I can't really see how we could, at the moment.

I'm being careful not to say that we can't *afford* it.

We'll just work in a fish factory and save up.

I'm so surprised that I can't emit as much as a peep. Edda's planning trips abroad with her little mom. The child must have picked some magic mushrooms this morning.

It's happened before, says Heiður. Two fully grown women scraping together money for a trip to more southerly climes.

The sands are a museum of many different time periods, to which no one has access except worms. There are human bones in the stomach of this sand, shipwrecks of the centuries, a Viking ship or two, of which no stories are told.

Few have gotten to know the sands up close, other than travelers of old and their horses, those who forded the rivers, who gathered driftwood, clubbed seals, who searched for gold in shipwrecks, who built bridges. If I could choose one of these roles, I would be a treasure hunter—searching for Chinese porcelain, diamonds, and gold bars in the flagship of the Dutch fleet from the seventeenth century. Its mast was still visible at the turn of the twentieth century, before farmers sawed it off and used it to panel their living rooms. Thereby destroying a clue for those who later tried to find the ship.

My life is a sunken ship, isn't it? Off which mischievous boys sawed the mast to use as fuel for a bonfire.

Sleep is what I yearn for. What I do not get.

Correctly used frustration is probably the most powerful pleasure by far.

Properly handled lovelessness, for example.

But insomnia is no pleasure, no matter how it's dealt with.

Ahead is a wall of fog rising between us and the glacier, between us and the sea, between us and everything that is in the here and now. This milky, soft wall in our path looks like a wall of silence. Beyond it, silence must reign supreme. I think it'll be useless for me to open my mouth once we reach it. Neither words would be heard nor sounds. A car crash would sound like colliding cotton balls.

The foremost layer in the wall is composed of loose wisps that condense and meet in a haze that thickens before our eyes, like simmering milk. Once there, nothing else is visible but a piece of the road ahead. To a tired mother it's a relief not to have to worry about missing a magnificent view. The view sails its own sea, like the sins that I've cast onto the highway behind me, to the west.

Heiður turns on the yellow fog lights, and we inch our way onward in the extensive blaze where there's no flame, just smoke, and the smoke isn't even harmful. The fog is like steam from a hot spring, though there's no hot spring. It won't harm the body, but it inspires claustrophobia. I don't dare say anything in this silent world, because I don't want to test whether it'll be heard. And I don't need to say anything. I close my eyes in defense against the unreliable external world, which is still not as unreliable as the internal human world. There's even more risk of becoming lost and perishing in there than out in what's called the big world. The biggest world is the internal world, the universe in a single person, the most horrifying of worlds, the least known.

A bird on its way to its next country has flown off course and flutters dangerously close to our headlight. It's so indistinct that it could be a tern or even a plover. Yet it is a bird, an unexpected bird, in the midst of white fog, like the fancy pigeon I saw in the pure white world of Laugardalur last New Year's Eve, a pigeon for which a black cat sat in ambush behind a snowdrift. A frozen cat that had probably lost its way, as cats do when it snows over their scent marks. It couldn't find its way home, or didn't want to go home.

The helm of fog is shaped like the snowfall was then, on New Year's Eve, which I spent walking home alone to Bollagata, from Heiður's place in Laugarás, not a taxi to be had at four in the morning. A woman walking in the night in rubber boots, thick tights, a wool sweater over a tulle dress. I'd brought my walking outfit in a backpack. I kept my dress shoes in it as I straddled fences in Laugardalur, a dwarf in a long coat on a dark night whose every corner couldn't be illuminated by the lights of the city, as the steam from the swimming pool ascended to the sky. There was no one out and about in Laugardalur except for me, and the silence was deep. But suddenly a record player was turned up. I didn't know where the music was coming from—maybe the house of the Botanical Garden's superintendent. It was Janis Joplin, the one and only, singing "Me and Bobby McGee."

I'd trade all of my tomorrows for one single yesterday.

Others would do so, too, dear Janis, if it were possible.

I gave my temporary freedom my full attention at Heiður's party. In unison with the united housewives of all countries, I'd finished the year by standing bent over pots and pans half the day. Dad had slipped me money for food, so I hadn't scrimped in that department. Edda didn't come home until eight o'clock, though I'd pleaded with her not to come later than six because her grandfather was coming for dinner. She was smelling a bit ripe, thanks to not having bathed or changed her clothes for many days and the stench of alcohol. Dad had grown agitated and distracted by the girl's absence, and it was difficult to carry on a conversation with him. I poured him a little wine and tried to get him to talk about the good old days, but I couldn't cheer him up.

The evening got better after Edda arrived, though she didn't stay for more than two hours. Apparently she wasn't granted leave from the gang for any longer than that. Gerti Chicken came to pick her up in the yellow van. Who knows, maybe Teddi wanted to take her along on a special project. I was thankful that she'd stopped in at all, because of Dad, since it cheered him up. My brother, Sibbi, picked him up around eleven, and when I was alone I went and stood in front of the mirror until the New Year, at which point the sculptor Tóti, Heiður's old boyfriend, stopped by to take me to her party. Heiður's one of those who keeps her old lovers handy, but that's a scheme I've never understood. I have my suspicions about it, and I imagine that Dietrich Bacon, her current boyfriend, would feel the same, if he bothered to think about it.

I had two dresses to choose from, a stretch dress and a chiffon dress, and after I'd tried both of them on five times each, I tossed a coin. The black chiffon dress, with its excessively plunging neckline, won. This dress, which is drawn in at the chest with sparkling black stones, had always looked surprisingly good on me, and I knew it. The tulle at the back slightly resembles little wings, but there's a certain humor in that. I took out Mom's emerald earrings, for which Dad had saved up to give her on her thirtieth birthday. The color of the stones perfectly suits my eyes and hair.

After the decision concerning the dress was made, I carefully applied my makeup, concealing the rings under my eyes, applying eyeliner, and mixing two lipstick colors to create a garnet-red shade. I put up my hair in a high bun to appear taller and more elegant, and finally I took my high-heeled black suede shoes with the golden clasps from the top shelf of the bedroom closet and removed them from their cloth bag.

Happy with Heiður's party, but feeling strangely regretful for reasons I didn't know, I left and took a shortcut home, through the Botanical Gardens. The snow came to my aid as I climbed over fences, leveling things for my short coat-enwrapped legs. The music grew louder, and hoarse drunken screaming could be heard through the large-flaked snowfall that settled on thickening trees and bushes. There was no one to be seen, but beneath a tall spruce tree standing alone in the middle of the gardens loitered a black cat, which cried out as I approached. It shouldn't have been out alone in the deep snow, the forlorn beast.

The cat, most likely a tom, followed me, mewing piteously at times, but I found its company better than none. For this was a sober and reasonable cat, if nothing else. And I decided to rejoice in it as I had rejoiced in the handshake and glance of Dietrich Bacon when I, all decked up, walked into Laugarás Hall. The handshake that warmed my soul and body, and which betrayed itself by lasting a few seconds longer than it was supposed to do. The highlight of that particular evening was the duet that he and Heiður performed: fifteenth-century Italian Renaissance. The most beautiful love song in *the world*, said Heiður, who played her gold flute as Dietrich sang in his silver voice. He repeated the word *cara* while looking at me, ever so gently and subtly.

So be it.

The cat and I came to a house reinforced with corrugated iron, not far from Suðurlandsbraut Road. And as we approached, a pigeon flew up from the white expanse of snow. I saw it by the light from a window. It wasn't an ordinary pigeon, but rather, a fancy pigeon, with a tuft on its head, pretending to be something it wasn't. It looked like a new species, in between a rooster and a dove. When the pigeon flapped its wings, that beggar of a cat got all excited, lost interest in me, and shot as if from a gun to the next drift, where it took a hunting position. To that little cat I was never anything but a small woman in the snow, just a temporary companion. At the start it was going to take shelter with me, but then forgot all about that when the tufted pigeon appeared. Was it just going to catch and eat this fine specimen, which had most likely been smuggled into this country under someone's coat? Maybe it would be rather easy prey if it were stiff with cold.

Then, right at that moment, I had an attack of apprehension. Where was Edda? What was Edda doing? Was she alive or dead? Was she fine, or hurt? Half-stoned, completely stoned, on what? Pregnant? Sick with AIDS? Or had she killed a few birds with one stone and was a number of these things at once? My thoughts were straitjacketed in a vicious circle. Same old story, over and over. A scratched horror record, that didn't change with the turning of the years. A new year starting, and I was screwed up once again.

Then I had to make it happen. I had to create angels throughout all of Laugardalur, lie down on my back, get up, make angel upon angel with wide wings until the day dawned and I turned into wingless stone.

The bird flew featherless,
alit on the wall, boneless.

It stopped snowing, and I tried to shake the snow off my black coat, then took off my black wool cap and brushed it. Along Suðurlandsbraut drunk people appeared as far as the eye could see, scattered here and there. Some stumbled, some stepped out onto the street and tried to stop cars crawling by in the wet snow. It didn't matter whether they were taxis or private cars. I made a detour so as not to be in the way of a loaded man behaving aggressively beneath a streetlight, punching the air, lashing out against some invisible opponent. The man was bald and had unkempt light-red sideburns. He was thick-set and wore no overcoat, only a suit, with his shirt untucked. Suddenly he gave a drawling shout: *Snorri!* At the same moment a resident on the middle story of the first Álfheimur apartment block began a traditional fireworks display from his balcony, shooting a great many rockets into the air, filling the night with loud bangs and showers of sparks.

He'd likely been in a drunken stupor before the clock struck midnight, and he was only now stirring to action on this first day of the New Year. This display couldn't have been popular among his neighbors, because the lights were off in most of the apartment building's windows. Even the man under the streetlight gave a start and shouted: *Why are you doing this, Snorri?*

The fireworks display dwindled to one rocket, which hissed horizontally off the balcony and sank with a mild whine to the ground by the basement window, while windows lit up throughout the apartment building.

It was as if the sparklers that burned earlier in the evening had been frozen and crushed and sprinkled over the fresh snow. It was a mass of tiny sparkling crystals, and I felt ashamed to leave tracks in it. That was more disrespectful than tramping in dirty rubber boots crisscross over the wide wet floor of the royal cleaning woman. I was therefore relieved when the snow started falling again and I knew that it would soon cover my tracks. I was guilty of walking on the earth, but then the snow covered that oversight, allowing me to tread lighter among the drifts, short-legged in boots up to my knees.

Only what was closest was visible, as in the fog we're driving through now. The world narrowed. There was nothing else in it but me. Now there's nothing in the world but the three of us, and yet, just me, because the fog-vapor creeps into the car. It envelops me until only I exist, alone in a car, a driverless passenger.

It's impossible to say where we've come, and how we're traveling, whether we're sailing or flying, whether we're being carried along by the fog river or sit unmoving in a viscous grayish-white substance. To me it seems as if the car's wheels could start spinning at any moment, and then it would be no use to switch on the front-wheel drive.

Now I lay me down to sleep, and so on. It would certainly best befit me to sleep after the unseemly toil of the night and honorable toil of the days.

This winter I'll have time to sleep enough. *To sleep enough*. It sounds like a line from a song in a dream. Insomnia's been one of my unwelcome mistresses this unlucky year. Thinking about Edda in her situation is like having a little child that's sick, and fearing for its life night after night, week after week, month after month. To sleep enough at the sea's edge farthest to the east, to the sounds of the waves. Is there a better dream than that?

Now I lay me down to sleep
I pray the Lord my soul to keep

Appearing at times through the porous fog are roadside puddles, and drinking from them are white sheep. Beyond them rise ravine-cut slopes with sturdy birch thickets. The sun gleams on the mossy-gray glacier that spills like porridge onto the plain. Wooded ridges and green patches of willow by the road. The world always comes to light once again. That's its nature and necessity. A widening world, out into sand and utterly gray stones.

At a house on Háteigsvegur Street stood two children, a boy and a girl, both of whom could hardly have been more than eight years old. They swung sparklers in circles, and I was worried that everyone might be dead drunk inside the house, meaning they the kids might end up outside until noon or longer that New Year's Day. When I walked by, the girl said to me: *Do you see that man?*

The human figure sitting on the steps and leaning against the railing was turning into a snowman, blending in with the background so well that I wouldn't have noticed him if not for the girl pointing him out. As I walked up the steps, it appeared to me that this white shape was a young man. He must have been sitting there for quite a while, judging by the amount of snow accumulation. His eyelashes sparkled white.

Wake up, I said, touching him on the shoulder.

He didn't wake up. I took off my wool mitten and touched his cheek. It was ice-cold. Yet the man wasn't dead; he was breathing. I tried to shake him, but he didn't move. I shook him more, perplexed, but at that he fell on his side and lay there with his knees at right angles. I was afraid he'd hurt his head when he plopped over. I rang four doorbells in a frenzy.

A young woman in a glittery dress of stretch material answered one of them. Her feet were bare in very high-heeled shoes. Before I said anything, she'd stuck her head out, looked at me and from me to the man who lay by her door, and assessed the situation in a flash: You're too late. The party's over.

No I don't need a party. We need an ambulance.

Are you hurt? Come in.

No, I'm not hurt. It's him.

Where's he hurt?

He might be frozen.

Is he dead, maybe?

I don't think so.

If he's dead, it would be more logical to call the police.

Start by calling an ambulance. Please.

The two kids had come all the way up to us on the steps. They'd lit new sparklers, very long ones that shot sparks over the man.

Go home, kids, I said. This isn't the place for you.

They headed toward the building next door.

We didn't dare move the man for fear that he was injured. The woman got a wool blanket decorated with the national insignia's four guardian spirits and spread it over him. It was strange to see him lying there like that, with a blanket up to his ears. An overturned doorstep ghost on New Year's Eve.

The woman put on a fur coat and high-heeled patent leather boots, and we hovered over the man and waited for the ambulance. A two-person wake, out in the cold. All we needed was for the bells of Háteig Church to ring. I started recalling old stories about corpses that couldn't be buried until spring, and I hoped that the frozen man would come to no harm, because when the paramedics wiped the snow from his face he turned out to be young and beautiful. Maybe he had a wife and child.

They asked me if I was coming, and I was on the verge of getting in the ambulance and accompanying him to the emergency room before I decided that it bordered on intrusiveness and abandoned the idea.

I hurried the rest of the way home to Bollagata. I felt as though I'd been delayed, that I had to hurry. That Edda needed me. I had a nagging feeling that I ought to be there, though it was uncertain whether my child would come home in an hour or three days from now.

Flókagata Street was littered with traces of the festivities: singed cylindrical stubs protruding from the snow on the sidewalks and yards; burned-out sparkler rods hanging from fences; black genever, champagne, and liqueur bottles from which fireworks had been shot standing or lying here and there. These pieces of evidence would remain as they were until spring, when the earth would start to turn green. Until May, when enterprising individuals and teenage work-groups would take to gathering the decaying remains of New Year's Eve.

In front of a house opposite Kjarvalsstaðir, two people were kissing. I found something mysterious about the couple, so I snuck over to have a look and saw that it was two women, one with a crew cut. *Once there were two lesbians on Flókagata Street, kissing outside while doctors thawed a frozen man who was found on a doorstep on Háteigsvegur Street by a short-statured assistant nurse.*

It had sometimes crossed my mind to try out a woman, but I felt it would be too much of an undertaking, and maybe show a certain disrespect for the male sex, about which I had no complaints, so to speak. It would have been impossible to complain about my most recent adventure, with Yves, if I hadn't simply forgotten about the man already.

On the one hand, the sun is shining, the sea is bright. On the other, there's fog, toward the land, which is a glacier. Fog that condenses and disperses according to a fast-paced pattern that no one can decipher.

Many a time I've watched my fjord to the east emerge from fog, but I've never seen the earth around my fjord emerge from snow from the very start. I know no season in my dream-fjord except for late spring and then summer, a hint of autumn. Next spring I'm going to document all of it: the coming of the migratory birds, one after another, the growth of the buds on the trees.

Ingólfshöfði is the headland of the settler Ingólfur Arnarson, said Dad as we sailed by on our way back to Reykjavík, or on our way east.

It isn't a headland; it's an island, I said.

No, it's a headland. I'm certain of it, said Dad, with a gentle smile.

Saga Kaaber, Heiður's mom, once said to me: You inherited your dad's beautiful, gentle smile. Was she trying to be beastly, or was she consoling me? Saying, Of course he's your father.

Fortunately, we can't read minds.

A Folksy Shop by an Iceberg Lagoon

I stir when the hum of the car engine stops, when the movement ceases. Heiður has parked as close as possible to an otherworldly lagoon. Turkish-blue icebergs glow with inner fluorescent light on water of the same color. Sunlight gleams on the ice cap, and smoky-black clouds hover behind dusky-blue peaks. The sky has taken on the color of the bergs and water, making everything equally blue: icebergs, sky, lagoon. A boat is moored, ready to sail between icebergs and rub shoulders with them. A seal pokes its head up, imitating a sea-beaten rock, and promptly dives down again.

A smoky-white cloud over the sea. Between us and the sea is a narrow strip of sand. Spanning it is a bridge, beneath which runs the glacial river.

Time to get some fresh air, sleepyheads, says Heiður. You really make great traveling companions. I wish I got to sleep.

You knew what you were getting into when you volunteered to drive us.

Get a move on, Edda. Be sure to stretch.

Leave me alone, says Edda, pulling a sleeping bag up over her head.

I make it to the ground through carefully planned maneuvers. I'm even stiffer than yesterday, and my inner-thigh muscles are sore, after my intense deed in the dark with a man I don't know. I'm going to try everything I can not to remember his name. It was nice while it lasted, and that's that.

The final tour group of the summer, wearing international headgear—headbands, ski caps, balaclavas, red tasseled hats—focuses multiple eyes on me from the windows of a minibus parked in front of a shop that wasn't here the last time I traveled the Ring Road. Even foreigners find me outlandish. They forget themselves and gape at me like tried-and-true Icelanders, even though they all know that staring is impolite. I'm not even in my white pants and moccasins any longer—just sneakers and light-blue jeans, like an ordinary person.

I rush down to the lagoon's beach as quickly as the state of my lower extremities allows. The sand-bearing icebergs are half-submerged and have the texture of foam. The ice chunks crack loudly as they split from the mother glacier. The cracking is amplified in the stillness of the wilderness, creating music to accompany the nearby ocean, which is as tactful and mannered as the inhabitants of the Skaftafell area.

The glacial air could easily drive my lungs mad. They rise and fall in sheer joy. If I could get Edda out of the car, her supple blood-rich lungs would suck in the glacier oxygen and refresh her liver and kidneys, prompting them to filter out the poison and the madness on the spot. The outcome would be a teenager who'd gone on a spiritual kidney machine, leaving no further need to worry about her.

I heed the demonic sorcery of the lagoon and transform myself into an elegant feminine arc diving in to swim among frolicking icebergs. Just as I'm about to hit the enticing surface, I feel the urge to pee, surprisingly abruptly, and I tear off stiffly to the shop's restroom before an accident occurs.

When I'm done, the last minibus of the year is gone, along with the international headwear. Parked here now are only our car and one other: the staff car, no doubt. If I hadn't had to pee so badly, I'd now be swimming in the lagoon like all the other bergs that calved from the mother glacier. The glacier is of course female, whether it crawls along or soars to the sky. I'm not sure whether everyone's aware of this.

A sign in front of me says BLACK DEATH AND SHARK, 400 KRÓNUR. I like that. A hot-dog-less shop at the foot of the largest glacier in Europe. I'm going to have a snack of these national delicacies without asking my overlords from the car. Have a schnapps though it's not yet noon. It hasn't happened often in my life, maybe never. That's fine. Ideally, as much as possible should happen that hasn't happened before.

When Heiður comes into the shop after a little stroll along the shores of the lagoon, I'm sitting at a table, staring out the window at the glacial fog, a gray vapor that plays around the luminous blue bergs at the glacier's edge. I'm finishing my schnapps and have two cubes of shark to go. Heiður plunks onto a stool and asks, astonished: What's that you've got there?

Schnapps and shark.

Are you nuts?

No, I just felt that this was what I needed.

You're really starting to go a bit overboard, Harpa. Day and night.

Shouldn't you be congratulating me?

Maybe if that shark didn't stink so much of ammonia.

It transforms into an internal fragrance. By the way, don't try filling the tank behind my back.

I toss three thousand krónur on the table. Heiður gives me a harsh look and says, You're exasperating, Harpa.

I won't go any farther with you unless you take it.

Heiður stands up, takes the money, shakes her head, and goes to the counter. I know exactly what she's planning to do. Order a coffee and apple cake with whipped cream, which is in fact advertised as a package deal for three hundred krónur. Once you've known someone long enough, every single little movement of theirs becomes predictable: what they eat, when they're going to be appalled, how often they need to go to the bathroom.

Here in this glorious refuge on the sandy wastes, where postcards, wool sweaters, and shark are sold, is where I would wish to spend the rest of my life, gazing out at the luminous lagoon and the tourist boat now resting ashore, waiting for the last cruise of the year.

I can easily imagine starting each and every day on a cruise around this lagoon filled with icebergs that have the texture of a sponge but break with a metallic sound. Listening to the amplified cracking when the sun shines intensely and watching the bergs split, melt, turn in circles—ensuring that the lagoon's appearance changes from one minute to the next. Between cruises I could look out to sea, awaiting ships that don't land because there's no harbor.

Now that I've begun, I find myself wanting to keep gobbling down more cured shark, the most revolting dish on the planet, chased with the worst schnapps in the world, Icelandic brennivín. This food makes you toxic enough to deal with the dead and the living, both equally hopeless.

Heiður eats so quickly that I feel queasy watching her. Studies suggest that the speed at which people ingest their food is inborn, and I suppose there's comfort in that.

Is it nice to work here?, I ask the girl at the counter as I get up to leave.

She gives me a silly look and says that it's good when things are steady. On the other hand, things are never steady, because everyone comes in groups, meaning the place is either packed or there isn't a soul.

Is the shark popular?

Icelanders don't want it, naturally, because they know how it tastes. Of the foreigners, it's mainly the Germans who dare to try it. They want the most for their money. In English it's apparently called *the full experience.*

How's the pay?

It comes out okay on a monthly basis, but the hours are long.

Do the employees live in this building?

There are sleeping accommodations for two.

And don't you find the natural beauty incredible?

It's beautiful when there's a full moon.

Who owns this shop?

Reynir Teitsson, from Höfn. He also owns GLACIER TOURS EVERY DAY OF THE SUMMER, INC.

Do you have his phone number?

I do. But he's also in the phone book. He lives at Hnúkarimi 7 in Höfn.

I need a job next summer, you see.

Are you in school during the winter?

No, I'm not in school. I should be, though.

My rude best friend, maybe my only friend, knocks on the window. I'm just waiting for her to press her nose against the glass.

I smile apologetically at the girl and say that it looks like I've got to get going. She smiles at me apologetically and even says, I'm sorry, as if it's her fault, as if she's held me up with her chatter and not the other way around.

. . .

My hot-tempered driver tears off with intense concentration and a gaze that's more piercing than the current visibility requires. As soon as she hits third gear, she screws up her nose and rolls down her window. I suspect that my breath reeks.

The monster in the backseat sits up, thrusts her head forward, and roars, Who's been drinking brennivín?

Not you, I hiss. Not this time.

The monster falls back and puts a towel over her head. I lean toward my window and pull my scarf over my trap to make my presence in the car as bearable as possible.

As I neared my apartment on New Year's Eve, I couldn't help but think about my child, and my hope flared that when I returned Edda Sólveig would be snuggled under the covers, and I could go to her bed and spread the quilt over her bare toes, just as when she was a child.

After that, I could indulge in half a glass of red wine from my open bottle, light a candle, listen to a recording of Dietrich Bacon singing *Leise flehen*, and be fifteen years old, not pregnant. I'd watch the snowfall through the arched window and recall how the singer looked at me as he sang at the second hour of the New Year.

I hurried to Edda's bed without even taking off my boots, but my daughter hadn't come home, of course. I felt quite sad as I systematically removed my coat and hat, folded my sweater, and put my wool socks in a drawer, and fear, my constant companion, welled up inside me. A piercing cat's wail came in through the window of Edda's room. It wasn't shut well, and I hurried to fasten it securely, because I didn't feel like talking to more cats today.

I did everything else I'd envisioned doing. As soon as I'd arranged myself on the sofa, with my legs up on the glass table and Dietrich singing *Durch die Nacht zu dir*, a new round of snow started falling softly—very, very slowly and sparsely. I imagined that I lived alone in this apartment, that I was an ordinary thirty-one-year-old single woman. I tried not to think about the unwashed dishes in the kitchen sink. Rare was the occasion when the crockery remained unwashed overnight. The thought of it assaulted me like the fiercest temptation. The dishes had such a magnetic power that my fingers itched to go and clean up, but I didn't give in. For the moment, I would do nothing, though it took an effort, and I hunkered down tighter on the couch and struggled to sit and gaze at the garden through the arched window. The snowfall wasn't serious; only a few unnaturally large flakes fluttered before the window.

The phone rang. Teddi asked for Edda Sólveig. I said she wasn't home and asked where he'd seen her last. He'd gotten separated from her downtown. What time?, I asked. It was around three, said Teddi. Is there something you should tell me?, I asked. No, he said, but I detected a sort of undertone to his voice, and the weakness in my lower back flared and poured straight down, so heavily that my knees buckled and I collapsed onto the stool next to the phone. Did she tell you where she was going?, I asked. She said she was going to lie down in the garden. Which garden? I don't know—she was just blathering. Was she completely stoned? Too bad I lost track of her. *Since when do you think you're looking after Edda, you who've brought her to ruin? Filthy bastard.* I hung up the phone and trembled with agitation. Then I lifted the receiver and slammed it down again, though the bastard wasn't on the other end anymore, of course.

She was going to lie down in the garden? Was she lying in the Botanical Garden in Laugardalur like a sick old snow-woman, in my footprints? Did she mean our little yard? There were plenty of other possibilities. It was only twenty degrees outside and Edda was always poorly dressed. No matter what I tried. Asking her to dress more warmly had cost me black eyes, punches, and shoves.

I took off my black chiffon dress with tulle wings and prepared myself for further outdoor activities on the first night of the year. I put on a Norwegian angora undershirt, thick tights, long trousers, a long-sleeved cotton T-shirt, a wool sweater, cotton socks, wool socks, boots, a winter coat, a balaclava, and shearling mittens. I would make the circuit of the neighborhood, look in people's yards and at Hlemmur bus station. If I didn't find Edda within an hour, I was going to call my cousin Rikki, the cop, and ask if he knew anything. I could also turn to Sibbi and ask him to drive me to several choice locations, or loan me his car if he were too hungover to drive. I put out the candle before leaving, but left a lamp lit in the living room window.

I'm going to lie down in the garden. I had a faint inkling that I'd heard Edda say this one spring, when everything was as good as could be. That one fine day she'd gone out into our Bollagata yard and sprawled out, covered with a sheet. Being a redhead, she can't tolerate sun.

The noise of caps and firecrackers assailed me as I went out the door. A group of teenagers or children was persistently shooting off fireworks in the playground across the street. One of them lit a flare, casting a red glow over the swings and seesaw and a sparkling slide of snow. It was just past six o'clock in the morning. Many a self-respecting person might wake at the noise now. What were children doing out at this hour? Who was taking care of them? What was wrong with this nation?

I started by sauntering into the yard as if I were going out for fresh air. The lamp in the arched window cast a gleam onto the snow. The lowest tree branches touched the ground beneath their white loads. The snowfall was still on its way toward stopping. A flake or two drifted to the ground and landed on a fence, branch, or the ground beneath my booted feet. I stood in vague cat tracks, probably made by Mr. Björn and ending at a small slanted drift in front of my arched window. I followed the trail as far as it went and stopped. Then I walked slowly around the corner of the house. There the pawprints were visible again, in the dim glow of a streetlight, and up over the pole shone the terrifically clear moon in full size, coming in low in the sky on approach, preparing for landing. The cat tracks led to the old spruce tree in the corner of the yard. A person's leg was sticking out from under the tree, and cat paws had stepped along its snowy trouser. At first it appeared to be a single leg, but when I bent down to take a better look, I saw that it belonged to a whole person, tall and slim. A cat sat on the person's chest. It hesitated before dashing off with a hiss. The chest was bare and scratched with blood, as if the cat had gotten to it. The person had long sparkling snow-hair that spread out over the ground. When I bent all the way over and peeked under the tree, I saw a lock of red hair. My daughter, Edda, had done exactly as she'd said.

I grabbed her legs and dragged her through the yard to the basement steps. I'd once heard of a woman out east who died of exposure. She'd bared her chest to accelerate her death. I put down Edda's legs when I reached the steps, grabbed the keys from my pocket, opened the door, ran up the steps, took Edda in my arms, and dragged her in, right into my bed, spread the quilt over her, and called an ambulance.

To accelerate death.

While I waited, I sat at the foot of the bed with my back turned to Edda's face. I wrapped the quilt better about her feet, over her shoes. I didn't check to see whether she was breathing, and wondered what had possessed the cat to settle down on her chest. I didn't even know whether this was our daily visitor or some other cat from around town, maybe a stray. Why had it scratched her? To wake her, maybe? But weren't cats just wild or stupid beasts, lacking the mind to save a person's life, as dogs sometimes did, or was it that they simply had no interest in doing so? Were there such things as Saint Bernard cats, trained to look for children buried in snow?

BURIED CHILD is the name of a famous play, but it's about something entirely different.

I hurried back out because I was sure that the ambulance would go to the wrong house. I was right. They were waking up my neighbor, a woman who was close to her delivery date. I heard the distant sound of her denying having made the call and directing the paramedics to my basement. The snow on my boots had left puddles on the floor by the bed. I noticed that Edda's face was wet and I wiped her cheek with the quilt before they put her on the stretcher. She was transforming from a frozen girl into a beached corpse.

Who are you?, asked one of the medics as we walked out the front door. He looked more horrified than surprised.

I'm an assistant nurse, same line of business as you, I said, to lighten the mood. My name's Harpa Eir.

Were you on Háteigsvegur Street just before?, he asked.

Yes, I came across a hypothermic man on someone's steps. He wasn't related, but this is my daughter.

We said nothing more to each other. I sat on a bench in the back with Edda. They drove so fast I had to hold on tightly. At one turn I nearly fell over onto the stretcher. I wanted to ask them to turn down the siren so that they wouldn't wake the child. I looked out the window. As we approached City Hospital, a firework shot into the air somewhere in the Breiðholt neighborhood, bursting with an incredibly expansive display of red, green, white, blue. It was irregular in shape, like an orchid, and appeared to me to stretch across the sky, from Hengill all the way south to Bláfjöll.

Edda had begun to shiver by the time we arrived at the emergency room. I'd never seen her so pitiable before, not even when she was bloodied and battered. I didn't want to be in the room while they were examining and treating her, so I waited in the corridor and watched the hobbling, bandaged people and white coats pass by.

A doctor came and showed me into a room where there were bandages and plastic trays on shelves, crutches in one corner, and crumbs of plaster on the floor.

I found her in the yard, I said, under a large spruce tree by the trash bins. She was bare-chested, with Björn, I think, sitting on her chest.

Were there two of them?

No, she was alone.

Didn't you say Björn?

Yes, but he left immediately.

What was he doing?, asked the doctor.

They know each other.

Did he make the scratch marks on her chest?

He must have.

How long had she been lying there?

She was in the yard the whole time. I'd just been sitting in the living room.

Can you come up with an idea of how long she was lying there?

Maybe since three thirty, because she became separated from her so-called friends around three, downtown. We live in Norðurmýri.

The doctor had a lot of freckles, including on the backs of his hands. He spoke with a lisp and had pointy yellow teeth. I thought he sounded stupid, and was certain he would make a mistake costing Edda her life.

Very drunk, on drugs?

On a lot of things, most likely. Ecstasy, for example. They must get it at the big festivals. Could she die?

No. Not unless there are complications, which I don't expect at all. Her body temperature is right around ninety-two degrees. We'll warm her up gradually. If freezing people are warmed too quickly, the heart pumps cold blood into warmer organs, with bad results.

COLD BLOOD INTO WARM ORGANS. An abrupt trembling came over me. I didn't tremble under my own power, but rather, it was as if the world shook me, the room, the chair. I tried to hold on to the chair's arms, but it was no use, because an outboard motor was shaking us both.

The doctor gave me an injection and had me lie down on a hospital bed. The tropical firework that stretched over half the surrounding mountains as we were on our way here in the ambulance lurked like a giant bird over a big map of the human musculoskeletal system. A sign not to give up even though the year had started like this.

I didn't fall asleep, and got up and called Heiður. It was almost nine o'clock.

I'll be right there, she said.

Aren't you drunk?, I asked.

Not really. I'm coming. And she hung up.

I wandered to the waiting room, a doped-up woman with springs for legs. I should have told the doctor not to give me a full dose, because I'm so small and light and so sensitive to drugs.

The waiting room was almost entirely packed, but I didn't notice anything in particular except a thin woman in her fifties with her head wrapped in a blood-soaked bandage. She was so plastered she could hardly keep herself in her chair. Next to her sat a very prim man of around thirty, bowled over with shame. I wasn't sure whether it was her son or a young lover. It dawned on me that the woman had the appearance of a foreigner, in much the same way I did. I took a good look at her to see how I would turn out after thirty years and didn't like it, even if I took better care of myself than she had. Not that anyone can be certain how long they'll live.

It felt as if Heiður arrived immediately, and I asked whether she'd come on a magic carpet.

What's the situation?

I don't know. Apparently she's not going to die, so I'm told.

Were you given a sedative?

I'm so doped up that I'm teetering.

Sit still, said Heiður. Don't move more than you have to. I'll ask.

Everything was on the right track. Edda was sleeping. I didn't want to disturb her. Heiður drove me home and helped me into bed. It was wet, of course, and I ended up in Edda's bed. Heiður lay down on the couch in the living room, and we both slept until late afternoon. She stayed at my place instead of with her golden boyfriend, even though he was going abroad the next morning. Through the mire in my head, I felt ashamed of myself for sabotaging my friend's love life.

I'm an exhausted child in a car, suffering from sore muscles after a one-night stand with the first man I met on the road, literally. You loose wench, shame! The first man you met. Tsk, tsk.

It's true, little Eisa, you certainly did an incredible job.

Mom, if you call me Eisa once more I'll never speak to you again. Now stop your rambling and come straight out with it. Who is my father?

Axel.

Fine. I'll ask Dýrfinna.

Do you think I care?

Where did you get hold of the poor foreigner who knocked you up?

At work, of course. I never went anywhere else but there.

At the Marine Research Institute?

It was called the Fisheries Department when you were conceived.

Mom gives me a cheeky look and purses her lips, which are done up with orange-colored lipstick.

A strange catch?

You might say so.

Was it wanderlust that compelled you to get hold of him? Did you have the affair in place of traveling abroad?

Your thinking has become terribly original.

Don't try to get me off track. You held up your wanderlust like a shield. You know, you're not the only one who wants to make tracks. Do you have to whine about it constantly?

Don't be so hard on me.

Mom, can't you be just a tiny bit of a guardian angel to me? Can't you be still, like the woman in the jingle? *There sits my mother, carding new wool.*

I have no interest in knitting.

A single-file line of sheep stares at me.

Meandering picturesquely between high tufts of grass.

The sparse vegetation is magenta-colored, with a purple weft, greening around the watery spots that aren't big enough to be ponds and are too big to be puddles.

It was really nice of you to come up to City Hospital when Edda froze. I could hardly have made it home without help.

That's what I'm here for, says Heiður. This visibility is really awful. It's good to be free of the landscape.

I don't understand you. You've never told me properly what happened afterward.

You're impossible to pin down, I say. You're on the move so much. Edda was utterly exhausted when she came home, with a bit of a fever and mild pneumonia, so I was home for two days taking care of her. Once when I was fixing the covers, thinking that she was sleeping, she started crying. I wiped her tears with the corner of the quilt cover and remembered that I'd done the same when she was starting to thaw, before she was taken to the hospital. I asked whether she'd intended to die and she said she didn't know. I also asked why her shirt was open at her chest and she said she'd torn it open herself, but she didn't know why. Once she asked me for a poem that she particularly liked in the *The Book of Verses*.

> A mishap! I am not to blame
> dear Mother, as I know you've seen
> the little brook down hollow green
> run swift in sport and joyful game,
> then broaden where the slope is tame
> to babble, bobble, guggle there!
> But not to fear! From here on out
> I shall indeed take better care.

> A merry life you have, 'tis true;
> when to embrace you, as you run
> your steady course 'neath slopes in sun
> are violets yellow red and blue;
> I stretched my hand for one or two
> and then you splashed so cold on me.
> You evil brook! From here on out
> I shan't forget, not once, you see.

My petticoat, white, pure and fine,
is now all soaked, right to my skin;
if then you'd heard and seen its grin,
the mischief that did from it shine—
I reached to make a flower mine,
and then it splashed so cold on me.
You evil brook! From here on out
I shan't forget, not once, you see.

Through hollow runs the brook in play,
and wets the maiden, toes to locks,
as there she steps upon the rocks,
so thoughtful of you, brook; I say!
Dear Mother, home is where I'll stay,
outside today I will not fare.
But not to fear! From here on out
I shall indeed take better care.

When I recited it we laughed, light as feathers, as if what had
happened to Edda was about as unfortunate as the girl's little accident in the poem.

Then Teddi arrived, without warning. I was going to slam the
door in his face, but was too late. Edda came out, and he slipped past
me. End of the dream. I've hardly been able to make contact with
her since then. She's like a malfunctioning lighthouse that emits a
faint light twice a month, one second at a time. I've acted toward her
as if she were dying, watched her in the hope of making the tiniest
connection, even if it's for the last time.

Harpa, is that him?

Heiður brakes sharply, nearly running into a bright-yellow van.

I'll be damned.

Gerti Chicken and company. These rascals certainly aren't engaged in an ordinary pursuit. They're ahead of us.

How clever. Progressive chasing.

I wonder where they spent the night.

What's that got to do with it?

I'll call Rikki. He'll arrest the bastards. I won't tolerate this.

Do you think he can arrest them for driving the wrong section of Highway Number One?

Delaying them would be enough to let us reach our destination. He only has to hold them up for about an hour. That'd give us more than enough of a head start. Once Edda's in Andey, these guys can't do anything. Doesn't their character make you shudder? They've seen her badly injured, wasted, half-dead. And right when she's about to get back on track, they come chasing after her. Would you call that human?

Maybe I should stop and try marksmanship, says Heiður. I can render them harmless by shooting holes in their rear tires.

Heiður, I can't believe you've got a firearm. You don't have a gun permit. And having a rifle near Edda? You know she's totally unpredictable. I'll have a nervous breakdown if you even mention it again.

Heiður gives me an irritated look, then steps on it and passes the van in the fog, honking the horn loudly. A little tirade about the driver finally losing her marbles comes from the sleepyhead in the backseat.

Heiður's getting good at keeping silent in order to preserve the peace. Would my poor friend ever have made this trip if she'd known how it would be? What her ears would have to hear, all those less-than-beautiful words. She's doing me the favor, sacrificing four days of her precious artist's life. The world's reward. I console myself with the thought that she'll have it far better on the way back, alone, left in peace with her own proper Telemann.

Menacing yellow headlights approach us rapidly from behind. They look like they're heading straight for us, but Heiður manages to turn aside at the last minute. Edda starts up with a shriek. We barely avoid running off the edge of the road.

Your wonderful friends aren't going to be content with just chasing us, I say. They want to kill us too.

Shut up, you old cow, says Edda.

Keep your barking to yourself, you poor thing, says Heiður.

You're both completely nuts, says Edda. I'm going to catch a ride back with them.

It's not going to happen, I say. I'll have the cops arrest them.

Ha ha. How are you going to do that? They're ahead of us, cackles Edda in her most loathsome tone.

I reach for my phone and there is a sudden ambush from the back: a blow to my shoulder, which slings me against the driver.

Always fucking sticking your nose in, you filthy old bitch, growls Edda, pulling my hair and jerking my head back.

Are you completely insane, kid? shrieks Heiður, fighting to keep the car on the road.

Now's the time. The accident that had to happen. A rash and fateful voyage leads to a fatal accident. What else?

Just stick to driving, bitch. Eat shit!

We hit a dip, nearly throwing Edda into the front seat. The car, now off the road, is tilted at such an angle that it's bound to flip as it joggles forward on the sloping bank.

No one says a word. Heiður and I jump out of the car. Even she, with her long shanks, has to resort to this method, since the door is high above the ground on her side. In the midst of all this, it strikes me that now she gets a chance to put herself in the shoes of Little Shortlegs.

Heiður waddles around in the gleam of the fog lights, kicking away a few rocks, and I try making a show of doing so as well, though I'm completely useless compared to her. I try imitating her, try not to be useless. She vanishes from sight, then ends up back within reach of the yellow gleam. The two fog-shadows, childhood friends, don't say a word, doing road construction bare-handed, without tools. Position: in the middle of nowhere.

Heiður suddenly leaps to the side of the car where Edda's sitting, or rather, half lying, and yanks open the door, which the girl barely manages to grab with one hand before she slides all the way out. Heiður, however, grabs the girl's free hand and jerks her out, causing her to fall and land on her side.

Are you nuts? My leg's injured.

Heiður steps on Edda's sprained ankle.

This is your very last chance. If you fuck up one more time, I'll leave you out on the road somewhere. If you're going to stay with us, you're going to sit in the front seat and get out of your mother's hair.

Just watch yourself, you old brute.

I really hope that you never realize what sort of burden you are on your mother, because if you ever did, *you'd be wrecked.*

Heiður takes her place behind the wheel. I sit in the back, terribly obedient. This time the dwarf doesn't have such a hard time getting in the car, which is lying almost on its side. A listing car, it's perfect for girls with short legs, if they're able to get in on the right side. But it's difficult to shut the door upward, toward oneself, and I'm a hair's breadth from falling out when I try.

A fumbling sound from out in the veiled world. The teenager in the fog. As forlorn as a dead girl buried in a nearby cemetery, with me given the task of looking after her grave because the family's nowhere near.

Heiður presses down on the gas pedal extremely cautiously, and the car crawls slowly up the incline on all four wheels. I'm still terrified it will overturn, but it rights itself on the road with a final jolt. Mission accomplished.

Well done, I say.

We barely avoided rolling over, says Heiður. If I'd turned the wheel to try to keep the car on the road, it would have flipped and we could have been killed. But I had the sense to turn the wheel in the same direction the car was going, which is why it stayed on its wheels.

No need to brag, says Edda. I've never come across such a rotten driver.

You have no shame, says Heiður. We nearly wrecked the car and died, and it's all your fault. You're like a wild beast.

Better than what *you're* like, says Edda, with a provocative laugh.

Listen, girls, I say from the backseat. Can't we make an agreement that you two not speak to each other?

I've got nothing to say to this old idiot. She's totally cuckoo.

I know you're used to better from your circle of friends. Maybe they're only slightly cuckoo, says Heiður. Cuckooed-out junkies who chase you out to the boonies. Let me tell you something. I've got a rifle, and if those damned fools come near us one more time, I'm going to use it.

Heiður, I say, that's *not funny*.

I'll shoot out their tires, and we'll see how far they go after that.

For God's sake, stop it. Both of you. One, two, and three.

Edda leans against the wool sweater that I'd been using as a pillow.

She glances askance at Heiður, with what seems to me fearful respect. That stands to reason. The only way to keep her under control was to trump her with violence, mental and physical.

I lean my head on a bag stuffed with bed linen and spread Heiður's down jacket over me. Yes, this will end with someone being killed. Maybe it'll be me. But I'm supposed to survive until then, thank you very much.

Oh, the mercy of being able to sit in the backseat, away from the bickering of the front seat. The grace of being free from Edda's supercritical eyes on the back of my head. Yes, shut up now, you bastards, and let me be.

For me, the trick to surviving has always been connected to car trips. The hum of the engine, the chance to be in your own world. Survival. Listening to the hum-humming, and not to Sibbi and

Mom squabbling over opening the window a crack, Dad trying to pacify them. Mom's grinding soliloquies about rites of passage among primitive peoples or the dysentery that killed Kamala the wolf-girl, interwoven with verses by her grandfather, the comic versifier and stalwart Antoníus, as well as her musings on the lives of the French fishermen in Icelandic waters. I've gradually come to the conclusion that a person is largely what he or she hears in childhood. Vulnerable to the rhetoric of others, unable to pick and choose.

Still hanging in the Andey living room is a photograph of Mom's surgeon, Martin, from the French hospital ship *Lodestar*, but there's no photo of the French fishermen who stood huddled by a stream, washing their clothing, their hands glacier-cold. The sea treated their poor hands so badly that they become swollen and cracked and bluish red, until they resembled vegetables and were called Iceland cabbages. The poor men never experienced summer warmth in their native lands, only the cold of the supremely bright Icelandic summer. They lived down south in little white houses by the sea, and in autumn when finally they were able to return home from the rough Icelandic fishing grounds, kids in wooden clogs ran to meet them, while bunches of blue flowers stretched up to their windows. When I was a kid, I drew pictures of all of this from stories told by Mom and Grandma and Dýrfinna. I understood that they all had their dream places where there was warmth and sunshine and great amounts of all kinds of fragrant herbs that didn't particularly need any special care to grow. I was sad that Grandma and Mom never made it to their dream places.

When I finally get to go see my dream place again, after three years' absence, it isn't by my own eager will, but rather as part of a desperate flight with my changeling from a host of phantoms and ghouls that wait in ambush for us on the Ring Road, planning to extinguish the little that's left of any spark of life within us. My dream place has become a destination to be dreaded. That's how it rolls if life is to continue, if we don't die early, before IT crashes over us. In my not-so-long life, I've experienced becoming a mother, as a child myself. I've seen my gentle child change into a new species that I don't recognize, and I've seen my dream place become a destination to be dreaded. PROGRESSION lets nothing alone if life continues; it grinds gemstones into dust, breaks people mentally and cripples souls, plows over pastures of plenty.

Stuck in a car with the tragedy of my life.

Back to the defensive mechanisms of childhood. I'm well trained for survival in a car. I survive by not existing. By considering the fluctuations of the speedometer as a Buddhist monk does a bowstring, by entering the rumbling of the engine as a dead Icelander does a mountain, by not existing in a way that the two in the front seat will never understand. Nor do my fellow travelers in the front seat exist, but their nonexistence is different from mine.

Different from the nonexistence of the light-gray bird loitering by the road, lost in existence. Soon dead under some car, my dear fat fulmar chick, unable to fly.

When my brother, Sibbi, was in the countryside during the summer, he amused himself by poking fulmars with a stick long enough so that the bird's vomit wouldn't reach him. Emptying out their vomit made it much easier to kill them.

Fulmar chicks are killed by biting them in the neck, grinding the neckbone between your teeth. Crack. A phlegmatic farmer, with a bitten bird in his mouth. That I'd rather not envisage.

Isn't it better for the nestlings to end up beneath car wheels than between a person's teeth?

It's all the same. All of it is just the same.

Heiður slips in a cassette tape, Schubert's *Unfinished Symphony*, which she knows pleases me.

All the beauty that man has created, in musical notes, language, images, buildings. The same species that uses its creative gifts to come up with innovative tortures and more efficient weapons, in the name of fighting against those who are almost like him, but not quite.

Those who don't quite belong to the same tribe, but almost. Those who have a slightly different religion, those who don't think quite the same. Man wants to eliminate those who resemble him, if they aren't exactly like him. I don't understand man. It's no wonder. I don't even understand the people next to me, my own dead mother, my best friend, my daughter. As for myself, never mind. There's something disgusting about people wallowing in thoughts about themselves, like weltering in a bathtub full of innards.

In a bathtub full of dead fulmars.

This bloody overturned bundle at the edge of the road isn't necessarily dead, but its brother with the tattered wing on the other side of the road is most definitely dead.

A dead bird across the highway.

It doesn't bode well.

I want to go home.

Nowhere is home.

Yet, oh, María, I want to go home.

. . .

Heiður puts the car in neutral and pulls the parking brake before taking off her sweater. Beneath it she's wearing a short-sleeved white T-shirt adorned with the Nike logo. She looks back at me and smiles. I shake my head and return her smile.

Heiður's arms, resting awkwardly on the steering wheel, are one of her most peculiar features. They're muscled like a man's, as if accustomed to intensive labor or weightlifting, but they end in the hands of a little girl, with slender, soft fingers that have hardly ever been subjected to manual labor of any kind. Yet it's strangely bulky where her wrists meet her hands. Someone should suggest to her old boyfriend, Plastic Tóti, that he should make a sculpture of Heiður's hands and arms holding a flute. This malformation of hers obviously hasn't escaped Heiður's notice either, because she always has the sense to wear long sleeves, preferably cuffed, when she steps onstage before an audience and raises her flute to her lips.

Once there was a master flutist who couldn't follow the score at the wheel of a pickup truck, or play it by ear. This remarkable female musician was a TONE-DEAF DRIVER, yet she drove anyway.

. . .

Edda Sólveig Loftsdóttir, my daughter, is snoring ever so softly, with her head leaning against the door. Her snores are like prissy maiden snuffles. A deceased elf-maiden with a golden band around her waist breathes through her.

The car rattles alarmingly on the potholes in the gravel road. This questionable staccato is the complete opposite of a supple, swift, hypnotizing dance.

The lovers' dance on the third day of the New Year was a series of continuous movements in which each movement was a preparation for the next, when an inkling of the one that came afterward was hidden in the movement that came before. A clearly formed dance from beginning until end. The dance following intermission was a logical continuation of the dance preceding intermission.

Lesser prophets may also have beautiful movements, but they don't harmonize. Each individual movement is separate and distinct.

No snow covers the dance of lovers in January. It emerges green from the snow in every season, and this movement will be there while the lovers live. My lover gave himself entirely to the heart-propelled dance, and his extremities danced accordingly. From then on, the man was mine. Wherever he goes, he's mine, but I keep this information carefully guarded.

How might that be, my friend in the west? Might happiness really exist? A man and a woman in love throughout time, a bit shy, slightly innocent—might it exist? A man and woman together for ages after starting off with a great love.

I think I know the answer. Years together with someone you love more than life itself is intolerable. A constant fear of not complying to his or her wishes, a never-ending anxiety that he or she will leave you. I think it's truly best to be with someone you care about, a good person who wishes you well, a pleasant person. Isn't love the most tedious thing of all? If grand, intimate love exists in the long run, it must surely kill off its lovers. Isn't love best in the form of an acute madness that seizes the soul and body? A madness that we must choke to death as soon as it's born, but that we're then allowed to remember for the rest of our lives, whether they're long or short.

Secret love. That's something for me, maybe for everyone. It costs nothing to desire in silence and stick to my own thoughts about things. There's something elegant about desiring what can't be had. Who was it that said he wished none such ill that his wishes were fulfilled? Could it be that the fulfillment of wishes in affairs of the heart is the slyest punishment meted out by the gods? How might it be to have desired a person for years, waited for him, fought for him, and in the end be granted the wish? To continue to love and be always in the red, because the other loves less. To discover latent defects, unworthiness. Not to be able to stop loving, not to be allowed to stop—because then life's purpose would disappear.

To be able to formulate your own thoughts is the greatest privilege. TO HAVE YOUR OWN THOUGHTS ABOUT THINGS, until death, undisturbed by the everyday: low-fat curds topped with skimmed milk, sour dishcloths. It's vulgar to compel dreams to come true. Am I really to devalue the winter night in Norðurmýri by battening it down to a double bed in the same bedroom for seasons on end? I should say not. Rather, it ought to be about extending the night, lap after lap on the racetrack of time. In any case, it's impossible to repeat it. Nights shouldn't be bound to particular locales.

To desire in peace. That's about it.

Like a doomed fulmar on the road.

Heiður swerves past an unfledged lump to avoid squashing it. The next car will surely tear a hole in the newly feathered skin and rip off a wing. For a young, obese fulmar on the road, about the only passable route is the one to heaven. I predict a rough end for it. Its fate won't be to fly up there, except in spirit.

The way east is marked with shredded, bloody fledglings. It would take a bulldozer to remove all these carcasses, hundreds of horrid carcasses. A carcass-dozer would be most useful and welcome on these roads in autumn.

In the densest of the fog, not even the next roadside marker is visible. It's doubtful we'll see anything living, unless some of the blood-smeared fledglings aren't truly dead. But at only twenty-five miles per hour, there's plenty of time to view the road's pathetic images. How nice it would be now to spend that time doing something else.

Stressed-out Heiður. There's nothing worse than driving blind.

I should head back to Reykjavík. This pile of carcasses isn't very promising. Nothing here looks promising.

Why don't I remember these doomed and dead birds from my travels with Mom, Dad, and Sibbi?

Autumn wasn't a time for traveling then. It's become so now.

Autumn is the time of dead fulmar chicks. I never want to witness this again.

THE TIME OF DEAD FULMAR CHICKS.

Are they obese, foolish, or unfledged? All of this at once, I suppose.

Heiður lays on the horn to save a bird. What does the bird do? Waddles like an old man on weak legs, two steps, off the road. Doesn't die now. Some time is left.

Why doesn't she use her stupid gun to finish off half-dead fulmars? It would be an act of mercy.

Did she really bring a rifle? Sneak it into a bag when no one was looking?

Heiður is tough on defense.

I'm soft all the time.

I don't deserve to be.

Don't deserve it!

Is it so desirable?

To be.

Like a doomed fulmar on the road.

Like a fulmar chick soon to be dead.

That's my story.

It's not interesting.

My death won't be interesting.

The day that I die will be a good day to breathe my last. Whatever day that is will be just fine for taking it. The last breath.

The day that I die will be a good day. But whether I look forward to it is another story. Even if I can't live as best as I'd like.

Can't live as best as I'd like. (Repeat and sing: NOT AS BEST, in chorus.)

I'd rather be dead.

If only I were allowed.

That's one among other things I'm not allowed.

We're not stopping at any gas station now, Harpa, in case those idiots are lying in wait for us.

I'm not afraid of those gangster runts.

How are you doing back there?

I was glad for the change.

It's more difficult for us to talk.

I'm so tired I don't feel like talking anyway. I'm in an utterly boring mood today.

You're so fun when you're boring.

Your typical double-edged compliment, Heiður.

The pickup truck takes a frighteningly slow pace up the steepest slope. The danger can't be seen except in short bursts, because the fog is merciful. A few sharply angled yards of scree and then the rising wall of black fog. The superhero Heiður drives very slowly, much too slowly even for these circumstances. She isn't used to this. My self-confident flutist isn't at home here.

The route up Almannaskarð is a route into the air, a kind of takeoff up into the fog roof. I'm afraid of heights and terrified of the most drastic slopes. Cars need suction cups for this mountain pass. I glance at Heiður. Yes, she's scared as well, the warrior herself.

I'm way too far over in the middle of the road, hisses Heiður. What if someone else comes along?

It's okay for you to move closer to the edge.

I'm too afraid.

Afraid that as we drive up the country's longest and steepest slope, a big rig will collide with us because we're on the wrong side of the road, or drive us off it, down the sheer scree. My mind tells me that at some point today we'll go off the road again. Maybe very far, maybe all the way. As far as it's possible to go.

Arriving at our destination on our backs. Where I can wallow.

Heiður, I say, trying to help, there's a sharp turn at the top, where it's steepest. Be prepared for it—we can't see a damned thing.

I'm fucking scared to drive here.

What else could you be?

If you were to ask me what I think is the ultimate countryside in all of Iceland, you'd think I would say my countryside, my fjord to the east. But I wouldn't say that, since my fjord isn't countryside, but more of a dreamland. I would say that Lón—which has nothing to do with me—is the ultimate Icelandic countryside. There at the lagoon between the majestic mountains of Eystrahorn and Vestrahorn, groups of sheep graze on sea-green grass and expand like fleece balloons. The sky above the sheep and adolescent lambs is a spotted floating sky, and a three-stranded peak juts up from clouds that wrap themselves like a fur scarf with a sparse fringe around the mountain's shoulders. The water in the estuary gleams as we draw nearer, and straight-beaked ringed plovers, so small that they should be called tiny plovers or plover pips, flock on the black glimmer, picking their way over the decoration beneath their feet. Incarnate ceramic birds from an Icelandic factory. To me *ringed plover* sounds modestly poetic. I write it behind my ear.

Ringed plover.

Ringed-plover stream.

Tiptoeing plovers are the antithesis to incapacitated fulmar chicks. Living birds are the liveliest of all that lives, but a dead bird is the deadest of all that was.

Over the iridescent estuary is an unbroken cloud band of turquoise light, a slightly cloying color. The western sky has assumed a hue of mild orange. I envision the past as having the color of an orange, but I have no idea of the color of the here and now. THE COLOR OF THE HERE AND NOW, though it's unknown, would be well suited for a poem or even as the title of a book; what book, I don't know.

Look, reindeer!

Wow, they're almost invisible in the landscape.

Their color is like eiderdown.

Keep your damned noise down, groans Edda.

Edda, look, there are reindeer.

Shove them up your ass.

The herd packs itself tighter and heads toward the car, with graceful movements, their heads bearing heavy V-shaped horns.

I thought they were supposed to be skittish.

A rust-brown stream rushes over a bridge spanning a powerful river running from Vatnajökull Glacier, past sweet summer cottages, paradisiacal foliage, and splendor.

I'm starving, moans Edda.

Good timing, I say. I actually have to go down to Útheimar to see Aunt Betty.

I'm up for that, says Heiður. I've never met her.

You've been missing out.

Is Betty the clairvoyant one?

Sure is.

But aren't we pressed for time because of those rascals? Don't we risk them catching us if we linger?

No, a detour will mess them up. Then we'll just finish the rest of the drive east all at once.

Plus, I continue, Betty's farm is fantastic. A lava complex rises there from the plain—and the farm is hidden within it, between hills, just a stone's throw from the sea.

We'll never reach the Eastfjords at the rate we're going, says Edda.

Are you in a hurry?

Damn, you make me crazy. I wish I hadn't come.

Heiður might not have another opportunity to say hello to Betty, I say. You might not, either. The two of you made such a good pair when you were little.

You think I really want to hang out with some supernatural old bat?

She's your great-aunt, after all.

Great-aunt, my ass.

It's down there. You can't see it until you've come all the way up to the door. And you know, Edda dear, Betty bakes the best cakes around.

I'm dying of hunger. You're keeping me starving, besides everything else.

Here, you can have a sandwich and a banana.

Ugh, gross, it's all crushed and shit. Besides, isn't the salmon poisonous? You barfed it up yesterday.

Let's go down to the farm. I'm hungry too, says Heiður, and this isn't picnic weather.

Heiður speeds up, accidentally honking the horn as she leans into the accelerator. Two little birds fly up from the other side of a rock, and a russet lump of a lamb hops across the road, right in front of the car, forcing Heiður to brake.

Lamebrained beast, says Heiður, hammering on the wheel and unintentionally honking the horn again.

Are you losing it?, howls Edda, scandalized. How easily she's scandalized, this scandalous girl.

Wasn't it Bettý who foresaw your mom's death in her dream?, asks Heiður, regrouping.

She sees everything in dreams. She should do live broadcasts from dreamland. There's so much going on.

Does it all happen?

Everything happens in retrospect, naturally.

Poor Grandma Sól, to die so early, says Edda. She was always so good to me.

What she means is: Not like you, Mom. You're always so awful. Which is an out-and-out lie. It's also a lie that her grandmother was always *so good* to her. The truth is that her grandmother was indifferent to her, albeit not as much as she was to me.

The indifference wasn't even the worst of it; the worst was her lack of constraint. She had so little control over herself that she clearly chose favorites between Sibbi and me, paid much more attention to him than me, spoiled him behind Dad's back. This she did so well that in the end my brother became an utterly spoiled mama's boy. Sibbi ruined his father, destroyed his life's work, financially speaking, put him in a rest home prematurely. I can hardly stand to think of it.

Dad: victim of my mother, victim of his son. He doesn't even get to have his own daughter, THE APPLE OF HIS EYE. She's taken from him as well. No, she was never his. My father's life, a tragedy that I can't bear thinking of.

Turn off the road there.

What kind of person is Bettý?, asks Heiður. More like Dýrfinna or your mom?

Hmm, I don't know, but she's really quite a show. That much I can promise.

Your mother was quite a show too.

Yes, but she was an evening show. This one's more like a matinee. It's absolutely astounding what she comes up with.

Strangely enough, I'm looking forward to visiting this aunt of mine, despite the circumstances. I've never really known her. In fact, I haven't had any interest in her before, except as a UFO that would best be kept above the clouds.

Aw, slow down, Heiður, you're breaking my back. Is this a road or a giant pothole?

Harpa, look! Oh my God!

A person dressed in a skirt and boots strides along the road with a big blue bag over his or her shoulder.

Is that a man or a woman?

I'm not surprised you ask.

Woman's skirt, man's haircut.

Now I see. It's Hrikka. Hrikka Kontaratandis, delivering the mail. She's from Lithuania or one of those countries. She's just had her hair cut.

Huh?

She came here after the war. She's married to an Icelander. Rumor was she had an affair with Valdi.

Betty's Valdi?

Yes. He was a handsome man.

I don't doubt it.

Postperson Hrikka waves as we drive past her. Her bulging blue bag must be heavy.

Why is she walking?

Don't ask me why people walk, I say. By the way, Betty apparently didn't care that Valdi was sleeping with someone else. I guess she's so busy with her contacts from beyond that it didn't matter to her.

A tidy, well-constructed barred gate appears on a road between lava formations. A road that leads nowhere, to no visible destination.

At turnouts on both sides of the road are numerous cars. Not the shells of them as at Arnbjartur's, but rather, real cars.

A party, says Heiður.

Let's leave, says Edda. The place is packed with people.

It can't be a party. The cars would be closer to the house.

It must be a family reunion, then.

Útheimar

G ood Lord, it's the yellow Bronco.
     Dead right, and they're tailing us.

May I point out to you that they obviously arrived before us.

At least I'll have the chance to ask Betty who on earth these people are.

I wouldn't bother.

As I walk past the yellow Bronco, I take a quick peek in its window. The farmer's lying on the backseat, with a russet sheepskin over him.

What did you see?, asks Heiður.

Nothing.

I can tell that you saw something.

On a moss-covered lava rock by the side of the road sits a man I can't quite place, though I know he's a distant relative. He's gesticulating, talking to himself.

Is that guy insane?, asks Edda.

Maybe he's an amateur actor from Höfn rehearsing a part.

How come I'm not connecting with you?, says the man sitting on the rock, tearfully. Can't I make any impression on you at all?

This relative of mine is all set to break down. I hurry past him, with Edda and Heiður close behind.

In the hollow to the north of the farm stands a cluster of tents: blue cabin tents with extensions, rescue-squad-red one-man dome tents, old Scout tents.

So it is a family reunion after all.

There's no one in view, but boisterous gossiping resounds from the tents. A jabbering monologue in my mother's style can be heard from a grand-looking cabin tent near the rise between the hollow and the farm.

I stop when I hear something said about Teitur, my great-uncle. Heiður listens with me, but Edda rushes up the rise.

This is the only existing photo of him, says a strong male voice. A handsome man until he was thirty, and enormously intelligent. Born and bred in Dylgja. He had a child with each of his two wives, Sabína the Younger and Sabína the Older. Their fathers' families were both from Kirkjubæjarklaustur, and it turned out that they were first cousins three times removed, so they were more closely related than it seemed at first.

Did the sisters have the same mother?

So they did.

Half sisters, then?

They were much more than that, of course, because the fathers were so closely related to each other. But this about the fathers' relationship wasn't discovered until later, because the paternity of one of them was misattributed.

But Teitur himself?

He had three children, and a fourth who died young, whom he had with Sabína, who later became his wife, and the wife of the two brothers the years that they lived at Litla-Klaustur. They had plenty of rough-hewn descendants, folks notorious for their scandalous verses, unscrupulousness, drunkenness, and bookishness, who couldn't wear green except when the moon was full because of the minuscule family ghost.

What was Teitur's first wife called?

She was called Sabína, the niece of his second wife, also Sabína, who died giving birth to their second child.

Oh, I thought they had three children together.

No, the third child had its own mother. He had that child with Regína when he was between female relatives, but he and Regína were half cousins, which wasn't exactly looked upon favorably by all. But no degeneration was observed in the child, who was named Ketill, although Yngvi, his son, was born lame in his right leg. Regína then married Teitur's brother Þorsteinn and had seven sons by him, all but six of whom died young. All of them worked clearing new hayfields in Suðursveit, including two twins . . .

The tent falls silent. Heiður trots off, and I follow her example. As we leave the hollow and head up the rise, a female voice in the tent asks: Identical?

When we reach the top, Heiður and I take a breather, smiling widely as we look down at sharp lava projections sticking up decoratively from the ground. In their shelter grow numerous foreign flowers, red-orange with yellow centers—even up here—and the grass is so vivid and so hardy that I foresee a green life for it through the winter and into spring. We can see straight down into Betty's garden—an orchard and vegetable garden and flower garden, which is remarkably colorful on the first day of September. In chubby red-currant bushes, thrushes pilfer red berries until they're full to bursting, their every peep stifled by gluttony.

Right up near the farmhouse, in a little clearing in the garden, we find an old tent. It resembles the tent we used on camping trips in days gone by, when Dad in knickerbockers and kneesocks heated Maggi soups on a Primus stove and squeezed Vals ketchup onto our hot dogs. As I recall, the old tent was pretty much the only place where Mom ever behaved like a normal person.

Heiður and I gaze over the plain and a small strip of the sea as well, where two boats dawdle idly on our side of the haze. The tranquility is so overpowering that it's as if a highly efficient silence-machine had been started in order to drown out all sounds, except for the dull babbling from the tents. Here, now, humans have the floor, and the animals make their absence conspicuous by saying nothing. The drizzle and the stillness have rocked both the domestic and wild animals to sleep. Not a whimper from the dog, no buzzing of flies. the migratory birds are either gone already or are silently gathering strength for their lengthy flights.

So it *is* real!, exclaims Heiður, skipping off down the slope along a path marked with glossy black sea stones.

Aunt Betty comes to the door with Edda at her heels, like a dog or Uncle Arnbjartur's pet lamb at Glóra. Betty seems even taller than I remembered, not an inch below five eleven. She's thin, and her curly, tangled, blackish-gray hair is formed in a peculiar wreath, its ends meeting beneath her chin. She waves to us with a discreet royal swing of her hand.

The welcoming ceremony at Útheimar is a CEREMONY OF SILENCE. As we make our way out of the garden, past the old tent, and through the garden gate to the farmhouse, we say nothing. The word *hello* isn't spoken until we come up to the door, and then it's spoken softly, as if it's sacrilege to utter a sound, as if we're guests at a funeral and the ceremony is about to begin.

Either my aunt has lost weight since last time or I'd forgotten about her sunken cheeks and spindly, wrinkled neck. Beneath her deep-brown eyes, dark rings reach down to her cheekbones. Her eyebrows, thick and steel gray, meet in the middle, like those of a Mediterranean male. Nothing about Aunt Betty is worth noticing but her eyes and their amazing enclosures, which draw all the attention. They're the center of this woman.

If you can manage to tear yourself loose from the overwhelming power of Aunt Betty's eyes and make an attempt to assess her overall appearance, it's clear, without any doubt, that it's more akin to beauty than ugliness, more akin to youth than old age. But this is a strange conclusion when considering each detail in and of itself.

Betty speaks so softly that even a person with perfect hearing has to focus hard to catch what she says, or even more, has to read her lips at the same time.

Would you like to come in?, asks Betty. I thrust my head forward in order to hear better. She misunderstands my gesture and thinks that I'm going to kiss her, so I give her an awkward kiss that lands near her ear.

Maybe you'd like to start by having a look in the tent?, she says, or so it seems to me.

What?

The tent here in the clearing.

It's just like the tent we had when I was a kid, I say.

It's the very same one.

Okay, I say with ordinary politeness.

Actually, people are generally much more polite than might be claimed. They take what's handed to them, and say, at their most prudent, *okay*, when they're served up some sort of crap. Does that mean I'm no exception, saying *okay* instead of asking how on earth our old tent has come to be here?

Your mom feels most at home inside it, says my aunt.

Edda dashes ahead, now with a cat suddenly at her heels. Damned if it doesn't look like Mr. Björn from Bollagata.

I didn't know about the family reunion, I say.

I wouldn't call it that, says my aunt, dragging out her words.

Betty leads the way while I take the opportunity to study her appearance. Her pink flannel garment is neither robe, smock, nor apron, nor is it a dress. It has short sleeves, reaches down to midthigh, and is tied at the back. The cut is reminiscent of a surgical gown, but its material resembles that of an infant's pajamas. Betty's wearing thick-soled sandals that increase her already considerable height. They don't look comfortable.

The tent is empty except for a thin mattress and an old Primus stove, just like the stove from the camping trips of my youth.

That's how Primuses were when I was a kid, I say, turning to Edda, who's sitting next to me.

In the dim light inside the tent, Betty's eyes are two black holes that shine, however that might be possible. Aren't black holes naturally opaque?

So you're on your way to Dýrfinna's.

Yes, I'm going to stay with her this winter, and Edda's staying in Andey.

I'm sure you'll both be quite comfortable.

Mom insisted, says Edda grumpily.

It will be grand, says Betty. Hasn't the trip gone well?

Sure, absolutely, I say. But I have no mind to discuss it in any detail.

It most certainly hasn't gone well, says Edda. Heiður's always running off the road, and was even going to head back to Reykjavík yesterday.

Yes, and why was that?, I ask.

There are five men following you, says Betty, without warning.

The Primus flame illuminates her hair-wreath and the black holes of her eyes. She looks like a foreign demon, from the heart of darkness. I decide to leave the tent to avoid being exposed to spiritual blather, but my rear end is so heavy that I can't be bothered to move.

Five men following you, repeats Betty.

I heard you, I say. I glance at Edda, who appears to be smiling.

There are only three men, says the girl.

The oldest has dark skin and dark hair. Tall, slim.

Similar to you, Aunt, I say. But it's like splashing water on a goose.

He's very fond of you, but I don't understand what he's saying. Something wrong with his vocal cords?

He's speaking a foreign language.

Can't you ask him just to speak his own language?

I think that's what he's doing. He's not Icelandic, that's for sure.

What a hopeless spirit—it can't even make itself understood by the medium.

Who said that it's a spirit?

Are you starting to see living people as well?

You know him, and your late mother knew him. He wants to get in touch with you, Harpa. He's a very sad man.

He'll have to stay sad. I'm not psychic.

You don't have to be psychic to see him, he's as alive as day and urgently needs to speak to you.

Then he should pick up the phone or drop me a line.

But the other four, aren't they alive too?, asks Edda.

One of them is a strikingly elegant man, very tall, but rather stout. He'll soon need to lose weight for health reasons. He's wearing a little hat and a woolen cape.

Good Lord, says Heiður.

You know him.

What more can you tell me about him?

His hair is grayish, face angelic. Big, beautiful hands.

Dietrich Bacon, I say.

Impossible, says Heiður. He can't be on our heels. He's my boyfriend, and I'm going abroad next week to see him.

I only say what I see, says Betty.

What about the other three?, asks Edda.

Indeed. It's just three little whelps, carrying an extremely dangerous book. You should burn it, little Edda, if they try to foist it off on you.

They've already let me have it. It's mine.

Burn it, along with everything that's in it.

Is that the book they let you have in Kirkjubæjarklaustur?

Yes.

What's the book?, I ask.

Vendetta and Voodoo, says Edda, trying to make her voice sound terrifying.

Heiður bursts out laughing.

It isn't funny, says Betty.

What type of vehicle is the foreigner driving?, asks Heiður.

He's coming by sea. Both of the foreigners are for Harpa.

That doesn't make sense, says Heiður.

I only say what I see.

I'm going to get some fresh air, says Heiður.

I only say what I see, repeats my aunt in an extremely soft, deep voice as Heiður squirms out the tent door.

Tell us more about the boys, says Edda excitedly.

They're slightly older than you, my dear. The driver, he must be seventeen. But you should beware of these birds. They're involved in all sorts of nonsense.

They're my friends, says Edda.

I don't think these are good friends to have. Stay away from them.

Is it sometimes possible to get through to Grandma in her old tent?, asks Edda.

She does hang about.

I inch my way to the tent flap, on all fours. It's impossible to listen to this.

Where are you going?, says Betty.

Out. You should be careful of what you say when adolescents are present. They're so impressionable.

I glance over my shoulder, still on all fours, and look into my aunt's face as I push aside the flap. Daylight falls on her uncommon head and hair.

We've come here mostly to bum a cup of coffee, not to listen to such . . . such . . . crap, if I'm going to be completely honest.

Don't be offended. All I'm trying to do is offer some guidance.

I hurry out of the spiritual tent and take quick steps to the farm-house. Heiður is sitting silently in front of the door, on a kitchen stool that has been used for paint jobs and is splotched with every color of the rainbow. Her expression is stony.

You hardly need any more proof, she says as soon as I'm within earshot.

What?

Harpa, this aunt of yours looks like a foreigner. And you actually resemble her. You can forget those incredible speculations of yours that your dad isn't your true father.

What do you mean I look like her? She looks like a walking joke.

What about the hair color, what about the skin color, what about her eyes?

Stop it.

The other two emerge from the tent and head toward us, young and old, tall and slender and limping, both of them, one with tangled gray-flecked hair, the other with red hair. My aunt in her pink variation on a robe and Edda in stretch pants and a black T-shirt, with a sneering white skull on the back. The cat follows them like a dog. I'll be damned. Everything here is after everything else. This cohesion at Útheimar isn't to my liking.

Wouldn't you know it? My aunt and her great-niece are holding hands. This sight startles me so much that I have to lean up against the fence for support. There's no denying that Edda is capable of surprising her opponents.

You must be hungry, says my aunt.

Yes, says Edda. I haven't had a decent bite this entire trip.

Heiður gets up and says: That's not true. Your mother brought gourmet snacks. Yesterday you had roast lamb.

I've got plenty of cakes for you, and there's no wait on the coffee. It's all out on the table.

Were you expecting visitors?

Yes, I was starting to expect you.

Did Dýrfinna call?, I ask, feeling a bit ashamed, because I know that the relationship between the sisters leaves much to be desired. Dýrfinna can't stand the way Betty messes with the beyond.

Dýrfinna?, says Betty. No. Not her.

A narrow foyer is the first thing to greet someone entering Útheimar by the main door, and then the kitchen. You take two steps inside and you're in the kitchen, just like that. The housewife forbids us from taking off our shoes.

The huge round table in the kitchen nearly fills the whole room. This table and the Aga coal stove that Betty hasn't had the heart to part with are like two independent but harmonious personalities, an old couple that rules over the home's nerve center.

LUCKAN SKAL VARA STÄNGD.

The Swedish runes on the Aga stove that no one could interpret when I was a kid.

Three megacakes adorn the table's white linen: one cream cake, decorated neatly with strawberries and kiwi; a chocolate cake with mousse and delicious-looking chocolate shavings; and a stout cake-roll with yellow cream, sprinkled with sugar. At the center of the table is a large porcelain dish of flatbread and smoked trout. My aunt has set the table with her best cups and saucers. I remember the Chinese porcelain service from my childhood. It's as thin as a shell, blue and white, with a peacock pattern. I count nine cups and one glass, and there's enough food for at least ten people. By my last count, however, there are only four of us.

Edda takes a seat at the table without being invited. Heiður and I follow her example. Edda grabs a piece of flatbread and munches it noisily, despite no one telling her to help herself.

Betty pours coffee and asks Edda whether she'd like some Coke. The girl is visibly thrilled, and even says *yes, please*. Betty goes to the pantry and returns with a one-and-a-half-liter bottle, pours a glass for Edda, and places the bottle on the table in front of her. The girl has already grabbed hold of a second piece of flatbread before

Heiður and I even begin, and she drains her glass in one draw. Betty hovers over her and refills the glass. Thanks, says the girl before bursting out with a long muffled belch. Heiður and I both nibble at pieces of flatbread, which are such sweet appeasement to our hunger that it takes enormous willpower not to gobble them down noisily like the teenager.

I'm going to stay behind, says Edda, as she starts in on a slice of brown cake, having finished her second glass of Coke.

I think that would suit you fine, says Betty.

I'm careful to keep my mouth shut. Heiður gives me a highly meaningful look.

You wouldn't mind, Mom, would you?

Wouldn't it be best for you to start with what we agreed on?, I say. If you don't like it out east, you can see whether your great-aunt is serious.

Where we are is also out east, says Edda, with a nasty laugh.

She continues to chow down. I'm appalled at the sight, but I'd rather not make it my business. Betty is still hovering over us, cutting slices of cake and pouring drinks and serving us, and crowning everything by going to the pantry to fetch a giant container of crullers. I dare not tell the woman to sit down. After all, it's her house.

Are you expecting people from the family reunion for coffee?

A lot of things turn up here.

I wonder why Dýrfinna didn't tell me about this reunion. I called her the day before yesterday.

This isn't the sort of reunion that would interest Dýrfinna. She's completely insensitive.

Are you saying it's not a family reunion?

Maybe not in a traditional sense.

What is it, then?

Mixed participation. We're experimenting with it.

How so?

People from here and from the beyond.

So all the participants must be psychic. The living ones, I mean, interjects Heiður.

To some extent, says Betty, sliding cream-cake slice number two onto Edda's plate. Of course we've had a bit of trouble, because not everyone sees everyone, which can make the overall relationships complicated in practice. I, for example, am the only one who sees your mother, and only in her old tent, but the others have some doubts about it—and about me as well, even though I've produced various evidence. When we held a closed meeting in your old family tent yesterday morning, we were overwhelmed by a perfume scent that everyone who'd met your mother recognized.

Madame Rochas, I say, in my finest pronunciation.

Heiður laughs out loud.

Lout, says Edda, her mouth full of cream cake.

I succeed in eating such a large portion of these baked delights in such an astonishingly short time that I'm more or less in sugar shock. You'd think that Betty kneaded drugs into the dough, because I feel almost unable to stop. The taste is irresistible. These aren't like country-girl cakes at the brink of the world but more akin to something you'd get at the finest patisseries in Vienna, Zurich, or Warsaw. The cake roll and cream cake might seem a bit too clunky for such places, but they're perfect on the inside, and the chocolate cake is impeccable both inside and out. How does Aunt Betty bake these exotic cakes having never stepped beyond this country's borders? It's true that Betty isn't Icelandic in appearance—I have to grant Heiður that. Still, she really reminds me of someone. I just can't think of who.

Please excuse me for a moment, I say.

You know the way, don't you?, asks Betty.

Yes, I say, and walk through the laundry room, which is adjacent to the kitchen, to the bathroom just beyond. I remember the unusual arrangement of the rooms at Útheimar from my childhood.

I feel queasy from my gluttony by the time I get to the bathroom, ever so tidy, without even a hint of the smell of cows. If anything, a scent of perfume hangs in the air. Madame Rochas.

Is that you, Mom, or is this just an earthly perfume scent, from a bottle?

I sit down limply on the edge of the bathtub and wish I could take a boiling hot bubble bath to alleviate my soreness. There are various methods for acquiring sore muscles; the method that I used last night is painless, and much more.

Oh, a nice soak in the tub would take too long. Hot baths are one of the things that aren't available on this long, long journey. We'd be unduly late to Andey, and end up spending the night with Dýrfinna.

My chin is more swollen and red now than when I looked in the mirror this morning. I haven't used a trace of makeup to cover over evidence of my nocturnal pleasures. I want to bear my war injuries like a man.

I fix my eye on the big, elaborate white-and-gold medicine cabinet hanging above the massive sink. Completely stuffed, I get up from the edge of the tub and open the cabinet. Despite its vastness, it turns out to be empty, apart from a brown pharmaceutical vial labeled *Peanut Oil*, as well as one bottle of Madame Rochas perfume.

I knew you were a fake, dear aunt, spraying the area with perfume and pretending that it's evidence of the afterlife.

At the same moment I realize who she reminds me of. She's nearly identical to my generous friend Gabriel Axel, a living, revenant replica. They're similar in height, similar in posture. They speak exceptionally quietly, and both have adopted the mannerisms and gait of the deceased.

When I return to the kitchen, I feel a bit sad seeing the three ruined gourmet cakes, devoured by three hungry female wolves from the wild roads of Iceland. At the same time I also notice that Edda Sólveig Loftsdóttir has almost completed what she set out to do: finish one and a half liters of Coke in ten minutes.

Small and full, stiff in all my joints, I don't want to sit down, because I might not be able to stand up again. I lean on the edge of the table like a drunken woman, and have half a mind to ask, in a drawling voice: Spirit of the glass . . .

Instead I say, trying to speak clearly through my sugar shock: I don't mean to be rude, but we really need to keep track of the time.

Heiður and Edda react astonishingly quickly, jumping up from the table. Bettý says that she fully understands our need to press on.

You're always welcome here, she says to Edda.

Maybe I'll come back, says the girl.

Think about it. There's plenty of time. You're also welcome, Harpa, if you need a break. It's not such a long drive.

I don't see myself in Dýrfinna's Israeli Willys jeep on the steep, icy slopes of Hvalnes.

It doesn't generally snow appreciably until January, and some winters there's very little snow at all. Time is on your side.

Maybe we'll come visit you if we can get a ride. I wouldn't dare to go far in the jalopy, even if the weather's good.

You'd attract attention on the road, says Bettý, with a slow, swelling laugh.

Edda bids farewell to her aunt with a kiss and says she'll come back soon. She skips off ahead of us into the garden and disappears between the rowan trees standing in a ring around the tent from my youth.

NIGHT QUARTERS OF MY DECEASED MOTHER. Yet not her grave.

Heiður and I silently plod along in Edda's track. On the rise, I turn around to see Bettý still standing by her door. I wave to her, but she doesn't wave back. I'm now less than certain that she's there, even though it looks like she is.

The murmur of voices grows louder in the hollow, mixed with outbursts of laughter. Once the drizzle stopped, the tent people started moving about.

I don't feel like talking to anyone, I say softly to Heiður. Let's just get to the car, quickly.

Stupid of us not to have taken the road, she says. We could have avoided this completely.

From the top of the rise, we see four thickset men in creaking nankeen overalls approaching us, carrying a little piano. They're followed by three others, two musclemen with mottled headbands carrying a piano stool with a little redheaded woman sitting on it. She's wearing a beige all-weather coat and flat-soled black shoes with laces. She laughs in a chiming soprano with a slow vibrato, like an old prima donna. The men who carry her and the stool laugh in a pulsating tenor, hohohoho-ho, their necks short and their thighs bulging. Just as the piano movers reach the crest of the rise, the two of us take a detour in order to avoid crossing paths with them, and whether it's because of that or something else, they start laughing even louder, in bumptious tones. The one who laughs longest drops into a baritone that dies out beneath the superbright soprano of the little woman. This is followed by a brief silence, but finally this choir is shaken together into a filigree of tenors, sopranos, and baritones. This booming prankster-symphony is like an eastern gale springing up out of the blue in the late-afternoon stillness of the first day of September.

Why are they carrying her?, asks Heiður.

Maybe she can't walk.

Is she a relative of yours?

Not that I know.

The little woman whose legs might be paralyzed plays the patriotic song "Iceland Scored with Inlets." Individual members of the side of the family from Dylgja, along with unrelated spouses and poorly behaved children in good-quality coats, arrange themselves around the instrument on the rise. The porters are the backbone of the choir, and the razor-sharp soprano of the accompanist slices through all other vocal ranges. The clan croons . . . *who have carried me at your breast* . . . children whine, a teenager puffs on a cigarette, and the swan couple on the pond has had enough of it. They take off and, flying low, join in the chorus . . . *as the Creator deems* . . . with a churlish honking and noisy flapping right over the clan's heads . . . *be blessed, Iceland, bless you* . . .

No one gives us so much as a glance as we walk off, except the mother and son from the yellow Bronco, as they stand there in nearly identical orange-and-bright-green rainwear, and wink at us as a two-year-old might. I don't wave in return, surprised that they see through the cloak of invisibility that Betty the conjurer or someone else must have wrapped around us.

Guess what I spotted in Betty's bathroom? An entire container of the perfume that my mom used. She sprayed the damned tent with Madame Rochas and acted as if it were convincing evidence of Mom's presence.

Heiður laughs, saying: The old lady sure is incredible.

Leave Betty alone, demands Edda. You know nothing about Betty. She misses Grandma Sól. They were such great friends.

They were always the best of friends. Both completely nuts. I always imagine them together with Seadevil. You remember that story.

I've never heard it, says Heiður.

Yes, you have. It's the most amazing story. Grandma told it to me every summer; I told it to Edda and, God willing, she'll tell it to her children.

I don't want anything to do with kids!, screeches Edda.

Not yet.

Never, you old crow.

Well, it all started when people on farms to the east thought it a sensible idea to raise puppies to give to the French fishermen when they came in the spring. Betty took a liking to a black puppy that was intended for the sailors and named it Seadevil. Then came spring. Grandpa Helgi and Great-grandpa Antoníus rowed out to one of the French fishing smacks with the puppy, in order to trade it for cognac and biscuits. Mom and Betty had gotten to go with them to the village, and they were waiting on the pier, half whimpering and holding hands. Father and son remained aboard for some time, before rowing away a bit tipsier than when they arrived. They'd only taken two or three oar-strokes when a splitting howl came from the French vessel, and a pitch-black lump cast itself overboard and made a beeline toward land, reached the shore where the sisters were waiting, and wrapped its wet paws around Betty's neck. When Grandpa reached land he said, Seadevil will stay with us. The puppy became the greatest of sea dogs—it had human wits about it. And it left behind a lot of tales worth telling.

So Betty called the creature back by magic, says Heiður.

. . .

The surrounding pastures bear the marks of autumn, in hues of red and tinges of yellow. I refuse to think about autumn, which is half-way or completely here, and the impending winter. An Icelander shouldn't travel in his own country after the thirty-first of July. On the first day of August, the land begins to display where it's headed. On the fifteenth of August, the first autumn leaves blow onto basement steps and the nights cool dramatically. The truth about Icelandic summer is that it lasts for just four weeks—that is, the month of July. It isn't until the start of July that the trees really get going and the flowers blossom in earnest. Right at the end of July everything starts showing signs of decline. But we shouldn't talk about that. Instead, we should try to avoid making it clear to ourselves just how frightfully short the summer is. For if we do, we despair.

Pale-red land
violet tinge
yellowish moss.

You fell asleep in a flash, says Heiður. Are you feeling under the weather?

No worse than usual, I reply.

The sleepless woman dozed. Aunt Betty put her to sleep.

SLEEPLESS BEAUTY, that's what I'll call my autobiography. How did I not think of that before?

The extremely dangerous book, according to Betty, which Teddi, in his Norwegian sweater, gave to Edda in Kirkjubæjarklaustur, has fallen to the floor of the car. I pick it up: *Vendetta and Voodoo*, a somewhat thick, shabby paperback. What a title, what a book.

What are the chapters called in such a work? Chapter One: Vendetta in the Family. It's clearly an absolutely marvelous scientific treatise. Chapter Seven: The History of the Evil Eye. When I try to go to that chapter, I discover it's not in the book. Its center has been cut out, and a petite plastic sachet full of white powder and brown tablets is glued neatly into the gap.

I pull the parcel from the book and open it, dip my finger in the powder and lick it. It tastes like potato flour. Do they mix potato flour into amphetamine powder? Or is this uncontaminated potato flour from Katla, Inc.? The pills have a suspiciously strong vitamin B flavor.

It would be easy to send Heiður to Reykjavík with this tomorrow, have her speak directly to Rikki, the cop, and find out what the hell it is. Suspicious Teddi would hardly expose himself by handing over drugs on Highway No. 1 in the presence of two witnesses. Obviously, he'd run the risk of the witnesses discovering the book's contents—as Heiður and I did.

I stick the bag in my pocket. God, what a piteous fuss this is on the part of these poor boys. A chase or pseudo chase, drug smuggling or pseudo drug smuggling using books. These stupid actions convince me that they can do nothing to us, and they know it. They're powerless little runts trying desperately to cause damage.

Of course they could have taken Edda with them back to town yesterday. But to take her where? What would they have done with her? Put her in a cage in some distilling shed?

The stupid, tattered old book goes into my bag as I send the gang in the Yellow Hen some virulent telepathic messages.

Oh, to be free to drive long distances at the water's edge. To glide along on the way east. It's almost like sailing. On the land side of the lagoon. Imagining the sea bigger than it is.

In the sea, solace and protection for sleepless women who sail wakefully into danger.

Women who want to be dead but do not have permission for that now

and make great strides in the art of survival, nondead, their minds mostly intact.

In the art of having my own thoughts about things.

Mostly about Edda Sólveig Loftsdóttir, my ex-child

who I grieve as I see fit

as if she were dead, as if she had died at the age of twelve when she was a normal child. When she was a girl of initiative, a girl who tidied her room and did her homework, chatted unself-consciously with everyone and looked her interlocutors in the eye, answering concisely the usual questions about her age and future prospects.

My lot. To have a child who destroys herself.

I'm like most people in how I compare my misery with the misery of others.

According to my calculations of comparative misery, no greater misery can exist. To have a child who treats her own dear life so badly that she could die from it, or even worse. To have a child who is sick or dies in an accident—that's something over which we have no influence. There's no one to blame. You nurse the child back to health if possible, you take care of her as long as you live or she lives. Those who lose a normal child will never be the same, but they have beauty on their side, the beauty in the memory of their dead child. There's no beauty in the memory of a child who's turned into a monster. If she dies, there's ugliness in the memory, and there's someone to blame, most likely the mother. The mother who didn't know how to raise the child, the mother who pumped polluted, sinful blood into her. In other words, I destroyed the child who's destroying herself. How did I do it? What cunning methods did I use? So cunning that I wasn't aware of them myself, so cunning that I still don't see what I did that was so incredibly wrong. Except for getting pregnant at the wrong time. But others before me have done the same.

I've calculated that no sorrow is heavier than that of having a child who transforms herself into a monster and frightens and torments its closest relatives, a child who is at the same time a victim of the unbearable ugliness of life.

To be afraid of one's own child and at the same time to cry over her fate.

My little daughter who once was, is now a delinquent child.

Enduring miseries like a woman in a war-torn country.

She's been abused, my little daughter.

My little daughter who once was lives in a bad place, and no one knows who made her that home.

It's my lot to suspect myself of doing her wrong.

My daughter, I'll grieve for you as my little one, as you were *before*, from the cradle to the grave. My memory of you is beautiful. Dead at thirteen. What followed never became a life.

I grieve for you in my dreams, my poor girl, weeping warm tears that heat my cheeks. My sobs heat me internally. I burn with sorrow because my child's life was beautiful, my only child, who died, and I'm burning because NO ONE WAS TO BLAME.

A mishap!
I am not
to blame,
dear Mother.

In waking moments the sorrow grows cooler, because my child isn't dead but lives a living death. My tears are hard as hail, my heart is chilled, because my daughter lives a life that's not a life. I don't recognize her as a person, and there's someone to blame for it, probably me, who got pregnant by an excited, shy peer, fifteen years old, and wouldn't have the fetus aborted. That was far beyond my imagination. The fetus that asked, when she was a nine-year-old child, Mom, why didn't you terminate me?

Why didn't you terminate me?

Is it this question that's so grating that my daughter can't live? Can neither live nor die. Or rather, lives in death.

Edda S
my pride
valiant and red-haired
came into the world at her mother's first attempt to create a child.

Edda S never misses the mark.

In her youth: her very young mother's helper
an ally in the struggle against chauvinists and counter jumpers who are
too good to do their jobs.
A booster when things looked bleak.
Had all the floors scrubbed, nine years old, by the time Mom came home.

Edda S
my pride.

No one was to blame.

I grieve for you exceedingly
tepid sadness that I swallow like boiled milk.

It's the cold shiver of grief that I fear.
Which is why I held your funeral at thirteen.

A funeral at the eleventh hour, before disaster struck.

My former pride and joy, Edda in her element.

Sweet-smelling nursling
a two-year-old whirlwind who spoke in tongues
a three-year-old strict and sweet mother of dolls
a five-year-old philosopher
a seven-year-old dusting girl
a nine-year-old principal of cows
an eleven-year-old devourer of books
Mommy's girl, Grandpa's girl.

After thirteen years, Edda S was sucked into a black hole.

Edda S,
take your quilt and go
back to your single mother
she needs you
she has nothing but you.

Don't cheat me of a daughter, my daughter.
Who will walk to the store for me on slippery sidewalks when
the time comes?

Don't cheat me of a granddaughter, my daughter.
Entertainer, helper, soul mate.

Granddaughter who will inherit the cocotte Cosette.

Don't cheat me of a grandson.
A vindictive baby
who slurps down mother's milk with loud moans.

A swaddling infant who changes into an impertinent schoolboy.
I'll tell him about Great-grandma Una, less about poor
Grandma Sól.
I'll tell him and his sister about Dýrfinna, less about Betty
and about my lethally obscure paternity when they're grown
up. Maybe.

I'll tell them of our flight to the east, three female refugees in a
pickup truck.
They were chased by little pricks in a pathetic yellow delivery van.
A nocturnal adventure in a transparent tower will not be includ-
ed in the narrative.
That's a private affair by a volcanic neck.

I've got to be able to talk about how it was
when Edda S was little
the clever things she said
the good things she did
the curse words she combined.

With whom should I talk
single, old
if not with my own daughter, Edda,
my only daughter.

I want to talk to you then
I should talk to you.

For this, you'll have to be Edda S
there won't be others for it. They won't be here.

Sit by me on the edge of the tub
spread a blanket over me softly
like a doll in a stroller when you were little

In the desert of sand and desert of stone, colors thrive in remarkable cohabitation.
Blue-gray sand with same-colored sea.
Giant light-red rocks with a violet tinge.

We've come to the kingdom of stones. The house by the sea is our destination, and around it is a wall of blossoming stones, which Dýrfinna has gathered during the long life she's been granted. Some I gathered myself. Others Edda gathered. It was she who found the stone that's shaped like a cow pie, russet and green. It was too heavy for her to carry it down from Slembigil Ravine. She stacked stones into a little marker so that we'd be sure to find it again. It took two of us to stagger back with it, and it was Edda who decided to give it to Dýrfinna, because, as she declared, she's the best in the world.

Dýrfinna is the kind caretaker in the kingdom of stones, and she knows where every single one of these thousand stones comes from, where it was gathered, and who found it. But it is I who own the stone of stones in this kingdom, the zeolite that I found up in a ravine when I was twelve. I'd climbed higher than I'd ever done before, when suddenly I saw the gleaming white opening, the sun due south and shining directly on it, and I clambered up and managed to tear loose one of the stones. As I pulled, I lost my balance and nearly fell on my back with the shining stone in my grasp. Yet I didn't drop it and somehow regained my balance. Didn't die. Not then.

A nimble-footed, erect-headed sheep struts slowly across the road, right in front of the car. It's this sheep who rules the roads. We can just slow down, thank you very much. An ankle-length fleece, carefully carded, tidy horns. An aristocratic gray sheep with a black-faced, a dusky-bellied prince, outside the sheeps' normal paths, on its way to rocky slopes

like us

up

to the brink of a precipice. They've left it unpaved, the rascals, and Heiður doesn't know how to drive it. Thrusts her nose forward, a terrified daredevil. A precipice that the fog partly envelops is worse than a precipice that can be seen. The mind's eye beholds an abyss even larger than it really is. The mind plays at harassing and frightening.

My solace and protection is the sea.

The presence of the sea can always be felt even if something blocks the view. It's the nature of the sea to make its presence known. The sensors of the inner ear feel it. The auditory canal picks it up remotely.

Two voluminous trucks bear down on our modest pickup at the most difficult point. I'm the one in the car sitting nearest the edge of the precipice. I'll be the first one to hit if we should plunge.

Heiður has the sense to stop.

I have the sense not to look down.

I'm frightened and cold. Now it's all going to roll. The agonizing cold comes from within and can't be lessened with wool sweaters, Álafoss wool blankets, down coats. This island is one universal peril. If she survives, little Harpa Eir will move away, after never really having belonged here for real. Harpa Eir belongs in Perpignan, where no one views her as a dubious intruder. Not there in the city where her friend for life, Gabriel Axel, lives, where people drink chilled white wine on a cherry square in ample sunlight. Harpa will return. As soon as she has the chance.

The chance to sail. It'll be a gentler cruise than the one today, taken by an unlucky woman who has to bounce through half the country with a sore body after having stretched herself quite far in various poses. Muscles made sore in the game of love are much more obstinate and cumbersome than muscles made sore by regular calisthenics.

I would wish to lose consciousness on the way down from the precipice, a precipice where rocks might fall headlong and kill people in cars, where a steering wheel might slip, where a car might plunge straight into the sea.

Oh, what did it did it did it matter if it fell?

I don't know. Act as if I'm sleeping. Yet I yet I yet I might wake up on the shore road where gentle sea licks red beach.

Seventeen swans saunter on the isthmus in the company of sheep that appreciate the vegetation of the sea.

Sea sheep.

Eva Sólgerður was exceptionally good at distinguishing sheep.

My late mother's chief asset, according to the obituaries.

The chief asset of a person no one understood is how incredibly good she was at distinguishing sheep.

I wonder if I'll have finished putting together the puzzle of my mother by the time my progress on earth comes to an end.

My soul to keep.

She who believed in nothing prayed with me and Sibbi at night, like a truly devout individual. During the day she pontificated about how religion was piffle. It was one of her most effective methods for hurting Dad. To her credit, however, she had choice words for all religions, whether it was Germanic neo-paganism, Zen Buddhism, or Christianity. She said it was all pure bunk, no matter where you looked. Fiction, in other words. Good literature in places—the Bible, for example, contains some very interesting bits—but that anyone should believe literally in what's found in these religious texts, by whatever name they were called, was incomprehensible, and was living proof of man's dreadfully primitive thinking. Even if he could get people to the moon and destroy the world several times over in an even shorter time than it took to create it.

She remained inveterate on her deathbed, never shaken in her conviction that religion was wishful thinking and gibberish, including the belief in an afterlife. If I were a poet, I would write about the time the hospital chaplain came to my mother to try to convince her about the afterlife. Yes, you priests, you know more than I do, Mom said. What I know is that I have only one heart, and when it stops beating no reserve generator takes over. Otherwise, suit yourselves. I also prefer to suit myself.

Mom had never bothered to be overly consistent except in matters of eternity. There she stuck to her guns, even to the point of shocking us. Mom at the end. My least favorite memory of her. Sticking to her guns even though she was going to die, and facing that fact directly.

Mom, who was the most masterful deceiver and ran away from facts faster than anyone, never deceived herself about her illness. It was she who turned out to be completely realistic as the end drew near. Perhaps it was hyperrealism she suffered from, not unrealism.

The mountains of the Eastfjords rise slantwise in an orange hue. A heavenly smoke-machine pumps fog systematically but submissively along their base, allowing sunlight access to a green field surrounded by reddish-yellow pastures. Mottled cows and perky calves chew their cuds, superintelligent according to the latest research. They're an unsurpassed comfort to the eyes of the traveler. It isn't possible to feel more inclined toward any animal than a cow. In my mind I'm more spiritually related to the cow than any other animal I know of, even physically. I have the forbearance of a cow, its moist eyes, slightly protruding, and a tongue that reaches up to my nose, though I rarely direct it there. I'm as clumsy in spirit as a cow is on the outside, and I feel as if I'm as stupid as a cow, which is what cows must feel as well.

The countryside here is rough and gentle, a rocky beach on one side, a sea of cotton grass on the other. At some point, all children think that cotton grass is cotton, until they find out it was used for wicks to illuminate dark and tattered turf farms throughout the entire country. It was one of the countless lessons of youth—that nothing, *nothing*, is as it seems. What looks like cotton is in fact a source of light. *It was like that with everything.* More or less. And it isn't getting any better.

The image of Mom isn't getting any better. Unpredictable Mom. There's no way to get a grasp on her way of thinking. I hear her in spirit praying for us, fervently, the irreligious woman herself, with greater conviction than Dad the believer. Mom's hoarse, jabbering voice:

The Lord my soul to keep.

Uff, this piffle about life after death is just wishful thinking, she said obdurately, a week before she died. People just can't accept the idea of disappearing once and for all because they're so terribly fond of themselves. That's all there is to it.

We should be careful with what we say, Sollí, said Dad, his lips quivering and his chin trembling. His eyes blinked rapidly, repeatedly.

I'm not a sucker for extra lives, said Mom. We don't need them. There are enough lives in this life.

Do you think that disabled children and people who are ill from birth would say the same?

There's no such thing as justice, said Mom. Injustice begins at conception. But that's an entirely different matter. It has nothing to do with new lives.

Justice exists if we're granted life after death, said Dad.

We're just not granted it, my dear. It's all unjust, and we can't do anything about it. To me it's unjust that I'm ill. But others have had to endure the same thing. I'm not worthy of any more pity than they are, and I'm not going to add insult to injury by saying to myself: It's not for real; now for the next life on a pink cloud.

Mom's death would have been easier for us to bear if she'd borne it worse. In any case, she didn't even bear it well. She simply didn't bear it. She just wasted away and, with her eyes, prohibited us from pitying her, even though she was quite far gone. It took far less time than the doctors thought. She'd even deceived them. Since then, I've seen many men and women die, but I haven't seen anyone go about it like she did. It was as if she remained outside of her illness. I still don't understand it. Even this part of my relationship with my mother is a mystery to me.

The night before she died, Mom, the master deceiver, put on her robe and was waiting for Dad and me in the sitting room when we arrived. She was even smoking. We sat with her for twenty minutes, and she lit another cigarette and kept the conversation going. She spoke only in brief spurts. That was all she could manage. I remember that she was amusing, but I can't recall a word of what she said.

Dad had to go to a meeting at school, and it would have been convenient for me to go with him in the car. Instead, I stayed with Mom in her hospital room. Dad helped me walk her to her bed. Or rather, we held her up between us as she tiptoed. She, who looked stylish sitting on her chair with her cigarette, so stylish that no one would have thought this smoking woman could no longer stand on her own two feet, so far gone that she couldn't live for more than another twelve hours. When I turned around to say good-bye to Dad in the doorway, he gave me a strange look, but I didn't know what he was getting at with that glance. I understood it the day after, when Mom was dead. He'd comprehended that she had little time left.

That night, the last night that my mother lived, I was on the brink of asking the question that had preoccupied my mind for so long—especially since I'd experienced personally what little it takes to get pregnant.

Mom, is Dad really my dad?

We were alone in the world, alone in the room. It was my chance. A perfect opportunity for opening up. I remember thinking, I've got no more than a few months, maybe six months at most. I never thought then that I'd have only that one hour. Actually, I didn't even have that, because Mom fell asleep soon after I tucked her in, and I sat and held her sleeping hand. Before she dropped off, I searched for a way to bring up the subject. To hint somehow at my unreasonable appearance, which simply didn't hold up in comparison to those of my parents and closest relatives. I wanted to try to sneak my way to the point, give her the chance to tell me everything, without my asking directly. I was going to say, Mom, do you remember when the boys attacked me in Dock Wood, thinking I wasn't a girl but a Wild One? It was probably no surprise, considering how small and dark I am. The "M" in "Mom" was on the tip of my tongue, but it was impossible to continue, because some sort of gleam in her eye warned me against taking even the slyest of detours to the matter. Then she closed her eyes and said: It's good that you hold my hand as I doze off, Harpa baby.

I was frightened when she started coughing in her sleep, because it was so hard on her. I was going to call a nurse, but then she stopped and a smile played on her lips. I stayed at her bedside a long time, hoping that she would wake, at which point I would inch my way toward the question. When she finally stirred, her eyes were more open to the big question, but then the words got stuck in my throat. I couldn't even say: Do you remember, Mom? I'll never forget when the boys thought I was a Wild Child and tried to kill me. It would have been easy for me to slip in this greatly rehearsed opening, because Mom was silent for a few moments after she woke. But it was I who couldn't utter a peep. Mom started talking, as per habit, going full blast into the nomadic peoples of the high plateaus of Tibet, who lived at a higher elevation than any other ethnic group. We would vomit in the thin air if we went to those parts. We wouldn't be able to survive the winter. She was so short of breath that I wanted to say to her: Don't exhaust yourself talking; let me tell you something funny instead. I'd heard this lecture many times before, in detail, but it was no longer possible to make nasty comments, so I said: You would have made a good natural scientist.

Everyone who lives and actively participates in life is a kind of natural scientist, said Mom. And that was the last thing I heard her say in this life.

She closed her eyes, and I sat with her for a long time after she was asleep. I gazed at her face, which had always been chubby, but was now emaciated. At the same time, it was also remarkably smooth and almost young and mischievous, her nose slightly turned up and her nostrils large, with long front teeth that bit her lower lip, leaving marks on it.

Now the thought finally crept in that perhaps she had no months remaining, only weeks. I sat with Mom until twilight crept through the windowpane and settled over her bed. It wasn't out of devotion that I sat there so long; it was because I wasn't in the mood to stand up. The entire time I just held on to her hand, which was as shriveled as dried herbs. When I finally released my grip and stroked the back of her hand, Mom smiled in her sleep, out to her ears. When I turned around in the doorway, she was still smiling, a long farewell smile.

Heiður, who'd been babysitting Edda, was restless when I came home. Still, she'd brought her flute with her and used the time to practice once Edda was asleep. Always using the time. How frustrating for people from whom time is stolen: young mothers, parents of troubled youths.

I saw that she wasn't happy with how long I'd been gone and how I hadn't even bothered to call to let her know what was up.

I told Heiður that I'd intended to ask my mom how I came to look the way I did, but that I couldn't bring myself to do it. Heiður said, as usual, that I could ask until the cows came home, but I would almost certainly get no answers.

She can't live more than a few weeks at most, I moaned, and suddenly found myself crying. Heiður tried to console me, and I wailed about how hard I thought it would be to live after Mom was dead.

She was never much of a support, Harpa.

Let's not talk about that now. It'll be hard to go on after Mom is dead, because everything between us is so unresolved. It's all been left unsaid.

Is it possible to resolve things with people like your mother? Aren't people like that constantly traveling all by themselves through incomprehensible spaces, as you yourself say?

So much can happen over time, I said. Many things change unexpectedly. If she were to live, maybe we'd come to understand each other, somehow. SO MUCH MIGHT BE POSSIBLE AFTER TEN YEARS THAT WOULD BE UNTHINKABLE NOW.

I remember what I said. I remember it very well. It figures I should remember it on this fateful trip, now, after these ten years, in fact, when channels are still closed that then I'd thought would open up. CLOSED CHANNELS would obviously be an excellent title for my story, which no one will ever write, and the best title for my life, which should never have been lived.

I need to pee. Once more. A wretched necessity, an endless disturbance. Broken sleep when you have to pee. A lot of people never sleep soundly because they have to go so frequently at night. Defective bladders are a problem throughout the world and a disagreeable ailment. Many women struggle with urinary incontinence, and it does nothing to increase their self-confidence.

No potty. Helmsperson Þuríður peed in a horn.

I need to pee.

This is a good place for it, my dear.

. . .

To pee outside in a thick fog would be an easy task for ordinary people who believe that if passersby see something, they'll think the shapeless mass is a rock, not a pissing woman. But I'm no ordinary person. I don't want to be seen squatting even if I might be mistaken for a rock. One disadvantage of a desert country like Iceland is how often you need to pee outside. It's been extremely important to me ever since I was a little girl not to be seen squatting. I must have spent quite a few hours of my life searching for a safe place to pee. And no matter how well I searched, someone always came. Such is destiny. It's unavoidable. You walk for half an hour up a gully in order to pee in peace, unseen by anything but the birds of the sky. Then someone comes walking by, always male: a shepherd, a backpacker, a dreamer.

Then, just ahead, a dreamland for outdoor pee-ers. Sea stacks standing upright, only an outhouse-distance from the road. I can crouch behind one of them in a covert operation, make it an intricate bathroom wall.

It's wet going to the sea stack, a minefield of little morasses. The peeing spot is usually farther away than the traveler thinks. Now, the only way is to hop prudently from one tussock to another, avoiding stepping in the little mudholes. Wet feet could ruin what's left of the trip, whatever's left of it to ruin.

Nature lies dormant beneath this wet hide. The blades of grass bend beneath the spiderweb of drizzle. The drizzle is healthy for the hair and more moisturizing than any cream. Balsam for my chin, chafed in the night.

The sea sluggishly splashes the land. It doesn't move on its own; it's the currents that move it without its having a say, eternally on the same course, onto the land and off.

The heather behind the sea stack receives the warm liquid. The gush is the umbilical cord between me and the earth. The posture I'm in is bad for a woman with sore thigh muscles. I would give a great deal to be able to urinate standing up, yet without having to be a man.

The respectable woman always has a pack of tissues in her pocket.

To pee outside hasn't been her favorite occupation, but here special conditions prevail, and even the most stable of characters could become addicted to this operation if they tried it, tinged as it is with salt air. HOW GOOD AND FAIR AND WONDERFUL ICELANDIC AIR IS ON YOUR BARE BEHIND. ACROSS YOUR BARE BEHIND would probably be a more poetic line.

Sheep bleat piteous *baa*s and troubled *meh*s, vomit-like sounds, no wonder, their being ruminants and all. A brownish individual, a bird that I name Móri, screeches and alights on the bathroom wall. A witness with wings.

When I stand up straight after a lengthy and voluminous urination suitable for an average-sized camel, I see my traveling companions preparing for similar operations, Edda squatting down behind a rock and Heiður behind a stationary lamb. It's picturesque. They both have their backs turned to me, peeing landward. For the sake of form, I'd thought it better to turn my back to the sea.

Five cars rush by. One slows down and honks, suggesting that they've seen the knee bends of two women with their pants down. If they had any sense of decency, they'd drive past silently. Act as if they didn't notice. Icelanders know no shame.

The bird, Móri, comes flying toward me, out from the soft white substance that covers the land. From where have you been sent, Móri, you worm, and how will you go about poisoning my toxic life today? It opens its beak and says that it's been sent from the uppermost regions. Sure you're not from Mom's place?, I say.

I'm careful to get in the car last, avoid argument, pretend to sleep, sleep if I can.

· · ·

If I had money, I'd build a house by the sea. Here, probably. Then I could water tussocks behind rocks on a daily basis, with my freeborn buttocks in the salty wind.

I built a house by the sea
and the sea said: Oh kay
Here I am and my name is
Hudson Bay.

If I had money, I'd build a house by the sea and the sea would say *oh kay*, and I'd build another house in the birch thicket at the end of a glacier. And if I had supernatural gifts, I'd live in both houses at the same time. Unfortunately, that toughie Heiður has a house in a dream place, though it's not a dream house as seen from the outside.

DREAM HOUSE. I was raised in Mom's dream house. Anyone brought up in a dream house can't live in a house of wakefulness.

A downpour. The windshield wipers at full speed can't keep up with it. The raindrops reverberate on the metal roof like hail. Rain streams down the windows.

ADDA AND HRÓI
VOPNAFJÖRÐUR

is written in bright-red letters on a tractor-trailer that we encounter. Heiður swerves at five miles per hour, and a liquid, muddy curtain splashes over us.

ONCE UPON A TIME WERE ADDA AND HRÓI. They lived in a little house and were initially poor but good. Then they got a lucky break and became considerably worse people by buying a big truck that ladled thick sewage over little cars that had done nothing wrong but drive along the road. The cars' drivers could see nothing and were in danger of ending up in a ditch.

Where the low-lying fog extends farthest up the mountainside it combines with its brother, the snow, in hollows here and there. It cuts the mountains with white lines, having settled in gullies for the summer, a year-round gorge-dweller that should have disappeared in summer but refused to go.

There's something beneficial in half missing the journey you're in fact taking—to miss it because of fog and drizzle, soft and gentle friends I enwrap myself in.

To creep into Harpa Hernandezdóttir's den. To rest after eighteen months of conflict. IN GLORIOUS HIBERNATION. Dreaming in my hide both covertly and overtly.

This winter I'm going to make love with my land, the land that is unknown to me. Out east there's not a man who loves me. Probably not out west, either, though sometimes I imagine it's so. How should I treat this matter? Think about it? My loveless lot. It's not even zero love. It's love below zero, and my one memory of a January night in the Norðurmýri basement, a memory of something that hardly seems as if it happened.

I should write at least one page about LOVESICKNESS when I'm done painting out east. It's high time that I write a report on this universal indisposition.

Are those who receive a lot of love when they're little, such as I did from my dad, better or worse equipped to deal with lovelessness than others? Do those who've received a lot of love search harder for it than those who've received little? Or are they better at accepting having little of it?

Mom didn't love me, or was bad at showing it. It was my father who took care of me. Can fatherly love substitute for motherly love?

Oh, how little I desire to spend my life as a lovesick assistant nurse. It's best to mourn and write a bit of poetry, cease to desire any man. Easier said than done. I should be content with my *one and only time*. Not everyone gets so much as that.

It's a crisp fourteen degrees, and there's brand-new snow, just before midnight on the second day of the New Year. It's been a half an hour or so since I heard anyone out on the street, the snow crunching beneath slow steps. Most people would hurry in the cold. A shadow-cat, probably Mr. Björn, shoots past the arched window, on a silent trip through the snow-crusted backyards of Norðurmýri.

There's no traffic, everyone's sleeping, pooped after the gluttony of the holiday. Even the cars are napping, and the noisemakers above me go to bed early. For one night at least I'm granted the mercy of not hearing them snore. I can't bring myself to break the silence with Jacques Brel, not even with Vivaldi's *Concerto per viola d'amore*. I'm alone in the world, in the mighty limbo of my Norðurmýri basement, and I ask for no more, not tonight. Instead, I'm going to breathe in indoor tranquility on a good sofa. I light two pink candles in the bronze candlestick from the estate of Grandma and Great-grandma, jetsam from the last century. *A good haul* was what people of the southern sands called it. The farms couldn't keep going without jetsam.

On the coffee table is a bouquet from Heiður, meant to cheer me up after the previous night, pink roses and delicate white flowers in bunches. The white flowers are waxy; I don't know what they're called. It looks dreadfully like a bridal bouquet or a bouquet for new parents. Accompanying it is a sympathetic message on a reassuring card, with an old photograph of a mother and her little daughter, exceptionally elegant women in frilly dresses and laced leather boots, promenading by the Pond downtown.

Heiður's going abroad in the morning to claim her fame. She gets to sit next to Dietrich on the plane. Lean her head on his shoulder. Then they'll go their separate ways, she to play in Italy and England, he to sing in Hamburg and Paris. Afterward they'll take a vacation together in Thailand. God, how I envy these people. And I'll have to endure the next few months Heiður-less.

Heiður is everywhere around me. The flowers from her are on the coffee table, which comes from her house of plenitude. My oval mahogany table from the garage on Laugarásvegur Road is the successor to the triangular glass table that I broke accidentally with a hot coffeepot when a certain man came to visit, which I haven't yet begun to forget for real. If I had the guts, I'd admit that his farewell kiss was still burning on my forehead eight months later. I hope the kiss will start to fade after one more month, the length of an entire pregnancy. You might expect that the exhausted single-mother-of-a-problem-child that I am wouldn't have terribly much to think about. One fucking *forehead kiss*, the kind given to deceased people and children. Is that really fuel for reflection?

I visit the fridge for cold apple juice that I bought in a fit of extravagance. Usually juice is never bought in my household. There's no need for it since the blessed water from the well of Guðmundur the Good runs from the taps. The first thing Heiður does when she returns from abroad is take a big gulp of pure Icelandic tap water. I understand her perfectly. I only wish that I got to return as often from abroad as she does in order to quaff the water at home.

I can understand how she has the heart to spend so much time away from Iceland, but I don't understand how she has the heart to be separated from her golden boyfriend for such long periods. I'm not certain that I would want that. Anyone with such a boyfriend must surely be willing to sacrifice a lot for the chance to hug him as often as possible and rest in his blissful embrace, to let her ears be stirred by his breezy baritone.

I'm lucky enough to possess an entire cassette with him singing, permitting me to remember how he looked at me as he sang on New Year's Eve. His voice is the only thing that's allowed to disturb the silence of mine this night. *Leise flehen.*

I can't bring myself to go to bed though I'm sleepy and I've put on my ivory-colored silk nightgown that I bought for a bargain at a flea market in Perpignan, in a little alley just off what I called Cherry Square. I can't bring myself to sleep even though I'm tired, because I want to think, in a blissful moment of peace. On one of the relatively rare nights when I know where Edda's resting.

In a hospital bed.

I was hoping to get her into therapy directly after her hospital stay, but she went berserk when I mentioned it. I was astounded to see such an animated response from such a sickly girl.

How far down does she have to go in order to change direction?
All the way?
To a place where there are no roads.
At this sweet moment, I shouldn't be thinking about it.
SWEET MOMENT.
The Lord is my shepherd, I shall not want.
He comforts my soul.

Here he sat, just before Easter, the man who drove me home from the supermarket, comforted my soul, and smiled a single smile that filled the room, adding light-years of memories to my life by doing nothing and saying nothing special.

I imagine putting my mouth to his mouth, getting to stroke the back of his hand, falling asleep with his breath on my cheek. Having a name for me when we were children—*the foreign girl*—must have been something akin to love, at least something that didn't disappear completely, whatever it was, and made its presence known when the foreign girl from the swimming lessons showed up again at the bar in Esja after all those years, still a girl, yet now the mother of a teenager.

Of course I'm foreign, kind sir, you're right about that, though I can't prove it. It was right before Easter, and now it's a new year. There were three phone calls from Ísafjörður. We spoke for a long time, laughed heartily. There's no denying that we're fun together on the phone.

Sirens come and sirens go. It's been only one and a half days since Edda and I were rushed to the hospital under flashing lights and an ominous wail. My child came so close to leaving and never coming back again. That's the last thing I could ever wish for. I don't know what I wish, but I mustn't be such a wretch as to wish that. I need to hold on to the idea that it often takes great storms to harness the winds so that the heavy clouds blow away to reveal the sun.

It will be a blessed day when my frozen child thaws out from the spells and changes back into a smiling person who draws pictures of turf farms by a round pond for Mom, the sun shedding rays on the turf roofs and water.

The snow crunches out on the street; footsteps draw nearer, but strangely slowly, as before. My heart beats faster. Why should someone walking down my street make it start doing so? *Beat slowly, my heart,* I order my heart, but it doesn't obey. Someone passes through the gate to my yard, at an accelerated pace, directly. Then the gate is shut and the steps to my apartment are descended, without hesitation. The bell rings. I go to the door immediately, as I am, barelegged in a nightgown.

Welcome, I say. I was just thinking about you, and I glance over his shoulder at the spruce trees across the street, heavy with sparkling snow, and at vivid pink northern lights dancing empowered across the sky.

Look, I say, pointing over his shoulder.

He doesn't follow my index finger, and instead places his hand on my cheek and plants a dream-prince kiss on my mouth. He puts his arm around my shoulder, turning around so that we both face the northern lights as we stand side-by-side in the narrow hallway. I lean my head against his arm in total silence, as I've done in many a dream.

In the sea-green hallway before the open door I shiver, wearing nothing but my low-cut nightgown. My guest shuts the door when he feels me trembling, nudges me into the foyer, shuts the hallway door to keep out more cold, firmly strokes my bare arms to warm me. He smiles halfway to his ears, giving a glimpse of his long white eyeteeth, a defect that looks good on him, and his cat eyes glow in the darkness.

> His green eyes
> are not of human kin
> but of the kin of cats.

> Eyes of the sea, not land.

Cat's eyes,
sea eyes.

Did they see me in the dark?

Would it be sweet to drown in them?

Are you home alone?, he asks.
Yes, but for bad reasons.
Oh?
I'll tell you afterward.
I'll tell you *afterward*, not later. There won't be any *later*.
My guest takes off his blue suede, fur-lined jacket and hangs
it up. He unlaces his well-polished boots, revealing his white card-
ed-wool socks. He takes the opportunity, while bending down, to
stroke the sole of my foot, my ankle and shin, up to my knee.
Maybe he found my bare legs a bit forlorn.
Your foot is softer than your hand, he whispers in my ear.
He leads me into the bedroom and lays me on the bed, lays
himself down beside me, and embraces me tightly. The darkness here
is perfect. I'm glad of that for now. He releases his grip, I stroke the
nape of his neck. It's a highly rehearsed scene from my dreams, like my
series of kisses along his neck.
He moves his hand beneath my nightgown, runs it along my
body, along my outer thigh, hip, and side, up to my armpit. Then,
with extreme care, he removes my nightgown, like I'm disabled and
unable to assist. He places the gown on the chair next to the bed.
Are you pressed for time?, I ask.
He doesn't understand the gibe, and says: I can stay until eight
thirty in the morning.
I realize that this is a serious matter and say: That's an entire night.

A fully dressed man, still wearing his sweater, kisses me carefully from tip to toe, spending extra time with my breasts and hands.

Kissing hands is an art that's practiced too little. It's said that the eyes are the mirror of the soul. But the hands are the gateway to it. By kissing the backs of the hands, the wrists, the knuckles, the fingertips, and moistening them slightly with the tongue, it's possible to pinpoint the bridge across which an individual stops being a patient soul and becomes an impatient body.

Take off your clothes. I can't wait.

He gets out of bed and goes into the living room, returning with a lit candle, which he puts on the nightstand. He looks at me in bed and stands there unmoving, for what feels to me like a long time.

Then it's as if he suddenly remembers what it's all about. He quickly undresses. First his sweater, then his shirt and undershirt. Next his socks, and then his pants.

He lies on top of me and takes a good long time slipping it all the way in.

He lies still, and our mouths and lithe tongues melt together, our teeth touch. In this stationary vortex I exist less than I did before. I who have lived for thirty years now scarcely exist, yet I feel that I'm only now living. Is this what we ultimately live for? To be less existent, or as a part of another, literally? I don't know, but I know that it's barely me, not the person I used to be, who lies here beneath a long-desired weight, having finally reached my intended destination, having come all the way.

My guest still doesn't move. He continues to kiss my lips, tease my tongue, but is otherwise completely still. The game is meant for me, the one who can't wait, who must keep going. He wants to make me move first, creating a perfect motion between two bodies that work together for the first time, in complete accord. Play, play fast, very slowly in between, or stop playing, rest and gather strength, dance around the common goal, avoid it, for a long time, then shorten the path in dizzying motion, to a low shout that echoes long and becomes a nursery rhyme that slowly puts to sleep a traveler drenched with sweat.

Day doesn't dawn brightly, not at this time of year, but when morning comes my guest remembers, having earlier been preoccupied with pampering my entire body, to ask me what happened with Edda. I tell him the whole story of my daughter and me, in a low voice with my mouth to his ear.

He embraces me with his entire body, arms and legs, lays his cheek against mine. He tells me to be brave, that I'll find a way, and it will turn out all right.

I'm supposed to promise him never to let this moment cast a shadow on life, but instead make it brighter. If you'd dropped into my arms, he says, and splashed water on me a year earlier . . . He stops speaking, and I feel a tear fall. I explain to the guest that the years don't matter, but to have an entire night until eight thirty in the morning means everything. No one can take it from us; we'll always have it to think back on.

He says again: *Just a year earlier.* My hands are tied now.

I laugh and say: Time is always crazy—let us not take notice of it. I grab his clenched hands, releasing them from each other, lightly bite his fingers and direct them down to my loins, where they're quick to find a special project. Nor do my hands remain idle. They can't restrain themselves from investigating this man's torso, the body hard with muscles, the soft skin, the masculine legs covered with rough hairs, as they should be. We're in no hurry in bed, because our time tonight will have to last us for a very long time, well beyond this one January night. There are moments when I let it be in the past, and I envision myself recalling it in my mind when I am old. The night is fuel for a time to come, a future time. Tonight the roads of all time conjoin.

The dance of lovers. A brilliantly coordinated pas de deux, as if performed by the most accomplished of ballet artists.

In my winter lair I'll program dreams about THE DANCE OF LOVERS AND SIDE ROADS OF THE EASTFJORDS.

I'm curious about that closed book: a hidden world within fjords that concerns me, where my people endured through rock-hard centuries. I've never explored a single road that heads inland from the fjord, winding up a hill, onto a heath. To cut between fjords, behind the mountains, is a future dream, as is Cherry Square in Perpignan. Where Harpa Eir wouldn't stand out, wearing a white T-shirt and sunglasses, drinking espresso from a tiny cup and water from a glass, beneath a striped umbrella.

In the spring, when the roads are turned muddy from melting snow, I'll use the last drops of power in the Israeli Willys to drive along tracks leading deep into the fjord, and then up to the high heath, to the next fjord, see the view change markedly with each passing yard, with each little twist, with each turn, a new landscape with new angles and indentations and curves, drastically changing mountains.

This spring I'm going to travel, Heiður, I announce. Even if I have to go alone in that junky jeep.

If I'm free, little one, I'll come in the pickup and we'll travel in style. Champagne in coolers—that's what I call traveling. You never know, I might just bring Dietrich along.

But we have no use for him.

Maybe you don't.

Through the back of my head, I see the yellow cat eyes in the backseat burning with suppressed malice, and I feel them burning two points into my scalp.

Edda envies us because we enjoy traveling together. That's life. Those who don't care to do anything envy those who do care to do things. But who would possibly travel with Edda? She has no one. Those who have traveling partners should be thankful and remember that many people never travel because they have no one to travel with.

I'll take you at your word, I say to Heiður. Come east and we'll have a romp through the area. We'll only walk over gentle terrain in good weather. And no camping. I'm not sleeping in a tent. I have my limits.

Heiður laughs, with whooping-cough-like wheezes.

Laugh it up. I'll besiege you when you take a break in between concerts and trips abroad. Then we'll journey on side roads, along zigzag paths, and discover new dells and pretty little creeks. We'll find remarkable rocks in new landslides, gather cuckooflowers and buttercups, the brightest flowers at the very start of summer, the season that never meets the need of an Icelander for summertime bliss. This season represents fear and desire, fear of rejection, fear that this precious time will be taken from us before it's hardly begun to take flight. But that's in fact what happens. It's taken from us just when we long most passionately for more. The Icelandic seasons should be named FEAR and LONGING. Summer is fear of winter; winter is longing for summer. Spring and fall don't exist in Iceland. They're part of winter.

The warm sea is greenish blue, like ignimbrite, and above it the scree is volcanic red, the sands of the beaches the same color. Red beach sand, the hottest colored of all the sands in the world, although the sand is in fact cold. Colors in cold countries are hotter than the things they color, hotter than the air. It's in style with the landscape, alluring in places, but actually useless other than to look at through car windows. Landscape that's unfarmable for anything resembling actual farming, useless for walking in except by those who wish to wander wind-dried in a rocky desert, stumbling their way up scree that's rushing in the opposite direction.

The word *ambivalent* is an imperfect word that doesn't describe how it's possible to have a variety of stances toward things. The word *ambivalent* is a coarse simplification of the complex feelings toward others that toss and turn inside people, toward their native country, toward all that is.

At the foot of a steep cliff standing at a perfect right angle to the ground is a hidden house, its roof just barely visible behind trees. I should ask Heiður to stop, get out, knock on the door, and tell the people that I'm here to stay. That I'll be taking over the house after their time. These exemplary people have cultivated tall, stocky, exemplary trees that are worthy of them in every respect. Evergreen trees to look at in the winter. Deciduous trees for the Icelandic summer, which is, I have to admit, longer than one month, considering that at that time of year the day lasts an entire twenty-four hours, round and round.

Rising from steamy veils, Iceland's Egyptian pyramid, Búlandstindur Peak, marks the most beautiful village in the country. Nowhere in Iceland is there more drizzly fog than here in its most beautiful spot. It's inside out, and completely in keeping with the behavior of this country.

I can't help it that the Eastfjords are my fjords, my country, and *that's where I've come.* I don't just love my own fjord—the entire region is Harpa's adventureland, which has bobbed underfoot and burned my eyes in my dreams ever since I was tiny. The people here are different, as is the climate. It's a fantastic world. There's more foreign blood in people of the Eastfjords than in other Icelanders. It can be seen in their external appearance, but they also stand out spiritually, though that's a quality I'm unable to put into words.

God, it's beautiful here, says Heiður.

This is nothing, I say. To arrive at Djúpivogur by sea at five o'clock on a spring morning—that's something. It's how I arrived almost every single spring that God gave me in my childhood. The pyramid appeared in the refreshing light, unless the Eastfjords fog was teasing us. But the fog made it fun, too, even though it isn't lively by nature. Mysterious fun—elves sprang from the fog belts around the cliffs and ridges. It wasn't possible to land, so everything was ferried by boat, piece by piece, people to shore, wares out to the ship. Sometimes the thick fog filled the fjord, making the world a white mass, concealing people and boats. But you could hear the oars striking the sea's surface, people talking, seabirds screeching, curlews warbling, eider ducks cooing, and plovers trilling, mingled with a soft bleating.

After coming all the way east, I'd prepare a floating outdoor festival in the style of the Workers' Weekend celebrations and fill the fjord with sails. I imitated Grandma Una in counting fifty-six sails in the fjord. I was going to sail away on all the fishing smacks, one after another. Remember the poem?

The sails on the smacks are wings of migratory birds.
Wings for sailing between sea and sky.
A sunstone points the way.

In my romantic musings I gave a novel the title THE MERMAID AND THE SEA. It began like this: So passionately did the young girl love the sea that she'd likely been a mermaid in a past life.

On the first trip, Mom and I got a ride from the pier on a tractor. Mom and I were close friends then, but it's actually before I can remember. The next time we were picked up in a jeep without a windshield. Yet most often, Aunt Dýrfinna gave us a lift in the Israeli Willys. A few such cars, which had been lengthened or something in Israel, made their way to this country. It's apparently the same age as I am, and I can have it, you see, though it would be a shame to stir it from its bedridden state. It hasn't been moved for a whole year. Dýrfinna stopped driving it then, though it might have been better if she'd done so earlier, if I understand Ingólfur correctly.

It's really making me tingle, seeing all the glory of your fjord, says Heiður. I can't believe that I've never come this way before.

Neither can I.

I've never had any such place out in the countryside, says Heiður. Except for the place of yours that you gave me.

This year, the start of September in Iceland's eastern depths has the blue color of May. There's a spring hue to the sea itself, a blue-powdered sky, the grass brilliantly green at the side of the road, and the fields succulent. The snow here hasn't quite melted away as it normally would. Streaks of snow cut the light-blue mountains between white troughs in the hollows. Everything conspires to distort time, making it seem to a female traveler in the land of her winter quarters as if it might be spring or early summer.

How good the land is to me. It puts its transformation on hold, so I can thrive as I did when I was a young traveler of the spring. Autumn lingers respectfully at the far horizon of the sea. Kind seasons, please take my side. Making it possible for many things to follow.

Every last inch of my soul is filled with eager anticipation. Soon she'll reach her destination, little old Harpa, a remote fjord whither she sailed. Her body is woken from a foggy slumber, as the countryside rapidly comes into view. It's my greatest lover, and I am its mistress. It will be a joyous delight to come to my place, to the fjord that's equivalent to young love. My young love was no man, but a farm within a fjord where foreign sails return from the beyond each May, the cruelly sweet month in which birds multiply while thick snowdrifts continue to rest in the hollows.

The greenest grass in Iceland grows in this elongated fjord, glowing at the edge of the fog this first of September. This fluorescent grass is for sheep to find even in the dark of night. Wouldn't it be typical of them, to allow themselves no break from eating while the rest of the universe sleeps?

Tiny peaks like avant-garde antennae stick out of a mountain that juts out over the fog river across the fjord. The peaks are lava splotches that froze on their way up into the sky.

Sloping mountain massifs north and south of the fjord fall together landward and rise in long lines toward the sea.

THE SEA IS MY LAND, skerries and breakers. The wave is my land. The waves.

A progressive traveler is camping at the bottom of the fjord, as close to the sea as it's possible to get without being washed away. He wants to be aboard a smack with sails but is modest and makes do with camping by the sea. This single man, American, I think, or Swiss, sits on a perfect chair at the water's edge.

A snow-white stream takes a twisted course down an elongated, rocky slope, helpless, with no soil into which to dig itself.

The mysterious island in the fog, Papey, takes its name from Irish hermits who came to Iceland before its history was written and left things behind—bells and crosiers, according to old books. There's nothing to find on Papey now, though; it's been rooted around on for decades.

What a specialized sort, this fog. How quickly it passes by. How slowly it passes by. Like the life we live, which passes and doesn't pass.

Tell me about Ditti, I say.

Ditti sang in *Elijah* in Bergen earlier this week, to rave reviews as always.

And where's he going next?

It's *Don Giovanni* in Berlin, answers Heiður.

How can this purehearted man be convincing as the immoral Don Giovanni?

He isn't particularly convincing in the role. But he sings like an angel. That's what matters.

So true. I envy you.

How could you not?

You're just so terribly different. I don't understand your relationship.

Music connects us.

What about birds of a feather and so on?

We complement each other. He's the gentle one, and I'm the one who makes the fuss.

But how are you going to go about it?

Go about what?

Establishing a home and bringing up children.

It's not on the agenda.

So you're just going to live out of suitcases, at hotels?

At hotels I don't have to clean up. I hate dishcloths, spools of thread, and rubber bands. I want to be left alone with my flute. I have one fixed place to stay, at home with my dad and mom. I don't need more.

They won't live forever.

I know.

Then what?

We'll cross that bridge when we come to it.

You two can't meet except now and then, and only for brief periods.

The rarer, the more intense.

I refrain from responding to this, because I don't want to hear what Heiður has to say about her erotic encounters with Dietrich Bacon. I sometimes call him the Piece of Bacon because of his family name, which he got from his English grandfather and which doesn't suit him too badly because he's so terrifically thick. It's partly out of envy that I don't want to hear more and partly because I find it embarrassing. It isn't right to get Heiður going about her sex life and penises. Once she started telling me, unasked, about Dietrich's beautiful member. An alabaster-white penis, perfectly sculptured and *big*, she said, adding that for her it makes a real difference how the penis itself is shaped, its texture and feel.

I'm sure I'd have a similar opinion if it came to that. It's just not something I'd bring up without being asked, especially not sober. What's more, there's no need to discuss it. Dietrich gives the distinct impression that there's little fault to be found with him in this area.

I was with Heiður at the concert at the Old Theater where they met for the first time. Ditti's one of the remarkable musicians who makes a habit of coming north as a result of friendships with Icelandic musicians. He was a rising star then, twenty-five years old, but he looked thirty-seven.

How to describe Dietrich Bacon in action? He's big as a mountain, but onstage he's a breezy, playful mountain, captivating the hall with his charming persona. His soft baritone voice is tinged with wistfulness, which really serves him well when he adopts a lighter tone. Back then his hair was black, whereas now it's sprinkled with gray, same as his eyebrows, and his appearance is mild, as in divine beings. His hands are artistic, big and fair of form, putting the finishing touch on his stage performances.

I swooned when Dietrich Bacon sang *The Dwarf*, and again when he sang *Leise flehen meine Lieder*. I wanted to take the man to a chamber and let him run his blissful hands through my hair and stir it with his baritonal whisper. Were I to look up, I would have seen the blue sky of his eyes, which gleamed with inner sunshine, not entirely human.

I heard Heiður take a deep breath when Dietrich finished the last note of *The Organ Grinder*, which she'd smugly informed me was the last song in Schubert's *Winter Journey*.

At the end of the concert Heiður went straight to Dietrich's best friend in Iceland, the conductor Holberg Ómarsson, and said: Holbi, no excuses. You introduce me to him.

Holberg is a grave young man from up north in Eyjafjörður; he was educated in Boston. He takes such inordinate pains with his language that those speaking with him confuse their idioms out of downright nervousness and conjugate words incorrectly time and time again.

I can't see any reason why not, said Holberg, and they rushed off, Heiður in the lead, as usual.

I loitered in the shelter of the cloakroom, intending to wait for my friend, but she looked over her shoulder and screeched out over the packed corridor: You're coming too, Harpa!

Little Harpa dared do nothing but follow, so that her friend would stop shouting, and little Harpa decided to give Heiður serious competition, seeing that she'd been so stupid as to bring her along. However, this plan didn't work, because Heiður had Dietrich pretty much all wrapped up. Even the conductor didn't get a chance to talk to his man. Holbi swelled with irritation, no doubt regretting that he praised Heiður's flute-playing upon introducing them.

Heiður played her hand like a professional, at first speaking piously about Dietrich's unusually wide vocal range, which was unique as far as she knew, and then turning to the quality of his voice. She concluded by saying: It would truly be worthwhile knowing German, even if it were only to be able to enjoy the finest nuances of the lieder. This comment stirred Dietrich's nationalistic and poetic heart so strongly that he immediately went too far and replied: Those souls who love lieder are a step above.

At that I saw an opportunity to take one step forward, saying that I particularly enjoyed *The Dwarf*, for obvious reasons. Dietrich snapped out of his sentimental coma, looked down, all the way into my eyes, and smiled a wide, mischievous smile. I saw instantly that if I put everything into motion, it would be fairly predictable where I would get with Dietrich.

Consequently, I thought: What does an Icelandic assistant nurse with questionable paternity need a German baritone for?

I couldn't answer my question at that moment and took two steps backward, allowing Heiður to continue at full steam. Even today I still regret this, as does Ditti, I can tell, the rare times that we see each other. But Heiður doesn't notice anything. Sometimes she says, unsuspectingly: Dietrich often asks about you—how you're doing, how it's going with Edda.

The dear man, fonder of me than he knows. I see it in the tiny twitch at the corner of his mouth when he looks at me. I can feel it in his grip when his big hand encloses mine like a living glove and pauses a few seconds longer than necessary. But he doesn't know what he feels. Men are often that way, and I find it beautiful.

Heiður managed, by crafty means, the precise details of which I've forgotten, to pretend to have some business with Dietrich Bacon. She handed him her business card with golden letters, and the snowball started rolling.

On the way home I did what I could to cast a shadow over the important singer in the eyes of my friend, and even asked her in for sherry from the single bottle I owned and had been saving for better times that never came.

He sings okay, I said. But he has absolutely no sex appeal.

What nonsense, said Heiður. German baritones are the most virile men in the world.

To me he sometimes sounds as if he's overeaten and has food in his throat. You know, sort of bl-huh.

Oh, come on now, Harpa. His voice is pure gold.

I know, I'm just an assistant nurse, can't even have an opinion about singing.

The man in the cape with the little hat is for Harpa, said the prophetic Betty of Útheimar. And Heiður rushed from the tent in a huff.

Two swans in a hayfield rest on their bellies and crop the grass, their necks curved.

A tall, slender, and supple lighthouse sits at the mouth of a fjord.

The fattest valley in the Eastfjords is sun-drenched in a mist of fog, the sloping mountains on the verge of tipping over.

Many paths are mysterious, but none like the paths of the Eastfjords fog, which passes by and doesn't pass by. The fog is a king's daughter under a spell, they say. I'm a little assistant nurse under a spell. I might be released from it tonight.

Little Harpa Eir, who stirred in the stone kingdom to the east and made up stories about rocks that were men, women, and children. When they spoke, some of them mixed up their vowels like Grandma Una. The couple Jakob and Ester, bottle-green and ochre-yellow jasper boulders, stood proudly in the Andey farmyard the last time I was there, and they haven't aged, and the same is true of their crowd of children, ten large stones with sparkling fillings.

IN THE STONE KINGDOM EVERYTHING STANDS STILL.

IN THE STONE KINGDOM THERE'S ENOUGH TO BE HAD.

The stone kingdom, where everything stands, still looks good alongside the kingdom of trees, where every inch of growth is a huge effort. The plants in the Icelandic tree kingdom have a harder time than other trees on the planet. They have to endure the gales all year round. Even the sun doesn't bless all the trees in Iceland. The evergreens can be badly burned by it in March and April. Never to recover.

ONCE UPON A TIME IN THE EAST, THERE WAS AN EXTRAORDINARY KINGDOM OF STONES.

The valleys are half-full of spar, jasper, zeolites, rock crystals, fossils. When the sun shines on such a valley, where twenty-one streams skip between crags, digging many a rhombus into the land, before flowing classically, jazzily, pop-ily through the valley, where the birch smells sweet, the dwarf willow fattens, and the chicks become fledged. The mortal assistant nurse does not ask for more.

I can't wait to get to Andey, says Heiður. I'm looking forward to it like a child.

You've been infected by how much joy I have in my heart right now.

How could I not have visited your fjord?

When we were little, it wasn't possible to drive here without taking the Ring Road the other direction.

We've been big for a long time now.

Things were easier when we were kids. Then the world swallowed us. The vortex of time sucked us in. Since when did we have time for anything, you and I?

I pestered my parents to let me sail with you, but they didn't listen. Everything I said was dispensed with as whining and nagging. It would have been so easy. We could have sailed together. I could have stopped for a week in Andey, and then gone back by myself. For me, being able to sail east seemed perfect, the epitome of prestige and bliss. I cried myself to sleep over never getting to go anywhere by ship except on that jog-trotting *Akraborg* over to Akranes.

You were the one who got to fly to other countries. I cried myself to sleep over having penniless riffraff for parents and never getting to see a foreign land.

I found flying to be shit compared to the idea of going alone on a round-trip to the east aboard the coastal ship *Hekla* or *Esja*. I always listened to the radio when you were on your trips to find out *Hekla*'s location. It would arrive in the Westmann Islands at seven in the morning, and I would think about what you were doing at that moment, hero of the sea. I imagined you to be a part of the ship's crew, not just a passenger. Preferably the captain, with a peaked cap, or else a ship's maid, with a little lace-bordered apron. A fairy-tale character.

Me? A fairy-tale character in other people's eyes?

Out-of-this-world beautiful.

I was like an immigrant before immigrants came into the picture. If I'd been born ten years later, I wouldn't have stood out so much.

You're exaggerating a bit.

Let's not dwell on my appearance.

You've somehow got to deal with all of this, Harpa.

I know. I'll deal with it tonight.

Dýrfinna will send me to see a shrink when I pluck up and ask her the identity of my real father. After all, aren't strange ducklings born everywhere? Aunt Betty doesn't resemble anyone I've seen in the family or even farther afield, and I'd never given that any thought, not until Heiður pointed it out to me. If I were in my right mind, I'd seek help and check to see whether there was a psychoactive drug that could eradicate obsessions and delusions and change Hernandez-daughters into Axel-daughters.

I knew your valley by heart, says Heiður. I took it all in like a foreign dreamland; I had no place of my own except for Laugardalur and Dock Wood. In my mind's eye I saw steep, rocky slopes beneath cliffs, where you found the stones that you brought me. Harpa Eir like a mountain goat up on top of everything, so high that no one could see her from the plain below.

You remember the agate that I gave you?

Do I remember? It hasn't moved from my window at Mom and Dad's house. It was the epitome of all heroic deeds, that you, so small and tender, managed to drag it down from Strýtuhlíð Slope wrapped in a blanket. How clever you were to see that there was something precious inside that grayish-brown stone.

I saw it in the light-colored spew oozing out through a crack on it. I was quite sure there was something in it and was terrifically proud after it was sawed in two and this delightful water-blue stone came to light.

The white house with the green butterfly roof comes into view, a solitary, sheltered house deep within the valley. Mountains on three sides, leaping waterfalls, and then Andey, at the farthest end of the valley, with two colorful jasper rocks in the farmyard. A dream place lying low beneath the sloping roof of white fog. As I know it, the foggy roof is lowest and densest at the mouth of the fjord and grows thinner the farther up the valley you go. Who knows, maybe I'll be able to see to the middle of the Andey slope and the whole of Grandma's Grove.

I used to call your fjord SWALLOW FJORD because I was so fascinated by the poor foreign birds that came to Iceland by accident, having intended to go to a warmer place. How they dashed low and fast and turned so sharply over the tussocks, like fighter planes performing aerobatics, in their hunt for flies to eat. And could hardly stand on their feeble little legs.

Remember, continues Heiður, when we both cried over stories of swallows that got caught in snowstorms just as they set off on their long autumn journeys to other lands? They would turn back and find their nests, then stay and freeze to death. Children who found them thought they were hibernating with their beaks beneath their wings.

Once a swallow flew in through a window in Andey, I say, settled on a cross-stitched pillow in the living room, and died. I never buried any bird with as much ceremony. I sacrificed a beautiful box I'd been using for my collection of napkins, whittled a cross, and carved on it

Little Swallow
Born   ?
Died   August 31, 1969

I wonder if my lot will be the same as the swallow's. Freezing to death in my nest or expiring on a pillow after this attempt to escape.

You won't freeze to death, Heiður replies. You'll get a boyfriend and he'll keep you warm.

Boyfriend, I say. There are none to choose from. They're all married sailors and truck drivers.

Sometimes desperate strangers can be found in fishing villages. They can be first-class musicians, from Eastern Europe, for example, playing the lute or trombone, maybe. So many things can happen. You just can't believe it until they do, like the fairy tale of Ditti and me.

Oh, shut up, Heiður. If there's one thing I can't stand, it's boyfriends.

Now I sit in the purring car, with my eyes closed in the limited visibility.

I open one eye a crack. Everything's in its place.

The islands at the mouth of the fjord both in their entirety. One of them unbelievably green, from the bird shit of the ages and the absence of men, the high crown of a bird-cliff that wanted to be a mountain. The other akin to a skerry, slanting and bare.

Everything is as it should be and more, because the generous sun inclines its rays over the shoulders of the mountain, under the wall of fog, illuminating the splendid pastures, warming geese on the home field, and setting in motion little horizontal fireworks displays for swimming birds on the surface of the fjord. The sea in this deep fjord is no longer of saltwater; it's a viscous molten pool of silk, the softest cradle in the world for ducklings tired in the evenings.

A sharp pinnacle rising up from a peak, a stony colossus high up the slope.

The mountain that blasted everything off itself, eternal sand seeping down its slopes.

Strips of fog hanging down to the middle of the slopes across the fjord, shrouding half the cemetery by the sea where my mom rests. Not exactly in peace.

They should tear these down, says Heiður.

The mountains?

No, these shacks.

I hope they'll leave them alone. It's been like this since I can remember. I could see them from the sea when I was a kid. You don't think it adds to the atmosphere?

It's ghostly, says Heiður.

The ghost houses scattered about the mouth of the fjord look as if dead souls had gone about trying to build a village but quit. They're stately dwelling places of stone-gray concrete with gaping windows that are just right for dead souls to look through. I'm going to move into one of these houses when I'm dead, like those souls, and do nothing else but look out at my fjord and conjure up fifty smacks under sails that resemble the wings of a flock of migratory birds. All in the hope that I'll find the good company of a brown-eyed Frenchman who's known his way around these parts of mine since the time of my grandma. Together we'll gaze at the stately farms across the fjord and the cemetery where this Frenchman rests, and my mom close-by.

She who spent half her days gazing at the fishing smacks on the fjord was given a place with a view over the fjord for eternity. The village is hanging on the hillside across the fjord, as if its houses had dropped down from the fog and stopped, luckily, just before the sea took over. In the house standing nearest the water's edge stays the runaway, me, and every morning when she goes out, two spruce trees the height of three people are the first things she sees. They shouldn't be able to exist, not in this place.

Bands of summer snow remain on the slopes, snow that won't melt now that it's not melted, a harbinger of snow, more snow this winter and even more snow.

The mountains are reflected in the tidal flats flashing their white drifts from last year.

Look, Heiður, just by the fish-processing plant lot, all the way down by the water's edge, there's Dýrfinna's house.

I won't believe that Dýrfinna and her house really exist until I see them right in front of me.

They do, I swear.

Does she live alone?

She lost her husband fifteen years ago. Asgeir was a marvelous man who cracked jokes until the day he died. Poor Dýrfinna. She's helped so many people and never lost a woman or child during her career as a midwife, but she lost her own little son and her husband so early.

I remember the photos of Unnar on your wardrobe.

That was one of Mom's whims. She had three enlarged photos of him on her home altar, the wardrobe where she kept Cosette, but his own mom had just one little photo of him on her chest of drawers.

Mom made a huge deal of this deceased nephew, but the mother who lost him never spoke of him. Mom acted as if she herself had lost a child and blathered on in disgustingly piteous tones about how her poor sister Dýrfinna would never be the same again. Unnar and

I played together when we were little and were great pals, but Mom even managed to ruin my memory of him.

I'll be damned.

She praised him so highly that Sibbi and I became allergic to him. Typical Mom. She had a way of sneaking embarrassing thoughts into our heads, thoughts that you wouldn't ever want to be associated with.

We concluded from what Mom said that it had been an ugly twist of fate that it wasn't either Sibbi or I who disappeared in place of Unnar. He was the most beautiful, most noble child that had ever been born in Iceland, a champion, sage, and clairvoyant, a son of Gunnar and Njál.

Your mother was colorful, that's true, says Heiður, laughing at me. But I don't always recognize her from your descriptions of her.

You know her better, of course.

Steady now.

A fiery-yellow buttercup slope. Untiring horses grazing down by the sea. A horse with a two-tone tail.

The village has become a city of toy blocks. If only it were toys, and not the destination for my winter sojourn, where the months of February and March will have to be endured. Half my life has gone into finding ways to survive. But this winter will be hard on the imagination. To find new paths in heavy snow far out in the countryside. Now the magician will be put to the test, Houdini of the mind, a person fleeing from the prison of the head, from the securely built cells of circumstance. I want out. To slip between the bars in a slippery box with folded wings that spread as soon as they have enough air to soar on.

I WANT TO LEAVE / IN A BOX WITH WINGS.

The dream place sifts in through the eyelids.

We cross the bridge at the foot of the fjord, bumping over the potholes at the tail end.

We take the turnout to Andey.

THE INNERMOST FARM IN A VALLEY. IT'S MY FARM.

From it branch additional valleys, with lush birch thickets, rich waters, and the distant sound of a stately waterfall that can't be seen until you arrive at its base.

One day, which actually existed, my dog Tryggur and I stretched out flat on the ground by the secret waterfall. A raven came and dived toward my companion. Tryggur began barking hoarsely and tried to get off the ground to grab the raven.

Yellow, red, green, and blue in the waterfall. I called it a FALLBOW. The black bird flew through the colorful bow, with a croak.

I'd started down a path that few people know about—it runs behind the waterfall, spraying those who take it. Come with me, says the waterfall to the one who looks through it into the light, eyes wet with spray, come with me, my way, *my way. This way.*

Come, I'll show you something, murmured the waterfall. *Come*, come.

Tryggur barked and snapped at my trouser legs. I jerked from my trance and took the same path as the dog, instead of going the way of the waterfall.

This day existed. I was in that day, and so was Tryggur.

A hawk-fly had buzzed in my ear. Its buzz proved that day existed. Before it all hit. And yet.

I was an immigrant from the very beginning, without a native country.

I supposed I should be ashamed of myself. There are people who have no roof over their head, many, many people.

But it's also true that I don't belong here, though I've had a bed to snuggle into and a quilt to spread over me. I belong in the other country, the one I do not know.

I open my eyes the whole way. The birch on the road is on its way from green to golden. At our destination the seasons are correct.

Big boulders scattered across the scrubby slopes. Everything rolls on.

Two birds in flight, to warmer lands
quickly over sheep at the crest.

Fog beasts of the wood.

Part of the very sky has sunk and laid itself over the mountain.

Damn, I'm disappointed not to see this properly, now that I'm
finally here, says Heiður, giving the dashboard a whack.

We can come back here tomorrow, before you leave, and have a
closer look, I say.

This damn fog could still be here.

We can always watch video of the place. Andey's been video-
taped, like everything else in Iceland.

Heiður guffaws.

Oh my God, what's that?, shrieks Edda.

Heiður slows down, grinding the gears.

The fog at the foot of the slope is moving, and within it something also moves, very slowly. Rocks covered in white sheets.

Haunting cliffs.

In the fog everything moves hauntingly.

The shifting rocks moo, and one has horns. They dance a clunky
little waltz in the sheets, and their tails swing in a slow rhythm.
DANCING COWS IN EASTFJORDS FOG.

At the gate stands a giant, swinging a hammer.

Can that be a human?, says Heiður.

My cousin Ingólfur is big and certainly doesn't grow any smaller
in the fog.

Three black dogs come rushing toward us, barking zealously. I
see them as parents and a naughty son uniting to defy the white car
that would be suitable for use as an ambulance for medium-sized
animals. Today all it transports is incredible women.

The dogs rush to meet us and run alongside the car, getting in
the way of the wheels as movie stuntmen would.

The white wall blocks the view of the abandoned farm Strýta,
but the roots of the slopes of Andey are visible ahead, the lowest of

the waterfalls, and rapids from my childhood memories. The white farm of my dreams, the old stone house with the green butterfly roof, a lamp lit in a window. Mom's house.

This is where she started to become who she was. In this house she nearly died, a five-year-old girl with acute appendicitis, if it hadn't been for her foreign lifesaver. She found this fact so exotic that she never got over it.

Not until she met another foreigner. Who gave life to her daughter.

The fence around Grandma's Grove is visible, as are the lowest of the big birch trees. They've grown taller since last time. In Grandma's Grove nothing stands still, though some things move at a crawl.

I hear the bleating of strong-voiced autumn lambs, but their snouts can't be seen, not a trace of a tail or tuft of wool. The wool and the fog are one. The only color in the fog is violet pink—in the dwarf fireweed that stretches over the islet in the Andá River, and in a cloud that has fallen from the afternoon sky, bathed with water on the one side and haze on the other.

Andey

I ngólfur, dearest cousin, hello.

He greets me with open arms, and then stretches into the car to kiss the monster. Not only does the monster kiss him back, she also puts her arm around my cousin's neck.

Ingólfur greets Heiður next. Tells her that he's seen her photo in the paper, heard her play on the radio.

I feel a stab of pain, unlocalized. It must be a pain in my soul. A stitch of jealousy of a woman who can do something. Who *is* something.

Ingólfur is in no hurry. He takes time to chat, holding a hammer in his hand. Mostly with Heiður, because she's guest number one.

. . .

Good Lord, he's cool, she says as we continue to the house.

Careful not to drive off the road, I say.

His voice, his presence.

He's taken, Heiður.

He's just like a movie star. Black hair, blue eyes, and a Roman nose. Such a muscular body. And he's so incredibly nice.

Just as well we're not staying overnight in Andey. I'm worried about you, dear.

So am I.

Fortunately, the man's happily married. A beanpole like you wouldn't tempt him.

Whores, says Edda from the backseat.

Heiður clenches her hands around the steering wheel, turning her knuckles white.

You should do us all a favor and shut up, says Heiður.

Edda laughs obnoxiously and says: Thould-thavor-thutup.

Is that the thanks Heiður gets for driving you all the way here?

I didn't ask to come, says Edda. You forced me.

Don't be ridiculous, says Heiður. Of course you've come of your own free will.

Courth-comth-fownthree-fill.

Shut up, Edda, I say.

I'm sick of listening to her. She's so pretentious, says Edda.

You're one to talk, says Heiður. All you are is attitude.

I'm never speaking to you again, says Edda. You're the most boring old cow I've ever met. Nothing but bossiness. Mom says so too.

What sort of bullshit is that?, I exclaim, in a tone that's God-fearing and gruff at once.

You did so say it, you liar!, screams Edda.

She's telling the truth, absolutely. I did say Heiður was bossy, though I would never admit it. I'm sure Heiður knows in her heart that at some point I must have blurted it out, but as long as I don't confess, she can still have a tiny bit of doubt.

. . .

When we reach the farmhouse, I hurry to leap out of the car, in terrified flight from this feud, nearly breaking the leg of a crazy dog. Three dogs circle me and the car in a little pack until Edda and Heiður get out. Then they split up their team and fawn over us, one dog each. It would make a decent act in a little circus, but Heiður and I aren't fond of our roles and try to get the bastards off us. Edda, on the other hand, seems quite happy; she pets her dog, then heads to the door, howling along with the four-footed choir of friends as her mother had done when she was in her prime, as the foster daughter of wolves. The circus animals abruptly cease harassing Heiður and me and run after Edda instead, taking turns barking away.

Margrét comes to the door with her youngest child on her arm. It's Unnar, two years old, named after his dead uncle. I freeze the image for long-term storage: Margrét with smooth, shiny brown hair, delicate cheeks, wearing a light-blue linen dress, with a barefoot baby in her arms, a happy-looking boy with long curls. A Madonna image on a remote farm, her farmwife hands like those of Mona Lisa, her fingers with knuckles that barely show, rosy-pink fingers and nails that are nearly merged, arching around the plump thigh of the Son of Man.

Into the frame of this heavenly image, in which marigolds blossom by the house wall at the lower left, runs a red-haired teenage girl, hindered by her leather-jacket armor, with three fawning dogs at her heels. She greets the Madonna with a handshake and receives a kiss in return. She then kisses the child animatedly on its suntanned cheeks and the child shrieks with pleasure, instead of letting out a surprised and fearful howl.

Edda holds out her hand toward the little boy and asks in a childish voice: Wanna co-ome?

He's all for it, and he leans immediately from the fragrant linen embrace toward the sour-smelling black leather arms. And what does the child do but sneeze in Edda's arms? Prompting the Madonna to say in a gentle voice: God bless you.

Her child imitates her: Gah bessu.

He's started to talk?, I ask, flabbergasted.

He's an early talker, says his mother modestly, with secret pride.

When we enter the kitchen, Edda takes a seat and holds her little cousin, clicking her tongue at him and making faces with her mouth and ears. His attention is focused one-hundred percent on the amazing delivery from Reykjavík. They're in their own world on the chair. The rest of us don't exist.

Now Guðrún and Rósa make their entrance, ten and six years old respectively, with white hair and dark brows, striking and attentive. They're wearing matching summer dresses, embroidered with bunches of little yellow flowers. They've decorated themselves to honor the arrival of visitors, Guðrún with sparkling barrettes in her hair, and Rósa with a ponytail and pink bow. They start by coming over to Heiður and me, initially not daring to approach Edda, though it would have made sense to greet her first. In truth, Edda doesn't take well to the angelic sisters, responding unenthusiastically to them, avoiding their handshakes, and muttering something that's impossible to make out.

You certainly have grown, Rósa, I say, to make up for Edda Sólveig's lovely behavior.

Yes, that's what everyone says, she declares in a bright, thin voice.

I think you're taller than I am, I say.

That doesn't mean much. You're so small.

No one laughs. Why should they? It isn't funny.

Margrét invites Heiður and me to have a seat at the kitchen table. I take my old seat facing the window and look out into the patchy fog that reaches almost all the way down to the Andá River of my youth.

In the area below the farm, I recognize all the curves of the Andá, every pool and depression, every little sandspit. It's wonderfully enriching to know a particular part of a stream or river by heart. It takes nothing more than mere acquaintance with a remote stream to feel infallible happiness upon coming to it and simply strolling alongside it, listening to it murmur. Wading bare-legged in it if it's sunny out and drinking from it with the palms of your hands. TO SPEND TIME ALONE WITH A STREAM IS THE EPITOME OF BLISS. Especially on a Sunday afternoon. It doesn't even have to be sunny.

Coming into this white-and-light-blue-paneled kitchen is like having climbed halfway up the stairway to heaven. The residents are prim and peaceful, as beautiful of color as Bible illustrations. And this paradise offers the aroma of oven-baking blended with a mild smell of the barn.

The sisters volunteer to set the table with cups and saucers, answering questions about farming and their school. Unnar, now restless, frees himself from Edda's arms. She turns her back to the company and stares out the window as if she were all by herself. The youngest girl peeks sideways, looking somewhat scared, at Edda's formidable back. I can't blame her. She scares me too, all the time, though I try not to show it.

Unnar is quite agile, considering his age, slipping between the chair legs and the table. There's nothing more remarkable on the planet than a two-year-old child. It has just turned into a person who is completely new, but waddles and babbles and sputters like an old person. It's still a little bundle that needs to be looked after very carefully, being unaware of cause and effect, and quite capable of killing itself as soon as it can walk. It creates its own language that we don't always understand, but the child understands us better than we think and better than we would care to have it do. This being is tragicomic, toiling and clumsy. It's very clever in many respects, and already quite sly though it comes across as simple and innocent.

Edda gets up and goes out, slamming the kitchen door behind her. I fear she'll wreak havoc in paradise. The children in this household will be the worse off because of her, and the adults as well, though in a different way. Somehow I don't think I would have agreed to this arrangement if I were a good person. It's best not to think right now about what I am. Best to think about it as little as possible.

I'd like to take a walk up to the grove, I say. Anyone want to come along?

No, thank you, say the sisters in unison. Heiður says she feels lazy after the trip and is just going to wait for me here.

It's drizzling. Are you sure you want to go?, says Margrét. Don't you want to wait for the cake?

It'll be waiting for me when I come back, I say.

I recall that Margrét's always been excessively cautious when it comes to trips, even if they're no longer than up to the grove or out to the springs.

Don't you want boots and rain gear?, she asks worriedly, as if I'm going to sea without oars.

Boots would be good, thanks, I say. But I don't need the rain gear. This isn't what I'd call serious precipitation.

It can be quick to change, says Margrét with a grave look.

If it does, I can jump back here in no time.

Margrét sees that this battle is lost, and asks me if I would please pick some rhubarb on my way. There's so much that she's hard-pressed to use it all.

Edda comes into the kitchen just as I'm going out. I ask her perfunctorily whether she would like to take a stroll with me to Grandma's Grove. She looks at me as if I'm nuts and says not a word.

Bye for now, I say, in such a hurry to get away that I stick my feet into the first pair of boots I find in the hallway. They're only one size too big; they could be Guðrún's, for that matter.

The boots of a ten-year-old child were too big for her at thirty would be a most outstanding line in my obituary.

I open the front door, and the water symphony plays around me: the brooks trickle, the streams skip, the rivers murmur. From three sides comes the rush of waterfalls, and it all echoes in the dream valley.

The fog is a lake whose bottom is at the middle of the slopes and whose surface is just below the mountaintops. Bubbling rills flow down out of the fog, and up from it jut peaks like the islands in Þingvellir Lake.

What do I care if I can only see a short distance? I know what's there, and I'll get to see my valley and its side valley tomorrow or the next day or the next. I can wait. The fog is no problem for me. It's a lukewarm vapor shrouding me and my easygoing land.

I'm in no hurry going up to the grove. Time doesn't exist, never has. Nothing exists but me and an old dog that slinks after me in silence. Poor old Lubbi, who was a puppy ten years ago. The last summer that my mother lived and just managed to make it east to say good-bye to her grove.

Anyone who leaves behind a tree hasn't lived in vain, Mom said not too long after it became clear where she was headed.

I bend down to pet Lubbi. Are you still alive, you poor devil?, I ask, feeling sorry for him. His fur is tattered, and his eyes are dull, with black sties in the corners nearest his snout. He's russet-colored, like a lamb, and his bark resembles a bleat, *meh-ehrff*. He taps me with his paw, in a way that feels distracted, not at all like the energetic, affectionate dog he used to be.

You're alive, you little wretch?, I ask again. *Awoof,* he answers, which I take to mean yes. He's of the opinion that he's alive.

The Garden of Fog

Come on, then, I say as I open the gate.

Lubbi plods happily into the good garden, where he and Mom and Edda and I had seen better days. Isn't that why one lives? To have seen better days.

Not *here*, Mom. No way.

Where do you want me to be, then?

Nowhere, Mom. Just stay in your place. I have other things to bother about than to carry your millstone.

Be sweet to me, Harpa baby. Do you remember when we spent entire days here together, rooting in the dirt? You helped me pull weeds and do the watering when you were just a chubby little thing.

Yeah, yeah.

You always were such a good girl.

Then why didn't you love me if I was so good?

I do love you, but I guess I'm bad at showing it.

Leave me alone. Let me think in peace.

You can't refuse to take a little stroll with your mother on old familiar paths.

I sit down on a rock beneath a birch tree, whose hanging branches protect me from the drizzle. Mom hovers over me with a hand on her hip. She's wearing checkered wool trousers and has an old backpack on her back.

Mom, why don't you help me, instead of just following me around? I can't go on. I don't want to exist, small and ugly as I am. I don't know how to live. I wish I'd never been born, and you won't let me be. How can you be so awful?

Be careful what you say, little Harpa. You yourself are awful. You never show me any sympathy. Poor me, who died before my time.

It's been ten years, Mom, a whole decade. Of course it was a shock for you, I admit that, but isn't it time that you pull yourself together and try to get over it?

A shock for me to die? You're funny, dear.

Okay, a turning point.

You should start writing obituaries for people. Mom laughs drily and has a coughing fit.

Did you forget your cigarettes?, I say. Why don't you blow smoke in my face like you're used to doing on this jaunt of yours around Iceland? I bet it's illegal for you to be here. Do you have a passport?

Mom looks at me in surprise, stopping in midcough.

You know what, Mom? After only a few hours everything will be out in the open. I'm on my way to ask Dýrfinna who my father is. Then you and your promiscuity will be exposed.

You're one to talk. You've already slept with more men than I'll ever manage. What, for example, were you doing last night?

I'm free as a bird. I don't have to explain my actions.

My word.

Mom, let's make peace, even if it's too late. I think we would have become friends if time had allowed. Things might have been decent between us now if you hadn't died. But you see how it is. You get in my way, and we're still fighting.

Mom fishes a tattered green-checkered thermos flask from her backpack and pours coffee into a plastic cup. I take a sip but it's the same old bad Braga Coffee. I don't want to insult her by criticizing it, though, so I use the cup to warm my hands.

All of a sudden, Lubbi is at my side, barking softly.

Isn't that our Lubbi?, says Mom.

Woof, he says.

Alone in Grandma's Grove with a decrepit dog and a stone-dead mother. Is it possible to be more bereft than this?

A tear rolls down my cheek. Down my left cheek, just like my friend Gabriel Axel in Perpignan.

What saves us is oftentimes the same thing that casts us into ruin, says Mom.

Should I write that down?

I stop looking at her as she hovers over me in her old traveling clothes. She appears to me to have grown younger, but I say nothing about it and look down, at the black boots I'm wearing in the wet grass, the boots of a child yet too big for me. They're becoming a part of nature, covered with ears of couch-grass blades. If I sit long enough, the soles of my shoes will become glued to the grass, moss will grow over me from top to bottom, my bottom will fuse with the rock, and a thousand years later children will come and say: There's the ogress who turned to stone, and the rock next to her is her old dog. She was talking to her mother, who was a ghost, and didn't watch out for the dawn, but her mom just vanished into thin air, because she no longer existed, anyway.

The children will sit in my lap, I who was once a person and an assistant nurse. They won't know what my name was: Harpa Hernandezdóttir Eir. Or that I had a daughter very young, and that it wasn't known what would happen to this daughter, but at least an attempt was made to rescue her from bad company and take her to the Eastfjords. And that it was precisely on that trip that the woman turned to stone, and she was very glad, because there was nothing ahead of her but damned hardship, but no one knew this except for her, while she lived.

How lucky the rock is that gets to be seen, though it doesn't know of its own existence. The lifeless rock attracts life that grows within it, lichen and moss, and maybe a little fern after a long time, if it should crumble in places, leaving gaps for growth. The rock might even be lucky enough not to be stuck in the same place all the time. It can travel if it rains a lot and there's a landslide, or if there's an earthquake, or if it's cloven by frost and is freed from itself and becomes two independent rocks.

OH, HOW I WISH I WERE TURNED TO STONE. It would have to happen quickly, however. I can't wait for the dawn. Back at the house is a situation I can't deal with, that I can't return to. I won't walk into the white paradise farmhouse that my delinquent daughter will be wrecking this winter. I'll lie low here, in Grandma's garden and Mom's garden and my garden, until Old Man Winter or some other ogre comes and grabs me here in this garden that waited, waited until I deigned to show up. No signs of autumn are on the trees here, and a pyramidal saxifrage blossoms contrary to the laws of the months. After roaming in the garden of fog, I sit on my rock and become it, beneath trees that Mom left behind, a slim birch and needly pitch pine.

Come here, Grandma Sól. I've found berries. A small, good Edda on a spring day long past. My mother went to her, ate the berries noisily, and said: *Yum, yum.*

How has it all gone like this? What's happened to the three of us since that good day?

Time has gnawed away at us. That's what has happened.

From the grove I see all the trees that I saw only partially from the farmhouse. The farmhouse can't be seen from here, fortunately. I don't want to see the place where Edda is. The Eastfjords fog is her best keeper. The daughter of a walking changeling, the Icelandic mulatto who doesn't know who her father is.

I have a seat on a rock by the Andá River, beneath the biggest pitch pine that Mom planted, a straight tree shaggy with needles. When the weather permits, it reflects in the pool, creating two trees fused at the roots. Now nothing is reflected anywhere; everything is dull. That's fine. It's enough today to have a little of something dull, as I myself am in spirit and in truth, an assistant nurse from Reykjavík with a wet behind. Completely dull. Thoroughly lackluster.

Something or other wails in the shrouded landscape. I thought I knew each and every sound, each and every bird, but I don't recognize this one. A bird, one that's tried to set course out of the fog, flies into an elastic window that gives in endlessly, wailing in fear of getting nowhere, that it will never winter in a warmer land, that it will be stuck here forever in this slimy fog in the season when any sort of weather can be expected.

Stuck in this stuff that covers the world and blocks the senses, but that doesn't debilitate my breathing, unfortunately. I'm forced to keep breathing. Breathe, breathe, breathe, one two, one two. When Dad is dead, I can stop breathing, and then I can finally do what I please. While he's alive, it's unfitting for me to quit breathing. Out of the question to take my own life with a good conscience. Remember that. Don't play with thoughts that will lead to nothing. When Dad is dead, I can reconsider the matter.

Edda will play no part in the equation. I've taken enough care of her. I'm done taking her into account. She ruined my life. Let's just admit it. I did, however, create her, of course, and had dedicated assistance in doing so. No, it wasn't like that. It wasn't assistance; it was nearly rape. I was a polite person, and I felt for this excited boy who breathed uncontrollably into my ear, panting and shedding tears, and who'd torn off my bra, even while I managed to hang on to my panties, but then I simply couldn't deny him entrance any longer. How grateful he'd acted when it was over, while I was hurting and regretted it all, a pregnant girl after the first time, though I didn't know it then, of course. But I was devastated. Maybe all women are after their first time. I just haven't asked. And who should I even ask? What should I read? Oh, what does it matter, after all.

Loftur Pálmason, the child's father, was not a poetic man. But after the first and fatal time, he called me a fairy-tale princess. It really would make a difference if people could keep quiet, during sex and right afterward.

The haze at the lowest part of the garden takes on a human form, which has come silently through the garden gate.

What should I do if Ingólfur tries to talk to me about Edda? I'm not here to think about her. I'm here to be alone, to fuse with rocks.

Careful not to get a chill, Harpa. Aren't you ready to drag yourself back inside?

Ingólfur hits the rock with his hammer. A resounding, haunting blow in the garden of fog.

Not quite yet. It's magnificent to see how well the trees are doing. It feels like the Garden of Eden, I say.

It's a tremendous bonus in life to have such a garden.

Of course, now I've brought a serpent to it.

Oh, the poor creature, Ingólfur says. Don't you worry, Edda's no match for us.

Seriously, Ingólfur, God only knows how this is going to go.

Maybe he does, but I have no qualms about the girl.

I'm afraid you don't know what you're getting into.

You could say that about anything.

She started acting up right away, back in the house.

It was probably worst while you and your friend were there.

She can't stand Heiður. And she hates me even more, that's for sure.

How did the rest of the trip go?

I don't know where to start. Heiður ran off the road on the sands. We could have died, and it was entirely Edda's fault.

She won't be a problem here. Here she'll start all over again. We're no part of her previous life, not since after the madness began. It makes a big difference.

Her gang was chasing us, or part of her gang, in a small yellow van, up until today. We last saw them around Höfn. It's absolutely beyond me what those rabble-rousers want. They spoke to Edda in Kirkjubæjarklaustur yesterday, and she got in their car to go back to Reykjavík, or at least that's where they said they were going. Then they turned up again saying they weren't going after all, because the sands were impassable, and they gave her a book. That in itself was funny enough, but I discovered by accident that they'd cut out its middle for drugs.

I've never heard of such a vile pack of thugs.

I'm not even sure it's real drugs. It could be potato flour. I think that Teddi, the crime boss, is too sly to take such a risk. I mean, Heiður and I both saw it when he handed her the book.

He might have felt confident it wouldn't be discovered.

Maybe. But Teddi's so paranoid that it borders on mental illness, and I just can't see him dealing drugs that way. I'm sending the stuff to Reykjavík with Heiður, and then we'll find out what it is. Whether they're serious about trying to ruin everything.

I doubt they know what they're serious about, Ingólfur says. As for Edda, though, you don't need to be anxious. She's completely safe from those rogues with us.

But she'll be going to school in the village.

Which means we'll have to keep an eye on her, of course.

How am I going to do that? I'll be working.

I'm sure we can find a way to keep track of one girl. The village isn't that big, and everyone would notice a stranger, especially in winter. We'll get the villagers to sound the alarm if she's seen talking to suspicious characters.

It might require an entire surveillance system.

We'll keep Edda secure and do everything we can not to screw up.

Are the girls out riding?

Edda's on Dreki and Guðrún's on Spói. Edda wanted to go for a ride and the horses were here at home, so it wasn't complicated.

At least she's showing a little sign of life.

She always was one for the horses. Just put her on horseback and all the nonsense is dead and buried.

I wish it were that simple.

There's something to be said for teenagers having work and play that suit their abilities. If they get interested in something, that's half the battle won. But we'll have plenty of time to talk about this, Harpa. We won't be that far from each other this winter, and you shouldn't work yourself up about it now. You must be completely exhausted.

Even if we manage to get her back on track here, I say, God only knows what kind of person Edda will become. And I can hardly imagine what'll happen to her soul. You wouldn't believe how much evil she's come into contact with in her short lifetime. Someday I may have to tell you all about it.

It's part of the package, that we learn about some things.

Remember, you must hide all medications from Edda, no matter what they're called.

It's already been done, Harpa. It would have been a little too conspicuous to empty the medicine cabinet after she'd arrived.

What an unbelievable situation.

We won't fix it by whining, dear cousin.

Ingólfur motions with his hammer toward the house.

Wouldn't you like to go before you grow into the rock?

I extend my hand and Ingólfur tugs. Upsy-daisy.

Don't forget to bring back some rhubarb, he says.

I pull up three stalks just for show, though I really want none of this abominable plant that gave me stomachaches when I was young. Besides that, it's deeply unaesthetic to walk while dangling rhubarb stalks.

Take some more, woman. That's nothing.

I'll come soon in your mother's Willys to get the ingredients for real jam.

You can go wherever you want in this country in the jeep. But I should warn you—it makes a hell of a lot of noise.

That doesn't scare me. I'm used to drawing attention.

You won't stand out so much here in the east. Every other person's half-dark, and a lot of them short. This is the perfect place for you, my dear.

It's true, I always felt more at home here than in Reykjavík. But do you really think I should drive the Willys?

Don't worry about it. I've given it a look—it's in good condition. I didn't do much other than change the spark plugs.

How can I thank you for everything you've done?

It'll be more than enough thanks to see you and Edda get things worked out.

Lubbi rubs himself on my boot as he plods past, on his way through the gate.

Aw, you poor old thing, I forgot you, I say.

He's grown so old. It can't go on like this much more, says Ingólfur. Not another word about that, though. I don't believe in talking about such things in front of the animals.

Edda and her cousin come galloping toward us, both wearing helmets and riding boots, like real jockeys.

She rides surprisingly well, I say.

Once you've learned, it can't be forgotten, says Ingólfur. She was always good with horses. Best to let her exert herself. Maybe I'll have her help me break the horses.

The wild beast would be perfect for it. I hope she can be of some help to you here on the farm.

Your Edda wasn't a lazy kid.

We wave at the girls, and my rascal of a daughter waves back, as if she's always been the best child.

Don't be long, I say. Heiður and I are leaving soon.

It doesn't matter if we're not back, says Edda.

I want to say good-bye to you.

We won't be that far apart.

Okay, Edda. Bye for now.

There's a sudden downpour, so Ingólfur and I run to the house.

The girls will be drenched, I say.

It won't do them any harm. It's like in the old days when kids didn't have extra clothes to change into. They had to hang around in their room all day if they fell in a stream or got caught in the rain.

Margrét's brows are knitted in concern as she opens the door between the kitchen and hallway at the moment we come dashing in. Both of us are dripping, and I'm holding limp rhubarb.

God Almighty, she says. Look at the state you're in, Harpa. I told you, you should have put on rain gear.

No harm done, says Ingólfur, smiling somewhat mischievously. He looks amused to see his wife's look of intense concern over such a small thing.

Margrét says nothing, but gives her husband a slightly accusatory glance, as if he's completely irresponsible.

You'll have to change clothes, Harpa. This won't do at all.

You're right. I'll go out to the car to get some dry clothes, I say.

When I open the door and hop back out into the rain, a startled lamb skitters away and vanishes around the corner—one of the cossets that have sought shelter right up next to the front door. All that draws breath is under protective wings at Andey. Sometimes I've suspected the couple of taking in more pets than necessary, just because they want to provide shelter to every living thing.

I change my clothes in the laundry room, among filled-up hampers, a battery of shoes, flowerpots with new cuttings, a rock saw, a rock tumbler, and glistening sawed-apart rocks in hues of bottle green, rust brown, and pink. Some resemble satellite images of Earth, others of sea-green and reddish northern lights, as I told the wandering Frenchman last night.

As I take off my pants and put on new ones, I notice that my thigh muscles still ache from the previous night's romp.

With rain-matted hair, worn jeans, and a shapeless, nearly color-less fisherman's sweater, this particular gal has lost all her city cool. As she was supposed to. That's why I came east. It's complete.

The kitchen's unoccupied. On the table are clean and dirty cups and a half-eaten, freshly baked rhubarb-jam tart.

I saunter into the living room, where Heiður's standing in a light trance, looking at the photo of Martin, the ship's doctor, with my mom and her sisters, out in front of the old farm. Martin's expression is slightly strained. He's wearing a uniform and a braided hat, standing with Mom, Dýrfinna, and Betty. Martin, Mom's lifesaver, was not the handsome man Mom made him out to be. His eyes are small and closely set, his nose long and sinking downward at the tip over his thin lips. But his peaked cap gives him an authoritative air, a man of an entirely different world from the turf abodes and the girls in the photo.

The sisters are about six, eight, and ten years old. Mom is blonde while the others are dark-haired. Mom is a small girl in her Sunday finest with a white bodice. All of them have spindly legs, yet Mom is pigeon-toed and Dýrfinna duckfooted. Both are wearing straw hats and have stout braids down to their chests, while Betty has tangles of hair that must have been utterly hopeless to keep under control, with or without a hat. Even at that age, Mom was funny to see, with her turned-up nose and one deep dimple. She'd put Cosette's head be-neath her cheek as if she were going to crush it, stretching her hands in a stranglehold around the doll. Dýrfinna, soft and Madonna-esque, is holding a tabby kitten, guarding it lightly at her chest.

In the photo Dýrfinna looks like a reduced image of her daugh-ter-in-law, Margrét, as she stood in the doorway when we arrived. They say that men marry women who look like younger versions of their mothers. Life's chain of love is strong and subtle, and is either entirely invisible, or invisible at times.

But I must tell the truth. Betty does look like me in photos from when I was a kid. Perhaps I shouldn't give up all hope that I come from my own family. It would please no one as much as me if I were really the daughter of Axel and Eva Sólgerður.

You sure did take long, says Heiður, a bit piqued, as if there'd been a minor accident.

I tried to turn to stone, but it didn't work.

You don't have to turn to stone. The matter's settled.

THE WOMAN WHO DIDN'T TURN TO STONE. That's me.

Rósa sticks her head through the living-room door and says: My mom says you should come have coffee.

I recommend the rhubarb-jam tart, says Heiður.

Call the girls, too, Rósa, and tell them to come in for a snack, says Margrét.

Let them stay outside as long as they want, I say, so glad to be free of my problem.

They're probably starving, says Margrét. That won't do.

I'm sure they'll find their way home before they die of starvation, says Ingólfur.

Heiður takes a bite of a fresh slice of tart and chews loudly. I find it hard to bear when people eat noisily, and Dietrich Bacon feels the same. I've sometimes seen lines of pain around his courteous song-mouth as his girlfriend's jaw makes smacking noises at the table.

Lordy, it's really coming down, says Heiður.

This isn't what we call rain, says Ingólfur. From our perspective, it hasn't rained at all, damn it. Not like it used to. In the past, it was common to be stuck inside for a whole week because of the weather. It rained and blew so hard that you couldn't even let the dog out. It's hardly ever like that anymore.

So you mean the weather's changed for the better?, asks Heiður.

That's not what I said. These days it doesn't start warming up until much later in the spring.

Really?

Plus, the moon is closer to Earth now, says Margrét. It's awful to see it sort of dangling just over the tops of the hills.

I think Edda's an ugly girl, says Rósa.

Rósa, if you can't say nice things, you can't stay at the table, says Margrét.

Edda's having a bit of a tough time, explains Ingólfur. She has friends who are mean to her.

I might pack my clothes and leave. She's so boring.

You don't have to do that, says Ingólfur. It'll all be fine.

Rósa frowns obstinately at her father and knits her brows.

I'm wrecking things, I think. I'm spoiling the lives of these good people who want to build up mine.

Let me fly to you, Jói, my good angel. It's the only place for me. The only place. Wherever he is. Since I didn't turn to stone by the Andá River.

Rósa, Edda's actually a bit ill, says Margrét.

There's nothing wrong with her, Rósa hisses. She's just a naughty brat.

Well, she may change.

I don't want to be in the same house as her.

She won't be around you so much. She'll be going to school in the village every day.

The director general of the journey east stands up, obviously irritated.

Shouldn't we be going?, says Heiður.

I guess we should, I say. Give my daughter our good-byes.

We'll be in touch, says Margrét. Have a good rest now, and don't worry about a thing.

I'm afraid I'll fall apart if I stop worrying, I say.

Margrét doesn't know how to take this. She's kind and has a golden soul, but no sense of humor. That could be her downfall as Edda Sólveig's mentor. No one survives in Edda's vicinity without viewing her nonsense from a distance now and then and laughing silently.

The space in Mom's attic is worry-free, says Ingólfur.

We two cousins grin. The company at the table looks away. No one understands me and Ingólfur but us. We've known each other forever. Ingólfur is my big bro.

NO ONE IS WHO HE IS. Cousins are brothers, aunts are mothers. Mothers are ogresses, children are beasts. As for me, I'm not me, but someone else in my paternal line. I'm at the point in life where no one is who he is.

Except for best friends. They're always friends, even now, or at least for the moment.

Heiður has put on her shoes impatiently and is expressing her thanks with nods.

She's made great improvements during our trip. If we were to travel the entire Ring Road around Iceland, she'd end up perfect. She doesn't interrupt as much and has almost entirely stopped abruptly ending conversations and situations. Long hours spent in a car with a delinquent teenager have taught my friend manners. The road to good manners is mysterious indeed.

In the yard at Andey, air cushions expand beneath my shoes. I teeter, like the drugged woman I was on New Year's Eve in the emergency room, with springs for legs.

The difference is that then, there was insecurity beneath my soles. Now I'm teetering on security.

Teetering on security in uncertainty. Uncertainty about the fate of Edda Sólveig, uncertainty about myself. A person with a stone baby in her stomach. A key question unasked.

It would be just like this person to forget what the question was when she finally reaches her destination. To forget that there'd ever been a question to ask.

Free of all concerns, we head for the sea.

No sunstone pointing the way, but rather a hazy star.

FREE OF ALL CONCERNS.

I wave at cheerful Ingólfur, gentle Margrét, dejected Rósa.

The fog-girls, Guðrún and Edda, ride Spói and Dreki out of the mist. When they emerge, we'll be gone.

From the penultimate destination, just a short distance to the terminus.

. . .

Might I then doze the final stretch, above rumbling wheels on a gravel road? Fall into the acute sleep of Sleeping Beauty and snore for a hundred years? Of course she may sleep, she who has cast her sins behind her and loses sight of them for the time being, perhaps forever.

The delinquent child behind her, under a sound roof in a valley attached to a fjord where everything is horizontal.

The village lies lengthwise on a slope, beneath long ribbed mountains.

Even the fog lies horizontally.

Harpa wants to go beddy-bye. Because Harpa's so tired.

What nonsense. She doesn't want to waste time sleeping. Life is waiting, has waited a long time, and now she's finally come to where it is. As soon as the pickup turns away from Andey and heads toward the fjord, I grab my own tail. Finally, I'm here, right now—not yesterday or the day before yesterday or tomorrow or the day after—and I roll down the window for further confirmation of that fact. I see what's to see here and now, hear the splashing of stream after stream, the rush of the river, how it all echoes in my valley deep on a tranquil evening, the first of September.

On the way out of my private valley, the sea looks like a little lake, and shining through the haze above it is an inflated Elysian moon. Yes, the sea itself is a homey lake where I could fish from a little red boat, and lucky fish would take the bait and kick about in a sparkling heap at my toes.

My sorrows aren't as heavy as lead. They dwell light as feathers in stuffed linen bags in the stern of a rowboat. I stand up and swing the bag over my shoulder, and see?—it's child's play. I put down the bag and rest my head on it, and the boat rocks me like an infant in a cradle.

Some morning at Dýrfinna's, preferably tomorrow, I'll open the bag by the water's edge and watch the feathers fly out upon the calm sea on a soft breeze. My sorrows won't disappear, but now they're feather-light, fluff from the quilt of the queen of the valley. They'll remain sorrows, but they can be left alone on their extended flight through my private sky.

Pink woolen cloud columns tower over the mouth of the fjord.

Between them dawdle violet islands of down.

What a relief to be free of the girl!, exclaims Heiður. I swear to you, Harpa, she's like a phantom that's been conjured up against you.

It would be easier to deal with a phantom than a living child.

This trip will be good for you—I feel it in my bones. I'm absolutely positive.

Was there something wrong? On a night like tonight, I can hardly remember.

Your Edda couldn't be in better hands. Your kinfolk at Andey are more akin to angels than humans.

How can Mom come from this family?

You know what, Harpa? It's time for you to make peace with her now, though earlier would have been better. I'll admit that I never had anything against your mom. She was really funny.

Either Mom was crazy, or she was a poet. For a time I was certain she was off her rocker, but I later came to think of poor Mom as just a poet who never wrote anything down. She was left alone with her original thoughts and associations, which no one wanted to hear. Dad's too down-to-earth to understand such a woman.

We're more or less miracles.

Mainly you, Heiður.

Though not like you.

I guess Mom would have done better with a man who was slightly nuts. Then she could have tossed some of her insanity over to him. Dad's so normal that it's impossible to foist madness on him.

He was always so patient, says Heiður. He never raised his voice, and he was constantly making mobiles and model airplanes with you and Sibbi. He built bookshelves for your rooms, while my books had to be stowed in the wardrobe.

As far as your dad goes, I say, there was nothing at all to complain about. He was always so amiable, offering us boxes of foreign candy as if we were little princesses.

Oh, Dad and Mom were fine. Their minds were just elsewhere.

That's the right way to say it about my mom, as well. Her mind was elsewhere.

What's so funny?, asks Heiður.

Nothing, I say. Nothing's funny.

Yet I continue to smile, unexpectedly. It's as if my mouth is incapable of holding back from a full smile, which continues to broaden as we drive past the fish racks in the innermost fjord at the bridge where horses graze between light-green tussocks. A black bank of clouds spreads out over the darkening sky, which is reflected on the level sea of the day that's passing and has been doing so since this morning on our winding road to the east.

As we turn onto the village's main road, where as a little girl I stepped onto land from my sea voyages in the spring, we're met with a strange sound from an avant-garde trumpet, like the purring bass of a giant cat. Or something from a noisy duck. Bagpipe-quackquack blues.

God, I can't believe it. A crumhorn, says Heiður.

What?

A crumhorn. It's a medieval instrument, and not so common. If you make an effort, you might be able to hook yourself an Albanian crumhorn player.

I don't need one.

No, probably not.

It sounds like a parody of a musical instrument.

The instrument that's going to be rocking you to sleep this winter is damned invigorating. I recommend quality earplugs.

What family is it in?

It's related to an oboe, and looks like a walking stick.

Blowing on a walking stick. Well, I never.

This place is glorious.

You're telling *me* that?

I am.

This is nothing. Wait until you come to the most wonderful gingerbread house, right by the sea. With a boathouse and everything.

This place has so much atmosphere that I'm starting to feel like *I* want to spend the winter in Dýrfinna's attic. Want to trade?

Trade! That's a good one. Where I am in life is stuck. I've painted myself into a corner.

The floor will be dry in the spring. Then you can take your quilt and go. Honestly, I'd really want to stay.

Not if you actually had to. My two rooms in the attic aren't in good condition. They're also under a sloping roof, which, admittedly, isn't a problem for a dwarf like me. Look, there it is.

God, is it that Pippi Longstocking house standing on its head in the sea?

Exactly. The third oldest house in the village.

It's a dream, says Heiður. Yellow, with a red roof, like in a child's coloring book.

It's even dreamier the closer you get. Entire beds of living rock in the garden, blooming in all colors, even in the winter. Other things that aren't so hard on your teeth grow there as well: strawberries, red and black currants.

In the semidarkness of my childhood village, a man is mowing his grass with a scythe. The first of September has come, but the optimistic man believes that the grass will keep growing.

Kids come running up the path alongside the stream, holding dock stems that they whack against the ground. Two women pushing colorful baby carriages take the same path, past the old physician's residence. An enthusiastic little kid comes zigzagging along the sidewalk toward us on a bike that's far too big. It reminds me of all the bikes that I rode in my day that were far too big for my short little legs.

On the stone wall around the community center sits a group of tourists who are probably from this place's sister village in Brittany, which has a name that no one can remember. French and Icelandic flags fly on a flagpole. We're in a foreign country in Iceland. Where the other country in the country is.

Where can I park?

Just here at this turnout above the house. We can skip bringing in the fridge tonight, unless reinforcements arrive to help carry it. For now, let's just bring in the vanity cases, the nightgowns, the chocolates, and the hardfish.

Are you expecting someone? Do you think that Yves might have tracked you here?

What are you implying?

I wasn't born yesterday.

I'd already forgotten about him.

And you say *I'm* forgetful. You can't remember who you slept with last night.

We didn't get much sleep.

No, not from the sound of it.

Sorry if we kept the driver awake.

It's great that you grabbed the bull by the horns.

Thanks for the moral support, even if it's a little late.

Dýrfinna's House

My old fjord lies tranquil in the growing darkness, accommo-
dating the dusky-blue mountains standing on their heads on
the other side. The whimsical Eastfjords fog has unraveled, only to
come together at the end of the world and gather strength for the
next assault.

Invigorated by the oxygen-saturated air and the scent of the sea,
I run down the wooden steps, making them reverberate beneath the
spruce trees, and stub my toe on a bucket of bilberries sitting on
one of the landings. I munch noisily on a handful of these tempting
fruits, not caring if I swallow moss and heather along the way.

The front door is unlocked, but I still ring the bell so as not to
surprise my aunt. Then I walk straight in, to the smell of sausage meat
and cabbage rolls. Margrét must have called and announced that we
were on our way. I recognize this chain of communication from the
old days. Alert: Visitors coming. Have coffee and food prepared.

Dýrfinna limps out of the living room in a Sunday dress. When
she reaches me, she puts her arm around my neck and strokes my
cheek like the most loving mother, and I remember what tonight is

all about: getting an answer to the question that's been gnawing at me since the story of my soul began.

THERE WAS ONCE AN ICELANDIC SOUL IN A VERY SUSPICIOUS BODY.

But I'm not uptight anymore. My soul is placid. Nothing falls or drips from it, any more than from the most well-behaved girl on her confirmation day. If there's an answer, Dýrfinna knows it. If not, then screw it; I'll keep living as I've done until now. I suppose it's less of a problem for me than others, though they have the advantage of looking more like average Icelanders.

The Atlas Crystal refrigerator of my youth, which I remember as being full of chocolate tarts and opened jam jars, hums in the little kitchen, and my salivary glands jump into action. I have to swallow to clear my mouth of saliva.

Dad once asked: How do you conjure up your cakes, Dýrfinna? Mom got up and went to the bathroom and stayed a long time, before returning with puckered lips and a red anxiety-blotch on her neck. She was a bit light-headed, having just stepped off the boat, but it was clear to me that she was also angry at her own klutziness at baking, and angry that Dad should dare to praise her sister to the skies.

After lingering outside by the spruce trees and rocks and the giant mirror of the fjord, Heiður has finally come inside.

Welcome, dear, and thank you for driving Harpa and Edda, says Dýrfinna. You deserve a medal.

Dýrfinna's living room looks exactly as it does in my earliest memories of it, from a quarter century ago. Little Harpa Eir, able to talk in quarter centuries now. While everything else that lives and breathes changes, the flowers in Dýrfinna's living room remain the same. Is it theoretically possible that they could live so long? Maybe if they were clipped regularly. Maybe these are the scions of scions of the flowers that I can first remember.

The big oleander is in the same spot by the window of the dining room, which faces the sea. As a little girl, I made a game of standing at a reasonable distance from the oleander, peering at the waves between the elongated dark-green leaves and fragrant pink flower clusters, imagining that I was down south at the Mediterranean Sea. I'd seen photos from Costa del Sol of man-sized oleander bushes, the beautiful blue sea sparkling behind them. But the plant was highly toxic. I feared it as if it were a wild beast, because Mom had come up with a clever trick for protecting me, saying: Be careful. Don't go too close, because if it gets hold of you it will strangle you.

Dýrfinna became so angry when she heard Mom scare me in this way that she reprimanded her in front of me. I was looking at the clock with the glass dome, following the perpetual motion of the carousel of brass balls that turned into chiming bells at fifteen-minute intervals. Hearing Mom being scolded made me feel terribly giddy, but I knew that I couldn't show it, because then Mom would punish me with an even bigger dose of indifference. Just at that moment the clock struck, and I counted out loud along with it in order to hide the tingling joy inside me over Mom's failure.

Now the balls have stopped spinning and the hands of the clock stand in place. Not a tick is heard in anything that measures time. What is audible is the rhythm of the sea, how it strikes the land, forward and back, always at the same pace, forever amen, until time comes to an end.

Everyone sends their greetings, Aunt. Dad, Sibbi, Arnbjartur, Erika, and Betty. The chocolates are from Erika, and the hardfish is from Dad.

Thank you, dear. What's new?

Well, Arnbjartur really wanted to come with us.

It would probably have done him good.

He has a handyman now, who takes care of everything for him.

Oh?

It's a Faroese fellow. Liggjas. He doesn't have anywhere to stay.

Things are bad for our neighbors in the Faroe Islands. I think we should do more for them, set up refugee camps if necessary, says Dýrfinna. How's Betty?

I really don't know. But she was awfully nice and served us such wonderful coffee, and the amazing thing is that she and Edda clicked.

I'm not surprised.

She was hosting some sort of event at Útheimar that she called a mixed-participation gathering. A family reunion with people from here and from the beyond.

Mixed participation. She's not all there, the dear. Dýrfinna laughs silver laughter, almost the same as Grandma Una's. The difference is that in Dýrfinna's laughter there's something a bit puckish.

Betty claimed that five men were following us, but they were all supposed to be alive, says Heiður.

That's something new, if they're starting to come from this world.

Yet hasn't some of what she's predicted happened?, asks Heiður.

If you swing enough, you're bound to hit something, says Dýrfinna. *Mixed participation.* Of all things.

Dýrfinna laughs again. It's ringing laughter, with a touch of crumhorn.

How did the rest of the trip go?

That's a story in itself, says Heiður. But we did one good deed by putting a roof over the head of a poor Frenchman we met on the road.

Heiður gives me an impish wink, which I pretend not to notice, though Dýrfinna does and looks at me curiously.

Yes, foreigners are often frightfully helpless in this country, she says. It can be an act of mercy to give them a hand.

Would you like to get settled in upstairs? I'll go set the table.

We aren't hungry yet, says Heiður. We just had coffee at Andey.

It's time for dinner, says my aunt. You must put something solid in your stomachs after all this traveling. You can't live on snacks and cakes alone. Do you have to head straight back tomorrow, dear?, she asks Heiður.

That's the plan.

Such a busy person.

Heiður and I ascend the steep stairs to the attic. Two small rooms with an open door between them. In the inner room a huge plant reaches all the way up to the ceiling where it's highest and leans against the wall, tied up so that it doesn't tip over. We have to squeeze our way through the door in order to get past the big lobed leaves.

What is this?, Heiður asks, shaking her head.

It's called *Monstera deliciosa*, which I think means bliss-monster.

Flashes of light dance a polka on the waves beyond the currant hedge. The silence of the village and the sea are carried in through the open window, interrupted by nothing but the chugging of a fishing boat, which isn't yet visible in the view provided by the dormer window. Heiður's falling into a lyrical trance, saying that it's wonderful to be here, that it defies her expectations. I'm so earthbound that all I say is that the rooms need to be painted.

If it helps you feel better, you should paint, says Heiður.

I start making Heiður's bed, which will be my bed this winter, a poor old divan against the outer wall, beneath the aggressive plant that's more akin to a monster than bliss.

Heiður sits down in an old square armchair in the front room and watches me take care of the housework. To her it's natural that I make the bed. And it *is* natural. She drove me all the way here, after all. She takes care of the big picture, and I the small details. It's been that way since the beginning. What's wrong with that? Harpa Eir, assistant nurse in spirit and in truth.

The monstera makes it difficult for me to tidy up the room. It's over me and all around me. I knock my elbow against it as I stuff the quilt into its cover, and bump it with my behind as I turn around. Heiður's worried that the room won't have enough oxygen because the plant sucks it all in.

If we don't wake up in the morning, we'll know why, I say.

Heiður laughs and says: We'll just open a window.

That won't do. The monstera doesn't tolerate drafts.

In other words, it's we who should give up the ghost, rather than the plant?

Have a look at this.

What is it?

It's Mom.

A photo of my mother, half-hidden behind ivy stretching an arm up the wall.

She was so elegant.

This is the picture of the mom I'd forgotten. My mom in shorts, binding hay bales. An attractive, well-built mother with wavy hair, Mom as she was a quarter of a century before I came into being, with her favorite mountain, Strýta, in the background. There's something provocative, yet at the same time dreamy, in her expression, as if she's waiting for something. For my mystery dad, I suppose.

If my dad's a mystery dad, then I'm a mystery daddy's girl.

Come and get it! Dinner!

I haven't put on the pillowcase, but I'm so reluctant about disobeying my aunt that I leave the bed unmade and tear off down the steep stairs ahead of Heiður.

Everything's on the table: freshly harvested small potatoes in a floral bowl that's older than I am, melted butter in a sauceboat, cabbage rolls on a platter, the same white-and-blue dishes that I ate off of in my childhood. Even the nick in my plate is the same, a comfort in a hard world that changes so rapidly, and badly. Both my private world and the outer world. No stone unturned, except in Dýrfinna's garden. Where there are, in fact, stones unturned.

I sit against the Atlas Crystal and listen to the hypnotizing hum; it's like the voice of an old man in his final moments, fully reconciled with his destiny. Dýrfinna takes up two spaces in a custom-built broad-armed chair covered with a sheepskin.

Help yourselves, says my aunt.

I see that Heiður is skeptical. She's extremely fussy, being accustomed only to the best, and preferring macrobiotics. Yet she serves herself, though she violates a cardinal rule by cutting apart one of the delicate light-green cabbage rolls, revealing the pale meat mixture inside, and taking only half.

You're certainly not going to be overeating, says Dýrfinna.

We've just had some rhubarb tart, says Heiður apologetically.

Always on a damned diet, of course, says Dýrfinna.

Heiður's not on a diet, I say, terribly nervous. She just never gains weight.

Out of the corner of my eye, I see the lines in Heiður's face harden. Her nose lifts and seems to grow sharper. Oh boy, I think, this is going to be fun.

Naturally, says Dýrfinna. Those who don't eat don't fatten.

Heiður's always eating, I counter in a quivering voice. She just burns so many calories.

That's what they all say. But they're really always dieting, all their lives.

Having said this, my aunt ladles a porcelain ladleful of melted butter over Heiður's half cabbage roll.

Good Lord, Aunt, Heiður doesn't eat butter.

That explains her figure.

Heiður blushes in frustration and watches the pool of butter branch out in the meat mixture's greasy broth.

Would you like a new plate?, asks Dýrfinna.

I wouldn't say no, says Heiður, with suppressed anger in her voice.

Dýrfinna positions her hands on the table and prepares to stand up, but I hop to my feet, take Heiður's plate, and get a new one. Heiður serves herself the other half of the cabbage roll, uncontaminated by melted butter, but is unable to hide her acid expression.

What would you like with that, my dear? I've got drippings, if you'd prefer.

Now I'm beginning to suspect my aunt of malice. She can't be serious, offering Heiður Jensdóttir *drippings*.

Seldom have I refused the drippings. But no. Just kidding. I don't want drippings.

A little bit of drippings would do you good.

It's completely unlike Dýrfinna to behave this way. There can be no other explanation than that she doesn't like Heiður. The expensive tracksuit, the pearly earrings, the unassuming diamond ring are more than my aunt can bear. It pains her to see Harpa as Heiður's poor, plain charity case, an orphan alongside the Laugarás gal who never needs to lift a finger, yet dashes around the world with a golden flute and a small hard suitcase stuffed with clothing of such fine silk that it never gets wrinkled.

Sorry, but I find drippings disgusting.

Drippings have nourished the Icelandic people throughout the centuries.

Fortunately, we don't have to eat the same old garbage anymore. How'd you go about growing that monstera?

You're not the only one who's asked, says Dýrfinna. My neighbor came here in the spring and measured the leaves and discovered that they're bigger than the book says they're supposed to be.

That's quite an achievement, says Heiður.

You just have to remember to water it.

Don't you have to go up to the attic every day to do so?, I ask.

Preferably twice a day. Big plants need a lot to eat.

How do you manage?

I keep myself fit.

Aren't you worried you'll kill yourself with all that scrambling about?, interjects Heiður.

I wouldn't be worse off breaking my leg on the stairs.

Heiður laughs, gasping.

Now I can start taking it easier. It'll make a difference having Harpa here to help me. Are you on your way overseas again?

Yes, I'm going to Copenhagen next week for a concert, and then on to Venice to meet my husband-to-be.

Isn't it dreadfully polluted there?

I don't know. It's my first visit.

Pollution and debauchery.

I think it's worse now in other cities besides Venice.

Aren't you always in those big cities?

Sometimes.

Do you enjoy it?

I enjoy it sometimes, says Heiður, standing firm.

I don't know what to make of this. I've known my aunt for thirty years and have never seen her like this. Yet isn't that what they say a person is? New sides until the very end.

I should call Dad, I say. He'll be done with his dinner.

By doing so I can kill two birds with one stone. Escape this puzzling bickering and speak to my dad before I betray him by asking Dýrfinna straight-out about the identity of my biological father. Just asking the question is a betrayal.

Dad's phone rings a long time. If he leaves his room, no one answers the phone. His roommate's so deaf that he doesn't even hear the ringing.

I call the duty desk and ask to leave a message for Dad, because I don't think I'll be able to speak directly to him in the near future if my forecast about the progress of the evening proves true. It certainly comes in handy now to have a dad who's so passive that I can rest assured he won't be the one to call first.

Please tell Axel Óðinsson that Harpa Eir called and that the trip has gone well and everything is fine.

I feel relieved as I hang up. Relief at not having had to speak to Dad. Not now. At how precious it is to have put one matter to rest. Until tomorrow or the next day.

I go to find Heiður to wish her good night. She's sitting on the bed that I started making for her, and I squeeze my way over beneath the overwhelming plant and sit down next to her.

Heiður?

Yes.

Do you think our friendship will be just as strong even though we said some nasty things last night?

We'll survive. Don't forget that if just the two of us had taken the trip, the knife wouldn't have come between us.

I'm sincerely grateful for everything. I would probably be dead, literally, if I hadn't had you to turn to.

I'd suggest you keep that to yourself.

No, I won't tell anyone.

I stroke my friend's cheek, and her eyes moisten a bit—the toughie herself.

You're my best friend in the world, I say, even if you're a little too impulsive.

I'll smack you, she says, choking back a sob, if you're going to be so sentimental.

Sleep well, my cutey flutey. Maybe one day I can repay you.

I hope not.

Beast. Good night. Sweet dreams.

Don't push your aunt too hard.

No way. She's made of reinforced concrete, as you can see. Good night and thanks for everything.

Good night.

I make my way downstairs. The only light in the living room glows from the lamp carved by my master-craftsman grandpa, as well as a few candles. The semidarkness hides how the walls are worse for wear. As soon as I came in through the door of the house, I noticed through the sea of plants and islands of photographs that it would be necessary to paint the walls on the ground floor. If I'm to paint upstairs, I might as well paint the living room, too.

Now is the time. *The time of questions.*
What's the deal with me, Dýrfinna?
To ask or not to ask
that is the question.
Show me the way, my lifeline,
Jói, my friend.
If you hadn't spoken I wouldn't be here, free from the little monster I was chained to. Free from my old life, maybe, soon.
What will happen soon?
A black-and-white passport photo of Jói is in its place in my wallet. His beloved face, enclosed in a dark frame of shiny hair. His classical facial features and rather heavy yet delicate eyebrows, long straight nose, and handsome cleft chin, give him the combined look of an Indian prince and Icelandic farmer from around the turn of the century.

Show me the way, Jói. You must see it clearly from where you are now, you who are in the light and the world before it became.

My aunt sails in slowly with a pitcher and cups on a tray. She puts down the tray on the table before sitting in her chair. Its high seat and sturdy arms are custom designed for handicapped people. The candle flames cast a mysterious gleam on a slightly tattered and stained Icelandic flag that has slipped halfway down a silver pole. Aunt Dýrfinna pours hot chocolate into gold-trimmed white cups and adds dollops of whipped cream. Her broad, smooth face has the same radiance one might find in a seventeenth-century painting by a Dutch master of chiaroscuro, and her hair is a halo of silver.

I feel as if I've come to an ancient temple, and that the sibyl will let the cat out of the bag soon—not in the oracular style, but rather in clear words that don't come as a surprise. That she'll tell me how everything will go, what will happen next, and what will happen thereafter. For Edda as well. Whether we live or die. Who we are. And above all who I am, though I'm not sure I'll care what she says.

It won't matter, since I've always known the truth and I'm doing nothing but gaining confirmation.

It's Dýrfinna who begins: Do you want to ask me something?

Yes. Do you know what it's about?

Let's hear it, Harpa dear.

I don't know how to start.

Just let out whatever it is that's bothering you. It's just me you're talking to.

I want to speak, but the words are fighting against being spoken. Dýrfinna is silent and steadfast. She's already portioned out to me all the assistance she has to give.

I look at my small feminine hands. The people on both sides of my family have big hands. Mom had masculine hands.

Everything has fallen silent in camaraderie with me: the land, the sea, and the people. Nothing ticks, nothing stirs. I hear nothing but the beating of two hearts, and even that beating must be my imagination.

Beating life.

Isn't that the line of poetry Heiður liked? The one that Alli the dwarf made fun of the most?

Bright death of the heart, beating life!

Oh.

Yet I have the sense not to publish these shreds of poetry.

If only the clock with the glass dome worked, if only the carousel were still spinning, if only the audible timer worked, to help and support me.

Now I've got to speak. That's why I've come, to push the leaden words out into the world, the unasked question that has thoroughly spoiled my days.

The time of questions has come.

I feel as if Jói is speaking, that it's he who finds the words and has borrowed my voice to say them.

I felt I could never . . . I didn't know how to ask Mom . . . because she surely would have told me first if she'd intended . . . if she'd wanted . . . to tell me . . . But I . . . I can't believe that I can look like this, and I've never believed it . . . that I'm . . . Axelsdóttir.

My aunt gives me a crafty look and says: Yet you are Axel's daughter.

It can't be.

Yes, it can more than be. It is.

Don't you lie to me, too. I'm sorry, Aunt, this has been bothering me for so long. I should go to bed.

There's more than one Axel in the world, my dear.

Don't talk to me like the oracle at Delphi. I'm so tired from the trip—from everything—that I can't do this now.

You're asking me about your true father. But you know him, Harpa. You know who he is.

You're not going to start telling cheap jokes now, not when I finally find the nerve to ask.

I get up in slow motion from this limitlessly soft chair with broken springs. I feel like grabbing Dýrfinna by the neck and calling her a witch of a midwife.

Witch of a midwife, I repeat to myself, careful not to release these bastards into the world of sound.

Think it over, Harpa. How many Axels do you know?

I only know Dad.

I'm sure you know another Axel.

That's true. The one who doesn't live here.

Well, I'll just sit back down in this deep chair, which could be the star of a nightmare, a bottomless hell into which one sinks and sinks, no solid ground beneath. Then I'll dip my face into the creamy foam of my hot chocolate, and shovel it up shamelessly with my tongue. Such a respectable woman, not giving a thought to using a teaspoon when *the truth* comes out, belatedly, after suffering and pondering morning, afternoon, and evening. Something that doesn't add up. Harpa Eir isn't who she's said to be.

Who am I, then, since I'm not me?

So the truth of it is a joke when it's finally told, and has always been plain to see. Axel Óðinsson, shop teacher, *is my dad*, though a foreign Axel, an acquaintance of mine, might have accidentally conceived me.

He lives in Perpignan, in France, I say.

He does, says my aunt.

It's not far from the Spanish border.

I finish my hot chocolate and immediately pour myself another cup, top it off with a big pile of whipped cream, and pat and shape it with a teaspoon. I'll have to down a lot of this drink before fully swallowing this joke.

How do you know this, if it's so?, I ask my aunt.

Of course it's so. Your mother told me the whole story soon after you were born. She suffered in silence while she was pregnant with you. Then you were born, and your appearance wasn't normal, but no one said anything, as you might expect, and your mother volunteered nothing. I asked her straight-out when you were several months old. Then she told me how it was. Otherwise, she probably would have kept silent about it forever.

Good thing you asked.

It was the only option.

Did Mom know immediately which of them was my dad?

She knew, because she and your father were no longer intimate.

I just stare at my aunt.

That's how it was, my dear. Your mother became involved in a completely unexpected passionate affair. She said she'd stopped thinking of such things.

She was lying.

Who knows, my dear.

Why was I always lied to? It was of absolutely no use. I've known for so long that it doesn't add up. Why wasn't I just told?

It isn't so simple, my dear. Consideration had to be shown to your father.

How can you possibly think that Dad hasn't known about this the whole time?

Your father is like other people in how he prefers not to face the facts. How would it have been better for him if your mother had hit him with the truth? Your father lives in the blissful illusion that you're his daughter. We don't tamper with it. That would be cruel.

Dad isn't stupid. He knows this.

It has nothing to do with stupidity, dearest. Maybe your father keeps the truth locked in some compartment. But he isn't aware of it. He can't reach this knowledge; there's a locked door in the way. He knows virtually nothing.

And my childless friend in Perpignan doesn't know that he has a child, who happened to present herself in the form of an Icelandic au pair.

You're wrong, my dear. *He* knows.

How?

Your mother wrote to him when you were a child.

Why?

I felt it was the right thing to do on her part, and I encouraged her to do so. It's better for people to know if they have a child somewhere. Even though it was clear to the poor man that he couldn't contact you. But he could do so under false pretenses, so to speak, after you'd found him. He could send you gifts as a neutral party, but not as a father.

So he knew who I was when we met that summer in Perpignan.

The blessed man. Compelled to say nothing to you. You can imagine how much he wanted to talk. The burden of silence can be so very heavy.

But how was it between Mom and Gabriel Axel, really? Were they in love?

Something like that.

Strange, the way Mom was.

Your mother was an incredibly beautiful woman in her time. She could be very amusing, and charming.

I've seen the photographs. She was beautiful, but it's hard for me to imagine her being amusing, or charming.

It's to be expected, perhaps, that you don't have many good memories of her. Once you started growing up, she left you to your father an awful lot. It was right for her to do so. She hardly had anything to spare. I think she always pined for the man in Perpignan. She spoke to me about him not long before she died. It was a very long love on her part.

Long love. So there's a measure. A length of love.

He's really great, I say. But he's nothing like me.

I've seen photos, but they were all taken when he was older. Judging by them, it's true—you don't look alike. But you could, of course, look like him when he was younger.

I suppose.

If the photos suggest anything, it's that he's a real charmer.

He is a real charmer. But damn, Mom's really lousy for doing this to Dad. With all the attitude she gave him, he scarcely lived a single happy day. How can two sisters be so different?

There are three sisters. Who does Betty resemble?, Dýrfinna says, before bursting into laughter. Then she pours hot chocolate into my cup, the third one for me, and tops up her own, adding more whipped cream to both.

Your mother was always a bit mentally unstable, and no one knew where it came from, she continues. She was tremendously obstinate when she was a child. She lived a great deal in her own world. She pretended to be French and called herself Mademoiselle Martin. She acted as if Martin, the ship's doctor who operated on her when she got appendicitis, was her father, even though Dad was alive and was tremendously good to her. She called the doctor "Dad," bade him a tearful farewell in autumn, waited for him all winter long, and chattered endlessly about him. It wasn't normal. The spring that he didn't come, she was inconsolable. We should have lied to her that he would come later, but she knew better. She cried and spent her time alone with Cosette.

I should have slaughtered that thing. If I'd only had the guts.

It would have changed little.

Was Mom just born crazy like that?

We shouldn't use such words. She was always quite odd, your mother. Her behavior was hard to understand. I didn't see her shed a tear when Dad died. But, as I said, she was inconsolable a few years earlier when Martin didn't return.

As if I didn't know how terribly contradictory she was all the time, I say.

Maybe. Also in the sense that she wasn't as she appeared. She was yapping away all the time and seemed to be so open, but in reality she was introverted. In retrospect, we knew little of how she really felt.

She sat all the time in the grove, Dýrfinna continues, looking out over the fjord as the fishing boats arrived and anchored. She wanted to go abroad ever since she was tiny. I've never seen that in such a small child.

Wanderlust or insanity, I say. What to call it?

Laughter simmers up in my aunt. Let's not judge so sharply. There are so many strange things in one's own chest, if one takes the trouble to look there.

Dýrfinna, don't you find people incredibly inconsistent in terms of being good for each other?

Certainly.

My poor mother wasn't good for any of us, and it's quite typical that she was worst for the one that she treated best.

Your brother's upbringing was certainly a failure. It's too late to save it. But your circumstances were different, despite your being siblings. Perhaps you were also more resistant toward your upbringing than poor Sibbi. In any case, you win. You have two extremely kind, living dads.

Maybe so.

I even have a letter that shows how good your French dad is.

He's more of an Andalusian than anything else, I say. Because he was brought up in Seville. His father was French and his mother a Portuguese Jew. So really, he's Jewish, since it's determined by maternity.

That's a brilliant mix. So you're half Icelandic, if we go by genes, one quarter Jewish, and one quarter French.

I'm quite the bastard. Such a mix doesn't exist in all the world. It's disorienting.

It shouldn't be.

Oh?

It's good when different nationalities mix. Good and necessary. Icelanders would have been a degenerate race long ago if they hadn't been so promiscuous, their women so excited about foreigners who were driven onto their shores.

You don't pity the poor strange-looking kids who emerge from this frivolity?

It's true that you don't look like anyone else, even though all sorts of things are born under the sun. It doesn't take a visionary to see that you must have been of foreign origin.

You weren't speaking literally when you mentioned a letter, were you?

Yes, my dear, it's a letter to you from Gabriel Axel.

Why didn't you give it to me a long time ago?

There were strict orders that you not be shown the letter unless you asked.

Why do you have the letter anyway?

Who else should have it? I got in touch with Gabriel when your mother died. I thought it right to inform him of her death.

And what would have become of this letter if you'd passed away, may I ask?

It was all taken care of. I put the letter in an envelope and addressed it to Ingólfur. He knows the details, since he had to help me with the English when I wrote.

Just a moment. Does everyone in the family know except me?

No, no. No one knows except Ingólfur and me.

Not even Margrét?

No, my dear.

My aunt stands up, supporting herself on the arms of the easy chair. There are traces of a whipped-cream mustache on her upper lip. It's appropriate that the sibyl would have a whipped-cream mustache while helping to solve one of life's mysteries, the one involving me.

She reaches for a key on a shelf that's the oldest piece in the house, embossed by my great-grandfather Antoníus, a craftsman and powerful poet. The shelf also holds a ceramic curlew, a row of rock crystals and zeolites, and a stuffed plover with a damaged wing. That plover won't be going far this autumn.

Aunt Dýrfinna opens the desktop cabinet, the piece of furniture that she sometimes let me investigate when I was little. In the shallow drawers she kept a locket with a photo of her Unnar, her wedding ring, which had become too narrow for her work-swollen fingers, old photos, and faded yellow letters, among them one from Great-grandpa Antoníus to Great-grandma Alda from when they were courting. My aunt opens the drawer where Great-grandpa's letter is kept and takes out a familiar folder of beige silk. Embroidered on it are carrier pigeons, which I've known well ever since I was a kid. Their wingspans are abnormally wide, reminding me more of eagles than pigeons. In this silk folder Dýrfinna has kept my secret. She pulls out a brown envelope with a rubber band around it. On it are the words INGÓLFUR ÁSGEIRSSON, in Dýrfinna's handwriting.

The letter to you is in here, explains my aunt.

Not even letters to me are addressed to me.

I tear open the envelope addressed to Ingólfur, and inside it find another smaller one, addressed to HARPA EIR AXELSDÓTTIR, in familiar letters made by Gabriel Axel's pen. His writing looks almost like typescript, each individual letter clearly shaped, the ink sea-green, appropriate for the person who owns a shop called The Art of Sailing.

Perpignan, October 18, 1984

1984! I should have asked earlier.

Dear Harpa Eir, my delightful daughter,

My heart is heavy writing you these lines, but I am also relieved. This letter will only appear to your eyes if you wish it yourself, if you ask the question. What drives me to write to you in this manner is that when we met, I sensed that you doubted your documented origin, and thus I have found the courage in myself to confirm that your suspicion is correct. I am the one for whom you searched, and the one you found, but you did not know that.

I felt certain that destiny would arrange for us a different, and better, meeting than our mere fleeting one that one particular summer, having brought us together as it did in the first place.

It was you, dear child, who made our meeting possible. I shall always remember as long as I live what you answered when I asked: Why did you choose this place, precisely?

I looked over maps of France, you said, and I liked Perpignan best.

In this, supernatural forces were at work. Your mind, dear child, your gentle intuition. I have never met a person your age so independent in thought, so pleasant in conversation. I am deeply proud to be your father, even if in secret, although no one knows that I am the father of anyone, no one but Elvíra, who nowadays I am able to call my life companion.

We must ask ourselves, dear child, what will come of you reading this letter while both of your fathers are alive. I venture to ask you never to reveal this secret to your father in Reykjavík. It would only sadden his heart and do no one any good.

I am aware that you have been beset by difficulties, and I wish that I could make life lighter for you. It is of great importance to me that you benefit from my decent means, to the extent that it is possible, without waking the suspicion of your father in Reykjavík. Over the years I have put together savings that will be more than sufficient to support Elvíra and me well into our old age, should God grant us a long life. As far as real estate is concerned, I own the entire building housing my shop, and last year I also acquired a rather small but well-built house by the sea, not far south of La Rochelle.

I understand that your economic situation has been quite constricted, and I ask you to do me the favor of accepting without delay, in cash, an advance portion of your inheritance. My house is always open to you and your daughter, both this one here in Perpignan and my cottage in La Rochelle, which is also delightful to visit in winter. I am able to give you the good news that when my assets are sold after I am gone, half of the equivalent value will be sufficient to secure the financial future for you and Edda, my beloved granddaughter. I sincerely hope to meet her before she is full-grown.

I know that you have had the inclination to educate yourself better. Nothing in life would make me happier than to be able to host you here, and Edda, of course, if you should wish to pursue higher education in these parts.

Now I ask that you send me a note, confirming that you have received this message. I have waited for this day with impatience and immense fear that I might not live to see it.

I wish you the very best, my beloved, distant daughter. Every day that I take breaths, I think of you. On the rare occasions that I received a letter from you, I lifted it with trembling hands, in the hope that the secret had been revealed, and that I would again be able to enjoy your company, wonder of my life, who God gave me in a roundabout way. May the good Father envelop you in love, and I pray fervently and sincerely that as things stand, the information that is confirmed in this letter may be to the advantage of you and your daughter, Edda Sólveig, and only to your advantage.

With love, always,

Gabriel Axel

Where in the world did they meet?

At the Marine Research Institute.

Oh?

Yes, Gabriel Axel came here because he had an Icelandic acquaintance who was a marine biologist. This friend showed him his place of work, and your mother was working in the café, where she served the foreigner.

Love at first sight.

Something like that.

Gabriel Axel never mentioned a word of an Icelandic acquaintance.

I know, my dear. He didn't want to waken the slightest suspicion in you. An extremely decent man, judging by all the signs.

Bettý said that I'm being followed by a tall, thin, dark-skinned man, speaking a foreign language.

What a bunch of nonsense.

She said he was alive, incredibly sad, and wanted to speak to me.

Pff, she must have sniffed that out.

How so?

She has a way of sniffing out all sorts of damned things. There's nothing supernatural about it. It's called prying.

Yes, but if no one in the country knows this but me and you and Ingólfur?

Naturally, your mother knew it while she was alive.

Do you think she told Bettý?

It's not out of the question. But it wouldn't have been wise to do so, because Bettý's never been able to keep secrets. Telling Bettý a secret is as good as broadcasting it.

You don't really put much faith in your sister's talents.

Yes, yes, she's a genius at baking, but she's completely irresponsible when it comes to conversation, and that's not the same as the gift of prophecy.

Silence descends, the silence that occurs when a question has been answered.

It's different from the silence preceding a question.

The time of questions hasn't passed, though one answer's been received.

A question that's been answered engenders new questions.

At what moment did he realize it, the owner of The Art of Sailing in Perpignan, that he was facing his daughter? When I told him my name? When did I do that?

He probably didn't recognize me right away, and indeed, a long time had passed since that day. The historic bright-weather day when I walked over to the tall man with the camera standing near the sculptor's domed studio, the man who gave me a gold chain that I told no one about, never ever, because he put a finger to his mouth and said *hush* in a foreign language as he waved to me before I set out for Dock Wood, crossing the plank over the little ditch.

The doorbell rings.

Who can that be, so late?

It's unusual nowadays, says Dýrfinna. It wouldn't be so surprising if I were still working.

Dýrfinna's heavy footsteps approach the front door. I'm uncomfortable waiting for her to open the door, and I move over to the old dining-table chair that's partially hidden behind it. I feel nauseous. I feel like I'm going to pass out. And why not? Poor me, whose line of descent has just been changed. A genuine changeling, on my father's side. Do the books say anything about whether people could be changelings on their father's side?

Might it be my man from Ísafjörður at the door? He could have tracked me down easily, of course. Impossible to know what that man might come up with. My palms become sweaty as I await what will come next. What if it's the boyfriend who's not a boyfriend? What should I say *then*?

Hello, Arnbjartur. Please come in.

Arnbjartur does as he's told. I sit tight on the chair.

My uncle walks to the living room in full Icelandic gear, wearing clogs and a typical angelica-green anorak, carrying a cardboard suitcase bound with a string, looking as if it could have been descended from the suitcase of Salka Valka and her mother, Sigurlína, when they stepped onto land, exhausted, at Óseyri in Axlarfjörður.

You'll have to sleep in the sewing room, says Dýrfinna. The women are sleeping upstairs.

I actually had the master bed in mind, says Arnbjartur, laughing and giving a glimpse of bits and pieces of his teeth, which seemed to be scattered randomly.

You'll start in the living room. You can't take everything by trump on the first night, says Dýrfinna.

Arnbjartur grins and sits on the couch, still in his anorak.

How'd you get here?

I hitched rides on trucks the whole way—first to Höfn, and then here. It didn't cost a single króna. The man laughs and rocks giddily on the couch. The vehicle from Höfn was called HERMANN AND LÍSA, REYÐARFJÖRÐUR. It was Lísa who drove. She's an absolutely lovely person. There were two of us coming from Höfn. I'm pretty sure the other fellow was French—handsome, wearing a red coat.

Did the backpacker continue onward?, I ask, a bit shocked at being reminded of my dead-and-buried one-night stand. Would he be staying in my fjord tonight?

Why do you ask?, inquires Arnbjartur, laughing with a chirpy trill.

Dýrfinna eyes me, saying: Might he be the same one who stayed with you in the summerhouse?

It can't be, I lie. He was going the opposite direction.

He got out of the truck here, says Arnbjartur. In case you're interested.

He was gone in the morning, forever. Then shows up again in the evening, at my destination. He hasn't come here to find me, but to find the fjord. How sensitive, and so very sensible. He wanted to fall asleep and wake up even just once in the dream fjord of the Queen of the Night.

Arnbjartur lays his suitcase on the couch and clicks open the rusty latches. From a brown paper bag he removes a plastic bag, containing the first harvest of autumn: small artistically shaped rutabagas, one head of lettuce, several bright carrots, potatoes. He lays out the slightly dirty fruits of the earth, creating a STILL LIFE, of freshly picked vegetables on a brown paper bag and posh cups and saucers.

The potatoes are from Erika. There are more in the bag in the hall.

You shouldn't waste them on me.

I've got to contribute something to the household, since you're putting me up.

Would you like some hot chocolate, my dear?, asks Dýrfinna.

Yes, please.

I'll heat up some more, I say, standing up out of the depths of the unspringy easy chair.

I'm sure Arnbjartur would like a little shot of something in it.

Yes, of course. Stay where you are. I'll take care of it.

I feel dizzy as I stand at the stove and stir the hot chocolate. Dýrfinna's made several liters in her old jam pot. I look into this honey-sweet brown liquid as the wooden spoon goes round and round, leaving tracks. I invent a new kind of sorcery, *hot-chocolate sorcery*, and empower the drink, intoning softly, like a witch just warming up.

Would you know yet more?

Had I known all along? Ever since the first tear ran down the cheek of my gloomy friend in Perpignan, in his apartment above The Art of Sailing?

Maybe I'd known it, but I didn't know that I knew. Humans are experts at raising mental screens: highly mobile, practical screens that conceal the facts. Yet maybe I can be excused for not exactly having let it cross my mind that the sweet ghost Gabriel Axel might be the one I was searching for.

Mom's wanderlust didn't ever take her overseas, only me. Maybe it could still save me—and Edda too. Mom's daydreams, or more accurately delusions, procured me two fathers and, according to the letter, some wealth, turning me into someone who might have *chances*.

I still have a chance to go to school. Can that be?

A chance not to have to spend my entire life tending sick people for shitty pay.

But would I really be better off, by educating myself, by having money, if Edda perishes?

The letter was written ten years ago. Higher education? I could have already been finished with that, if I'd had the sense to ask my question earlier.

By now, I could have been DOCTOR HARPA EIR. Though a doctor in what, I have no idea.

If I'd had the heart to ask, even as late as two years ago, I could have gone abroad with Edda, and she never would have wound up in this mess.

Those who don't ask, don't get any answers, find no solutions. Not asking can be fatal.

Yet I'm thankful for having finally stammered out the question.

Which yields answers.

And the answers propagate stealth.

Stealth in dealing with my dad, and stealth in dealing with Edda, at least as long as my dad is alive.

Maybe forever.

But where to begin? How to answer the next questions?

Should I betray my *father in Reykjavík*, as my genetic father in Perpignan so deftly called him? Betray him in his old age and go to the other father, the man Mom had an extramarital affair with during the blackest winter days more than thirty years ago? Wouldn't that be beautiful? Is it even possible to use the word *beautiful* in such a scenario?

On top of everything else, Arnbjartur's come all the way here, like a representative of his brother, the artificial dad in the capital.

I stop stirring the hot-chocolate sea, stop intoning, having gotten nowhere with my sorcery. The unmagical little sorceress arranges snacks on a metal tray—flatbread with butter and smoked lamb, homemade bread with egg and cucumber—and then brings the treats into the living room.

As soon as I put down the tray on the coffee table, the phone rings.

It's probably your boyfriend, says Arnbjartur, in his squeaky voice.

I don't have one.

Not that you know of.

Hello, Harpa, it's me, says the nervous voice of the man I bring with me everywhere—even on this journey east.

Is that you? Hello. Wait a moment.

The telephone cord is short. I can just barely slip inside the kitchen door, and speak with my mouth at the door crack as if I'm whispering an immense secret into the foyer.

You're not alone?, he asks.

No. Can you hear me well enough if I speak this quietly?

Yes, I can hear you.

You found out where I am, the first night.

I also tried yesterday, but your aunt said you were coming today.

Strange, she didn't mention anything.

Strange. Can you come see me?

It depends a bit on where you are.

I'm in Ísafjörður.

I'm not on my way there.

No, of course not. I have to go to Egilsstaðir.

I see.

Could you meet me there?

I don't really think I trust myself to travel from fjord to fjord in my aunt's Willys.

Could you take a bus?

I suppose so.

Can I come to you?

When?

The day after tomorrow.

I don't know, I say. I need to paint my room.

So?

Would you be able to stay a while?

Two nights.

Would you need to leave between evening and morning?

Yes.

Is anything special going on?

I've got to see you.

Has that become a reason?

Don't be cold to me, Harpa. I think of you day and night.

Yes.

How was your trip?

There's so much to tell, I wouldn't know where to begin. It would take volumes to make a full account of it.

Did something special happen?

Nothing that I'm able to discuss on the telephone.

It's awful to think of you way out there and worried about your girl.

Actually, things are pretty darned good here. I've stopped worrying about Edda. I've had so many worries that there's no room for any more. Now I'm just raring to get away and start some serious learning.

Oh, Harpa, you're not leaving Iceland, are you?

Do you want to keep me here so that you can use me twice a year?

It might be possible to increase the number of times.

How many do you offer on an annual basis?

We'll see. Please, can I come visit you?

Uh, no.

You must be completely exhausted. Can I call you back tomorrow?

I can't prohibit you from doing so.

Oh, Harpa, I feel like my tongue's pasted to the roof of my mouth. I can't seem to say anything that I want to say.

You could try writing it.

Are you hiding something from me? It's like you've changed.

We haven't seen each other in over half a year. A lot can change in that time.

Have you met someone else?

Would you find that strange?

Harpa, you have to tell me what's going on.

Of course I don't *have to*. Besides, who's to say that I know what's going on?

Listen, I can hear you're in no mood to talk right now. Let me call you tomorrow. You probably just need some time to figure things out.

You think so?

I'm hanging up now, Harpa. Talk to you tomorrow. Good-bye and good night.

Bye.

I fully expect Arnbjartur to be eavesdropping, but he's still in the living room, with his paws in the silk folder, having a look at Gabriel Axel's letter to me, without his glasses. He sure knows how to pry into other people's business.

What do we have here? A foreign letter from '84, in a freshly opened envelope, it looks to me.

Dýrfinna gives me a collusive look. She expects me to try to wriggle my way out of this.

What's an old letter to Harpa doing here with you, Dýrfinna? And who's this Gabriel Axel?

It's from my dad.

I'll be damned. That's what I'd call news.

I thought you weren't interested in genealogy.

I'd say this is a bit more than the usual names and dates. Is the man's name really Axel?

His family name is Axel, yes.

It's practically an act of providence to have them both named Axel.

I can't see that it matters, says Dýrfinna. The main thing is that little Harpa is of such fine character.

What does poor Seli have to say about this?

This is a secret, Arnbjartur, says Dýrfinna. No one invited you to read that letter. I strictly forbid you to mention this to anyone. Your brother has no idea. You can imagine how he would react.

I can't fathom how he wouldn't suspect something. Anyone in his right mind can see that he's as much Harpa's father as the cat's. Her mom never played with a full deck.

Many a person missteps without being branded crazy as a result, says Dýrfinna gravely. We shouldn't judge so sharply. There are people here and there who don't fall for temptations, but who's to say that they're any better than the rest?

Thank you for the kind words, Finna dear.

A door slams violently somewhere in the house.

I don't know what that can be, says Dýrfinna.

Arnbjartur replies excitedly: *The leg's here.* I'll never be rid of it.

When Dýrfinna asks what he means, she is treated to the entire story. Arnbjartur curses the ungrateful limb that he took under his wing, the damned gam that he placed in a well-crafted box in consecrated ground and sang a hymn over, and which repaid the favor by returning from the grave and kicking down doors. And now, it's obviously followed him out here to the Eastfjords.

Do you think Bettý might be able to help you get the bastard under control?

I'm scared shitless of your sister.

Uff, I'm far more dangerous than she is.

Quite possibly. People never have the sense to fear those who are truly dangerous.

Sæmundur the cat dashes in, light on his feet, and jumps into my lap.

Where've you been, Sæmundur dear?

He answers only when I start stroking him devotedly, as in the old days. It sounds to me as if he's been sitting at the seaside, meditating, as the very last rays of the sun played in his fur.

Sæmundur's purr reminds me of my late mother's voice. Yet how much more pleasant it is to listen to him.

How much purring cats have over speaking mothers.

Mine, at least.

Are you melancholy, my dear?, asks Arnbjartur.

No, no. I just find it quite sad to have left Dad behind like that.

There's no end to poor Seli's troubles. But he has only himself to blame. I told him to stay away from your mother. She was an incredibly dubious character.

I forbid you to talk about my sister like that, says Dýrfinna. She wasn't perfect, but neither are you, dear.

I didn't mean to offend you, but as far as I'm concerned, my brother definitely deserved better.

He was in love. That's all there is to it.

I've never understood what people are going on about. I'm not in love, says Arnbjartur.

I'm sure you were at one time, says Dýrfinna.

Then it would have been with you, Finna. Arnbjartur's face turns purple from laughter.

Well, what's so funny about that?, says Dýrfinna. I'm rather offended.

Don't be. No, Finna dear, you and Eva Sólgerður are really the most different of sisters. Poor Seli didn't have a chance in that misadventure.

I'm going to finish making my bed, I say. I'll be back in a moment.

Sæmundur senses that I'm ready to get up. He beats me to it and leaps off my lap with a mew of complaint.

It's just so sad to leave Dad behind.

It was sad already, sing the stairs as I march up, but how will it be after tonight? With his brother sniffing out the secret just as soon as it was revealed to me.

My old dad, who has lost everything. A wife who betrayed him, producing a strange-looking daughter. A daughter who has fled and, besides, is not his daughter. A bungler of a son who let his father shoulder the responsibility for his own debts, completely fleecing him as a result. At that rate, he should thank his stars that he still had his poor little Blaupunkt radio, several items that he crafted himself, and a few books about nature in Iceland and other countries.

Now the false daughter, the apple of his eye, is going to flee even farther, to her other dad in a southern corner of the world. If I know my dad, he'll do me the favor of dying before it comes to that.

In the sweltering heat of the inner bedroom, Heiður is snoring quietly but vigorously under the shelter of the wonderful monster-plant. Experience has taught me never to sleep without earplugs in the vicinity of my best friend. For the long trip east, I invested in silicone earplugs, but I highly doubt that anything would suffice to defend against this snore-phantom. I once called Heiður that out loud, the *snore-phantom*. It's one of the things that'll not soon be forgotten.

I use my strength to push my pillow into a pillowcase that's too small, forming a hard ball that hardly resembles anything for laying a head on. And the bed's more like a plank than a divan. But no matter—tonight I'd sleep soundly on anything, even a bed of nails with a boulder beneath my head. Those who have gained a new paternity must surely sleep more soundly than those who have nothing but a dilapidated one and no chance at any metamorphosis whatsoever. I really should celebrate this tomorrow with a Coke and Prince Polo.

I take the well-swaddled Cosette out of the brown leather suitcase that my dad in Perpignan slipped me before we parted ways. It was stuffed with paper, beneath which was another gift, just as he said there would be, and which I was supposed to unwrap when I returned home to Iceland. When I did, I found a golden heart-shaped box, and in it the scarab, my Egyptian beetle of lapis and gold. A lucky charm for an unlucky creature, a lucky charm that I lose and find, lose and find.

I lay Cosette on my bed, the raggedy doll that my mother loved more than she loved me.

It would be better if I tossed her into a bucket of water.

If I soaked you, Cosette Plaster-Cocotte, you'd dissolve.

But it won't do to soak Harpa Eir. She'll never dissolve.

I could also bury you in a shoe box, Cosette, up in Grandma's Grove, next to the little swallow. Put up a cross and sing "Over Cold Desert Sands."

BAK PÚ VÓ, Mommy Mare.

FISH, replies Mom, as of old when she found me howling on the kitchen floor in my foster-daughter-of-wolves game, after returning from the fish shop, with me thinking she'd gone into town.

Pillow in hand, I turn around to find Mom sitting curled up in the stocky easy chair, with her head beneath the huge shade of the floor lamp just beyond the doorway. If I pull the string and turn on the lamp above Mom's head, maybe she'll disappear. But I'd need to reach over her to do so, and I tremble at the thought.

The spotlight in the fish-processing plant's parking lot sends a dull beam in through our window, instead of lighting up the lot as it should. The gleam from this crooked light reveals that Mom's hair has turned white, thin, and straight. She's wearing a long yellow bathrobe of flax. Her legs are crossed, and the upper part of her inner thigh is visible, revealing old folds of skin that appear powder white. She's finally aged these past ten years, and not particularly well.

Are you feeling better now, girl?

It's good to have some certainty.

Aren't you terribly scandalized?, asks Mom, sounding distressed.

That's hardly the word for it.

I loved him, says Mom tearfully, pointing at the place of her heart with her middle finger, an exaggerated movement and carefully conceived finger position, as if from some sort of modern dance. At the same time, she gives me a penetrating, melancholy look, with her eyebrows raised and her eyes half-closed, like a first-year theater student.

I loved him, she repeats.

What does it matter?

Mom starts sobbing. Her body shakes, her face is chalky white, her mascara smudges. If a very elderly man were to play a female role, he would look something like this. It's the most horrifying look I've ever seen on Mom, but I don't want to laugh. I want to lie down on the floor and wail, or jump on her and smother her with the pillow. I think she'd be relieved.

You have no idea how I've suffered.

I let my hands holding the pillow sink, and Mom continues in a raspy masculine voice, as her sobs dwindle.

Then I died and left you and Edda. You have no idea what it's like to be dead, witnessing everything and not being able to do anything. You just keep on suffering.

Come on, Mom, if we search a bit, we can dig up some good memories. Remember when you and Dad came east on board *Hekla* at the sunniest time of the year, and I made up the bed for you, in this exact same room, because you always got seasick and wanted to lie down as soon as you arrived? You were fine that time. You were in a good mood, bright and cheerful.

You're a wonderful girl, Harpa baby, but I'm a terrible disgrace.

It turns out it was great, what you did. I don't have to worry about money. That's really important. I can go to school and everything, Mom.

Yes, but what does that do to help poor me?

Mom has started crying again, and this time I can hardly bear it. I go over to the chair to embrace her, to comfort her. She stands up, and the yellow rag she's wearing falls open, revealing a tired and forlorn old breast. I wrap my arms around Mom, around empty air, and fall onto the chair in a heap.

Mom, I say, my face buried in the rock-hard pillow. Mom, I love you more than anything. I wish you were still alive.

I hear Arnbjartur's clogs clacking, and he shouts up the stairs: Aren't you coming back down?

Shh. Do you want to wake her?, I whisper loudly.

I can't hear you!, the man shouts.

I get up, throw the pillow onto Cosette, who's occupying my bed, and hurry down.

Did you need to make such a horrendous ruckus?, I ask. My friend is sleeping upstairs.

Dýrfinna is sitting with her hands on the chair's arms, as if she's about to stand up. Her head glows with light that comes from inside. She's an angel of the evening, next to a still life of potatoes, rutabagas, carrots, lettuce, and a porcelain pitcher of hot chocolate with a stately spout and a gold knob on its lid. She wants to say something, and I'm inclined to think it'll be prophetic.

Would you mind making up a bed for Arnbjartur in the sewing room?, is what she says.

No problem. I'm a professional bed-maker, after all.

You'll find quilt covers and sheets in the bedroom closet, says Dýrfinna.

I know.

Everything's the same in Dýrfinna's closet as the last time I looked in it I don't know how many years ago. It could very well have been when I made up the bed for Dad and Mom during the heat wave, early in the morning, before Dýrfinna and I went to pick them up. The same pink-striped bed linens lie ironed and folded on the same shelf. How appropriate to pick up where I left off after all these years to make up Arnbjartur's bed. I bring the set into the sewing room, and fish a quilt and pillow from a drawer.

I swing the door shut and am alone in my world. The quilt and pillow give off a strong fresh-air scent, as if everything's just come off the clothesline. The same vibrant smell as when I made up a bed for my dad and mom twenty years ago, on the world's sweetest summer morning.

Dýrfinna and I took the Willys to go meet them. They were standing at the ship's rail, looking like the happiest married couple in the world. Mom leaned into Dad's shoulder, and Dad had his arm around her. It's a great exception to remember them getting along well together, both happy at once. In general, each was in his or her own particular mood. Happy, sad, whatever.

That day, each of them tried to outdo the other in waving, and Dad took off his cap and bowed. When Mom stepped ashore, she said: My, how you've grown, Harpa baby, and I'd swear you're becoming even more beautiful.

There, you see, I wasn't always so awful.

I know, Mom. I said that just now.

I heard you.

The hardest thing to forgive is how you behaved toward me when I was pregnant. How could you act like that? You who'd had an accidental child yourself.

Naturally, I was like most people, in the sense that I didn't know what I was doing.

I'm starting to understand that, Mom.

There's so much that you don't remember, Harpa baby. Like the summer in Andey when it was just the two of us.

Most of the good that happened is before I can remember.

Aw.

Were you terribly sad because of that man?

Gabriel? I had a cheeky little girl who was so cute that she caused people on the street to turn and look. It was better than nothing.

Then I stopped making you happy?

Don't you remember? I was always stitching clothes for you and ordering clothes for you from foreign catalogues.

Yes, I remember.

We also had good times in the grove when there was no haymaking. You know, I planted almost all the trees in the strip highest and farthest to the east, mostly during the summers when you were two and three years old, but of course you don't remember that.

I think I *do* remember it, Mom. You had a big shovel, and I had a little blue shovel and a red bucket. You know, I went straight up to Grandma's Grove today, despite the fog. The pitch pine grew about a foot and a half over the summer. It must be a record. The birch is also healthy-looking and fat, and it's spreading wildly. I'm going to do the rounds sometime in the next few days and tend to the little birches. The gale the other day nearly blew them from their roots. But first I need to paint my two rooms. It's impossible for me to feel good in a place where the walls are so patchy.

You've been neat and tidy all your life. I won't delay you any longer, Harpa baby. You need to make up that rascal's bed. And I hope everything goes well with Edda.

At least I tried. The worst thing is not to try, as Dad said.

You can still end up blessed, Harpa. Just be sure not to make the same mistakes I did.

You didn't exactly make mistakes, Mom.

Maybe not.

Mom? Where are you? I can't see you now. Why do I only hear you?

It's because of something you said earlier, upstairs. I don't need to bring anything more into the light. Now I'm in the light.

In the same place as Jói?

That's not what I said.

Out in the dark, an unfamiliar light flashes, with pauses of varying lengths—a malfunctioning lighthouse that I'm unable to place, or a beam from a ship rolling on the waves in the fjord.

The weather must have turned quickly. The sea crashes against the land, bellowing as if it's going to snatch it all away, flood it, spare nothing, as if it can no longer contain itself in its own spacious compartment that covers over three-quarters of the globe.

Dýrfinna steps into the doorway and says that Arnbjartur's starting to yawn.

I'm coming, I say as I shake the quilt with the pink-striped cover one more time, to fill my senses with more of that invigorating fresh-air scent.

Did you have an interesting phone conversation earlier?

Yes, it was with a man who called me the foreign girl when I was a child.

There's something between you two?

The entire country. He moved to Ísafjörður.

Oh?

He's an accountant. He got a good job offer there.

Right. It takes two years to get over heartache, if it isn't nourished, that is. It also takes two years for the most passionate love to evaporate, if people are together.

I'll consider that, if it ever comes down to it. But don't you need to get some rest, Dýrfinna, after all these ghostly visitations?

Try to get some rest yourself. I hope you sleep well.

There's a definite undertone to her voice. A peculiar emphasis on *sleep well.* I suppose she thinks I'm upset. Which is precisely what I'm not. Upset is what I was, before my question was answered.

Good night.

Good night, my dear, she says, wrapping her arms around me like the most caring mother, kissing me on the cheek, stroking my hair.

Thank you for everything, dearest Dýrfinna.

Thank you for wanting to stay.

I call out to Arnbjartur that I've finished making up his bed and bid him good night.

Good night yourself, he says, in a strangely slow warble.

I make a vow by the window upstairs, over the continually glittering waves, not to sleep in even if I'm tired. Tomorrow morning I'll be up and about at the crack of dawn, and the past and future will merge as I change into myself, a girl who was at the water's edge and still is.

The future has stopped looming like a vicious cat with its claws out. It's a pet cat with downy paws stretching on the sunbaked sand of the beach tomorrow morning when no one has risen in the Eastfjords but me: HARPA EIR AXELSDÓTTIR.

I take out a kimono, a gift from that rascal of a partner Alli the dwarf, and lay it on a chair by my miserly bed, in case I should need to go downstairs in the night.

My head falls comfortably on the lousy pillow. My body's wrapped in one of Dýrfinna's delightful down quilts. I do exercises to stimulate my circulatory system after two days of sitting in the car—curling and straightening my toes, in rhythm with Heiður's snores.

How curious I am to know more about Mom and Gabriel Axel. What on earth was their story?

Met at the Marine Research Institute. Then what? How did they meet again? Where did they meet? How could they communicate? His English isn't good, and Mom was never much for languages. Maybe they didn't need to say anything. But Mom was always so talkative. Where could they have done it? In his hotel room? If he even stayed in a hotel. How often? Was my late mother hot-blooded?

Well, I certainly can't ask about all of that, but I'm planning to ask Dýrfinna for more details, unless my dad, the one in Perpignan, tells me everything now that this much has been revealed.

I should be grateful that he's somewhere, that I found him, that there's still a story about who I am. I hope my father cares enough to tell me the entire story when the time comes.

Toes out, toes in.

I run my finger along the old gold chain and the recently twice-discovered scarab.

There's something that I need to ask you, my father and friend in Perpignan, the next time we meet, and I imagine that it won't be many months until then.

Do you recognize this gold chain?

Might you have old photos of a curly-haired girl in shorts, with an orange in her hand, up against Sæmundur the Learned on the seal, next to the sculptor's domed studio?

The man was standing not far from the domed building, tall and slim and very dark, in light-colored clothing, a camera around his neck. I was on my way to Dock Wood on the warm day about which the stories were spun. I'd planned to go straight over the plank bridging the little ditch, but I had a feeling that the man with the camera wanted to talk to me, so I walked toward him. Then he came over to me and smiled a radiant, sad smile that's haunted me ever since.

He wanted to take my photo by the statue. As I approached it, I looked up and saw that one tear was about to fall from the tip of his nose. I blamed it on the breeze.

He said that I was beautiful. That word I understood: *bea-u-ti-ful*.

I remember the three clicks from the camera. Three photos of Harpa Eir, Axelsdóttir, of course, eight years old with an orange, half an hour before she was nearly finished off in Dock Wood.

The tall man in the light-colored suit sat at the base of the statue of Sæmundur on the seal and indicated that I should sit down next to him. He stroked my hair so gently that in my mind I called his hand *angel hand*. How I wanted to reply in kind and pat him on the head, on his curly raven-black hair that reached below his ears, but I was uncomfortable about doing so, because the man was not Icelandic in any way.

To me he seemed most like a gypsy. Dad had just shown me pictures of gypsies in *National Geographic*. From his appearance, it would have fit if he played wild songs on the violin well into warm nights. Yet that seemed a bit off, because he was wearing a suit.

After we stood up, I got the idea that he was a photographer from a foreign country who'd heard of the Wild Children and happened now to be searching for them, just as I was. I pointed at myself and him and Dock Wood to let him know that I could show him the way. He looked at me and smiled and shook his head.

He then took the gold chain off his neck and put it around mine. Thank you, I said. He put a finger to his mouth to indicate that this was a secret and said something in a foreign language that I understood to be *hush*.

The secret that I've kept so well that I didn't even tell it to myself: it was him, the one I've always searched for. More than ten years later, in Perpignan, I didn't recognize him, so discreet was I with myself. His hair had turned gray, and he looked a bit frail.

I can tell my father and benefactor when I meet him that I never got into any trouble because of the chain. That I've always just said: *I found it in Dock Wood.* No one ever made a single comment. Even Mom didn't ask about it. I was above suspicion of having pilfered it, and it didn't cross anyone's mind that it could have been a gift from an unknown traveler.

When I meet the man again, he'll learn that I told the secret to no one, not even myself.

He won't be told what happened to me in Dock Wood half an hour after we met, since that would lead to a trail of tears down the left side of his neck, and that wouldn't do.

How I look forward to meeting you, my sad friend, the man I searched for and found, without knowing what I'd found.

Let's visit him if it's so fun at his place, said my delinquent child somewhere along the way. Did I hear her right?

How am I going to break all of this to Edda?

I haven't come that far. Tomorrow is another day, and tomorrows are for searching for new paths.

Today is the last day, and tomorrow is the first.

All days are the end of something, even if only of themselves, and at the same time they're a start, if we remember that they're new.

No longer will my days be nothing but waiting.

How many days did I wait for a man who stopped for a night? For a man who doesn't want to visit me tomorrow, but the day after tomorrow.

How many days of my life have I waited for an answer that was free for the taking?

Heiður, who knows me better than anyone else, advised me against searching for an answer. It certainly will be fun to tease her now.

I tear myself out from under the down quilt and enter the sweltering heat of the inner room, beneath the lobed leaves of the wonderful monster.

I was right all along, I say loudly. I knew it—he's foreign.

Gabviel Athel, says Heiður, turning to the wall with a sharp jerk.

What do you mean? How do you know?

I dun-no.

Are you sleeping?

Yeth.

It's no good wasting very many words on sleeping sibyls, so I just look at her. She certainly knew more than she let on. Of course she knew. Just as I did.

Tonight it's not to be wondered that everything is as new. That it's turned out to be as it should, no matter how that is.

A rasping bagpipe-quack from a nasally mallard is heard out in the passing night, a solo piece in the middle of a symphony of snores that increase in volume in three corners of the house. Dýrfinna snores like a fireworks display, to the accompaniment of the short, decisive, cheeky snores of the flutist and Arnbjartur's traditional pastoral puffing and whistling. I'm not going to sleep well. My clairvoyant aunt must have emphasized *sleep well* because she knew I wouldn't, due to the snoring.

What do I care? I don't feel like sleeping, even though I'm exhausted. A woman with a new paternity has no use for sleep. She who is the only hybrid of her sort in the entire world has every right to remain awake. I'm very proud of my heritage, though it's by no means my doing. This well-fabricated new person sits down in the square chair where her recently aged mom sat before, pulls on the lamp string, and there is light.

Maybe I'll sit in this chair until the future begins, until the early-rising cat makes his rounds. In the morning I'll follow my Sæmundur down to the beach and watch him stretch by the sea, the same as his father Þangbrandur did before him, as preserved in my childhood memory. I can hardly wait for tomorrow to dawn, for a tomorrow to come in which Sæmundur and I can lie there and meditate.

Nearly horizontal sunbeams will stretch diagonally across the entire fjord, baking Sæmundur's gleaming fur as he dozes stretched out on a board by the old overturned boat. When he sees me giving him the eye, he'll stand up venerably and take several slow and seductive steps toward the sea. He'll toss himself onto his back in the sand of the beach and stretch, making himself incredibly long and thin. He'll wipe his head with one foreleg, stretch out his hind legs, and spread his claws. He'll perform these well-rehearsed morning exercises specifically for me, his cat eyes flashing like undersea suns on the world's first day.

A car door slams, right outside the house. I didn't hear a car drive up.

Who is slamming the door of no car?

A rustling noise comes from below. A very light knock on the door. Teddi? Yves? Who knows. I'm not answering. Help.

Again comes a knock, excessively modest yet slightly harder. If I don't answer, it will wake Dýrfinna.

I hope you *sleep well*, she said. So she wasn't talking about the snoring. It was about this visitor, whoever it is.

I put on the kimono, a silken artistic creation, with wide arms covered in cherry blossoms that turn into light-pink expanses of clouds in the spring Japanese sky.

I hurry down the stairs and hop to the floor from the third step, as I did when I was a little girl. I'm in good form after my hops out of the pickup truck on the way east.

Dietrich Bacon is standing on the veranda, right between spruce trees that shouldn't be able to grow at the Icelandic seaside. He's nearly as tall as they are, this international singer in a brown wool cape and green Tyrolean hat.

From the silence of the village, the crumhorn blows.

A crumhorn, here? These are Dietrich Bacon's first words. He looks around in fear, as if expecting to be ambushed and set upon by the instrument.

Exactly, I say. Please come in.

Thank you, he says, with a final cautious glance. So I found the place.

There are five men following you, said Bettý. *One in a cape, with a little hat.*

I suppress the laughter that's churning up inside and, in order to keep the visitor from thinking I'm making fun of him, transform it into a maiden-like smile.

He takes off his high-quality gloves, and we shake hands, a bit too long, as usual. A heavenly touch.

I was singing in Bergen, he adds apologetically.

The blue-gray clouds of his eyes scintillate with the light of his soul beneath the brim of his green hat.

I knew that, I say. Step inside, and watch your head.

Thank you. I wanted to surprise Heiður.

The prophetess at Útheimar said something else. She said: *For Harpa.*

What a great idea, I say, taking the man's coat. She won't be expecting it.

I certainly wouldn't think so.

You made her tell you precisely where she was going, didn't you?

He smiles that mischievous smile of his, which kindles a supernatural light in his eyes.

I was very crafty. She told me your aunt's name and the village where she lives. The rest was easy—though I did, of course, have to get help looking her up in the phone book in order to find the address. And I'm familiar with the pickup, as you know.

Heiður has gone to sleep, Herr Bacon. How about if I warm some hot chocolate, and then we can wake the lady?

Sounds like a good idea, he says quietly.

His baritone whisper has tingled my senses.

Sounds like a good idea.

The voice is an echo of the soul.

The voice says it all. It can't deceive. Hands and eyes and mouths can deceive. Everything can deceive but the voice.

Durch die Nacht zu dir.

Dietrich takes off his sweater. He's a hardy one, this man. Beneath it he's wearing a short-sleeved blue shirt, meticulously ironed.

He walks into the living room and sinks into the dark-blue sofa where I've sat through the years, at every age, with my mom, dad, Dýrfinna, Edda.

Why couldn't I have covered over the night-scrape on my chin? Now that it's my destiny to share a room with the singer before daybreak.

I light a candle in the silver chandelier, and the glow illuminates the mottled miniflag that Dýrfinna hoisted to full-staff from half-staff before she went to bed.

You took the ferry to Seyðisfjörður?

He's come from the sea, like the others: Martin, Mom's lifesaver; and Gabriel Axel, Harpa's lifesaver.

It was sheer luck that I managed to book passage. There were some no-shows. It was the last trip of the season.

Autumn arrives quite early here.

Another knock comes at the door.

What's that?, asks Dietrich in surprise.

Something's blown against the house, I say, not wanting to mention a word of the cut-off leg that lives an independent life and kicks at doors in this part of the country.

There's no wind outside. It sounded to me like someone pounding on the door.

Strange.

The singer goes to the window, with me following, and we look at the fjord spreading out beyond the two walls, one of sparkling rock and the other of leaves.

You should take a look at Dýrfinna's stone kingdom when you wake up tomorrow, I say. There's a huge variety of stones, gathered over a long period of time: shiny, dull, bright, dark, light, heavy, oval, even horned. There's also one shaped like a choice cow pie, russet and green—Edda found that one. But the treasure of treasures is the zeolite that I found. It sparkles like a snow crystal, whatever the season.

It's a world of fantasy, this fjord, every inch of it, says Dietrich Bacon, after a silky smooth throat-clearing, as if he were going to sing. Then he clasps his beautiful hands as if to accentuate his words, and I nearly lose myself in gazing at them.

In the flickering gleam of the candlelight, we remain silent, to our pleasure.

He looks at me with divine tenderness, like the benevolent Sarastro himself, and again it seems as if notes will emerge when he opens his mouth.

What can you tell me about Edda? How's it going with her?

We don't know yet. We'll have to see. Right now, I think she'll be fine, but I'm not sure I'm seeing things in the correct light tonight.

Dietrich Bacon repeats: *Tonight?*

Tonight I'd actually forgotten that I have a daughter.

Is that even possible?

I have to forget her now and then in order to survive. It's been incredibly difficult. Besides, I had her so young that I often feel as if she can hardly be my daughter.

That you can hardly be her mom, maybe.

The light of his eyes warms me, to my very bones.

Silence descends, the same as before the question came crashing down on Dýrfinna. The crumhorn makes no sound, the snoring has ceased, every single thing is silent, other than two hearts that beat, alternately light and heavy—slow down, speed up, slow down—like the footsteps of people searching along complex paths for a target that remains obscure.

Now he looks at me as he did the first night of the year, when he moved his lips to the most beautiful love song in the world, ever. *Cara.*

My friend. Yes, I exist. Differently now.

But what use to me is metamorphosis when I'm stuck with the most dreadful of all that is dreadful? My savior is upstairs, the snore-phantom who stole my man from me one fateful moment backstage at the Old Theater and believes that he's hers.

For Harpa. That's what the prophetess said.

He doesn't know it himself.

If he learns who I am, if I tell him my secret, he'll understand himself. If I reveal myself, a new fateful moment will arrive and everything will be turned around.

I want to say to the visitor: Please excuse me, I'm just going to think it over a bit, whether or not I should tell you something.

Please excuse me while I warm the hot chocolate.

The Atlas Crystal refrigerator welcomes me with a click and a loud hum. The fjord's flashes of light increase in number beyond the wall of living rock, and I start in on a new hot-chocolate sorcery, stirring clockwise in the vast opening of the jam pot with Dýrfinna's long wooden spoon, round and round.

I step onto a stool and grab a little crystal cask from a shelf, pile whipped cream into it, put it on a tray. I arrange two Sunday-best cups and two silver teaspoons, and step back up to grab white napkins with golden edges from the shelf.

I take a new position at the stove, stirring and stirring with the spoon that's too long and bending the floating light-tracks of the sea, intoning until a whirlpool forms in the middle and sucks in all creation.

If I tell him the question I asked this evening and the answer I got, he'll understand who he's come to find.

If I say nothing now, my fate will be the same long love that Mom had.

I'll be remembered for seemingly endless monologues on peculiar topics.

Damn it, I'm stamping my foot now. If I wake Heiður, this matter with the colossus in the wool cape will be finished. Forever, amen.

I start in alarm when the symphony of snores from the house's sleepers revs up again, this time with increased strength. Dýrfinna's fireworks going off at full steam, Arnbjartur's whistles lengthening, and Heiður's short snores transforming into Kamala howls.

Surely Heiður will wake up to this racket of hers, not later, but now, and the matter will be resolved for good.

The sea of hot chocolate has reached the boiling point. I pour it into the stately pitcher and add it to the tray.

On my way into the living room, I hear that the singer's soft baritone snores have been added to the sleepers' symphony, which resounds from the four corners of the house.

I step over the threshold and see Dietrich Bacon filling half the couch, leaning back with his Sunday-best arms crossed over his chest. I put the tray down on the coffee table, next to the little flagpole. The cherry-blossom clouds on my wide sleeve brush against the singer's arm, and he smiles, his eyes closed.

Glossary

Bollagata:

Sculptor's domed studio: The sculptor referred to here is Ásmundur Sveinsson (1893–1982). Sveinsson's domed house/studio in Laugardalur in Reykjavík, which he donated to the city, is now a museum. The "hulking cement folk" are figures in the nearby sculpture garden.

Fáskrúðsfjörður: A fjord and village of the same name in the Eastfjords of Iceland. It and five other villages comprise the municipality of Fjarðabyggð. Harpa refers throughout the novel to Fáskrúðsfjörður as "my fjord" or her "dream place."

On the Crest of Kambar:

The Foster Daughter of Wolves: This is the title of the Icelandic translation of Arnold Gesell's *Wolf Child and Human Child* (1941), which tells the story of the Indian "wolf-girl" Kamala, based on the diary of Reverend Joseph Singh, who ran an orphanage where Kamala and her sister were kept and looked after by Singh after he supposedly "rescued" them from a wolf den in 1920. The Icelandic version *(Fósturdóttir úlfanna)* was translated by Steingrímur Arason and published in 1946. The story of Kamala was refuted as a hoax by Serge Aroles in his book *The Enigma of the Wolf-Children* (2007).

Selfoss:

"The days have come": See Ecclesiastes 12:1.

The Shop on the Plain:

Gunnar and Njál: A reference to Gunnar of Hlíðarendi and Njál Þorgeirsson, main characters in the famous medieval Icelandic saga *Njál's Saga*. The mountain Þríhyrningur is where the character Flosi of Svínafell hid out after leading a band of men in the burning of Njál and his family in their farmhouse.

Curse-pole: In Germanic pagan tradition, a curse-pole (in Icelandic, *níðstöng*) was used for cursing one's enemies. It was a long wooden pole to which a horse's head was affixed and directed toward the enemy. The curse could be carved in runes upon the pole. A famous example is found in the medieval Icelandic saga *Egil's Saga*, when the eponymous hero, Egil Skallagrímsson, raises a curse-pole against King Eiríkur and Queen Gunnhildur of Norway.

"Mary, lofty and mild": From a hymn dedicated to the Virgin Mary (in Icelandic, *Maríuvers*), composed by the Icelandic composer and organist Páll Ísolfsson (1893–1974), with text by the Icelandic poet Davíð Stefánsson (1895–1964).

Yule Lads: In Icelandic folk tradition, there are thirteen "Yule Lads" (in Icelandic, *jólasveinar*), one of whom comes down from the mountains on each of the thirteen nights preceding Christmas to put rewards or chastisements (gifts or rotten potatoes) in children's shoes left by the windowsill. Their mother is the ogress Grýla, and their father the ogre Leppalúði.

The Corral at the Foot of Eyjafjöll:

Le déjeuner sur l'herbe: A reference to the painting of the same name (in English, *The Luncheon on the Grass*) by the French painter Éduoard Manet (1832–1883).

Orla Frogsnapper: A children's book (in Danish, *Orla Frøsnapper*) by the Danish writer Ole Lund Kirkegaard (1940–1979). A 2011 film version of the book is titled *Freddy Frogface* in English.

Höfðabrekka, Glóra, Útheimar: All of these places are on or near Iceland's south coast. Höfðabrekka is near the town of Vík in Mýrdal. Glóra is a fictionalization of the farm Ásar in the Skaftártunga region, West Skaftafell County (between Mýrdalsjökull Glacier and Skaftafell National Park). Útheimar is a fictionalization of the farm Hraunkot in Lón, in East Skaftafell County (the area along the southeast edge of the glacier Vatnajökull, between Skaftafell National Park and Lónsheiði Heath).

All as the one blossom: A reference to the Icelandic funeral hymn "Allt eins og blómstrið eina" ("All as the One Blossom," also known as "On Death's Uncertain Hour"), whose text was composed by the Icelandic priest, hymnist, and poet Hallgrímur Pétursson (1614–1674).

Soon heralding the morning: Lyrics from the quartet "Bald prangt, den Morgen zu verkünden" in act 2, scene 6 of the opera *The Magic Flute* (*Die Zauberflöte*) by Wolfgang Amadeus Mozart (1756–1791). The popular Icelandic children's song "Hann Tumi fer á fætur" (text by Freysteinn Gunnarsson, 1892–1976) is based on this quartet.

Efri-Hæðir:

Lati Geir: A reference to a popular Icelandic verse (unknown author): "Lati Geir á lækjarbakka / lá þar til hann dó / Vildi hann ekki vatnið smakka, / var hann þyrstur þó" ("Lazy Geir on the stream bank / lay there until he died / He didn't want to taste the water, / although he was thirsty").

Njál's Saga: Again, a reference to the famous medieval Icelandic saga, whose author, like that of all the Icelandic family sagas, is anonymous.

Glóra:

Bimbirimbirimmbamm: A reference to the "chorus" of an old-fashioned Icelandic children's rhyming game, which involved teasing about boyfriends or girlfriends. (Harpa's mom is playing on the game's idea of finding someone.) One version runs: "Who's knocking? Bimbirimbirimmbamm. It's Gunni. Bimbirimbirimmbamm. Who does he want to find? Bimbirimbirimmbamm. His dear Zukkat. Bimbirimbirimmbamm. What does he get in reward? Bimbirimbirimmbamm. A can of beans. Bimbirimbirimmbamm."

Kirkjubæjarklaustur:

"A kindly blossom": From Hymn 507 in the Hymn Book of the Lutheran Church of Iceland, "Ó, faðir, gjör mig lítið ljós" ("Oh, Father, make me a little light"). The text, by the Icelandic poet Matthías Jochumsson (1835–1920), is a translation of the hymn "God make my life a little light" by the English novelist and poet Matilda Betham-Edwards (1836–1919). This stanza, in the original, reads: "God make my life a little flower / That giveth joy to all, / Content to bloom in native bower, / Although its place be small" (*Littell's Living Age*, 117).

"Never seek to tell thy love": From the poem "Never pain to tell thy love" by the English poet William Blake (1757–1827).

Passion Hymns: The *Passion Hymns* (in Icelandic, *Passíusálmar*) are a set of fifty hymns written by the Icelandic priest and poet Hallgrímur Pétursson (1614–1674). They are sung during Lent in Iceland.

The evil net: See Ecclesiastes 9:12.

In the Shelter of Lómagnúpur:

"From the sky drip big drops": Part of a verse by the versifier and shop owner Ísleifur Gíslason (1873–1960). The verse in full reads: "Detta úr lofti dropar stórir, / dignar um í sveitinni. / Tvisvar sinnum tveir eru fjórir, / taktu í horn á geitinni" ("From the sky drip big drops / wetting the countryside / twice two makes four / take the goat by the horns").

A Folksy Shop by an Iceberg Lagoon:

Iceberg lagoon: This is Breiðamerkurlón, also known as Jökulsárlón, the large glacial lake on the border of Vatnajökull National Park in southeast Iceland. It is a very popular tourist destination.

Brennivín: An Icelandic schnapps flavored with caraway. Also known as "Black Death," it is considered Iceland's signature alcoholic drink.

Leise flehen: A reference to Franz Schubert's (1797–1828) *Ständchen* (Serenade), with the lyrics "Leise flehen meine Lieder / Durch die Nacht zu dir" ("Gently goes my song's entreaty / through the night to you") by lyricist Ludwig Rellstab (1799–1860).

Buried Child: A play by the American playwright, actor, and director Sam Shepard (1943–). First performed in 1978, it deals with the disintegration of the American family.

"There sits my mother": Lines from the nursery rhyme "Tunglið, tunglið taktu mig" ("Moon, moon, take me"), by the Icelandic poet Théodóra Thorodssen (1863–1954).

"A mishap! I am not to blame": From the poem "Illur lækur eða Heimasetan" ("Evil Brook, or, Staying at Home") by the renowned Icelandic romantic poet Jónas Hallgrímsson (1807–1845).

"Yet oh, María, I want to go home": A line from the song "Ó, María mig langar heim" ("Oh, María, I want to go home"), an Icelandic version, with text by Ólafur Gaukur Þórhallsson (1930–2011), of the song "Mary, Don't You Weep" by Mel Tillis (1932–) and Marijohn Wilkin (1920–2006).

Útheimar:

"Iceland Scored with Inlets": The lyrics to this song (in Icelandic, "Ísland ögrum skorið") were written by the explorer and writer Eggert Ólafsson (1726–1768), and the tune was composed by the composer and physician Sigvaldi Kaldalóns (1881–1946).

Helmsperson Þuríður: A reference to Þuríður Einarsdóttir (1777–1863), otherwise known as Þuríður *formaður* (helmsperson Þuríður), who lived in Eyrarbakki in southwest Iceland and was renowned for her prowess as a sailor as well as her investigative abilities, having helped to expose those responsible for the robbery known as "Kambsránið" (The Robbery at Kambur).

"I built a house by the sea": From the poem "Hudson Bay" by the Icelandic poet Steinn Steinarr (1908–1958).

Guðmundur the Good: Guðmundur Arason (1161–1237), elected bishop of Hólar in 1203. In his travels around Iceland, he blessed springs and wells, some of which still bear his name today.

The Dwarf: A lied for voice and piano (in German, *Der Zwerg*) composed by the Austrian composer Franz Schubert (1797–1828).

Dýrfinna's House:

"Seldom have I refused the drippings": An Icelandic idiom ("Sjaldan hef ég flotinu neitað") meaning "I never refuse what I'm offered" or "I don't bite the hand that feeds me."

Salka Valka: A reference to characters in the novel *Salka Valka*, by the Nobel Prize–winning Icelandic author Halldór Laxness (1902–1998).

"Would you know yet more?": A refrain (in Icelandic, "Vitið þér enn eða hvað") in the Old Norse poem *Völuspá* (*Prophecy of the Seeress*), probably the most famous poem from the *Poetic Edda*, a collection of mythological and heroic poems preserved in the medieval Icelandic manuscript Codex Regius.

Prince Polo: A Polish chocolate bar, one of the first confections imported into Iceland and for decades probably Iceland's biggest selling chocolate bar. It is still popular today, in the classic configuration "Coke and Prince."

"Over Cold Desert Sands": A popular song (in Icelandic, "Yfir kaldan eyðisand"); originally a verse by the Icelandic poet Kristján Jónsson *fjallaskáld*, poet of the mountains (1842–1869).

Sæmundur on the seal: A reference to Sæmundur Sigfússon, also known as Sæmundur *fróði* or Sæmundur the Learned (1056–1133), an Icelandic priest and scholar who became a popular folklore character. In folktales he often tricks the Devil into doing his bidding, as here, when he has the Devil in the form of a seal transport him back over the ocean to Iceland from France. Upon nearing the shore, Sæmundur brains the seal with a psalter. The scene is depicted on a sculpture by Ásmundur Sveinsson (see note for the chapter "Bollagata"), which stands in front of the main building of the University of Iceland.

Durch die Nacht zu dir: In English, "Through the night to you." See the note for *Leise flehen* under A Folksy Shop by an Iceberg Lagoon.

The benevolent Sarastro: A character in the opera *The Magic Flute* (see note under The Corral at the Foot of Eyjafjöll). He defends and protects the main female character, Pamina, particularly from her mother, the Queen of the Night.

About the Author

Born in Reykjavík, Steinunn Sigurðardóttir studied philosophy and psychology at University College Dublin. She made a name for herself at the age of nineteen with a volume of poetry entitled *Continuances* (*Sífellur*, 1969). Sigurðardóttir has since become one of Iceland's most frequently translated writers, and one of the most lauded, having won the Icelandic Literature Prize (for *Place of the Heart*) and the national Bookseller's Prize in 2011, among many other nominations. Steinunn Sigurðardóttir's extensive body of work includes eleven novels, seven volumes of poetry, two volumes of short stories, radio plays, television plays, and a children's book. Her novel *The Thief of Time* (*Tímaþjófurinn*, 1986) was adapted to film in France (*Voleur de vie*, 1998), directed by Yves Angelo and starring Emmanuelle Béart and Sandrine Bonnaire. After an extensive and fruitful career abroad, most notably in Germany and France, *Place of the Heart* is Steinunn Sigurðardóttir's English-language debut.

About the Translator

Philip Roughton is an award-winning translator of modern Icelandic literature and a scholar of Old Norse and medieval literature. He holds a PhD in comparative literature from the University of Colorado Boulder, and has taught literature both there and at the University of Iceland. Roughton's translation of Bergsveinn Birgisson's *Reply to a Letter from Helga* was listed among *World Literature Today*'s 75 Notable Translations of 2013.